She Dies at the End

By A.M. Manay

Pythoness Press

Livermore, California

Enjoy!
Best Wishes,
AM

Table of Contents

Acknowledgements

Many thanks to my husband for his unwavering support, to my son for his smiles, to my friends and family for their encouragement, to my high school English teachers for their knowledge and wisdom, and to the staff of Starbucks Number 6532. I could not have completed this project without your help and kindness.

Chapter 1

She watched them bury her again.

Four people stand in a garden. The short redhead, an impatient fireplug, has a dusty shovel in his large hands. His wide shoulders stretch his clothes. A tiny teenager with caramel skin stands beside him and places a hand on his arm, her tunic marred by drops of blood. A tall waif stands apart, distraught, shaking; blue tears fall from her eyes, eyes the same shade of electric blue as her hair. Closest to the grave is the bloody businessman, his dark suit stained darker still with blood, his white shirt ruined, his shoes dusty, his designer tie twisted, now turned more noose than accessory.

His face is stone. His eyes scream. His fangs catch the light. A girl is dead because she tried to help him. His girl is dead, just like the ones before.

Her corpse waits patiently, cradled in the gnarled roots of an old tree. Blood has soaked through her blue silk dress. It stains her mouth, covering the blue tinge of death. The businessman bends down and kisses her forehead. He lifts her up, leaps gracefully into the grave, and places her carefully into her resting place. Her dark blue eyes are still open, but she doesn't look frightened. She looks relieved. He closes them gently, touches her cheek. A drop of blood wells in his eye, rolls down his cheek, falls silently onto her dark hair, evidence of his grief: her killer's grief.

She watched them bury her again.

***

November Snow awoke with the certainty that she'd overslept and promptly bashed her head against the bottom of her table. That was the one drawback to her little nest, but she'd take a sleeping bag on the ground and a knot on her head any day. It was far preferable to sleeping in her mother's trailer and the consequent possibility of waking up to sounds she'd rather not hear. It was rather cozy, actually, along the lines of a blanket fort.

The girl crawled out into the dim light inside her tent and began to prepare for another day of work. She jumped to her feet; a quick glance at her watch confirmed that she had better hustle. Her oversleeping was no surprise, really, after the previous night's shenanigans. She sighed inwardly and ran her hands through her long black hair, yanking out the worst of the tangles and steeling herself to face the day.

Her first task was to wash off the previous day's dust and sweat, which she did with a quickness as the shower in her mom's motor-coach lacked hot water. *What I wouldn't give for a scalding hot bath*, she thought. Pulling on her thrift store jeans and t-shirt, she caught brief glimpses of their former owners. Detergent could wash away many things, but not the imprints of those who'd previously worn the clothes. Thankfully, such visions tended to fade with time as she made her the items her own, but the first few days in someone else's castoffs were always a real headache. She then attempted to wake her mother from her stupor, which this morning was a futile effort. *Not that I'm surprised.* The next job was breakfast.

She walked quickly down the midway toward the food stands. She grabbed an apple from Sally's candy apple counter. Most everyone was busy preparing their games and rides for the influx of marks soon to ensue. Her few friends greeted her. More, however, crossed themselves, called her a freak under their breath, and kept on working.

Some of those were men or boys whose advances she'd awkwardly rebuffed. Her usual reaction to flirtation was alarm. Physical contact was difficult for her, as it made it much harder to

8

block visions, and she never knew what horrible or funny or embarrassing thing she was going to see. She cultivated an air of coldness, but when that failed, she usually resorted to channeling their dead relatives. That was remarkably effective: almost no one wanted to make out with his dead grandpa.

Her general unpopularity stemmed from her severe shyness, her occasional collapses, and her thankfully rare outbursts directed at people no one else could see. There was probably also some professional jealousy at play. She was only 17, with two years as part of the carnival, but she took in more money than all the old-timers. Her relative financial success was likely the only reason the two Snow women hadn't long since been kicked to the curb.

This time of preparation was the calm before the storm. In truth, for November, all that existed was a storm of varying degrees. On a good day, she sat in the eye of it, a dispassionate observer, plucking moments out of the wind and relegating the irrelevant or unhelpful or uninteresting to the background. On a bad day, the hurricane picked her up and tossed her against the side of a barn. Her world was never quiet, never empty; the past and the future were always battling to be heard over the present.

Her best defense was an occupied mind. Reading, studying, drawing, calculating – these gave her enough moments of peace to get by. Music helped, too. She sometimes listened to a beat-up old radio as she fell asleep. It tended to calm her and gave her more pleasant visions as she slept. Once the gates opened and the crowds poured in, November didn't leave her tent until the carnival closed. Being among so many strangers was dizzying, nauseating. Their echoes swirling around along the empty midway were quite enough for her.

"Here you go, sweetheart: funnel cake, the breakfast of champions." A sunny, weathered face full of smile lines, crowned with hair more salt than pepper, shone down on November.

"Thanks, Neil," she replied in her quiet, low-pitched voice, smiling back at him, her eyes brightening for a moment. Neil was one of the few people she could call a friend; he always tried to look out for her. He also had the distinction of never having enjoyed her mother's favors, which gave him a number of gold stars in November's estimation.

She hadn't trusted his kindness at first. She later found out that he simply missed his daughter, whom he hadn't seen since his wife had wandered off. Neil was a lifelong carnie, born and raised; he'd grown up spending half the year on the road and the rest back on the family farm. His brother Mike owned the carnival, having bought it from their parents when they retired. Neil had no interest in retiring himself any time soon. Being around people, making them smile—it was all he was good at.

"Oh, I almost forgot," added Neil. "I found something for you yesterday when I went by that strip mall. They had a used book shop." He pulled out a textbook. "Physics. That's the kind of stuff you like, right?"

November was touched. She didn't get many gifts. The black cover was still in good shape. She flipped through the pages, which were almost unmarked. She caught a brief image of a boy with glasses and acne burning the midnight oil along with the smell of some nasty energy drink before she turned her attention back to the contents. It seemed impossibly challenging, which was exactly what she looked for in a distraction. The harder she had to think, the less likely she was to succumb to stray visions.

"It's wonderful, Neil. I really appreciate it. I'm almost finished with that calculus book, so perfect timing," she replied, glancing up at him again. She didn't so much as blink when she saw a knife sticking out of his chest. Phantom blood began to stain his flannel shirt; the contrast to his smiling visage was almost funny in a morbid sort of way. *Let it wash over you like a wave and then back out to sea.* She took a slow, deep breath.

Such intrusions were a constant irritant. Someone would brush her shoulder, and suddenly November was watching a car wreck or a mugging or a quintuple bypass. She did like Neil quite a lot, so she hoped that he would avoid that stabbing, but November had long since learned to hold herself apart from the possible fates of the people around her. Too much interest, too much empathy, too much wanting to save people from the inevitability of death – that would lead her right back to a hospital.

Even when she tried to warn people, it often backfired. A person was always willing to believe her about the return of a lost love or a financial windfall but usually just got angry if she suggested that the client get a mammogram or a divorce or a handgun. Besides, most of her visions were only possible futures that depended on how people made their choices. Most of what she saw of the future was not set in stone. She'd seen Neil die three different deaths over the past year. The best thing to do was to ignore what she saw as much as possible.

Neil's face grew more serious. "How's the arm healing?"

November looked down at her sleeve. "Fine," she answered. "Not infected. You did a good job with the bandages. The aloe helps." Neil had been a medic in the army for a few years right out of high school, and he served as their go-to guy for injuries and minor illness. She couldn't quite meet his sad eyes. She didn't like him feeling sorry for her, and she was afraid that one of these days he was going to call the child protection people, despite her pleas to the contrary.

November's greatest fear was getting locked up again in a mental institution. She'd been sent to one when she'd wound up in foster care after her grandmother had died. She could fake being normal for a few minutes at a time when she was in public, but in close quarters, her foster family had quickly realized that November saw and heard things that weren't there.

She was much older now, of course, and could put on a much more convincing act of sanity, but she really didn't want to take any chances with getting caught up in the system. The life she'd built here wasn't easy, but it was hers, and she still found happiness in it. She would not permit her mother to take it from her. She had explained all this to Neil, and he'd agreed that the foster care system would not be a good place for her. Still, he wished he could get her away from her mother. Only one more month, and November would be 18 and Mike could kick her mother out and still keep November around, which Mike had promised Neil he would do.

"Well, that's good, I guess," Neil replied. He seemed like he was about to say something more and thought better of it. "Better hurry, kiddo. Ten minutes until the gates open. Time for you to turn into the Great and Powerful Oracle."

"Right. I should also make sure Mom is up. Thanks for the book." She tossed her trash in the bin and high-tailed it back down the midway.

"Sure thing," Neil said with a wave. "I'll bring you lunch about four o'clock."

***

12

The trailer was a mess, of course. November hated messes. She began compulsively tidying. Her mom was up, miracle of miracles, and was actually drinking a cup of coffee as if she were a normal human being. *Perhaps today won't be a disaster after all.*

Julia had the same pale skin, dark blue eyes, and jet black hair as her daughter, but there the similarities ended. Her skin was prematurely aged by drink and drugs and trouble. Her clothes were always dirty and too large and her eyes haunted by all she'd seen and done and was planning to do. She never smiled for fear of showing her ruined teeth. One regret after another was scrawled across her face. When Julia looked at her daughter, love was poisoned by grief and guilt and not a little fear.

A toddler screams, inconsolable. She bangs her head against the wall. A terrified mother struggles to calm her. "Dada no go!" the child screams, again and again. A policeman bleeds in the road. A gun is dropped into a storm drain. A uniform stands at the door. Empty glass bottles fill the trash bin.

November's gift denied her the amnesia most people have about their early childhood. She could revisit every detail of her father's death: the scratch of the carpet under her face as she screamed, the crack of the gunshot, the smell of her father's blood mixed with that of asphalt and exhaust, and the sound of her mother's muffled weeping and clinking ice. The St. James Mental Health Center was also always near at hand. The institutional smell of lemon cleanser or the squeak of rubber shoes was enough to make November queasy.

The bright spots in her childhood came courtesy of her grandmother, who'd taken her on when Julia had dropped the child off and failed to return. All November had left of her was a rosary, worn smooth from years in Grandma's pocket, then a few more years in November's own. It had gone with her to foster care and from there to the hospital, where it had been returned to her when she had been released. She remembered the epic breakdown she'd suffered when the staff had taken it from her upon her arrival. They'd had to sedate her for days. Getting it back had seemed like a miracle.

It was her little oasis; fingering the beads, November could hear her grandmother's voice and smell her cooking and remember the years that she hadn't been all alone. She didn't do much praying with it, unlike its original owner. November was a little on the outs with the Almighty. Her grandmother had told her that God had blessed her with her power, but to November, of course, it seemed much more of a curse than a blessing.

"What happened last night?" her mother asked quietly, fingering her bandages and gingerly palpating her bruised face.

"You tried to steal from your . . . guest. He caught you and beat the crap out of you. You're lucky you didn't end up in jail or the hospital," November answered in a quiet voice. *I wonder if she even felt it.* The previous night she'd been furious, screaming at her mother, but in the morning light, the woman looked so small and fragile. November just couldn't summon up the rage.

"Who patched me up?" Julia asked.

"I did. Neil was busy dealing with the guy, getting him to leave."

"Thanks." Her mother just stared at the coffee cup.

"Mike read me the riot act, Mom. I'm surprised he didn't call the cops. We weren't even closed yet. There were still families here. Kids, for God's sake! This is the longest we've lasted anywhere, and Mike is going to put us out if you keep on with this,"

November said in an even voice. She couldn't even work up any anger.

"I'll do better," Julia said. "I will."

"Go to work," November ordered as she let the screen door slam behind her. At this point, she knew better than to get her hopes up.

***

November laid out the tools of her trade on the table in the center of her tent: a five-minute hourglass, a sketchpad, some sharp pencils, a bowl of sand, and a lamp. She worked barefoot. Contact with the dirt floor helped to ground her, just as the bowl of sand somehow cleansed her palate between clients, washing away the last vision and making way for the next. Her costume was a white, Grecian gown she'd found for three dollars at a secondhand store. In the dim light, her fair skin and wavy, inky hair made her ghostly and beautiful rather than sickly and pale as she appeared by daylight. Her cash box sat at her feet, to be turned in to Mike for the count as soon as the gates were closed. A lamp and a fan were plugged into a generator outside; early fall in the San Joachin Valley was brutally hot. She opened the flap of her tent, put out her sign, and sat down to wait.

She hoped it would be quiet tonight. The first few days in Tracy had been ridiculously busy. She'd had lines halfway down the midway due to her reputation from the year before. This was their second-to-last night, and usually this was when the crowds started dying down. She was exhausted, though she was glad to have a little more money to put by for the winter, assuming she could keep it away from her mother. In theory, her dad's death benefits from the force should easily get them through a few months in a trailer park in Nevada, but money went through Julia's hands like water. During the day, November's business was light, and she was grateful for some cool weather for once as she did math problems and sketched. Work began to pick up at sundown, after Neil had delivered her a dubiously nutritious lunch of a hot dog and some cotton candy.

Things quieted down for a spell, so she broke out her new textbook: *Modern Physics from A to Z.* She was just finishing the first chapter when she heard her next visitor.

"I hope we're not interrupting you," came an amused voice at the entry.

Oops. She could usually hear her clients' footsteps or see their shadows on the canvas in time to hide her books, but these people had been completely silent. "Not at all," she said quickly, then stopped short as she looked up to see her visitors. *They're here*, she told herself, disbelieving.

Her heart came into her mouth as the blood left her face. Her whole body shook once in sympathy as her world reordered itself. Finally, the Oracle remembered to breathe again.

She began to put her book away, carefully marking the page, pressing the bookmark into place, struggling to find calm and control in the ritual. She made herself look back up at them, willing her face not to show her fear. She forced a smile and welcomed death through her door.

Chapter 2

The businessman wipes his hands on a linen handkerchief after he lays the body in her grave. His hair is slightly silvered, his severe features strangely young and slashed with a thin scar. "The shovel, William," he commands the redhead. The son, who appears to be the older man, tosses the tool to his father, who catches it deftly without even sparing it a glance. The businessman looks down at the girl lying in the dirt.

"Don't be frightened, little one. I'll be here when you wake up," he whispers as he begins shoveling dirt atop November's remains.

"Wait," cries the tall girl with the blue hair. She snatches a flower from a nearby bush. She tosses it into the grave and resumes her weeping.

November wasn't sure when she'd begun having the vision. It seemed to have always been with her, a frequent presence in her dreams, and the sole vision she had ever had of her own future. When she was very small, she could pretend that the bloody little corpse was a stranger, but as she grew older, resembling the deceased more and more, she was forced to admit to herself that she was watching her own burial. She knew that she would die, violently, and much too young. The vision tasted like fate, not possibility. That certainty, that inevitability, was part of what drove her into the hospital after her grandmother's death, along with guilt over her father's death and the mental exhaustion of a power she could not control, a power that seemed to grow stronger by the day even as her mind tried and failed to keep up.

Grandma Reggie had been the only one who acknowledged the reality of November's gift. She'd tried to teach her granddaughter that her second sight did not make every tragedy her fault. She'd tried to devise ways for November to cope with the visions. It had been her idea for November to begin drawing what she saw as a way of getting it out of her system. Regina had gotten her art lessons as soon as the child could hold a pencil properly. Too, soon, however, she had died and left November to the abuse and neglect of her floundering mother and the ineffectual-at-best treatments of a series of increasingly depressing hospitals and doctor's offices.

At first, without her grandmother's help, the effort needed to cling to sanity just didn't seem possible or even worthwhile. Why struggle if she was going to die before she could even begin an adult life? Eventually, November had come to an acceptance of her fate. She began to find her happiness in little things, as grim as her life in the hospital sometimes was. Once she got a little older, got a handle on her fear of mortality, she began to gain some control over her power. None of her varied visions frightened her any longer; she no longer scratched at her eyes in her sleep. She found ways of coping with her sightings, blocking them with some success, and seeking them if she wanted to find them. Her periods of lucidity became longer, and her attempts at suicide ceased. Finally, she was able to convince a new doctor at the hospital that she was cured enough to be released. She had found a path through her madness. She'd long hoped her mother would be able to do the same with her addiction, but in this, November was forever disappointed.

Now, here stood three people in her tent, two of whom she knew for a fact would help put her in the ground before she was old enough to rent a car. The redhead was a little on the short side, with the solid build of someone accustomed to physical work, but his clothes were those of a wealthy man, his aura one of leader of men. He was handsome and imposing, with his dark red hair and the fairest skin November had ever seen. A sprinkling of freckles and a crinkle of laugh lines softened his serious face. The blue-haired girl seemed even more graceful in person than she had in the vision, and she was even lovelier looking happy than she was in grief. Her hair and her eyes were the same improbable shade of electric blue, her ethnicity difficult to guess. The boy was new to her. He looked like he'd just stepped out of a frat house on the way to a beer run – cute but not very impressive. He was blond and cocky and very "California beach bum," though lacking the requisite tan.

November closed her eyes briefly, trying to regain her balance. They would not kill her tonight; she could be pretty certain of that. The clothes were wrong; there was an extra man, and two of her gravediggers were missing. She clung to that assertion. This focus helped her to slow her runaway heart, and she opened her eyes again. Her fear was gone. After all, she did not fear death anymore. Pain, she feared, but not death. And in the vision, they seemed to be her friends. They were sad that she died, so she didn't think they would try to hurt her. She was actually more excited than scared, she realized. She had spent her whole life wondering how she was going to come to such a strange end. Now she seemed on the verge of finding out. *Showtime.*

"Please, do sit down." Perhaps a display of power was in order, to get rid of the feeling that they'd caught her flat-footed. She looked at the redheaded leader. "Your name is William, yes?" Now it was their turn to be surprised. They glanced at one another as they sat down in November's sanctum.

"Yes," he allowed. "It's William Knox. Microphones planted around the carnival, is it? Or scouts to relay what people are saying?" His lips were pursed with amusement. He had the air of an adult humoring a lying preschooler.

"If only," November replied with a tired smile. "I've been waiting for you for quite some time – well, two of you, at least. I just didn't know we would meet tonight."

William raised an eyebrow. "Is that right? And what do they call you when you're not playing Oracle, little girl?"

"November," she answered, surprising herself. "Em, to friends." She never shared her real name with clients, but she guessed there was no reason to dissemble with these ones. They would get to know each other soon enough, after all.

"That is a different one," commented the girl with a friendly smile.

"Mom accidentally put the date on the name section of the birth certificate form, and she and Dad decided that they liked it. And what shall I call the rest of you?" November replied.

"You can't tell with your magic powers?" sneered the blond youth.

"I probably could, but it isn't very polite." November didn't mind skeptics, but he didn't have to be so obnoxious about it.

William gestured toward his companions. "Zinnia and Ben." Zinnia gave a wave and a smile. Ben just rolled his eyes.

"How does this work?" Zinnia asked, tucking an errant lock of her short blue hair behind her delicate ear.

"Five minutes for five dollars." She held out a gloved hand into which Knox placed a crisp ten dollar bill. November dispensed with her usual theatrics, assuming correctly that they wouldn't play with this crowd. "I will begin with the past, to establish my credibility. I then will probe the future, which is so much more uncertain. Much of the future is fluid and can be changed by decisions that lead you down different paths," November explained.

"Trying to prepare us for this turning out to be a crock?" chimed in the younger man. November raised an irritated eyebrow.

"May I continue?" she asked with a touch of hauteur. William silenced Ben with a look. November began again. "In each person's life, however, there are usually one or more events that are unavoidable. All paths lead to those points, however circuitously. Some things are just inevitable. Some people call these moments fate."

"So how do you tell what is fated from what can be changed?" asked Zinnia. Her voice lacked Ben's condescension. November realized that this member of the party, at least, was actually interested in her work.

"I can't know for certain, always. But so far the visions that come unsought and that come again and again, unchanging: those ones seem to come true no matter what people do."

"Why the notebook? And the sand?" Zinnia probed.

"Sometimes I draw what I see, faces mostly. I'm not always able to catch names when I'm under. Plus, clients get a kick out of it, and sometimes they tip," she said with a crooked grin. The sand was harder for November to explain clearly. She'd never tried to put it into words before. "The sand helps me transition from one person to the next. It kind of, like . . . washes away the old vision, so I don't get too distracted and muddled. That and digging my toes in the dirt seem to blot out some extraneous noise and fragments."

"Did someone teach you that?" The girl seemed genuinely curious.

"I discovered it by accident when I was little, playing in the sandbox. My grandmother had to drag me away kicking and screaming. It was the only place I had any peace." It was kind of nice, actually, sharing some of her own story with these strangers, though it made her exposed. People came to the Oracle to ask questions about themselves, not about her, and she hadn't been able to discuss her gift honestly with anyone since her grandmother had died. She was accustomed to people looking at her without ever seeing her.

"Can we get on with this ridiculous waste of time?" asked Ben with an impatient sigh.

William offered his hand, and November removed her gloves and turned the hourglass over. "Let's begin at the beginning," she said. She braced herself and touched his hand.

The first thing she noticed was that he was cold as death; the next was that this was unlike any reading she'd ever done. She expected it to be painful. Her readings were usually a disorienting agony, but she was pleasantly surprised. It was like looking over a cliff and down into a pool of water so deep that she couldn't see the bottom. Normally, she was sucked right out of time, pulled under like some kind of thrashing drowning victim in a horror movie. But with this man, she had to consciously choose to jump. She fell and fell until she hit the water, then she swam for what seemed like forever, past memory upon memory, year after year after year. She could see William's life shimmering around her; she could reach out and touch events as she chose, tasting a moment here or there, but they did not reach out to grab her like the pasts of other people.

A creaky ship with black sails, a battlefield littered with men and horses rotting in the sun, a woman great with child, laughing in a garden. Her businessman, dressed in an ancient style, cradles William's mangled body, aided by a beauty with golden hair. William bites a man with a hook for a hand and drinks until the light goes out of his prey's eyes.

Alternately horrified and fascinated, she wanted to stop and explore everything, and at the same time she longed to flee back to her tent and forget every bit of it. It took all her discipline to keep going, back and back, further into the depths. At last she found it: the beginning.

A mother rocks her child, singing a song in an ancient tongue, singing in the sunlight to quiet the fussing baby with his bright red mop of curly hair.

November began to sing along, singing words both foreign and somehow familiar, since every lullaby is the same, really. They all say, "I love you, baby. Sleep well, baby. Sleep safe, baby." November felt wrapped in the warmth and the safety of the scene.

Suddenly, she was back in her chair in her little tent, shaking with exertion. William had snatched his hand away as if burned and looked at her with a new respect. "What are you? How could you possibly know that song?" he asked quietly.

She shrugged her shoulders. "I don't know why I can do this." She paused, trying to assimilate what she'd seen, having difficulty believing what she'd experienced. "You are . . . really old," she said, forgetting her manners in the face of her shock. William nodded in confirmation. She glanced at the hourglass just as the last grain fell. She absentmindedly turned it over again as she began to quickly sketch the faces she'd seen. "That was . . . unusual."

"You are quite impressive, I must say," he admitted, staring at her hand as faces began to appear on the paper.

"Do you impress easily?" November asked with a little smile as she sketched, fishing for complements.

"No," came his curt reply. "Besides my age, how was this unusual?" he asked after a moment's pause.

"Less painful than most other readings. More information, but easier to control. More vivid but less . . . suffocating." She held up the paper. "Your mother?"

William nodded, shocked anew. "My human one. I'd almost forgotten what she looked like. I haven't seen her face in nine hundred years."

November finally screwed up the nerve to look into his face. "Are you really a, um, vampire?" she whispered. William nodded. November took a deep breath. "All of you?" William shook his head.

"I'm a fairy," said Zinnia with a playful smile.

November closed her eyes. "Seriously? Fairies are real, too," she said, taking a deep breath. "I, mean, I've seen such things in dreams, but I didn't put much stock in them. People thought I was crazy enough as it was. I told myself that those visions were metaphorical or something." She sighed. "I suppose there's also a werewolf waiting in the car?" she added jokingly.

"Of course not. Werewolves are our enemies from time immemorial. We are allied against them," replied William severely.

"Right . . ." She shook her head in disbelief. "Well, this is all a bit overwhelming." November pressed her fingers to her temples. "Shall I try to see your future, then?"

"Oh, I think that's rather enough for today," William said quietly. "And as for being overwhelmed, you'll feel much better after I make you forget that this ever happened. That will give us some time to figure out what to do with you without your running away or telling anyone about our existence. Zinnia," he said, turning his head, "would you do the honors?"

The girl's voice took on a strangely sonorous quality as she said, "Listen carefully to me, November. This never happened. You've never met William, Zinnia, or Ben. There's no such thing as vampires or fairies or werewolves."

November burst out laughing, giddy from the adrenaline and the strangeness of it all, covering her mouth and raising a quizzical eyebrow. "I'm sorry, does that usually work?"

William swore. "Yes, usually. And now we've violated the Precepts. Terrific."

"Precepts?" November asked.

"We have laws, November, and one of the most important ones is to prevent the human race from learning that supernatural creatures exist," explained the fairy. "So we enthrall humans to erase the memories of those on whom we feed and others who discover our existence. It seems, however, that you are immune."

"How old are you?" William demanded.

"I'll be eighteen on the first of November," the girl replied. "Why?" she asked.

"Damn it. You're too young to turn for three years yet," William muttered. "The Reforms are such a nuisance sometimes. Sometimes I really wonder why I wrote them. What am I supposed to do with you?"

"We could kill her," said Ben. "Problem solved. I'm hungry again." He leered at her. November looked right at him, showing no fear. She supposed she should be more alarmed. Honestly, though, he was more irritating than scary. Maybe that's why he was acting like such a jerk: overcompensation.

"Stop it, youngling," William growled. "Magic humans don't grow on trees. We're not wasting her blood on you. Perhaps we can make a good case for an exception, since she's so valuable." He turned to November to add, "Please excuse him. He is a toddler who hasn't yet learned any manners." The blond youth glowered.

"No offense taken," she carefully replied. "I'm not going to tell anyone about you," November tried to assure them. "And who would believe me if I did?"

"You would have been smarter to lie, to pretend you didn't see what we were, to pretend that you're a fraud, a con artist." William looked at her, almost regretfully. "Now you're stuck with us. You'll have to become part of our world. Your fate is sealed."

November's smile was a touch wistful. "Oh, not to worry, Mr. Knox. My fate was sealed quite some time ago. I could only have perhaps delayed the inevitable. Here, I'll show you." She pulled one of the binders out of the battered army surplus trunk that contained her few prized possessions. She'd never shown these drawings to anyone except her grandmother. "Now, you must excuse the quality of the early ones. I was only this many when I started drawing you," she explained, holding up three fingers.

The three creatures gathered around her record, flipping through the drawings November had made of her visions. Her habit was to draw all sightings that disturbed her. It helped her process her emotions and put them out of her mind. She kept the ones that seemed important and destroyed the rest. This binder was labeled "My End."

The early drawings were stick figures in crayon, sometimes labeled with misspelled words: "blu ladee, ded body, shovl." They grew more detailed later. Some showed the whole scene, others the faces in detail. On some she'd jotted the spoken words she could make out, or pictures of the flowers. There was a tenderness in the later drawings, almost like affection. These specters that once had frightened her into madness had gradually become old friends, like any frequent visitor is apt to do. "This is the only vision I've ever had about my own personal future. I know nothing else about my fate. I've tried to look, but it's all fog and smoke." She paused. "I assume you know the others in the scene?" she asked as the visitors flipped through her work, stunned into silence.

"Yes," the man in charge finally answered. "The vampire who made me is the one you call the businessman. The Indian woman is my sister Savita, made by the same vampire." He closed the book and inquired, "May I take this with me? I will return it."

November hesitated. It felt like giving away a part of herself. Then she relented, realizing that she didn't really need it anymore. "Sure," she said. "Please don't let anyone normal see it. I don't want to end up back in the madhouse."

"Do not worry about that. I am not in the habit of consulting humans," he said with a small smile. "You seem awfully calm about all this. Human beings are not usually so sanguine about their own deaths. Nor are vampires or fairies for that matter."

"It's kind of a relief, honestly, that you've finally appeared. I've spent my life waiting for the ax to fall," she confided. "I stopped being afraid of dying some time ago. I know that's insane, but the world beyond is better than this one, based on what I've seen of both."

Her guest stood up. "Based on these drawings, you're going to be stuck in this world even after you die, poor child." He studied her for a moment. "We will be back for you. I must make arrangements. Do not run," he admonished her. "We would surely find you, and as much fun as it would be to hunt you, I really don't have the time to waste. Besides, if you eluded us, you could well find yourself in the hands of someone worse. Diamonds don't stay hidden forever. When does your little band leave town?" asked the vampire, standing up to depart.

"Day after tomorrow, at dawn," November answered truthfully. She had no intention of trying to evade them, knowing that it would be futile. "Are you going to bite me?" she asked with some trepidation.

"Almost certainly," William answered with a grin, "but not right now. I wish we had more time to prepare, but we will have to make do. We shall see you tomorrow night, November. Stay out of trouble."

"Wait," she cried. "I have more questions!" And in the blink of an eye, they were gone, silently and invisibly, and she was left alone once again, with only her visions for company.

Chapter 3

November stumbled through the rest of the evening on auto-pilot, tremendously grateful when the last patron made his exit. It didn't seem real; it simply didn't seem possible that she'd just met two vampires and a fairy, a dream come to life. She wondered briefly if she was losing her mind again but quickly dismissed the notion. In fact, she was strangely calm. The shaking and crying would come later, when she lay down to sleep and found her mind abuzz with questions and fears and strange images from William Knox's too long life.

November realized she was ravenous, changed clothes quickly, turned in her cash box, and headed down to the communal supper they held together late each night. As usual, she brought a book with her, but she found herself looking around the table rather than burying her head in its pages. There were a few faces she'd miss: Neil, of course, and sweet Mrs. Kravitz who had made her a birthday cake the year before. The workers chatted loudly, blowing off steam after a long day. She kept accidentally catching Mike's eye; he would then quickly look away. That was odd. The carnival owner usually avoided even glancing at her, unless her mother's behavior made it unavoidable; November had the impression he was a little afraid of her. Her mother was picking at her food with shaking hands. November knew better than to get anywhere near her when she looked that desperate for a fix.

None of them knew anything of the revelations that had taken place that evening in November's tattered tent. None of them were aware that the world they inhabited wasn't theirs alone. November couldn't imagine what their reaction would be to the idea that there were magical creatures among them, wandering the world with their own plans and their own laws. She wondered what her own reactions would be to what was sure to be a stream of disturbing revelations to come. Tomorrow, the troupe would pack everything up to move on to the next town, and for the first time in years, November wouldn't be going with them. She wondered how long it would take them to notice she was gone. She wondered if they'd look for her. She wasn't sure if she wanted them to or not.

As soon as she crawled into the warmth and safety of her sleeping bag, her usual stoicism fell away, and she began crying out the shock that she'd had to keep bottled up all evening. She held tight to her grandmother's rosary as she confronted her fear of being taken away into the unknown, into a world she knew nothing about, into the hands of ancient and dangerous predators who would somehow lead her to an early grave. Would she be miserable? Would they be cruel to her? She thought not, based on the little information in her vision, but how could she be sure? Would her mother be able to manage without her? What would become of that broken woman?

After November had wrung out all her fear and trepidation, she fell into an exhausted sleep, watching William Knox forge weapons and shoe horses and bite people until the sun rose. Her dreams that night were vivid but not horrifying or terribly violent, to her great relief. She'd feared the scenes of war and murder she'd caught glimpses of during the reading would return in force, but she had been spared more of that for the moment.

The next day, working all day and then striking and packing kept her occupied enough that she didn't have too much time to think. She filled her small suitcase and trunk and kept them aside along with her sleeping bag, not knowing whether or not she'd need them in her new life. Once her own tent was packed up, she wandered around the camp offering a hand to those who needed some help with their gear. After years in this nomadic life, November was stronger than she looked, wiry and hard beneath her worn clothes.

As she walked and worked, she caught snippets of conversations from the previous night. Normally she would ignore such clutter, but there came a moment when she thought she could hear William Knox's voice. November had assumed that the mysterious trio had left the carnival directly after they had high-tailed it out of her tent. It appeared she had been mistaken.

She began to listen more deliberately: it seemed that her new friends had been asking around, gathering information about her: "Frigid little witch, that one . . . Nice girl. Too bad about her mom . . . Nose in a book all the time . . . I hear she spent time in a hospital . . . Works hard, never causes trouble . . . Did you see what her mother did to her arm?" She spied Ben talking up the girl who ran the cotton candy stand, her hair dyed the same pink as her wares. She saw Zinnia deep in conversation with Neil, and she caught a glimpse of William having a quiet talk with Mike, but she couldn't make out more than a few words. *What was that all about?*

As the night wore on and she had no more work to keep her busy, November grew ever more anxious. Everyone else gathered to eat and celebrate the successful run. November hung back. Her appetite had left her; she was increasingly nervous, and she didn't think she could manage acting normal in front of the others while they feasted.

She wondered how long she would have to wait. Maybe the vampires would change their minds and leave her alone? She knew in her heart that this was highly unlikely. Would she have a chance to say goodbye to her mother? Did she even want to? What would she say? She didn't imagine the woman would be happy to lose a source of income. November turned to the always helpful coping mechanism of indulging her nerdiness and sat reading on her trunk for the next hour, waiting for the hangman.

"You didn't run. I'm a little disappointed," Ben whispered in her ear with no warning whatsoever.

"Jesus!" cried November, jumping up and away from him. "What is it with you guys and the sneaking up on people?" She was thoroughly creeped out.

"Sorry," he replied with a grin that said he wasn't. "It's kind of our whole bag."

"You seem to be in a much better mood today," November said grudgingly as she willed herself to calm down. *Stop shaking*, she told herself sternly.

"Yeah, sorry about that," he allowed. "Baby vampires get cranky when they're hungry." He shrugged.

"So you're not hungry now, then?" she asked hesitatingly, keeping a wary distance.

"Nope. You can thank the young ladies of Laney College for that. I ate before we left Oakland." He looked awfully pleased with himself.

November wondered if these college students had survived being Ben's dinner.

Ben must have caught her expression, as he added, "Relax. I didn't kill them or anything. We don't kill every time we eat. It's wasteful, and what would we do with all the bodies? We try to avoid killing warmbloods, actually."

"Good to know," November said, a bit awkwardly. "So, now what?"

"Come with me," Ben replied mysteriously. "There's something Lord William wants you to see."

"*Lord* William?" she asked incredulously, both eyebrows and arms akimbo.

"I know; it's ridiculous. Vampires have a rather antiquated governmental structure. They're crazy old fashioned," Ben explained as they walked. "It takes some serious getting used to."

Ben stopped her as they came up behind Julia's trailer. November's stomach filled with butterflies when she saw William Knox deep in conversation with her mother, their backs turned to the young eavesdroppers. Ben and November stood in the shadow of a tree, close enough to hear their conversation without being noticed by Mrs. Snow. November listened closely, fighting a feeling of foreboding. Was the vampire going to harm her mother? To enthrall her into not calling the police once her daughter disappeared?

"I'll give you five hundred dollars for her," William coldly proposed. Julia was twitching, unable to keep still. Her dealer had raised his prices, and she was in a really bad way. November's eyes widened in horror. She pressed her lips together to keep herself silent. She knew at once how this was going to go, but she refused to believe it.

"She's my daughter," Julia protested unconvincingly. "What kind of monster do you think I am?"

"Don't insult me by pretending you care enough about her to refuse," William answered. "Do you have a counteroffer?"

Julia hesitated, but only for a moment, such a painfully short moment. "A thousand. And the watch." She pointed at William's Rolex.

November had to lean on the tree to keep from falling to the ground. She knew she had a bad mother, but this betrayal was a knife in her stomach. Her injured arm began to throb anew. She pressed her fist against her mouth to keep from sobbing out loud, but she couldn't stop the tears from pouring down her face. That Ben was standing there watching her only made it worse, one humiliation on top of another. She had no desire to have an audience for her agony, especially that cocky man-child. She tried to hide behind her hair. *Why do I feel so ashamed when I'm not the one doing something shameful?* Part of her wanted to confront the woman she could no longer call her mother. The rest of her wanted to flee, to find a dark hole to climb in and never come out.

"Done," William replied, counting out the cash and taking off his watch. "You will leave the carnival and have nothing to do with any of these people ever again. You know they will turn you in to the police if they see you with this kind of money after your child goes missing. I told the owner that Child Protective Services was taking her away, and you'd best let them continue to believe that. Listen carefully: you don't remember what I look like," he said, his voice suddenly different as he enthralled her to cover his tracks. Then he swiftly turned and began to walk away. The former blacksmith turned back to add, "You didn't even ask me what I want her for. How do you live with yourself?" He strode away, shaking his head in disgust.

November turned to run, unthinking, just desperate to get away. Ben stopped her, grabbing her by the shoulders. "I'm sorry. I didn't know that was what he wanted you to see." His face and voice were earnest.

She looked at him for a moment, silent and uncomprehending. Then she let Ben take her by her gloved hand and lead her away. She was too dazed to argue. They found Knox standing by her meager pile of belongings. When she saw him, her pain turned to anger.

"Why did you make me see that?" she cried. "What did I do to make you want to hurt me?"

William turned to face her rage. "It was not my desire to cause you pain, child, but I needed you to see the truth. I need you to understand that there is no coming back to this place for you. You will be homesick in the coming days; you will grieve for the life you left behind. You will miss your mother, God knows why. But you will. You will think of running away. That is normal for someone entering our world. Such dramatic change is bound be difficult. But you need to understand that there is nothing here for you. There is no home for you here. That woman isn't worthy of you. You owe her nothing. She doesn't deserve your worry or your love."

William paused. "I also needed to be sure she wouldn't go to the police after you disappeared," he admitted. "You have every right to be angry with me. I hope that in time you'll forgive me and come to understand my reasons. I hope you'll be able to turn your anger to your mother who deserves it, and that in time you'll let go of that burden and make a clean break with your human life. And I assure you that we will take better care of you than she ever has. Now, we must go."

"You're a monster," she spat.

"Sometimes." He reached for her hand. "Come."

November refused to let him touch her, but she walked with them, silent and calm, too numb to fight or to feel much of anything. She let William help her into the back seat of a black sedan, not even registering the swanky brand and the leather seats. She took the handkerchief he offered and wiped her face of tears. Ben took the wheel, and Zinnia turned from the front passenger side to give her a sympathetic look.

"That must have been awful. I could feel it all the way from here. I'm sorry." The fairy reached for her hand to give it a squeeze. November let her. Zinnia looked at the bandage peeking out of November's sleeve. "Hey, would it be okay if I healed your arm in the morning? So it doesn't scar?" She glanced at both November and William for approval.

"Good idea, Zin," William replied. "And Ben, we'll need to stop at the ranch on the way. I haven't fed in days."

"Livermore it is, boss," Ben said with a grin as he pulled out of the dusty parking lot. "I can always use a snack."

"Just roll up your sleeve so I can see it, November. If it's really bad, we'll have to ask someone else to take care of it. Healing isn't my best gift."

Zinnia winced as the wounds came into view, three burns across her forearm about an inch wide and an inch apart. For an instant, November could see fury fill William's eyes as he looked at the swollen welts. In that moment, she softened a bit toward him. His anger at her suffering seemed genuine.

"What happened?" Zinnia asked in a near whisper.

November was reluctant to answer at first, but seeing the concern in Zinnia's eyes gave her the courage to come out with it. *What the hell? Let's give having friends a try.* "She thought I was hiding money. She needed it for drugs, and she wanted me to tell her where I was keeping it. I had the curling iron out. My hair had dried funny, and I was trying to get ready for the customers that afternoon." November hesitated. "So, when I wouldn't tell her where it was, she just picked it up and . . . It was impulsive. She

36

didn't plan it or anything. She's not as bad as that. She just . . ." November trailed off, unable to say the words.

"*Were* you hiding money?" Zinnia asked, appalled.

"Of course I was. She can't be trusted with it. Winter is coming, and I've worn out my shoes." She paused. "I hate being cold."

"Did you tell her where it was?" William asked in a soft voice.

She turned to look him in the eye. "No," she answered firmly.

Knox gave her a sad but approving look. "Good girl."

November smiled slightly at that, surprising herself and the vampire both. She looked back toward Zinnia. "So, how does this healing thing work?"

"Fairies can heal injuries by laying on of hands. See, to eat, we use physical contact to feed on the life energy of other living creatures. When we heal, we're basically giving some of it back. But it only works during the day," she concluded with a shrug of apology, then turning back around and leaving November alone with William in the back seat.

After a somewhat awkward silence, November ventured, "So, where are we going?"

"We'll stop briefly at a ranch I own in Livermore. I keep a variety of animals there, for hunting," William explained. "From there, we'll go to my house in the Oakland hills. We've set up a room for you there. We should probably do one at the ranch as well, but we haven't yet had time." The vampire's smartphone buzzed. "Excuse me, I need to take this."

November turned to gaze out the window as her host conducted his business. She tried not to eavesdrop as her kidnapper/rescuer/pall bearer discussed the stock options of some tech company he was involved with down in Silicon Valley. She looked around the car with calmer eyes, and what she saw was money, money everywhere: designer clothes, state-of-the-art phones, expensive haircuts, manicured hands. Whatever these creatures did for a living, it was lucrative.

She looked down self-consciously at her own hands: her broken, dirty nails and dry skin and rough cuticles. She looked at her clothes: ill-fitting and worn and someone else's before they were hers. She wasn't ashamed of herself; she didn't consider poverty a sin. It was just one more reason for her to feel off-balance and out-of-place. Her new companions weren't just from an alien world— they were also from a very different class.

November returned her gaze to the window. They were speeding along the curving interstate through the Altamont Pass. During the day, the arms of the windmills spin their welcome as the same wind that turns them ruffles the grass, tall and brown and ready to burn after the long, dry summer. At night, it is a bit eerie, the unlit hills rising black on each side, the road curving out of sight into the dark. She smiled as they came out of the pass above the Livermore Valley, looking down at all the lights as they began descending the long hill down into Livermore. When the wind is high, drivers feel like they are going to be blown off the road, but this night was calm. The valley below had a busy sort of beauty to it. It was hard to believe that amongst all that frantic development, alongside national laboratories and strip malls and subdivisions, there were still working farms, still people tending vineyards and raising cattle and sheep and horses. It was even harder to believe that a vampire lord kept a ranch as a snack bar amongst all the scientists, commuters, ranchers, vintners, and suburban families.

They soon exited the highway, as empty at this time of night as it was gridlocked during rush hour. The roads became smaller, and soon the luxury sedan approached the gated entrance to William's ranch. It seemed likely to be the best-fenced property in the area, national labs included. November looked up at the ten-foot-high electric fences topped with razor wire and her body gave an involuntary shiver.

"It's just to keep the neighbors safe, November," William explained, noting her discomfort. "We don't want animals or humans or, God forbid, children wandering onto the property while we're hunting. If a vampire in pursuit caught scent of a human . . . there are very few of us who would be able to resist."

"I don't think I find that as reassuring as you intend it to be, given my, um, humanness," November replied as the main house came into view. Automatic floodlights came on as they drove down the driveway. It was quite a lovely house, all timber and stone and large windows. It was well-landscaped, with drought-resistant trees and shrubs scattered artistically about. November wondered what it would look like during the day. It looked like there was a garden in the back, perhaps a gazebo.

"You will be perfectly safe in the house, I promise you. Zinnia and my sister will keep you company. She spends most of her time out here, with her wife and a few of our staff who take care of the land and the animals. The city doesn't suit her," William explained as he helped her out of the car and into the cool night air. November wrapped her arms around herself against the chill, prompting William to remove his jacket and place it around her shoulders.

"Thank you," the young woman said, touched by the gesture in spite of herself. An Indian girl appeared at the door as the four of them climbed up to the porch. She was wearing a cotton *salwar kameez*.

"You are most welcome," she said in greeting, smiling at November. "My brother has told me about you. My name is Savita. I'm afraid I can offer you nothing but water. We are not accustomed to having human visitors here."

"Hey, Savu *akka*," he greeted his sister with a kiss. "You're actually one of the first humans to set foot on the property since the construction was completed," William added cheerily.

"How . . . um . . . flattering," November responded uncertainly, drowning in the large coat that had been made for a blacksmith's shoulders. She caught a glimpse of Knox sitting at a large desk in a very well-appointed office.

"We'll be back in 30, *akka*," William called to his sister as he descended the steps. He smiled back at them, and the two hungry vampires disappeared in a blur of speed.

"Wow," breathed November.

"One of our more useful tricks," Savita replied. "Into the house with you."

They sat in a homey room full of comfortable furniture facing a large fireplace. Zinnia pulled out what looked like homework and settled down on the floor to study. As November sank into the leather couch, she saw her binder of drawings sitting on the coffee table.

"William came straight here after meeting you, to show me your drawings and to tell me of the reading you conducted with him. He was amazed, and believe me when I tell you he is very rarely impressed by a human," Savita began. "It seems that you are a very powerful seer."

"I don't know about that," November replied, looking at her hands. Powerful was not a word that she associated with herself.

"We do. Young one, my brother has been alive for nearly 900 years, and I have 50 more years than he. Seers, wise women, healers, mind-readers – they are extremely rare among the humans. And visions of the future are rare even amongst our people, the vampires and fairies. You may well be the most powerful soothsayer to fall into vampire hands in centuries. You are extremely valuable." Savita watched the human carefully, sensing her trepidation. "I am frightening you with this talk."

"I don't understand what you want with me. I thought your brother was taking me mostly because I found out the secret of your existence, but you seem to have very high expectations of my abilities. All I am is a crazy teenage girl with a power she can barely control. What if I'm not what you want me to be?"

"All we want is for you to help us as best you can with certain problems we face. We will not hurt you if you fail, November, and we will do everything we can to protect you from those who would," Savita reassured her earnestly. She reached out to touch November's knee but pulled up short when the human flinched.

"Those who would what?" November asked softly, thinking of her bloody corpse lying in the dirt.

"When your gift becomes known in our community, a day we will do our best to forestall, there will be others who covet you, others who have less respect for humans and who would deal with you more harshly, others who would do whatever is necessary to stop you from helping us," Savita explained with somewhat brutal honesty.

November took a deep breath, trying to steady her heart and her voice. "Other vampires?" she finally asked.

"Vampires, fairies, even werewolves. You are a rare jewel. It's a lucky thing we found you before anyone else did," Savita added.

"Lucky for me, or lucky for you?" November ventured boldly.

"Both, I hope," said the vampire with a twitch of a smile.

"You've endangered me. You've brought me into a fight that isn't mine." November was circling back towards anger again.

"Yes. But the truth is, you would have been dragged into it by someone. You don't seem to understand the reputation you've built travelling with this carnival. We did some research after we heard about you. You have quite the internet fan base, November. You're all over Facebook, Instagram, Tumblr, Twitter, YouTube. Some powerful creature was going to find you and use you. It was inevitable. You were never going to be left alone to live a normal life in the human world, if your gift would even allow you to do so."

"Here, show her," Zinnia chimed in, passing her laptop to Savita.

November looked at the screen, stunned into silence. There was a picture of her, presumably taken with someone's phone. It was in black-and-white, part of her face obscured by her hair, which had the effect of making her look mysterious and exotic. There were testimonials from clients singing her praises, a few complaints from others, sketches that had been scanned and uploaded, and the carnival's projected schedule for this year and next. There were even audio and video files of readings, probably also taken surreptitiously with a phone. November felt naked.

"You really didn't know, did you?" Savita said, reading the look on her face. November shook her head. "In this modern world, nothing stays secret or anonymous for long. Besides – you told William yourself that you knew this was fate, for you to wind up with us." November nodded.

Suddenly, November was sucked from the comfortable room out into the grassland behind the garden.

A deer is running for his life, but his death is running faster. The hunter is exhilarated and hungry; the prey is desperate and afraid. William leaps onto his quarry's back and sinks his teeth into his neck; the deer stumbles and falls to his knees, surrendering to the inevitable. The animal gives no cry of pain; he does not thrash or fight. He slowly weakens as the vampire feeds until his breathing stops. William pats his dinner's neck, whispers, "Thanks," and begins striding back to the house.

November came back to herself with a gasp, looking into Savita's concerned face. "Are you alright, November?" the vampire asked with concern.

November nodded. "Just caught sight of your brother, ah . . . eating breakfast," she answered. "Sometimes visions come upon me like that, without warning. I wonder why . . . oh, the coat, of course! Personal objects, especially when they are often worn -- they can give me very vivid sightings."

"That is as it was for my sister, as well," Savita replied with a sad smile.

"You have a sister like me?" November asked excitedly. She'd never met anyone else with a gift like hers.

"Had. When I was human. She was so beautiful. She couldn't bear her gift. She took her own life when we were teenagers, shortly before I was made a vampire." Savita looked across the room and shook her head.

"I can certainly understand why she would. I tried more than once," November confessed quietly. "I finally gained some control over the visions, but I had to learn to harden my heart. I'm sorry for your loss," she finished weakly, reaching her hand tentatively toward the vampire, not knowing what to say.

"It was a very long time ago," she said. "Your strength will be an asset to you now. It sounds like you're half vampire already," she said with a weak smile.

"May I ask, how old were you when you were, um, changed?" November was curious because William had said she herself was too young to turn, but Savita looked to be barely more than a child.

"I was 15. We have since decided that is far too young. The world was different then. I was an adult by our standards, already married and widowed when I died. But going through eternity looking like what is now considered a child is a bit of a burden, and many people your age are not mature enough to handle the transition from a human life to a vampire one. We lose a lot of young vampires. And a disappearing minor tends to attract police attention. So, about a century ago we made a law that humans must be 21 to be turned."

At that, William strode in, seeming more relaxed than he had in the car, and with a bit of color in his ivory face.

"By the way, where's Noemi?" he asked his sister.

"My wife is still in Las Vegas, helping Father install his new artwork," she replied before adding, "It seems you gave our new psychic friend quite a show."

"You saw me feeding?" he asked, concerned that he had frightened the human. "Are you . . . upset?" he asked gingerly.

"No, it was fine. I've had much worse, believe me. It was actually kind of beautiful and exciting, to be honest," she admitted, coloring slightly. "And he didn't seem to suffer or fight. It looked as if he was falling asleep," the seer finished.

"Our saliva contains analgesics and a substance that induces calm and a sense of wellbeing, so our prey don't suffer unless we hurt them on purpose. There are those who like to torment their food, but I am not among them." The imposing redhead paused. "Not unless it's someone who deserves it," he finished ominously.

William sat down next to November. "Which brings us to the next part of your adventure." He paused, and the human's anxiety returned in full force. "We must exchange blood."

"I beg your pardon?" she blurted, sliding away from him. "Why would we need to do that?" she asked with alarm, turning to Savita to look for aid.

"So that other vampires and fairies know that he has a claim on you, that you are not prey available to them," Savita explained gently. "You only need to swallow a drop of his blood, and he will need a sip or two of yours. It will not harm you. Then our people will be able to tell when they meet you that you are bound to William. He is Lord of California, so none of his vassals would dare molest you."

"They'll think I'm his pet human?" she asked with some distaste, wrinkling her nose.

"Essentially," William admitted. "That will make them curious about you, as I have not had a favorite human in many years. They will be even more curious if they find out that you're living in my home. That simply isn't done unless a vampire plans to turn his human in short order, and you are too young yet to turn legally. You will be meeting dangerous people who will want your blood and your body and, once they find out about it, your gift. This blood bond will make them at least think twice about trying to take you, as it would be an act of aggression against me. It is well known that I am not a good man to have for an enemy, and I have a powerful family. The blood will also help us to find you if you are ever stolen."

William leaned in to look into her alarm-widened eyes. "I know it must be horrifying, the thought that people will think of you as property. But it will help protect you. It must be done."

November nodded. The idea of being seen as someone's pet *was* horrifying; the idea of being seen as "free prey" was rather more horrifying. "Will it hurt?"

"A little, as the fangs pierce the skin. Like a needle. After that, no," Savita assured her.

"Okay," November said softly after a brief pause. She swallowed. "I'm ready."

"You really are a brave girl," William said with a touch of regret. Fangs appeared in his mouth, transforming his features in a rather terrifying fashion and quickening November's heartbeat. He pricked his finger with one fang and held out his hand. November took a drop of blood on the tip of her finger, braced herself, and licked the crimson liquid from her hand, grimacing with anticipatory disgust.

Her mind was filled to bursting with image upon image, too fast to process or appreciate, one bitten victim after another, a millennium's worth of hunting and feeding and fighting and sex compressed into thirty seconds of whirlwind. She heard someone cry out in pain or pleasure; she couldn't tell which. It took her a moment to realize the voice was hers. When she opened her eyes, she was on the floor, William, Zinnia, and Savita hovering over her with worried faces.

"That was rather intense," she said, placing her hand upon her forehead as the struggled to sit up.

"You looked like you were having a seizure of some sort," Savita said, helping her back onto the couch. "That is not the typical reaction to consuming our blood. What did you see?"

November hesitated. "A lot of feeding. A lot." She colored again as she remembered what else she'd seen. "I'm alright. It wasn't painful, just really, ah, vivid."

William looked like he would blush if he could. "By the way, whatever you see of my life, tonight or any other time, I need you to keep to yourself. I am a private man, and neither my enemies nor my friends need to know my every secret. I must say, having to place so much trust in a human makes me uncomfortable. Though I expect it's no more than I deserve given how I've upended your life."

"I don't discuss my visions with people who aren't in them. If I draw any of you, I'll give the papers to you, and you can decide whether or not to destroy them," she replied. William's request made her realize that she was not, in fact, powerless. William was exposing himself to the very real danger that she would see things he wanted kept secret. The moment he first touched her, he put a weapon in her hand. *I am not helpless. I have something they want. Something they fear. I am not helpless,* she breathed to herself.

"Thank you," William said. "Are you recovered enough to proceed?" November nodded. William lifted her feet onto the couch. "Lean your head back against the armrest," he directed. "Don't forget to breathe. It'll only take a moment."

He brushed her hair away from her neck and leaned forward. It felt strangely intimate to November, who had never been this close to any man or boy before. It was what she'd imagined a first kiss would be like when she finally had one: awkward and exciting at the same time. Then she felt a sharp prick like a large needle, and she heard William swallowing – swallowing her life's blood. It was a strange thought. William lifted his head, pressing a tissue against her neck.

"All done. You did great, young one. How do you feel?"

"Good," she said with surprise. "Relaxed, strangely enough."

"Did you see anything?" Savita asked.

"No. Everything went still," November replied, pleased at the unexpected peace.

They heard a knock at the door, which opened to reveal Ben returned from his hunting. "Does she taste as good as she looks?" asked Ben with a wink when he spied the bandage.

"Better," answered William, almost growling. "Fangs and hands off."

"I was just teasing her," he said stiffly. Under his master's glare, he managed to squeeze out the words, "I apologize."

"She will need friends in our world. I expect both of you to look out for her without trying to eat her or bed her. Is that clear?" William asked Zinnia and Ben in the lordliest possible manner.

"Of course," replied Zinnia, smiling at her new friend. Ben nodded, his eyes resentful.

November yawned, which William took as a reminder to depart. "Good night, *akka*. We'll talk tomorrow," he said, kissing Savita on the cheek one more time.

November barely made it to the car before falling asleep. She stirred once as William placed her in a soft, sweet-smelling bed. She heard, "Go back to sleep, soothsayer. See you at sunset," and fell back into the only dreamless sleep she'd ever had in all her life.

Chapter 4

November woke up in yesterday's clothes, momentarily confused by her surroundings. All was quiet and sunshine. She was shocked to look down at her battered watch to see that she'd slept until nearly two in the afternoon. She had to admit, though, that it felt incredible. She'd never had such peaceful sleep, no matter how exhausted she'd been when she'd put her head down.

She sat up to begin taking stock of her new home. She was lying in a queen-sized bed with soft white sheets, a pale silver blanket edged with satin, and a quilt patterned in silver and white. Feather pillows cushioned her; an alarm clock and a modernist lamp stood sentinel on the nightstand along with a smartphone charging next to a set of speakers.

She realized with a start that no one had ever slept on this bed before. Everything beneath her was brand new. The idea that they had purchased it for her was a bit alarming. What were they going to expect in recompense? In November's experience, nothing worth having came for free. She tried to catch a glimpse of what the room had been used for before she arrived in it. Cardboard boxes along with a couple of guitars and music stands were all that she could find. Apparently, it had been used for storage, which was reassuring. She should sleep well here – there was no one else's past to pace the floor, waiting to invade her dreams.

She turned to look out the window. The view was lovely. The home was perched high on a ridge overlooking Oakland, and she could see all the way to the Bay. The immediate environs were filled with greenery. She could not see the neighboring houses; William's home was an isolated and surely costly sanctuary.

November stood and walked toward the door. She was filled with momentary panic when she realized that it was locked from the outside. She kept trying to turn the knob, to no avail. Her hands began to shake; her mouth filled with saliva, and a wave of nausea overtook her as she realized that she was more prisoner than guest, at least for the moment. For an instant, she was back in the rubber rooms of St. James' Hospital, full of a desperate ache from all the tears and the hours spent banging her head against the padded door. Fortunately, she quickly returned to herself, and anger soon replaced fear. November checked the windows, not surprised to find that they were also sealed shut.

Resolving to occupy her mind in order to stave off panic, November returned to her exploration. In one corner stood a miniature fridge topped with a microwave and a small cabinet stocked with dishes and flatware. *Well, at least they aren't going to let me go hungry.*

Opening the fridge, November had to laugh in spite of herself. The eclectic collection of foodstuffs evinced the fact that this household was not accustomed to sheltering human residents. The contents of the fridge, in no particular order, included an artichoke, a jar of pickles, a bottle of ketchup, a box of teabags, a quart of now-melted vanilla ice cream, a jar of peanut butter, salami, goldfish crackers, a loaf of pumpernickel bread, a pomegranate, a package of chewing gum, green bananas, a bag of apples, and a box of raisins. November hoped they'd let her help with the shopping in the future, but she appreciated the effort. She paused her investigation of her new domain to break her fast with a peanut butter on pumpernickel sandwich accompanied by raisins, a glass of melted ice cream, and a cup of tea.

Thus fortified, she went to the wall opposite the window to examine the desk. Surprise and delight filled her heart as she discovered that the desk was packed with art supplies: heavy paper, pencils, charcoals, pastels, paints, pens, brushes. It was like Christmas. A bookcase alongside was also well-stocked, with room for her own books to find space with additional textbooks and novels. She also found a somewhat reassuring note on the desk blotter:

November –

> Please make yourself at home. I apologize for the locked door, but it was the safest thing for all of us. Zinnia will be home from school around 4 pm. You'll see the rest of us after sunset.

--William Knox

She then turned her attention to the other doors in the room, which she assumed correctly would lead to the bathroom and the closet. She picked one at random and discovered a closet full of clothes. Someone had helpfully removed all the tags and hung up the outfits. She reached out her hand, sliding the smooth fabric between her fingers. Like the bed, these clothes had never belonged to anyone else. The quality was fine, but the clothes were not ostentatious. She was strangely grateful not to know how much they had cost. They looked to be the right size and included ensembles appropriate for a variety of occasions. A dozen pairs of shoes were stacked neatly in a shoe rack one the floor. There were a variety of flats and low heels that seemed pretty practical along with a couple of pairs that looked to be threats to life and limb. This was shocking extravagance to a girl who'd never had more than one pair of shoes without holes in them at any one time. The bureau alongside the closet was stocked with pretty underthings, socks, stockings, and t-shirts.

Finally, she opened the door to the bathroom. November shook her head in pleased disbelief at the enormous tub and fluffy white towels, the perfect blue tile and shining faucets. The room was stocked with every toiletry item imaginable, and November immediately decided that the next order of business was a bubble bath. She couldn't remember the last time she'd had anything more than a quick, cold shower. She stripped off her dirty clothes, unsure what to do with them until she found a cleverly disguised hamper, and drew herself a piping hot bath with copious bubbles.

After a good long soak and thorough scrub, she emerged smelling of tea tree oil and feeling ready to face just about anything. She slathered herself in lotion, wrapped herself in the softest bathrobe known to man, and combed out her hair. Not knowing what was on tonight's agenda, she dressed simply and neatly in jeans, a blue v-neck sweater, and some low-heeled boots. Everything fit, by some miracle. *Who put all this together, and in only one day?*

When November looked at herself in the mirror, she was surprised and pleased to see that she looked like a normal girl for once. She was accustomed to having a general air of neglect. Her clothes never quite fit. There was always a hole that needed patching or a stain she hadn't been able to get out in the sink. Today, she looked like someone cared. November examined her neck, expecting to see an awful mark from the previous night's bite, but she found only faint pink spots where the fangs had pierced the skin. She'd never have been able to find them if she hadn't known they were there. *That vampire saliva is good stuff, apparently.*

The tour of her quarters complete, it was time to explore in a slightly different fashion. Her hosts could lock her body in a room, but they could not close in the rest of her. She had discovered this aspect of her psychic ability by accident when she had been about 11 years old. It had appeared of necessity one afternoon when November had been caught by a terrific thunderstorm while out walking alone. Before joining the carnival, this was how she had spent much of her time as it was the surest way of avoiding human contact. The lightening was growing closer; she was drenched to the bone. In her desperation to find shelter she'd managed to create a mental map of the terrain, enabling her to find and take cover in a shallow cave. She hadn't had much need for this gift lately, but she enjoyed practicing it; it was a good break from her other, more upsetting abilities. She would look for underground water, for instance, or try to map the bottom of a lake, or try to see what stores were inside a mall before she went inside.

November took a deep breath and began to feel around beyond the door. The first thing she noticed was how huge the place was: room after room, three floors worth plus a basement, separated into two wings. The house was largely empty. She caught glimpses of the vampires at rest in tastefully appointed rooms in the basement. They really did look dead when they were sleeping. She caught a glimpse of a fairy in an office. He had deep brown skin, lime green hair and eyes, and had the hurried air of the extremely busy. Another fairy was arranging flowers in a granite-countered kitchen. November picked up a smattering of decorative details here and there: the black and white marble floor in the foyer, the blue door on the guardhouse by the gate to the grounds, the mosaic of a rose and a sword on the bottom of the outdoor pool.

As she continued to look around, November slowly began to realize that this was no mere mansion: it was a cunningly disguised fortress. The walls around the grounds were over 12 feet high, a foot thick, and topped with spikes, with only one well-guarded entry gate that looked like it had been lifted from Fort Knox. There were external metal shutters poised to block every window in the house as well as every exterior door. There appeared to be some kind of system of escape tunnels. There were generators in case of loss of power and a water storage tank, she presumed in case of fire, since she didn't think vampires and fairies drank water. There was an armory stocked with crossbows, stakes, knives, guns, and weapons she didn't even recognize. It was alarming. *These people are loaded for bear.*

To combat her growing unease, November broke out her physics book, a notepad, and a pencil and started working problems. She played with the streaming service on the phone, searching for a few of the bands she liked from her many hours spent listening to the radio. She passed the afternoon lounging on her bed, nibbling goldfish crackers and working problems, until she was startled by a knock on the door.

"Hey, Em, it's Zin. Can I come in?"

"Of course," November replied, placing her books to the side. The fairy opened what sounded like several locks on the door and came bounding into the room, wearing a long, patchwork skirt with a black tunic embroidered with flowers and a bright scarf. Between the outfit and her hair, she looked like a punk hippie.

Zinnia plopped down on the bed beside November, asking, "Did you have an okay day in your gilded cage?"

"That isn't funny, Zinnia. The room's very nice, but that locked door really scared me." Her voice cracked, but November forced herself to continue the speech she had prepared. "I came with you quietly because I know from my vision that I am meant to be in this world, but I thought it would be as a member of this household, not as a prisoner. I want to be treated like a friend. I could probably accept being an employee. But I will not be some . . . some dog kept on a chain. I won't be treated like a criminal or a crazy person."

54

Zinnia looked sympathetic as she tried to explain the inexcusable. "There are eight vampires living under this roof, and during the day they rest, hidden away from the sun. It's the only time that they're really vulnerable to attack. It's unheard of to leave a human free to roam a vampire's home during daylight, especially one who isn't enthralled. To have you wandering around their home plays to their most primal fear. Lord William will try to convince the others to make an exception for you, and they respect his authority, but his nestmates are some of his most important supporters. Most are part of his government, and he can't risk losing their loyalty. He has to tread carefully. This is uncharted territory."

"I suppose I can understand that," she said quietly, still uncomfortable. "Though I would point out that being kidnapped and held in a building full of predators plays to *my* most primal fears." Em paused. "So it isn't to keep me from running away? Not that I have anywhere to go, really."

"Well, I suppose that's also a consideration, to be brutally honest," Zinnia admitted. "To tell you the truth, you are safer here than wandering out in the world. If we heard about you, you can bet that other supernaturals have, too. We just got to you first." Zinnia looked with curious revulsion at the bowl of multicolored goldfish crackers on the bed. She sniffed one and wrinkled her nose.

"So, you came looking for me on purpose? How did you know I was even there?"

"Ben heard about you from some human he was feeding on. He thought it was bull, but he was telling me about it, and I told Lord William, who became very interested. He cleared his schedule, and off we went to the boonies searching for you."

"And what if I had fought coming here, or run to the cops or something? What if I hadn't already accepted my fate?" November asked, not sure she really wanted to know.

Zinnia at least had the decency to look her right in the eyes as she confirmed, "Then we would have kidnapped you for real and tried to win you over after. That would have been especially hard for me, since I can sense other people's feelings, but we'd still have done it. Lord William can be ruthless when he thinks he has to be, and we are all sworn to obey him and to serve his house." Seeing the horror in November's eyes, she added, "He is fair, and I've never known him to be gratuitously cruel. He is gentle with humans, criminals excepted. You don't need to be afraid of him."

"Then why does he think he needs me badly enough to be willing to kidnap an innocent stranger?" November asked.

"That's his story to tell, November. And I promise you, he will." She gave the human a reassuring pat on the knee. "Here, let's fix that arm." November held out the injured limb, curious and nervous. Zinnia laid her hand lightly upon the injury and closed her eyes. "This might be uncomfortable," she warned. The warning was accurate, as November's arm began to ache, burn, and itch intensely all at once. She caught flashes of Zinnia's life, glimpsing the fairy as a tween making out with a boy behind some bleachers as well as a night sky full of twinkling lights of many colors. Zinnia was quickly finished, and November looked down in wonder at her completely healed, unscarred arm.

"Thank you!" November exclaimed with an amazed smile. "I thought it would scar something awful."

"No trouble at all," her new friend replied. "Why don't I give you the grand tour? The bloodsuckers will be up soon," she said with a smile.

November pulled on one of several pairs of gloves she had found in her underwear drawer (They really had thought of everything.) and followed the fairy, not mentioning that she had already conducted her own partial tour earlier.

"So, what are you studying?" November asked as they walked down the tastefully decorated hallway.

"Double major, music and history, at Cal," she replied. "Everyone wants me to be a lawyer." Going back to the tour for a moment, she added, "The house was rebuilt after being damaged in the Oakland Hills fire. Your neighbors on this hallway are all fairies. There are five of us who live in the house. Willow and Pine run daytime security with some other fairies who live offsite, and Birch is Lord William's right hand man. Rose is the house manager, and Birch's wife. Pine is their son. Rose set up your room, which used to be storage. There are also a number of guest rooms up here, for fairy visitors."

"Were the instruments and stuff in my room yours?" November asked. Zinnia replied with a nod. "Would you rather be a musician or a lawyer?" November had never really given any thought to her future, given that she didn't have one. She'd also never lasted at a school more than a few days, so college wasn't really ever on the horizon.

"Fairies don't sleep, so there's plenty of time to do both," she explained.

"Never?"

"Only when severely wounded. We're more vulnerable at night, though, so we don't go out alone after sunset, especially during a full moon. Werewolves are the biggest threat to us. Our power to absorb living energy doesn't work at night, nor does our ability to change form. So, we can neither feed, nor fight well, nor flee. That's why I didn't go hunting last night with the boys."

"What do you mean by change forms?"

"We have a fairy form, a tiny body that glows and flies. You know, like Tinkerbell in that book you humans like so much." Zinnia made a face. "Man, that girl makes us look so pathetic. We kind of hate her."

"I saw a group of them, when you healed me, but I didn't realize what I was seeing. It was beautiful." November felt rather overwhelmed by all this information, but Zinnia's matter-of-fact demeanor aided her effort to avoid freaking out.

"Yeah. A bunch of us together makes a pretty good show," Zinnia replied. While chatting, the two girls had made their way past the fairy bedrooms and down a couple of impressive staircases to the large entryway. There was a matching staircase on the opposite side of the foyer leading into the other wing. November had never been in such an enormous home. The foyer was quite modern in design, lots of glass and metal and the color white, with the marble tile she'd seen in her mental tour. The only rather incongruous touch of the antique was the collection of portraits, most of them obviously centuries old. They featured the faces of the three vampires in her burial vision, unchanged by time of course, plus a statuesque blond woman, portrayed as wife and mother to this vampire family. There were a number of other vampires and fairies she didn't recognize.

"Who is the blond woman?" November asked with curiosity. "I saw her when I did Lord William's reading."

Zinnia looked sad for a moment. "That's King Ilyn's late wife, Queen Marisha. She died about 200 years ago, so I never got to meet her. They say the king has never been the same. They were together over 2000 years."

November gasped. The scale was incomprehensible. "How awful! What happened?" she asked.

"No one knows. She was murdered, they think, but no one could figure out how or by whom. There were suspects, and the king and the whole family moved heaven and earth, but they could never find any proof of guilt."

Zinnia returned to the tour. "Now, the wing where our bedrooms are is the residence, with the kitchen, living areas, game room, theatre, swimming pool, music room, and ballroom. The opposite wing houses the offices, conference rooms, auditorium, war room, and courtroom. This house is the seat of government for vampires and fairies in California. No human has ever been permitted in the government wing, so I recommend that you don't go wandering over there."

Zinnia took November through the domestic portion of the house, which was homey and comfortable while remaining thoroughly modern and stylish, courtesy of what must have been an excellent decorator. The kitchen was amazing: huge and bright and stocked with lovely high-end appliances. It seemed a shame that it was wasted with the exception of the refrigerator, which was filled to bursting with the blood of various creatures, neatly labeled and dated. November wondered how the human blood had been obtained but had no desire to actually reach out her hand and find out. "They had to have the builder include a stove and all. To do otherwise would have aroused suspicion," Zinnia explained. "And it gets used occasionally, for human business partners and people like that."

What truly impressed November, however, was the library. The brief glimpse she'd had of it in vision really didn't do it justice. The room was two stories tall, with ladders on rails, stocked floor to ceiling with books both ancient and contemporary. It smelled of leather and old paper. Several large mahogany desks furnished this temple of learning, with couches and armchairs and reading lamps scattered about. For a bookworm like November, it was heaven. She must have looked as thrilled as she felt, for Zinnia grinned, saying, "I'm sure Lord William would let you read whatever you like." November was wonderstruck.

Zinnia continued playing tour-guide. "The vampires have their bedrooms underground, of course. The various entries to the basement are hidden and very well-secured. Their rooms are light-tight and impervious to fire."

"What did the contractors think of that?" November wondered aloud.

"Lord William told them they were vaults for a priceless collection of artwork," Zinnia replied. "People are pretty credulous when they're being paid an awful lot of money. Also when you can enthrall them with the sound of your voice into believing anything you say."

"I bet."

The two girls sat in the library chatting and reading the newspaper. November avoided the news sections and the depressing visions they would inspire. Zinnia told her a little bit about herself. She was living with William while she went to school. Her father, originally from Japan, had died when Zinnia was small. She went to visit relatives in Japan every summer, but it was awkward. "I'm too American for them. Too white. Sometimes being mixed is hard," she said.

Her mother Amandier, who hailed from Quebec, was now Lady Governor of Oregon and a close ally of Lord William and his clan. "Lord William is even one of my bond kin," Zinnia added. When November raised an inquiring eyebrow, the fairy explained, "When fairies are born, they impress on anyone they come into contact with in the first 24 hours of life. So, fairy parents invite their close friends and family to visit during that time. We have a feeling of well-being when close to them, and we can sense distress. Only works both ways between fairies, though. I can sense Lord William a little, but he can't read me at all. The bond lasts our whole lives, many centuries."

November tilted her head in surprise. She hadn't realized that fairies were as immortal as their vampire friends, since the only one she'd ever met happened to be the genuinely teenaged Zinnia. Only nineteen years old, Zinnia was still a child by the standards of her people, and she was still quite vulnerable to injury or death by misadventure. "They watch me like a hawk," her friend said, half-complaining through a smile.

November wondered what it was like for all of them, to live for centuries, to have such a long view of history, to watch generation after generation of humans be born, make the same mistakes as their forebears, and die off. She supposed they must share her cynicism. *Nothing ever changes.*

Zinnia got out her laptop as November continued to read the paper and began exploring the books in the library. The girls kept chatting until sunset brought the vampires upstairs. Lord William entered the library, inquiring, "I hope you had a good rest, November?"

"I slept like a log," November confirmed, "Better than I ever have. You should bite me every night," she joked, blushing as it hit her just how forward that sounded.

"Don't tempt me," he said with a grin that thankfully rendered the comment less creepy than it would otherwise have been. "Zin's been showing you around?"

"Yes. I might even be able to find my way back to my room." November felt strangely awkward. She just didn't know how to be around him. He had essentially kidnapped her and installed her as some kind of servant in his house, but, then, she hadn't exactly put up a fight. Part of her thought she should hate him, but she somehow couldn't quite manage it.

The truth was, this place already felt more like a home than she'd had in some time, and she had been waiting for these people her whole life. He was taking advantage of her gift and of her unfortunate situation, but if he was giving her something of value in return, a safe home, a family of sorts, perhaps she could forgive him for the initial transgression. *We'll see*, she thought.

Then there was the complication of their blood connection. The intimacy was both exciting and strange, and she did not fully understand it.

"Do you feel ready to meet the rest of my people?" William asked. "Some of them are very curious about you. I've told them of your gift. Otherwise, they would have objected to having you living in the house. They are loyal to me; they will not reveal you to outsiders. I would trust them with my life." Of course, he was trusting them with November's life as well. That made the locked bedroom even more offensive to November: she had to trust them, but they had no trust in her.

"I should warn you, most vampires are used to thinking of humans as prey or entertainment or useful tools, not as people worthy of consideration or concern. I realize that must offend you, but that attitude is part of what allows us to survive. We maintain an emotional distance; we have to in order to be able to live with ourselves. Imagine it, November: one day, you are human. The next, you have to hunt humans in order to stay alive. Humans do the same thing: dehumanizing their enemies, and ignoring the suffering of the animals they use for food. Any other humans we bring here are so enthralled that they have little memory of what happens to them. Please, just be patient with my people, and try to forgive them if they offend you with their words. They are going to need some time to get accustomed to you, as you will need to get accustomed to us."

November grew more and more nervous as William spoke, but she did understand probably more than most humans would. She knew a little something about keeping oneself remote from the suffering of others in order to maintain one's sanity.

"What about fairies? Do they feel the same way?" November asked, biting her lower lip.

"It has always been easier for fairies to blend into human society," Zinnia answered. "We could wear a wig or dye our hair, live among them, and feed with a handshake or an embrace. We don't have to shed blood or lure our prey to a remote location in order to get a meal. So, we don't tend to see humans as quite so foreign, at least when we're young. The older we get, the more isolated we tend to be from the humans around us, especially when we mostly associate with vampires and other fairies. The next youngest fairy in the house is almost 300 years old. So, everyone finds me amusing," she finished a bit sadly. "They find me precious and naïve and overly emotional."

"Also refreshing and sweet," William added with genuine affection. It was obvious how fond he was of his bond niece.

"Alright," November said, trying to unclench her jaw. "I think I'm as ready as I'll ever be. Let's run the gauntlet."

William tapped on the door of the library, and the members of his inner circle filed in and surrounded their unusual houseguest.

"This is Greg, keeper of the exchequer," William began, "and Savita's son." Greg nodded at her, little interested, then turned his attention to the newspaper November had discarded. He had been about 30 years old when he was turned, November guessed. Dressed in a yellow shirt and designer khakis, he was a tall, slender African-American with close-cropped hair, a goatee, and heavy, black hipster glasses. She wondered if a lot of vampires did that, wearing glasses to blend in. It seemed like that would play well with accountants and bankers and stock brokers.

"Birch, my lieutenant governor," William continued. This was the man she had glimpsed earlier in the office, the one with tight lime-green curls and skin the color of good earth. Birch gave her a searching look when he was introduced, as though trying to find something wrong with her. Another skeptic, perhaps. He looked like one who rarely smiled.

Lord William continued the introductions, and November tried to focus on learning the names. Felix, Megan, and Daniel were described as knights serving the household along with the fairies Willow and Pine, so she pegged them as the security personnel Zinnia had mentioned. November wondered what their actual duties were. Whom were they trying to keep out? Or in? Did they make arrests? Fight battles? All five knights looked to be in their mid-twenties, but of course, November had no idea of their actual ages. They looked her carefully up and down in an almost clinical fashion. November didn't know if they were evaluating her as a threat or as a meal. Willow was quite fair, with shockingly purple eyes to match her hair, compared to which Pine's light brown skin and amber hair and eyes seemed much more sedate.

A tiny Asian-American vampire named Amy was the Lord Prosecutor, dressed to the nines from her spike heels to her perfectly coiffed hair. Her counterpart, the Defense Advocate, was a tall, dark, and handsome vampire named Josue who was wearing a shiny three piece suit. November wondered why there wasn't a judge. She suddenly realized that William might well be judge, jury, and executioner, which made her stomach do a little flip. The diplomat, Mary, had been middle-aged when she was turned, and sported a wild grey spiked hairdo. She, too, wore a suit, a more conservative wool number. Her job was liaising with other state lords and with the king's court.

Rose, the fairy house manager, looked just like the stereotype of a high society hostess: she had a short blond bob, pearl jewelry, conservative designer clothes, and manicured nails. November wondered what her real hair color was. She supposed it must match her violet eyes. She was the only one who smiled at November, for which she was grateful, even though she knew it might just be part of the woman's job. "Please do let me know if you need anything, dear."

"Thank you for my lovely . . . accommodations," November replied.

"You're most welcome, darling. Were the clothes acceptable? And the food?" the hostess inquired.

"The clothes are wonderful, just perfect," November assured her. "I did wonder if I might have some influence over the grocery list," she admitted, thinking about the strangely stocked fridge. Rose shot an annoyed look at Zinnia.

"That was my fault. I didn't get the right things, did I?" Zinnia asked with a self-deprecating expression. "None of us eat food, and we don't pay all that much attention to what humans eat, because it all seems so disgusting. I should have asked Ben to help, since he's young enough to remember what you people actually like."

"It's okay. You did fine. It was just a rather odd assortment, that's all. It's a better stocked fridge than I've had in a long time, believe me," November reassured the two fairies.

"You see why I insist on doing everything myself," Rose mock complained.

The more interesting comments began after they'd all given her the once over. "She's pretty enough, I guess, but a little scrawny for my taste. I suppose I'd be willing to take her off your hands once you're bored with her," Josue remarked offhandedly in William's direction.

"You might be able to fatten her up a little by then," Daniel suggested.

"I'm surprised, my lord," Mary commented. "You usually go for a more ... experienced woman."

"Yeah, this innocent virgin thing is a bit of a departure, isn't it?" Felix agreed. "That's usually more my line," he added with suggestive eyebrow wiggle.

"Oh, I bet she'll be a fast learner," Willow said with a wicked grin.

November flushed bright red at the casual inappropriateness of their statements. *He did warn me, but ouch.* "I'd appreciate it very much if you would all stop talking about me like that," she said firmly, pressing her lips together. Everyone in the room turned to look at her aghast. The silence was broken only when Amy burst out laughing.

"This is going to be fun. A human who talks back!" the elegant lawyer whooped delightedly.

"How many times do I have to tell you people that she isn't enthrallable? She can actually understand the words coming out of your mouths, and she is not here as a source of blood and recreation," William said, irritated at how the introductions were going awry.

"Sorry," Josue said with a smile and a wink. "No offense meant. I've never met a magic human before."

"Well, I've never been kidnapped and installed as a prisoner in a vampire slash fairy household, so I guess it's new experiences all around," November replied with an edge in her voice. Apparently her latent anger and anxiety had been seeking a way out and had finally found one via her smart mouth.

"I'm afraid you'll all have to fight me for her," Greg finally chimed in matter-of-factly, looking up from the business section of the newspaper, "if these notes she's made in the newspaper are what I think they are." He raised his eyebrow at November, asking, "Are they?" His interest in her appeared to shock everyone in the room.

"The dates on the left are when the stock hits its next low point and the ones on the right are the next high," November confirmed. "It's just a game I play when I have a newspaper around. I pick a few stocks and see what I can see. You know, after I finish the crossword." *Like you do.*

An unaccustomed smile brightened the financial advisor's face as he shook his head, saying to William, "You pay this girl whatever she wants. She'll make you ten times as much." He laughed, "I just need to make sure we don't get investigated for insider trading."

November smiled, pleased to be appreciated for her gift instead of her blood. After this little victory, it seemed like as good a time as any to bring up the difficult topic of her bedroom door. "Can we talk about the lock on my door?" she asked, looking around at them. William nodded permission. "I have no intention of trying to run away, and I have no desire to do any of you harm. I came here willingly, even though I know full well that things are going to wind up with me going into the ground. I want to be able to sit in the library or eat lunch outside or go for a swim instead of being trapped in my room all day. I want to feel like a person."

She took a deep breath and screwed up her courage to continue. "I could not stand living here as a prisoner. I've spent time locked up at the mercy of unkind people, and quite frankly, I'd rather die than feel again the way I felt back then. I'll be a hell of a lot more useful to you happy than miserable, I guarantee you." November exhaled loudly. She'd been working on that speech all afternoon.

"Why not?" Ben said. He'd snuck in the library during the introductions and sat down on top of one of the desks, holding himself a little separate from the rest of the group. "She'd never be able to escape the grounds. As for our resting places, the doors are hidden and secure. How could she even get in?"

November swallowed. "Actually, I've already found a few of the doors by accident, and finding out the codes would be trivial. I am here because I'm a psychic, after all."

"I told you we should get bio-scanners," Birch piped up.

"You are honest to the point of self-injury; you do realize that, right?" William said to November, exasperated.

"One of you would have figured it out eventually," she replied. "Withholding the truth when I'm trying to convince you to trust me seemed inappropriate. Besides, it doesn't matter if I got into the basement. You must have motion detectors in there, and the doors to your rooms look like they belong in a bank vault. I assume they're locked from the inside. I'd never be able to hurt anyone before the fairy staff stopped me. Look, if you can't trust me in your house during the day, how could you trust anything I told you about my visions? I'm forced to trust all of you, even though apparently you'd all be happy to feed on me and do God knows what else. Why shouldn't you have to trust me a little bit?" She sat down awkwardly, her speech complete.

Her new housemates at least seemed to be taking her seriously, the patronizing looks having disappeared from their faces. "Well," William said, "While we digest that, we need to get on with our evening. Feed quickly. Gavel is in an hour, and the defendants have started arriving and are in holding. Ben and Zinnia," he continued, turning to face them, "keep November company. Watch a movie or something. We'll be done working in about 4 or 5 hours."

"I need to go hunting," Ben countered.

"Use something from the fridge," Lord William ordered as he strode out the room, retinue in tow.

Ben heaved a sigh. "The apex predator of planet earth, reduced to drinking cold blood and babysitting a human housepet."

"So sorry to inconvenience you," November snapped. "I wouldn't even be here if it weren't for you, or so I'm told."

"Children, let's play nice," Zinnia said. "Ben, it isn't her fault that Knox doesn't trust you with important things yet. It takes time with Lord William."

Ben nodded, chagrinned. "I know. Sorry. It just gets old, being treated like a child all the time."

"Tell me about it," Zinnia and November said at the exact same time. All three burst out laughing. "Come on. You both grab some snacks and meet me in the theatre. Let's see what's on streaming," Zinnia suggested.

The three teenagers settled in to watch the previous summer's biggest blockbuster, which none of them had managed to see in the theatre. November could count on one hand the number of times she'd actually been to the movies, so this was quite a treat. It felt like something three normal teenagers might do together, and November wondered if this was what it was like to have actual friends your own age. As it turned out, Ben was pretty funny and not such terrible company when William wasn't around.

It was nice to have a distraction from her ever crazy life, and she was finally beginning to relax when she was jerked out of her body and dragged to an isolated roadside where two vampires were interrogating an unfortunate woman.

She is a curvy brunette with a shag haircut and a pretty face, dressed in ripped jeans and a lace camisole totally inappropriate for the cold night air. He looks to be barely more than a child, turned before he'd had to shave more than once a week. His eyes are the only thing that give lie to his cherubic face: they somehow manage to be both amused and merciless.

The man holds his victim down on the ground as the woman rifles her purse and asks the wretch what has become of her daughter. Terrified into honesty, the mother replies that she sold her daughter to a man whose name she didn't know and whose face she couldn't remember. She is crying from fear, her mascara running down her face. It looks like she tried to get away. Her left ear is bleeding where the earring has been torn away; her shirt is torn and a bruise is already starting to form along her jaw.

"So, vampire or fairy then, since she's been enthralled," the man remarks to his companion, "Not werewolf." He continues by asking Julia, "You sold your own young to a strange man?" He shakes his head. "Humans. Such savages."

"He was dressed so well. He sounded educated and all. Promised he'd take care of her," says the wayward mother, trying to justify it as much to herself as to these strangers. "I figured she had to be better off with him than she was with me. She'd be better off with anyone else than with me," she replies, closing her eyes in shame, for some reason wanting her attackers to understand and absolve her.

"We should hurt her some, make certain that she really was enthralled. The boss doesn't like things half done," the female vampire comments in a disinterested voice.

"No, please!" their victim cries. "I'm not lying. I'm trying to remember, I just can't." Her eyes are wide with desperate pleading.

"Don't worry, puppy," the creature replies, changing her mind as she pulls her hand out of the purse with a smile. "I think we have everything we need," she says. "Look familiar?" she asks her accomplice, flashing the watch she'd found in the bottom of Julia's knock-off handbag.

He grins. "William Knox has been wearing that watch for at least fifty years. He wants that little freak as much as our employer does."

"It is interesting that he gave it to this crack whore in exchange for some human weirdo," the woman remarks casually, trying to cover her hurt feelings.

"I was skeptical that some cow could be important enough to justify our paycheck, but maybe the boss is onto something, if William thinks so, too. He's not easy to fool. Well, not most of the time," he says, provoking a bark of laughter in his companion.

The two predators gaze down at their victim, whose face has lit up while they talked with a pathetic hope that she might escape with her life. "Take it," Julia says. "Take anything. There's drugs in the trailer, too, under the couch cushions. Just please, don't kill me."

"Time for breakfast?" the man asks.

"I've worked up a pretty good appetite myself," his companion replies.

Julia begins to scream when she sees their fangs descend. Her eyes go wild, rolling as though they belong to a wounded animal. Her mind cannot not make sense of what is happening. For a moment she thinks it is a drug-induced hallucination, until the pain comes. The vampires tear into their meal. There is nothing of William's careful feeding. The predators revel in the fountains of blood and the torn flesh, groaning with pleasure at the kill as Julia's blood soaks the dust below her into a gory mud. Screaming. The smell of blood. The only mercy is that death comes quickly under such savage attack. She passes out almost immediately; she does not have long to wait before her final breath escapes and her heart stops pumping her life away.

The moment her mother was gone, November fell back into her body in William Knox's little palace, the impact as stunning as falling onto concrete. She looked around, disoriented. She found herself on the floor, Zinnia and Ben on either side, clutching her hands tightly. The movie was still playing in the background, all explosions and gunfire behind their troubled faces. Zinnia's expression was one of concern. Ben's was harder to read.

"Why does my throat hurt?" she asked in confusion. "Why are you holding me down?"

Her new friends let go as November struggled to sit up. "You were screaming rather a lot," Zin explained with worry in her voice. "And you started scratching at your eyes." She paused before asking, "Is that why you wear the gloves?"

November looked at her gloves, puzzled, as if seeing them for the first time. "No, though I guess it helps with that, too."

William came bursting into the room with Greg hot on his heels. "What happened?" he demanded. "We heard her screaming." He looked at his underlings as if they might be at fault.

"I had a vision," November replied calmly. She felt frozen inside. She had no desire to weep. She wondered what was wrong with her. She'd just watched the woman who'd given her life get mauled to death, and she felt nothing much about it.

"What did you see? Are you alright?" the lord governor asked, kneeling beside his new charge.

"My mother is dead. And the creatures who killed her now know that you have me," November answered, finally sitting up straight. "I need paper and pencil."

"Oh, November, I . . . I'm sorry. I . . ." William trailed off, not knowing what to say.

"Why?" she said, puzzled and thinking out loud in her altered state. "You thought she was vermin. You've killed plenty of people and watched plenty more die, haven't you? What do you care about some random human whore?" She sounded nonchalant, as if they were discussing the weather.

"I do not enjoy seeing you suffer, nor do I celebrate a waste of life," he said quietly, his eyes sad. "I'm not a monster, November." He watched the girl warily as she began to rock back and forth with her knees hugged to her chest, clenching her teeth as they began to chatter from the adrenaline.

"I know you're not a monster. I wouldn't work for you if I thought you were," November said evenly, completely placid despite the shaking. "I need paper and pencil," she repeated, hyper-focused. "I need paper and pencil." She needed to follow her normal procedure for upsetting visions. If she could work, she could stave off her collapse just a little longer. She could put off facing the reality of what she'd seen if only she could treat it like any other vision. She kept insisting, over and over, "I need paper and pencil," unable to answer the questions they were asking her, unable to respond to their expressions of concern.

William finally took her by the hand, led her down to a desk in the library, sat her down in front of a stack of paper, and put a charcoal pencil in her hand. She began to draw with a savage concentration, only intermittently aware of what was going on around her.

"Greg, stay with her along with Zinnia," Lord William ordered. "I have to go back to court. They all heard her scream, of course. I'll tell them . . . I'll think of something. Don't leave her alone, and don't let anyone but me see what she draws."

Ben asked, "What about me?"

"You're relieved. Enjoy the rest of your evening," the lord replied curtly.

"Why? I can only be trusted when nothing's happening, is that it?" Ben's mouth was suddenly full of fangs as his temper began to get the better of him.

"It's not a punishment, boy. Look at yourself. She's got your blood up. It's the screaming, the smell of her adrenaline. It's my fault; I should have let you go hunting. You stay here and your teeth will wind up in her neck, and my stake will wind up in your chest. Now get out, go feed, and try not to kill anyone," William said in a low and dangerous voice. Suddenly, the lord had the youngling by the collar, pressed against the wall, his own sharp teeth now bared. "And the next time you question one of my orders, you'll find you're not the only one in this house with fangs." William released his ward, who stalked quickly out of the room. Greg's face betrayed neither surprise nor interest in this altercation. Zinnia bit her lip and twisted her hands. November took no notice.

She drew for hours, stopping only when the cramp in her hand grew too painful to continue. William joined the vigil at some point during her marathon. Her aching fingers finally drew her back to herself. She noticed for the first time a cup of tea placed by her hand, cold to the touch when she picked it up. She wondered briefly who had brought it for her and caught a flash of Rose setting it down. She looked at her three companions and saw a worry in their faces that edged close to alarm. They looked at her almost like her mother had after her father died, the way some of the nurses did after one of her episodes. Zinnia looked like she had been crying.

"Please don't look at me like that," November whispered. "You're making me feel like a freak." She handed William the stack of paper. "I think you know them," she said quietly, rubbing her throbbing hand ineffectually. Her voice sounded almost like her own again. The shock was wearing off.

"I do, unfortunately," He replied, shuffling through the stack of drawings, showing one to Greg, who raised an eyebrow. Knox looked at her carefully before he continued, "How do they know it was I who took you? Your mother couldn't have told them."

"She still had the watch," November answered. "They recognized it."

William closed his eyes in self-reproach. "I am a fool," he said. "I told you I'd hide you and protect your secret, and two days later my enemies know who you are and where you're living. And I've managed to get your mother killed."

"I'm glad she had the watch. They'd have tortured her otherwise," November replied honestly, brutally. "At least she died quickly." She paused, swallowing convulsively as bile rose in her throat. Part of her wanted to talk about what she'd seen, but she was afraid that saying the words out loud would make it all real.

"They asked her how she could have sold me, before they killed her. Do you know what she said? That she knew I'd be better off with anyone but her." November choked on the last word. She felt the ice inside begin to crack. The last thing she wanted was to fall apart in here, in front of these near-strangers who'd set this violence in motion. "I'd like to be alone for a little while," she said urgently, standing up, ready to flee.

"I will check on you in an hour," William said after a pause, the reluctance in his voice betraying the conflict between his need to question her further and his respect for her pain. November nodded and walked briskly out of the room, breaking into a run as soon as she hit the staircase.

She barely made it to her bathroom before the nausea overtook her and she began to vomit, a violent, painful heaving that didn't stop even after she was completely empty. She curled up on the floor, the cool tile a comfort to her flushed face as she finally began to weep. At first the tears came silently, but soon she was sobbing so hard she could barely breathe. She was keening, wailing, making noises she'd never heard come from a person's mouth in her life.

When she finally grew too exhausted to continue, she managed to pull herself up to her feet to brush her teeth and wash her face, smeared with tears and snot. She pulled off her clothes and managed to get herself into a nightgown before she curled up in her bed, completely wrung out.

That was how William found her. She had her rosary in hand, seeking her grandmother's comfort, her lips moving in prayers she didn't really believe in but couldn't help turning to in the moment of her extremity. At the moment when William knocked softly and peeked his head in, her nose was still red from crying, her eyes and mouth still swollen despite her efforts with cold water.

"It's alright," November said. "You can come in. I'm done freaking out. For now." She sat up, put away the rosary, and pulled in her knees, small and alone in the middle of the bed, feeling like a little girl in her pastel nightgown.

"May Zinnia come in, too? She wanted to come up and comfort you when we heard you . . . grieving, but you said you wished to be alone, so we waited."

"Okay," November replied hesitantly. The fairy ran in, jumped right up on the bed, and wrapped her arms around November, who stiffened at the unaccustomed affection before finally relaxing and placing her forehead on her new friend's shoulder. William waited at a respectable distance, obviously uncomfortable with this gratuitous display of affection. The fairy's kindness was almost enough to set off another crying jag, but November managed to keep herself together. To her relief, the physical contact set off no visions.

"Thank you," she replied softly, looking away when Zinnia drew back to sit next to her on the bed. She was touched by the young fairy's concern. "So, you could hear me? All the way up here?" she asked, flushing with mortification as she realized that the grief she'd tried to keep private had still been on display. The exposure was almost more than she could bear.

"Vampires and fairies have very acute senses. It's difficult to keep things private in this house," William admitted. He took a deep breath before adding, "Please know that we don't think less of you for your reaction, November. We've all lost people to violence. We know loss. We're simply . . . uncomfortable with human feelings. We spend centuries isolating ourselves from them as much as possible, but with you, we cannot."

After an awkward pause, November changed the subject. "When are you going to tell me who those people are and why they want me so much? I need you to finally tell me why I'm here," she demanded, voice firm, unwilling to be patient any longer.

"Are you sure you don't want to rest now and talk about it tomorrow?" William asked.

"I want to know why she is dead. I need to know. I also need to know what we're up against. Things must be pretty bad if you're looking to a human for help." November was determined now, meeting his eyes without fear or anger, grief or anxiety. She had cried all of that out on the bathroom floor. In that moment, she felt only resolved to fight.

Lord William began to explain. "I'll give you the short version tonight, and we can fill in the rest tomorrow. In the last year, there have been a series of attacks on various lords in the kingdom. Three lords governor have died, and several others have been grievously wounded, along with numerous bystanders, including fairy children. They have all been suicide bombings, committed by fairies or vampires. They have carried either explosive belts filled with silver and wooden shrapnel or incendiary devices. All the murderers have been killed in the attacks so they cannot be questioned about who sent them and why. No groups have taken responsibility. There have been no manifestos expressing their purpose."

"Why silver?" November interrupted.

"All supernatural creatures are vulnerable to silver. It burns our skin. It causes painful wounds that resist healing. It saps our strength. Bound in chains of silver, even the oldest, strongest werewolves, vampires, or fairies cannot escape. In high enough quantities, it can kill. Young fairies are easier to kill and are especially vulnerable to silver poisoning," he explained patiently.

William continued, "Every ten years, the Assembly of Lords meets in legislative session. The Assembly is scheduled to begin in three months. The fear is that someone is planning some kind of revolution, to try to overthrow the government and take control of all or part of the kingdom. The lords that have been killed were old and powerful, with war-time experience. Most of them have been allies of our family for centuries. It could be that these are preliminary attacks designed to weaken the ability of the government to resist a takeover, to weaken the states which would be most crucial in winning any civil war. It is rare that all the leaders in our world are gathered in one place. Attacking the Assembly is too rich an opportunity to be passed up by whoever is behind these murders."

"Have they come after you?" the psychic asked.

"No, not yet. As you know, I have taken great pains with our security here. No one enters the grounds without being searched.

Many of my fellow lords are too proud to take adequate precautions. They are powerful and arrogant and think themselves untouchable. Not that I am immune to arrogance myself." That drew a smile from Zinnia, who quickly covered her mouth.

"And the two vampires I saw tonight?" November inquired, trying not to shudder.

"Mercenaries. Thugs for hire, loyal to whoever wrote the last check. They are well known and very good at their jobs. Almost everyone has used them for dirty work at one time or another, though not I nor anyone of my household. It's dishonorable, hiring people like that. They also have a fairy they often work with, by the name of Dogwood."

"Then how did they recognize your watch?"

He bit the inside of his cheek, stalling, in a rare sign of feeling. "One of them is my daughter," William admitted with a sigh. November eyes widened. "I don't know where I went wrong with Agnes. I haven't turned a human since for fear of repeating the mistake. I think now that she was not a good candidate for turning. I was blinded by my infatuation with her, but looking back, she was flighty and shallow and a bit greedy when she was human. Being turned into a vampire doesn't usually improve one's personality. It tends to amplify what was already there, the good and the bad. That's one reason we're supposed to be careful about whom we choose." Grief thickened his voice.

He continued, "The other vampire is named Philemon. He's much older, nearly as old as I am, a veteran of many wars. He's the one that led my Agnes down the primrose path: easy money, no family loyalties and obligations to deal with, giving free rein to all of our hunger for blood and sex and violence – these things can be very seductive to a young vampire. There's a reason we have such rigid hierarchies and laws. There would be no vampire civilization without them. We'd all be savages like Philemon and Agnes."

"So do you think whoever hired them is the same person who is behind the assassinations?"

"Maybe. Maybe not. You would be a serious threat to him and whatever his ultimate plan is, especially now that you're in my possession. They know I would fight to the death for my father the king. So, if the terrorist leader didn't send these two looking for you, he'll send someone else. Every supernatural creature on the continent with ambition is going to want to get his hands or paws or fangs on you, November. I wanted you because I think you can help us defeat the terrorists and defend the kingdom, preserve the peace and prevent war. Others will have other reasons, some of them not so noble."

He continued, "I wanted you to know that I'm sending Willow and Pine out at dawn to go find your mother's body and give her a decent burial. The map you drew looks quite detailed. I'm confident they'll find her."

"I want to go with them," she said, looking up at him.

"I don't think that's a good idea. The last thing we need is for you to be in danger, and the body won't be in very good condition. There's no reason to put yourself through that," William replied. "Besides, you need to get some sleep."

"I already saw what they did to her, believe me." November replied. Her chest tightened as she tried to take her next breath. "I'll never be able to forget. Besides, I might be able to see something about Agnes and Philemon and their employer if I'm on the scene." She looked down at her hands before continuing, "She is my mother. Was my mother. She may have been a bad one, but she's still mine. She still gave me life. I didn't get to say goodbye to her when we left the carnival, thanks to you," she said, reminding him of the previous night's cruel departure. "Please," she said, the tears beginning to flow again. "Let me bury her and say goodbye. Goodbye to her. Goodbye to that life."

William wavered. The information could be invaluable, and her tears were discomfiting. "Alright. You stay with my people at all times. No wandering."

"Of course." She had no desire to run into any more danger. "Thank you."

"I don't suppose you'd allow me to go with her?" Zinnia piped up.

"I'm afraid not," William replied. "I swore an oath to your mother to keep you safe, and I'm disinclined to take any chances." Zinnia looked disappointed but knew better than to argue.

"I am sorry for your loss, November, truly. I should have thought to protect her, but I allowed my contempt for her to cloud my judgment," William confessed.

November absolved him after a moment of thought. "I don't blame you. They probably hoped I would, so I wouldn't be helpful to you. I blame Agnes and Philemon and whoever sent them. My mother was never going to make old bones. I've seen her die of an overdose. I've seen her beaten to death by a pimp. I've seen her hang herself in prison. I've never seen her dying peacefully in bed. She's been trying to kill herself for about 15 years. Part of me is relieved that she's free now, though she didn't deserve to die like that," November admitted, more to herself than to them.

William looked at the window. "It's nearly dawn. I must retire," he said. "You handled yourself well, November. You're a formidable child."

He walked over to her and touched her hair lightly, as though blessing her. "Be careful today." November nodded, and William walked briskly out the door, leaving her to prepare to depart.

Chapter 5

November quickly dressed and packed her worn, military surplus rucksack with food and bottled water. Zinnia helped her find the garage, where Pine and Willow were loading some gear into the trunk of a grey 4-wheel drive Audi, one of an incomprehensible variety of vehicles filling the cavernous space. Pine and Willow looked extremely competent and slightly annoyed. She suspected that they resented being sent such a long way just to bury some human. Zinnia gave November a quick hug and a whispered, "Good luck," and disappeared back into the house.

"Ready to go?" asked the violet-haired Willow, opening the back passenger-side door. November nodded and clambered into the car.

"You drive," Pine said to Willow, tossing her the keys. "You're less likely to get pulled over for no reason." Willow snorted and did not argue. Fairy or not, what police saw when they looked at Pine was a black guy in an expensive car.

The ride was long and uneventful. November's mother had been killed near Inyokern, in the middle of nowhere in the high desert. She had no idea why her mother had headed in that direction, but then again, Julia was never known for logical planning. November was able to get a few minutes of sleep, for which she was grateful.

She also used her gift to take a little peek into the cases in the trunk. The abundance of weapons secreted therein was both alarming and reassuring. She kept quiet for the most part, though she did speak up at one point to thank the two fairies for performing this unpleasant task. Pine responded, "We're not doing it for you." He smiled, though, as he said it, taking some of the sting out of the words.

When the miles and miles of farmland gave way to the trees of the Sequoia National Forest, November knew they were getting close. The closer they got, the more tense she became, and the more difficult it was to block from her mind the violent images of her mother's murder. She did her best to hide her discomfort. The last thing she wanted was to seem weak to these two warriors.

"Pull off here, please," she said, directing them down a tiny road off of 178. Very quickly they were out of sight of the main road and seemingly isolated from civilization. The two fairies gave each other looks indicating some degree of skepticism of her navigation. These looks were soon erased when her mother's beat-up motor-coach came into view. The fairies wanted to check the scene for dangers before letting November out of the car, which gave her a few moments to steel herself for the unpleasantness ahead.

Finally, they signaled her and she emerged, walking slowly towards her mother's body. Julia lay where she fell, in the dirt next to her home. The smell was awful, though thankfully her body was still in the shade of the trailer and hadn't been baking in the sun all day. There were flies, of course, attracted to all that blood. For some reason, that was the hardest thing for November to see, flies covering the flesh of her flesh. As much as the body, they testified to the reality of death. She did not cry, nor did she flinch from the carnage. After all, she'd already seen it countless times and shed many tears.

She swatted the insects away, took out a wash cloth she'd packed in her bag, moistened it with water, and washed the blood from her mother's face. She was prettier dead than alive. Death had taken life's hardness out of her face. Kissing her on the forehead, November whispered, "Goodbye, Mama." The fairies were keeping a respectful distance. She stood and motioned them forward. "Now what?" she asked.

"We'll dig her a grave," Pine replied. "Won't take long. We're fast workers." Willow was already pulling two shovels out of the trunk.

"I'll see if I can sense anything of Agnes and Philemon, alright?" November responded. He nodded, and the two fairies got to work. Their movements were efficient and speedy and graceful, a strange little dance of death.

November began circling the murder scene, looking to see if there was anything left behind. No cigarette butts or chewing gum or other human detritus, of course, the attackers being vampires. She tried to pretend she was a detective, not some terrified little girl now orphaned in a cruel world. She tried to pretend this was like the countless other deaths she'd been forced to observe over the years. Not finding anything on the ground, she returned to the body reluctantly, examining it with great care. Her thoroughness was rewarded when she found a strand of light brown hair. November smiled for the first time that day. She and her mother had black hair. November had a piece of Agnes, a piece that with a little work and a little luck might betray both the vampire and her employer. She pulled an envelope out of her bag and placed the hair inside for safekeeping, then searched a few more minutes but found nothing else of use.

Checking the trailer's interior was more difficult than she'd expected. The awfulness of the body, she'd prepared herself for, but the flood of memories that assaulted her as she entered her former home were something of a surprise. The surprise was that they were not all bad: nights spent doing each other's nails while a thunderstorm raged outside, birthday parties kludged together with candles stuck in Little Debbie Swiss Rolls, breakfast for dinner. She was expecting all the bad days to come back in full force, all the neglect and abuse and drugs and men. But somehow, as November said goodbye to her mother and to her old life, the happy moments were what rose to the surface. Not sure if that was merciful or cruel, she wept quietly for a few moments before drying her eyes and closing the ratty screen door for the last time. She found no useful evidence within those flimsy walls. There was nothing there for her anymore.

The fairies were waiting outside. "We're ready. We need to get a move on if we're going to make it back before dark," Willow said. "Is there anything in the trailer that could lead anyone to you, even to your name?"

"I don't think so. I don't have school or medical records. She didn't keep pictures. We didn't get much mail other than overdue bills."

"We'll torch it just in case," she said. "Shall we proceed?"

November nodded and watched as Pine lifted her mother as though she weighed nothing and carried her a little ways into the brush, where they'd dug Julia's grave. Willow cleared a wide firebreak around the trailer. November wondered if they had to do this sort of thing often. They seemed to have a system down. Pine hopped into the hole, placed her mother gently at the bottom, and jumped back out. He looked to November, and when she nodded, he began filling in the hole so quickly that November could barely follow his movements. When he was finished, November knelt and patted the mound a few times. She rose to her feet, saying, "Thank you," and walked back to the car without another word. As she watched the trailer go up in flames, the three of them began their drive back to civilization, back to November's new home.

The first few hours of the drive were uneventful. November ate her packed lunch and the fairies argued over the music. They sounded like an old married couple. She supposed they'd been working together for some time. Outside Bakersfield, a monstrous traffic jam brought them to a dead stop. "Wonderful," Pine said. "I'll check the traffic on my phone."

They were still waiting for the traffic map to load when November piped up from the backseat. "Overturned tractor trailer, maybe 7 miles away. It's on fire. All lanes blocked. We're going to be here for awhile," November reported, pleased to be useful. The fairies raised their eyebrows at each other.

"I'll look for an alternate route and report back in to the boss," Willow responded, while Pine swore impotently at the other vehicles. "Let's circle back and take 99 instead of I-5, go through Merced and Turlock." As Pine moved to comply, she dialed the house in Oakland. "Willow. Give me Birch. Yeah, traffic's awful. We need to take 99 to 205. I doubt we'll make it back before dark. We'll have to stop for gas, and presumably the human will require something. They always seem to. Yes, please inform Lord William when he rises."

One advantage of their change in route was the beautiful scenery through the Sequoia National Forest. November couldn't help smiling as she looked up through the window at all those trees. The quiet and shade lulled her into a much-needed and mostly vision-free nap.

The traffic jam and change of plans cost them a lot of time. By the time they stopped for gas in Manteca, it was getting dark. "I need to use the bathroom," she told Willow quietly, a little embarrassed by her human needs. The bathroom was in a separate building rather than inside the little convenience store. Willow came inside with her to get the key from the cashier and followed her to the entrance, waiting for her outside the door after peeking to check that both stalls were unoccupied. It felt strange, to be the subject of all these precautions. It was not until she was washing her hands that she realized that Willow's efforts had been both necessary and ineffective.

November heard a struggle begin outside the door. Before she could react, she herself had been flung against the wall, a hand around her throat. As she struggled to breathe, her assailant gloated. "Waited on the roof. Came through the window," crowed a large fairy with bright yellow hair and eyes. "Now we wait for my partners to finish with your guards, and then we're going to take a little trip. If you scream, I will make you regret it. Understand?" November nodded, and he released his hold on her neck. She could hear Willow and Pine outside and caught a mental glimpse of their violent struggle. There would be no rescue from that quarter. She was on her own. "I wish it was daylight," the fairy whispered right into her ear. "So I could have a taste. Ah, well – there's always tomorrow."

Her thoughts began to race. Her mind flashed back to a lesson from her mother. Once puberty hit, Julia had taught her daughter some basic defensive strategies. It was perhaps the only useful mothering she had ever done. "Make them underestimate you, think you're not a threat. Then go for the eyes and the groin. Fingernails are good. Car keys are better." November's fear crystallized into an icy clarity.

November looked up at the unknown fairy and allowed her mouth to tremble. "Please don't hurt me," she whispered, tears beginning to flow. A moment later, she slumped down to the floor in an apparent faint. As the fairy swore and bent down to check on her, her hand came up with the crucifix of her rosary between her fingers, and she planted it firmly in his left eye as she brought her knee up between his legs.

He began to scream, tearing at his face. November tried to run past him to the door, but he grabbed her ankle and gave it a yank, knocking her to the floor and climbing on top of her. He began to hit her even as her rosary was still sticking out of his eye, landing blows on her ribs and her face as she tried to protect herself with her arms.

"I should kill you, you little whore," he screamed, but then seemed suddenly to weaken. "What have you done?" he whispered as light suddenly began to pour from his wound. She closed her eyes reflexively as the light grew brighter and brighter; her eyelids glowed red. There was one more scream, and when she opened her eyes, her assailant was gone. Her rosary sat in the middle of an empty floor.

The adrenaline was such that she felt none of her injuries as yet. Her shock held her still for a moment as she sat on the floor, staring at the place her attacker should have been, not comprehending what her eyes were telling her. The sound of screaming out in the parking lot reanimated her; she grabbed her rosary and stood up, having absolutely no idea what she was going to do. Her clarity of mind returned, and she used her ability to peer at what was happening on the other side of the door. Willow seemed to be holding her own, but Pine was in desperate straits, on the ground, his attacker above him.

November finally remembered the case of gear the two knights had loaded into the trunk. Praying that Pine had left the car unlocked, she took a deep breath and ran as fast as she could to the car. Relieved to find the car open, she popped the trunk, pulled out the shovels, and opened the case.

Carefully cradled in foam sat a variety of silver weapons with leather-wrapped handles along with a couple of firearms. Having no idea how to aim and shoot, she grabbed a silver-tipped mace and placed a coil of silver chain over her shoulder. She began to move toward Pine. His attacker had his back to November, and she hoped he was too engrossed in enjoying his imminent victory to notice a

90

weak little human. He turned to look at her just as she got close enough to strike, and she hit him full in the face with all her weight behind the blow.

The painful shock to her arm and shoulders caused her to drop the heavy mace, but she was still able to throw the chain over her enemy while he was on the ground, clutching his head and recovering from her assault. The injured fairy's cry distracted his remaining partner-in-crime just enough for Willow to get the upper hand. She sliced into her opponent's neck, and at the instant his head was separated from his body, he turned to a flash of light. Willow placed her hands on her thigh, bent over with exertion, and assessed the scene with a few efficient glances before she began issuing orders.

"November, move everything currently in the trunk to the floor in the rear. Then help Pine get in the back seat. Start the car and sit in the front passenger side. Understand?"

"Yes, ma'am," November replied, moving quickly to do her part. As she did, Willow secured the surviving assailant and tossed him in the trunk. She then turned her attention to the crowd of witnesses who were watching from the entrance to the store. She enthralled them into forgetting it all and tampered with the surveillance system, moving quickly enough to be practically invisible. They sped away and were already halfway up the on-ramp by the time they heard sirens approaching the gas station.

They got about a mile down the highway before Willow turned to her and asked, "How bad are you hurt? Do you need a doctor now or can you make it home?"

"You can take us home. I think I'm just banged up and bruised, but I can't really tell how badly. The pain hasn't kicked in yet," she answered, patting her limbs and feeling around for injuries. Em leaned her head against the window and tried to slow her breathing and her stampeding heart. She looked back at Pine, who had passed out as soon as she'd gotten him into the car. "Is he going to be okay?"

"I don't know. He needs to make it to morning to be healed and to feed. If he can last that long, he'll be fine." Willow looked grim. "If he dies, Lord William had better let me kill Dogwood," she said fiercely, anger and fear dueling in her voice. "How could I have missed them?" she asked with dismay. "Pull my phone out of my pocket," she directed November, both hands on the wheel as she sped for home, heedless of traffic laws. "Call 'boss' in the speed dial and put it on my shoulder."

November did as she was told. "My lord, we were engaged," she reported without prologue. "Three fairies, commanded by Dogwood. The girl and I are lightly injured. Pine's in bad shape. Two assailants dead. Dogwood is in the trunk. ETA about 90 minutes." November could hear William cursing on the other end; he then began peppering his knight with questions. Willow replied, "I don't know how they found us. We had no tail on the way out there. I'm sure of it. No sign or smell of any fairies out at Inyokern. We changed our route due to traffic and informed Birch, per instructions. We called in our plan to stop in Manteca, per instructions. We should sweep for bugs, everywhere."

After a pause, she continued, "I failed you. I should not have been surprised by them. Of course we looked for hostiles when we got there, before we allowed the human to exit the vehicle. They hid well. It was dusk, and our powers were limited. The gasoline and exhaust covered up their scent. We'll go over every detail once we arrive, of course." There was another pause as the vampire spoke. "I agree. I think the prisoner will be more secure in Oakland than Livermore. And November doesn't seem to need immediate medical

92

attention." William gave some instructions, to which Willow replied, "Roger that, sir. Over and out."

Willow looked back at November after dropping the phone in the cup holder. "Who taught you to fight? Not that you don't have a lot to learn, but that wasn't bad for a little human girl."

November decided to take that as a compliment. "My mom. She managed to do one thing right," she replied with a ghost of a smile.

"What happened in the bathroom? How did you get away?" Willow asked, eyes on the road.

"I, um, tricked him into dropping his guard and stabbed him in the eye with my rosary. He couldn't seem to get it out. I tried to run, but he grabbed me and knocked me down. He was hitting me when light started to pour from his eye, and then I closed my eyes and he was gone. Then I saw through the door that Pine was in trouble and remembered that case in the trunk."

"It must be silver. Your rosary. I'm surprised William let you in the house with it," she commented. "Glad he did, though."

"I had no idea it was real silver," November replied. "If we'd known, my mom would have pawned it ages ago." It seemed appropriate somehow, to have her grandmother's rosary wind up protecting more than just her sanity.

"Must have been a very young fairy, to die from such a small wound," Willow said, musing. "I guess they figured he could handle the weak human while the experienced ones killed me and Pine." Willow smiled wolfishly at her. "I guess you showed them. They underestimated you." She paused before adding, "They're not the only ones."

They drove in silence for a while, and November's pain began to set in. A nasty bump was rising on her head where the fairy had slammed it against the wall, and it hurt to take a deep breath. A steady ache was settling into her shoulders. Her jaw throbbed. Her tongue probed her mouth, tasting blood but finding no missing or loose teeth, which was a relief. Her forearms were bruising purple where she'd tried to use them to protect her face. On the whole, though, she was grateful for being lucky enough to escape serious injury.

Pine, on the other hand, drifted in and out of consciousness, moaning occasionally in pain. She heard nothing from the trunk. She wondered what Lord William would do with Dogwood. She suspected it would be rather awful. She caught herself hoping it would be.

It wasn't until they hit the Altamont that she began to process what had happened. She had killed a man – well, a fairy, to be more precise. She had nearly been kidnapped by the same group of people who murdered her mother. *You killed someone*, she told herself. *Then I brained another man with a mace. You killed a man. A boy. I killed a boy.*

She began to shake but did her best not to make any noise. Her fairy companion, however, noticed the change in her breathing. "Hey, it's alright. You did fine. You did better than fine. We all got out alive," said Willow in an unusually soft tone for her. November nodded but said nothing. "Is it the shock coming out, or are you starting to feel the injuries?" she asked.

"Both. I think, um – I think it's also just realizing that, ah, I seem to have killed someone," November admitted in a whisper as the tears began to silently fall. Willow's unexpected kindness had undone her.

Willow peeked at her. "You know you were totally justified, right? It was self-defense, after all."

"I know," November replied, drying her tears on the back of her hand. "I know it wasn't a crime or immoral or anything. But still, it just feels . . . I don't know how to explain it."

"The first time is hard, even for us," Willow confided. "It gets easier. But you don't want to let it get too easy."

November leaned her head back, feeling a bit better after the tears and the unexpected pep talk from Willow. She tried to focus on the music once Willow turned the stereo back on. She just didn't want to think about anything for awhile. She found herself checking the mirrors, trying to see if someone was following them. She couldn't take any more excitement. Relief filled her as they finally arrived at the compound she was already starting to think of as home. How strange her life had become, that a house full of people who could eat her was now her only place of safety.

Willow pulled up to the front door. Half the household was already waiting outside. Daniel helped Willow lift Pine from the car and carried him inside. As soon as November climbed out of the vehicle, Lord William's hands were on her shoulders and he was examining her for injuries. Judging from his expression, she looked about as bad as she felt. "Are you in pain? We have a doctor inside," he said. "He'll patch you up and in the morning, one of the fairies can heal you."

"Okay," she said, wincing as pain shot through her head. "Sounds like a good plan. What else happens now?"

"I'll debrief Willow. Then we'll see how useful Dogwood can be," he said in a dangerous voice.

"If you're going to want me to do a reading on him, I'd rather do it before any, um . . . unpleasantness occurs with respect to . . . uh . . . his person," she suggested as euphemistically as she could manage.

"Are you sure you're up to that? You've been through a lot today already," he said, but November could sense his eagerness to put her gifts to the test. The vampire obviously wanted her to examine the prisoner but had been afraid of pushing her too far by asking himself.

November thought a moment. She was not keen to get near the savage fairy, but she wanted to know who was after her. "If I can see the doctor and eat first, then yes. Just, you know, hold off on the torture."

"Deal. I'll send someone out to get whatever you want, brave girl," he said.

"Pizza. Salad. Coke, please," she said, suddenly ravenous. "Also, can we do this little séance in a room where no one's been, um . . . harmed?" She did not want to see twenty years worth of vampire violence just by crossing the room's threshold.

"As you command," he replied with a grin. "The doctor is in your room." He turned from her and directed one of his men to take the car down into the garage where they could move the prisoner more easily.

November made her way slowly to her bedroom, taking her time on the stairs as every deep breath felt like a blade in her chest. In her room, Zinnia was waiting with the doctor. Her friend jumped up and was about to fling herself into a hug when November warned her off, saying, "Careful, Zin. I'm a little banged up."

"Right, of course," she exclaimed. "This is Dr. Cedar." He rose to shake November's hand. His eyes were an unnatural shade of electric blue that screamed fairy, but his hair was dyed brown. "Do you want me to stay?" Zinnia asked. November nodded and sat down on the bed for her exam.

He checked her over thoroughly, tsking audibly at the livid bruises that had already formed on the right side of her face. He listened carefully to her breathing. "No indication of a rib puncturing the lung, which is very good, but there are definitely fractures. I'll need you to take off your shirt so I can tape up your ribs."

"Zinnia, can you help me?" November asked. "I don't think I can lift my arms above my shoulders." They wound up having to cut off her shirt, revealing livid bruises across her torso and swelling around her shoulder. If November hadn't been in such pain, she'd have been embarrassed about being half-naked in front of this strange doctor. He shook his head some more, finished his exam, and wrapped her in a copious amount of tape. Zinnia then helped her into a button-up blouse.

"Take things very easy tonight until dawn when someone can heal you. The last thing you want is to turn a cracked rib into something more serious. I'll leave you some Vicodin for the pain. Get some food. Get some rest. Any shortness of breath, straight to the hospital. No physical activity, you understand? And no one is to bite you." November nodded and thanked the doctor. She made a quick trip to the bathroom, avoiding looking at her bruised face, then returned to sit on the bed with her friend.

"All Lord William told us was that you were all attacked but you all survived. What the heck happened?" Zinnia demanded, her eyes full of worry. November had finished giving her the short version when Ben knocked on the door.

"Special delivery for the fairy slayer," he said, coming in with a pizza and a take-out bag. The smell reminded November just how starving she was. *There's nothing like a desperate fight for survival to whet the appetite.*

"Bless you," she said, reaching for sustenance. She was glad he seemed to be choosing not to get angry about being sent on such a menial errand.

"I got you a milkshake, too. That's what I always wanted when I had a sucktastic day," Ben said in a rare reference to his human life. He joined the girls sitting on the bed.

"Thank you, thank you, a thousand times, thank you!" November said with a smile as she took the treat from his hands. "Ah, chocolate. You're a prince among men."

"I know," he grinned.

She ate while her new friends peppered her with questions. They demanded to see the killer rosary, so she pulled it out of her pocket. The two supernatural creatures were careful not to touch it. "Yep, definitely silver," judged Zinnia as she held her hand above the crucifix. "Lucky you had that."

"Seriously, though," November replied, finally done eating. "I'd probably be in the trunk of their car or something right now. Or worse." She put the leftovers in the fridge and concentrated on finishing her milkshake. A bath and some sleep, and she might actually feel like a human being again. "I still can't believe I did those things. I fought a fairy kidnapper in a gas station bathroom and stabbed him in the eye and killed him. Me, a person who has to get her nerve up to kill a spider. And then I whacked another guy with a mace. A guy who is a centuries-old professional hit man. I hit him right in the face." She looked down at her hands as the reality of her day once again overtook her.

"You don't feel guilty, do you?" Ben asked. "They were your enemies and had it coming."

"No, I don't. Maybe that's the problem. I feel like I should, but I don't." After a lifetime of seeing death everywhere she looked, her general attitude was that everyone dies and there wasn't much point in expending a great deal of emotional energy on it. She knew that made her a freak by human standards. There was one real fear November had about her future after her upcoming death. She was afraid that if she became a vampire, she would lose whatever empathy she'd managed to retain after her years of seeing far too much suffering and death. Vampires were bloodthirsty by nature, after all. They had to learn to view humans as prey. And, it seemed, they fought with other supernatural creatures rather regularly. November didn't want to become a monster. *Am I a monster already?* she asked herself, not for the first time.

"You did great," Ben said. "You really are amazing." His eyes no longer had their usual mocking look. November was rather alarmed by his sudden change in tone. She was even more alarmed when he scooted closer to her on the bed, reaching his hand towards her face. Zinnia looked equally concerned.

This awkward moment was mercifully interrupted when Willow knocked on the door and called, "Our lord wants to know if you're ready to examine the prisoner." Ben jerked his hand back as if burned and affected a slightly bored facial expression.

"I suppose I'm as ready as I'll ever be. How's Pine?" November asked.

"Still hanging on. Thanks to you," Willow replied. November grabbed her drawing pad and a couple of pencils and headed out the door. They walked down to the library, where she and Willow used one of the secret doors to descend to the basement.

It turned out that there were several rooms down there that locked from the outside. The dungeon area was separated from the vampires' resting places by a long, well fortified hallway. As they approached Dogwood's cell, November hesitated. Willow looked at her with concern, saying, "You don't have to be frightened. He is well-secured. He cannot harm you, and several of us will be in there with you. You are in no danger."

"I know," she replied. "Lord William does not seem to be a careless man. It's more that . . . I've never done anything like this before. I mean, I've never done a reading on purpose without permission, with the intent of doing the subject harm. I realize he deserves it, but it disturbs me."

"Well, try to think of it this way: the more you find out, the less we'll have to hurt him afterwards," Willow said brightly. November suppressed a shudder. She didn't like to think these people she was coming to care about did such cruel things.

Willow turned to face her, bending over to meet her level. "It must seem barbaric to you, but this is how our justice works. It's how human justice works, too, in many places. They just hide it from you so you don't have to think about it. We don't torture people over petty crimes. And at least we don't lock people in boxes all alone for 50 years like humans do. That's barbaric. We have four punishments only: fines, pain, banishment, and death. Dogwood knew what he was risking, attacking Lord William's people, in his own territory. He does not deserve your pity."

"I know. Let's get this over with." November and Willow walked to the door of Dogwood's cell. The fairy was dressed now in beige hospital scrubs and was bound with many yards of silver chain to a cast iron chair that appeared to be set into the concrete. She felt assured that he would not be going anywhere any time soon. His face had healed from the mace's blow. It was a face that she suspected had started life handsome but had wound up twisted by misdeeds. William, Daniel, and Birch were also in attendance.

100

There was an empty folding chair, presumably for November. "I'll need a few minutes to get used to the room before I start in earnest." William nodded his understanding, and they crossed the threshold.

A parade of previous prisoners passed through November's mind. There were fairies, vampires, werewolves, in varying degrees of distress. There were not as many as she had feared, and William had listened to her request and used a room with no history of cruelty to torment and distract her. Perhaps they had a separate room for suffering. The thought of that repelled her. When she opened her eyes, the prisoner spoke. "So this is the prize for which I lose my life. She hardly seems worth it, all the bodies piling up at her feet."

"On that point, Mr. Dogwood, I believe we are in agreement," November found herself replying. He looked surprised to hear her speak coherently.

"Oh-ho, Knox, you don't keep her on a leash, then? Is she more fun that way, unenthralled? Or maybe just more useful?" Dogwood asked snidely. No one gave him the satisfaction of a reply.

November sat down in the chair, saying, "I'm just going to touch your arm for a few minutes. Please forgive the intrusion."

The prisoner barked a laugh at her unexpected civility. "Poppet, it will be rather the highlight of my evening, I expect."

November braced herself, unsure about the strange waters she was entering. She pulled a deep breath into her lungs and reached out her hand to touch the fairy's bare, hairless arm.

She began with the recent past, hoping that would be the best bet for relevant information. The visions were more fragmented than she was used to. This being the first fairy she'd really tried to read, she wondered if this was true for all of them. While reading William had been like swimming through deep water, reaching out to caress the visions as she passed by, reading Dogwood was like sifting through debris as it fell and piled around her, as she tried to grab enough broken pieces to put together something coherent without cutting her hands. It was still easier than reading a human, when she often felt as though she were drowning and smashing against submerged hazards, dragged through the visions by unseen forces.

She tried to block out as much as she could of Dogwood's brutal fight with Pine as well as her own intervention in it. She saw a flash of him speaking on a cell phone and caught the word "Manteca." She then saw him speaking to a cruel-mouthed man in expensive-looking black clothes.

The man has one brown eye and one blue. They are talking about a plan and the need for patience. Dogwood bows to him at the end of the conversation. Their words are unclear. Dogwood carouses with Agnes and Philemon, all taking turns feeding on a doomed man. Their victim dies with his eyes open as Dogwood sucks away the last of his life

That one made her shudder, but she forced herself to continue and push further into the past. Sexual assault also seemed to be a popular activity for the three of them. Cruelty after cruelty she picked up and discarded in the search for something useful, forcing herself to wade through many violent deaths of vampire and werewolf and fairy and human. She was rewarded with the sight of him helping a vampire woman put on a vest of explosives and hide it under a purple jacket. He seemed to be encouraging her, preparing her. She caught the names "Clara" and "Victor." That was a satisfying find. The next scene she found was a surprise, as she watched Dogwood and the late Queen Marisha in what appeared to be an intense conversation, about what, she could not tell.

November returned to her body with a jolt, looking up at William's face as he cradled her head and held a handkerchief against her nose. He had pulled her chair away from the prisoner, breaking their contact. "What happened?" she asked, confused and wondering why he'd stopped the session.

"I decided that enough was enough. Your nose started bleeding," he said. "Does that happen often? When you do readings?" November shook her head. She'd never been affected like that while working. William held up a handkerchief soaked with blood and took a box of tissues from Willow. November grabbed a few and pinched her nose. In a few minutes, the flow stopped and she looked around the room. Dogwood looked amused. William looked hungry, for blood and information both, November suspected.

"You better hope she doesn't do that in front of a younger vampire. You can barely restrain yourself," said Dogwood with an ugly smile. "Even a teetotaler like you, who eats animals like a filthy werewolf. She's wasted on you." He turned his attention from November back to the psychic. "What did you see of my future, fortune teller?" Dogwood asked.

"I didn't bother looking," she replied honestly. "I think we all know that it will be neither very nice nor very long." Her tone wasn't mocking or cruel, simply matter-of-fact.

"They won't be able to protect you, you know. My master will have you for himself or he will see you dead. You should wish he'd found you first. He would enjoy you and then make you a queen," Dogwood called out to November as William helped her to her feet and out the door. As she passed Willow, the fairy reached out and squeezed her less-injured shoulder, a much appreciated and unanticipated gesture.

"I strongly suspect that I would rather be a corpse with these people than a queen with your master," November responded firmly. She did not turn around for a last look at the doomed man.

As they slowly climbed the stairs back to the library, Birch following close behind, Knox requested that she give him a brief report to inform his questioning, after which she could draw and write down her impressions in more detail. As they settled into some chairs, Savita walked in. "Perfect timing, *akka*. November has just done a reading on Dogwood and was about to give us her initial thoughts. Hopefully they will give you somewhere to start with the prisoner."

November looked questioningly at Savita. The vampire explained, "I'm the Royal Inquisitor. I suppose I'm similar to a federal prosecutor. I handle major criminal investigations on behalf of the court. As the assailants likely came from out-of-state and may be involved in significant ongoing criminal activity, my brother has invited me to participate in the inquiry."

"How did you end up with that job?" November asked.

"I'm a mind-reader, November. Even when I was human." November's eyes opened wide. "Don't worry dear girl; I have to touch you in order to hear anything much. You are harder to read than other humans. I refrained from telling you the other night because I suspected that you were already rather overwhelmed."

"Fair enough," the human replied. She was intrigued that Savita had possessed her ability even when she was human. November had never met anyone like herself. She was also relieved to find out that William had tools other than torture at his disposal.

"Shall we begin?" William asked as he pulled up a chair. "I've already briefed Savita on this evening's events at the gas station."

"You acquitted yourself quite well, I'm told," Savita complimented the human. November tried to shrug and regretted it.

"Well, first of all, I saw Dogwood talking to someone on his cell phone about us stopping in Manteca," she said, and William nodded, unsurprised.

"We're already looking for bugs and tapped phones," William replied. "I rather hope we find one, as the alternative is unpleasant to contemplate."

"Even if we do find one, we have to consider the possibility of a mole. After all, someone would have to plant the bug," Birch replied. His deep voice matched his always somber face.

William gestured for her to continue. November shared, "I saw Dogwood speaking with a man he seemed to treat as his superior. They kept referring to a plan, and the man said that they would have to continue to be patient. I didn't catch a name, but I'll sketch him for you. His eyes were two different colors, his hair graying. Handsome in a creepy sort of way. Something about his mouth. Black clothes."

Recognition washed across all three of their faces. Apparently this man was no stranger. "Could you tell how long ago they were speaking?" Birch asked. "Recently? Centuries ago?"

"Based on the style of clothing, I would guess recently, within the last few years. I'm sorry I can't be more specific," she apologized before moving on. "I also saw a lot of random violence, which may or may not have any significance given his predilections and line of work. I'll draw them. Sometimes he was with Agnes and Philemon."

William nodded sadly. "No surprise there. Please continue."

"This one seemed quite important: I saw him helping a girl with what looked like a vest of explosives."

William's eyes lit up, and even Birch managed a small smile of satisfaction. "Oh, November, do you have any idea how long we've waited for a solid lead like that? We may finally be able to begin unraveling this mess. Do you know anything else about it?"

"The names 'Clara' and 'Victor' seemed to be associated with that part of the vision."

"Victor, the lord of New York, was killed 8 months ago. Clara I'm not sure about. Perhaps it was the name of the bomber? At least this gives us somewhere to start," the Lord of California replied.

"There's one more thing," November said, hesitating before she continued, "I saw him talking to Queen Marisha." The room went completely silent as the three listeners looked at one another, suddenly on edge.

"When? Were they fighting?" Savita asked intently.

"The clothes looked like latter 18th century to me, maybe, turn of the 19th? I'll draw them and you can confirm. It looked like an intense conversation, but not like an argument. They were seated close together, and the body language wasn't particularly hostile," November reported. "I couldn't make out what they were saying."

"I can't imagine what she would have been doing talking to a creature like that," November said incredulously.

"We shall look into it," Savita replied. The three of them stood.

"We'll check on you before dawn. If you need to rest, please do. We can pick up again tomorrow evening. Office supplies are in the armoire over there in the corner if you need anything to help you with your work," Savita instructed her as the vampires headed for the hidden door. November nodded and began drawing.

As they opened the door, Birch turned and said, "I thought it was folly, when Lord William went to find you. Evidently, I was mistaken." November nodded her appreciation of his gesture of goodwill, and the three creatures disappeared back into the basement.

A few moments later, Willow came up from the basement and walked through. "Boss said I should check on you and Pine and then get some rest," the fairy said wearily by way of explanation. November gave her a weak smile and then set about her work.

November started by checking the armoire, where she found ordinary pens and pencils as well as charcoals, colored pencils, pastels, and paper. She also appropriated a binder and sheet protectors. She liked to be organized in her work. It gave her a sense of control her life often lacked.

She focused first on the scene with the explosive vest. She wanted to be sure to include all the details she had seen in case it would help Savita and Knox match her to a particular attack, like the one in New York. The bomber herself looked quite calm. She certainly didn't appear to be having second thoughts. Dogwood was the one who looked anxious.

The scene with Dogwood and the man with strange eyes also seemed quite important, and she hoped the details of the clothing would help them all to date the conversation. She then quickly sketched the cell phone vision and the scenes of random violence, focusing on the faces of the victims in case any of them were identifiable.

Finally, she turned her attention to the vision of Marisha. This one had such obvious emotional significance for William and his family, she wanted to get things exactly right. She did one sketch focusing on the clothing, again for the purpose of dating the scene. Then she did a series of drawings focusing on facial expressions and body language.

She was frustrated that she hadn't heard more of what was going on in the conversations, but she did her best with what she had. By the time she looked up from her final drawing, the night was half gone. Every cell in her body was exhausted, yet she feared going to sleep, sure that given recent events, she would be woken by visions every hour. Nevertheless, she had to try to get some rest. She organized her drawings in the binder and moved to one of the couches to await her companions. Someone had left an afghan draped over the back of the sofa. November curled up and lay down, struggling to find a position that didn't hurt, then pulling the blanket over herself. She was asleep as soon as her head came to rest on a throw pillow.

As she expected, her sleep was troubled. Flashes of her mother's murder interlaced with scenes of Dogwood's depravity and her own memories of that evening's attack. She had long ago trained herself not to scream in her sleep, but tonight it was a very near thing. Whimpers of fear escaped her throat as she relived her recent traumas, and she woke up to William gently shaking her by the shoulders. The blanket was tangled in her limbs, evidence of her desperate thrashing as her churning mind had thwarted her attempt at rest.

"Are you unwell?" Savita asked, kneeling beside her.

"Bad dreams," November answered. "To be expected after the last few days I've had. I didn't scream, did I?" she asked, embarrassed.

"No," William replied. "But you sounded . . . distressed."

"Did you get anything useful from Dogwood?" November asked, sitting up straight.

"Indeed we did, with your help," Savita answered without revealing anything more.

"I meant to ask you, did you find any personal items on Dogwood when you searched him? Jewelry, or anything like that? It could be useful for me later," November inquired, not that she had any desire to romp through Dogwood's past any further.

"Yes, actually," William replied. "He had a necklace. We'll save it, of course. We also sent someone to retrieve his vehicle. Perhaps the phone will still be in it, since it wasn't on his person."

"Can I ask, how long are you going to keep him here?" November ventured. It made her nervous, having him so close. On the other hand, she felt guilty for hoping for someone to be killed, however much the creature deserved his fate.

"A few days, most likely. We want to get as much information as possible, but I don't like keeping prisoners indefinitely. It invites trouble. He is not protesting innocence, so there will be no delay for trial before the penalty of death is administered. Hopefully Pine will be well enough to strike the blow himself," William answered. "Don't worry. He will be carefully guarded. You are in no danger." William checked his watch. "It is nearly dawn. You should go to bed. I'm afraid we're pushing you much too hard. The nosebleed concerns me. We can study and discuss your drawings this evening."

"They're in a binder on the desk," she said, standing to head upstairs. "I could definitely use some rest. I'd love to have a few days with nothing traumatic happening, just to recover and work and get used to living here."

"I shall do my best to give you that respite," William promised.

November hesitated, painfully self-conscious about what she was about to ask. "Speaking of sleep, as you've just seen, I have trouble sleeping soundly. But the other night, after you bit me, I slept like a baby. No dreams or visions at all. I know the doctor said not to, but I'm just so tired, so I was wondering if it wouldn't be too much trouble, I mean, would you mind, um –." Before she could finish the request, William had her pressed against the wall, his hand cradling her head and his fangs at her throat.

"Ready?" he said softly.

"Uh-huh," she replied, breathless. She gasped as he bit, relaxing against his arm and the wall as he swallowed her blood. Savita looked slightly concerned.

"Will that do?" William asked as he pressed another handkerchief against her neck.

"Yes," she squeaked, suppressing the part of her that suddenly wanted more. "Thanks. I, um, guess I'll see you later then," she said awkwardly as she ducked under his arm and escaped out the door. She walked as quickly as she could manage toward her room, trying to ignore the strange feeling in her stomach. She suspected that she'd enjoyed that rather more than was appropriate. She refused to consider the possibility that she was falling for William, so she put it out of her mind. There was way too much going on for shenanigans like that. And then there was Ben – he was being awfully solicitous all of the sudden. And he was beautiful, and more age-appropriate. Cursing herself for having hormones, she dragged herself up the stairs and down the hall.

She walked past Pine's bedroom on the way to her own. The door was open, so she peered in to see how he was doing. Birch, Rose, Zinnia, and Willow were standing vigil around his bed. He
110

was still unconscious but didn't look any worse than he had when they'd taken him out of the car. Rose looked like she'd been crying. Her white silk handkerchief was stained with tears the same champagne color as her hair. Apparently those violet eyes were contact lenses. Birch was holding her hand, their fingers tightly intertwined with love and anxiety.

"It'll be dawn in half an hour, and then we can heal him," Birch said.

"We would have lost our son if it weren't for you," Rose said, smiling at November through her tears.

"He wouldn't have even been attacked in the first place if it weren't for me. I'm glad I was able to help him," she said. "I'm so relieved that he's going to be okay."

"We were there in service of our house," Willow replied. "None of this is your fault. Lord William brought you here, remember?"

"Thanks, Willow . . . I suppose I'll leave you to it, then," she said. "I'll see you all after I get some sleep." Zinnia gave her a gentle hug before November slipped out the door.

She headed straight for bed, barely mustering up the energy to take off her jeans. She left the blouse on, knowing that it would be impossible for her to get into her nightgown on her own. Her pain was catching up with her, so she took one of the pills the doctor had left and curled up in her warm bed, falling quickly into a blissfully quiet sleep.

Chapter 6

The sun was already low in the sky by the time November opened her eyes. She glanced at the clock and realized that she'd slept nearly 13 hours solid. Sitting up to stretch, she was forcibly reminded of her injuries. She ached everywhere and felt so stiff that she could barely move. She took a deep breath for which she was immediately punished as pain stabbed through both sides of her chest. November gingerly made her way to the shower, hoping the hot water would loosen her battered limbs. Being clean did at least lift her spirits.

She ate an improvised breakfast while dressed in her bathrobe. Leftover pizza seemed appropriate given that it was only an hour or so before sunset. She somehow managed to get dressed, very slowly. She chose a skirt and a pretty blouse that looked easy to put on. Slip-on flats were her only option for shoes, as she couldn't bend over to tie or fasten anything. She pulled on some gloves that almost matched. At least they were clean, which had often not been the case in her previous life.

She looked in the mirror that she'd been avoiding and winced at her battered appearance. She looked worse than her mother ever had after even her worst night. Her face was a mess of bruises. She tried to make her hair at least presentable. She found a trove of makeup in the bathroom and considered trying to cover the injuries, but with her lack of experience with cosmetics, that seemed to be a losing proposition. She did put on some lipstick, for probably the first time in her life, then laughed at herself for thinking that anyone would notice her lips when most of her face was purple and swollen. Still, the gesture somehow made her feel a little better. The sooner she could find a fairy miracle worker, the better.

She walked bravely over to the door and hesitated, mentally crossing her fingers as she reached her hand out to touch the knob. It turned easily in her hand and opened to reveal the hallway. November smiled. That was one victory, at least. Someone had removed the locks while she'd been sleeping. She looked down and found a copy of the Wall Street Journal on the floor in front of the door. Someone had scrawled a note in the corner: "If you get bored . . . Thanks, Greg."

November burst out laughing and was punished again by her broken ribs. No longer feeling such a prisoner, she went looking for a fairy to put her body back in working order. She found Zinnia, Pine, and Willow in the game room.

"Pine! You're better," she cried in relief. To her immense surprise and discomfort, the fairy in question hurried over and knelt at her feet.

"To you do I owe my life, and to you do I pledge my friendship and service," he said solemnly, looking up into her startled face. November's eyebrows shot up high enough to hit her hairline.

Catching her reaction, Willow explained, "It is our way, when one's life is saved by another. If you're ever in trouble, he is honor bound to do his best to help you. You look really alarmed," she said, laughing. "It's okay. It's just how we roll."

"Okay, um, thanks," November replied, reaching down to take Pine's hand as he stood. "I could certainly use a friend, never having had many," she said with a little smile. She was worried that maybe Pine resented being saved by a little human weakling, but she didn't see any evidence for that in his face. "Speaking of which," she said, pointing to the green and purple bruises on her face, "Can someone do something about this?"

"Of course," Willow replied, gesturing for her to lie down on the couch.

"This will take longer than your arm, Em. It might feel rather strange. And of course, I suppose you'll see things," Zinnia said.

"Don't sugar coat it. You should warn her that it will hurt a great deal," Pine said seriously. "Nothing comes free." November nodded, grateful for the warning. "Regrettably, I'll have to sit this one out. Still on the mend." He sat in an armchair across from the couch.

November stretched out with a little help, and the two women knelt next to her.

"Ready?" Willow asked.

November nodded nervously, and the two of them placed their hands on her, closing their eyes in concentration. She suddenly felt very warm. Her skin burned uncomfortably, especially in the places where she had been wounded. Fragments of visions began to swirl around her. November didn't want to pry, though she was quite curious about her new friends, but as the pain of healing increased, she yearned for a distraction. Finally, temptation got the better of her, and she reached out for one of the fragments.

A very young Willow hides inside a hollow tree in the dark of night, curled up as small as she can make herself, shaking with fear, covering her ears, surrounded by carnage. Injured and dying fairies bleed light. One by one, they disappear in blinding flashes while huge wolves howl in triumph.

November felt horror-struck and a bit guilty about spying on such an awful tragedy. No wonder Willow was so tough, having survived something like that. Wary and chastened, she tried to ignore the events piling up around her as her friends worked their

114

healing magic. She attempted to focus on her breathing as her wounds knit painfully together, but it was difficult. She found herself fighting the pain and becoming afraid of it, which only made it worse. She finally turned to the skills she used to get through the worst of her visions and managed to let go and ride the waves of pain. For a brief moment, the discomfort ceased, and she thought the ordeal was over. Her relief was short-lived, as suddenly every wound blazed with an intense pain that wrung a cry out of her throat, and then it was over. Her friends helped her to sit up as she breathed in little convulsive gasps as the pain slowly ebbed.

When she had recovered, she wiped away the tears, accepted a glass of water from Pine, and asked Zinnia, "Why did it hurt so much? It didn't hurt like that when you healed my arm." She sounded a little betrayed.

"Those wounds had already almost healed. These ones were new and much more severe. You had a number of broken ribs. The difficulty of healing rises sort of exponentially with the severity of the injury," Zinnia explained. "I'm really sorry," she added, looking like she might cry. "I don't have a lot of experience doing this. Maybe I did it wrong."

Willow shook her head. "You did fine," she said.

"That's just how it is. My parents healed me this morning. They've done it many times and it still hurt like hell, and my mom is an especially good healer. It's as though months of pain and healing are compressed into just a minute or two. That's what makes it so awful," Pine explained.

"It's alright," November said, beginning to feel better, a little embarrassed now by her emotional reaction. "I know you didn't mean for it to hurt. Thank you for putting me back in working order." She looked at Pine. "It must have been really bad for you this morning."

Pine nodded. "There were a few minutes there when I almost wished you hadn't been quite so handy with that mace." His smile and wink took the edge off the comment.

"Yeah, about that . . . would it be possible for someone to teach me how to fight better? I got lucky this time, but next time . . ." November blushed as she flashed back to her desperate improvisation.

"It wasn't just luck. You could have hidden. You could have gone with them. You chose to fight, so you've already got the heart for it. That's the most important thing," Pine countered. November warmed to hear encouragement in his voice. It was nice to feel like she had won the soldier over. "You'll never be as strong as any of us," he continued honestly, "but I'm sure we can teach you something. We'll have to adapt the lessons we're already giving Zinnia and Ben," Pine answered. He seemed pleased to be able to do a favor for the girl to whom he owed his life. His confidence made November feel calmer, and the idea that Ben and Zinnia also had things to learn made her feel less alone in her lack of fighting experience.

Rose walked into the room. "I take it from the screaming that you've healed my favorite human?" she asked. Dressed to professional perfection, she had a clipboard in hand.

"Yes, I'm feeling much better now," November answered, managing a true smile. She really did feel fully recovered, but she had no desire to repeat that experience if she could help it, hence the request for self-defense lessons.

"Excellent. I need to talk to you about food. I've decided to hire a service to deliver meals and groceries for you each week, since we

116

fairies and vampires obviously have no idea what you people actually like to consume." Rose aimed a pointed look at Zinnia, who blushed blue with guilt over her grocery shopping failure.

"Well, thank you so much," November replied. "I don't want to be any trouble, or cause some huge expense," she said self-consciously, unaccustomed to generosity or even an ordinary amount of care.

Rose rolled her eyes. "Please, child, Lord William can afford it. For God's sake, it's the least we can do to feed you, not that you look like anyone else has ever bothered. Besides which, you already seem to be earning your keep quite handily." She glanced first at her recently-saved son and then at her clipboard. "Anything you need, you will have. Obviously, going out shopping is not safe for you right now. We've gotten you a credit card on the company account, and we've ordered you a computer. It should be delivered today. You can order whatever you need. If you can't find it, ask me."

November widened her eyes. *What else could I possibly need? And my own computer?* She was used to fighting homeless guys for time on library computers. Rose just kept going as November's incredulity continued to grow. "We'd like to set you up a bank account for your salary, but it is complicated by the fact that you are a minor with no legal guardian and have no identification and are being hunted by nefarious animals. Until things settle down and we can get some decent forgeries, we'll just keep track of what you're owed."

The fairy finally noticed November's befuddlement. "For heaven's sake, dear, you aren't a slave. You have very useful abilities and deserve to be compensated commensurately. And my husband and I will make sure Lord William doesn't try to lowball you. He can be unnecessarily frugal sometimes." The others laughed knowingly.

"Thanks so much," was all November could manage as Rose handed her a black credit card.

"Here are some menus from the service I hired. If you can mark what you want and get it back to me tonight, they can deliver tomorrow afternoon."

"Sure, thanks," she replied, taking the proffered papers and pen. Regular meals of healthy, well-prepared food certainly sounded like an appealing change of pace.

"Lord William wants you to take things easy for the next several days," Rose said.

"Yes, I asked him for some time to recover and get used to my new, um, situation," November replied.

"Obviously, the whole residence is at your disposal, aside from others' resting places. If you need anything, just let any of us know. Do not go into the government wing unescorted. The alarms give me headaches. And now I have to get on with my real work," Rose said.

"No rest for the wicked?" Pine asked his mother with a wink.

"You hush. You know the king and court are coming for Christmas this year," Rose replied.

"It's October," her son replied.

"Exactly! Barely two months left to make arrangements," she said, throwing up her hands at the impossibility of it all as she strode out the door. Pine laughed.

"Well, I've got homework," Zinnia announced. "I'll be in the library."

"We've got a meeting," Willow said. She and Pine said their goodbyes and headed out the door.

November went with Zinnia to the library. She worked on filling out Rose's paperwork and set about fulfilling Greg's request. She was putting off dealing with the envelope in her pocket. She did not look forward to seeing anything about Agnes's ugly life. Perhaps she should procrastinate, put it off for a few days and take things easy. But what if something she saw was time sensitive? What if she could have prevented an attack, or another attempt at her own kidnapping? She would never be able to forgive herself.

She took a deep breath and pulled out the envelope. She reached in and drew out the strand of hair, lowering her defenses and willing herself to go wherever the hair took her. Unfortunately, it took her straight back to her mother's death and no further. She tried to push past it with no success. Growling with frustration, she returned to herself and put the hair away again.

Zinnia looked up from her truly formidable pile of books. "Problem?"

"I found one of Agnes's hairs on my mother's body. I was hoping it could tell me something, but all I'm getting is my mother's murder. Maybe it was on her body too long? I don't know. I'll try again another time. Maybe I'll have better luck," November replied, feeling a strange mixture of disappointment and relief. Now she could relax without any guilt, once she washed the images of her poor mother out of her head.

As she turned her attention back to the *Wall Street Journal*, Savita and Lord William arrived, heralding sunset.

"All better?" Lord William asked, walking over and kneeling next to her chair to get a good look at her. To her great consternation, his nearness made her heart leap.

"I'm fine," she said, willing her voice to sound normal.

"Excellent," he replied. "I have some unfortunate news. Dogwood is dead. He somehow managed to poison himself with silver; perhaps he took it when he was in the trunk of the car. We were hoping to question him further. The only consolation is that with your help, last night was very productive. Also, that he died a slow and very painful death."

November was secretly a little happy at the news. It was hard to relax knowing he was down there in the dungeon. William continued, "I mean for you to have those quiet days that you requested. We've put you through a lot." He reached out and touched her hair, brushing the heel of his hand lightly against her cheek. The contact gave her chills. "I'm proud of you," he added, and then he walked back out the door. "I need to inform Pine that he's been robbed of his chance for vengeance. Then I'll be in my office if anyone needs me," he called in their general direction. November looked after him, feeling both relieved and perturbed by his exit.

Savita sat down on the floor next to November's chair. "Your work last night was very helpful. I am wondering if you would be willing to work more closely with me on the investigation of these bombings."

"Of course, I mean, if you think I can add something," the human replied a bit nervously. "I've never done anything like that before. What would it entail?"

"I would like you to examine the evidence I've already gathered, to see if you can offer any additional insight." Savita looked up at her. "I could certainly use the assistance. I have made very little progress, sad to say."

"Sure," November said, steeling herself in advance for what promised to be a very unpleasant task.

"I'll set something up with my brother. I'd better make a move and get back to Livermore," she finished, rising gracefully.

"Have a good night," November said as Zinnia gave the vampire a friendly wave without looking up from her books. The fairy had a test the next morning, apparently.

Ben joined them a few minutes after his elders vacated. "Well, you've certainly got your pretty face back. You sure you feel alright?"

"I'm fine. Really." All this attention was beginning to alarm her. Ben backed off a bit, reading her face.

"I hear that fairy healing can be pretty painful," he said sympathetically.

"Yeah, I hope to avoid needing it in the future," she replied.

"Unfortunately, I need to go out and find some food," Ben said with a voice full of reluctance.

"Unfortunately?" Zinnia asked, confused.

"I'd rather stay here with you two," he answered. "Be back in an hour." He gave November a lingering look before he rushed out the door. November blushed furiously. Zinnia laughed.

"What in the world was that all about?" November asked her friend when they were once again alone.

"He obviously wants you," Zinnia replied, amused at her cluelessness.

"Two days ago he was complaining about babysitting me," November countered.

"Things change. You've shown yourself to be more than the typical, disposable human," her friend said. "Nothing can come of it, of course."

"Why not?" November demanded. She wasn't sure that she even *wanted* anything to come of it, but the decisive statement offended her nonetheless.

"You belong to Lord William. You cannot steal your lord's human, seduce her, feed on her blood. You just can't," Zinnia explained. "Especially when Lord William seems to be taking rather a shine to you himself. I've never seen him so affectionate toward a human before, and I've known him all my life."

"I'm not his property," November said. "And who says anyone wants to feed on my blood? Maybe Ben just has a little crush on me."

"Don't think of it as being his property. It's more like you're under his protection. He would have to give another lower ranking vampire or fairy permission to pursue you. They would never dare otherwise. And of course Ben wants to bite you. Blood and sex go together for vampires. Same goes for fairies and life energy. It's all bound up together." Zinnia paused. "You should be careful, with Ben. If you encourage him, and Lord William sees that Ben's after you, or if he bites you, heaven forbid, Ben could get in serious trouble. I'm talking scourging, banishment, who knows what. Lord William would view it as defying his authority. Ben is the one who would be punished, not you."

"Eek! This is all so confusing," November complained, throwing back her head in frustration. "*You* seem to be pretty fond of Ben. Unlike everyone else in the house."

The fairy sighed. "Yeah. I feel bad for him. He's in a tough spot. Here's the story I heard: his maker turned him as a gift to his

122

young daughter. The girl was having a really hard time adjusting to being a vampire, and she took a liking to Ben. So their maker turned him to try to make his daughter happy. Ben liked her, too. He fell for her pretty hard. But she was still miserable as a vampire. She wound up killing herself. Then his maker got killed, and he was left all alone for about a year, until Lord William forced him to move up here when the locals in So Cal got tired of his drama. And now he doesn't really fit in here," Zinnia continued. "It's been almost a year, and he just can't seem to get along with most of us. He and I are friends, maybe because we're close to the same age. But the others find him irritating and arrogant and careless. Lord William doesn't trust him, and Ben doesn't even really try to improve his reputation."

"Wow. What a mess," November replied. She had more sympathy for him now. His attitude seemed a bit more understandable now that she knew the back story. "So, you don't like him in a romantic way?"

"Of course not! He's too much of a slacker. Besides, it's pretty unusual for a fairy and a vampire to be involved. They can't drink from us, which is kind of their whole bag. For a fling, we all prefer humans we can feed from. For a serious thing, we mostly stick to other fairies because our population is so small. We have a duty to preserve our people." Zinnia sounded like she was reciting something her parents had drummed into her head. "Do you like Ben? Or maybe Lord William?" Zinnia asked in a sing-song voice, a mischievous gleam in her eye.

"Ew!" she exclaimed, throwing a pillow at her friend. "Jeez, I don't know," November replied more honestly after a long minute. "Maybe? There's just too much happening all at once, and I don't want complications or trouble right now. This is not a good time or place for me to try to learn how to date." She stopped for a moment, hit with an unpleasant realization. "Of course, it seems this might be the only chance I ever have," she said slowly, considering her upcoming, oft-viewed burial.

"Just be careful and smart about it. And don't do anything you're at all unsure of. It seems like you've got your head on straight, as far as I can see. You're not acting like most people our age seem to, throwing themselves right into bad situations," Zinnia said, trying to be supportive.

"Thanks. It's good to have you to talk to, Zinnia. I'm not used to having a girlfriend." November smiled.

"Me neither. It's kind of awesome," Zinnia agreed, grinning.

"Do you have a boyfriend?" the human asked.

"There's a boy in one of my classes, Rigo. He plays piano. We have lunch together. He eats. I pretend to eat. Then I feed on him. Sometimes we make out. The circle of life. And then there's Acorn. We're betrothed." She sighed heavily. The engagement did not seem to be a source of joy.

"You're engaged. To be married. And you have a human sort-of-boyfriend. Wowzers."

"We've been engaged since I was, like, 5. I'm almost 20 now, and we probably won't marry until I'm 50. That's about the age when we have the best chance of carrying a child to term. I've met him once. My parents picked him because his dad is Lord of Georgia and we're not too closely related. It's all about politics and making baby fairies. Love is not the objective."

"That sounds incredibly difficult." November responded.

Zinnia shrugged. "It is what it is. Hopefully, we'll come to love each other. If I don't find love in my marriage, I'll find it elsewhere, and no one will think any less of me. When you live for centuries, monogamy isn't that prized. Most married fairies and vampires take human lovers as well. That's just how our world works."

"But don't people get their feelings hurt?" This system sounded to November like a recipe for disaster.

"Sometimes."

"So if you fall in love with a human, you can never tell him who you really are," November said. "And you'll almost certainly outlive him."

"Yes. Vampires get to make a choice if they fall in love with humans: they can make them vampires. We can't make someone a fairy. It's a hard knock life," she shrugged. "So, most of us try not to get too emotionally attached to humans. We try to save our love for each other. It's safer that way, for everyone," Zinnia said, a little sadly. "Pine had a human husband, though, but that's pretty unusual."

"Huh," November said, thinking of her own efforts not to get too close to other people, isolating herself as a survival mechanism, a way to protect herself and her sanity. People had always found her to be cold and unfriendly.

She wondered why she felt closer to these strangers after only a few days than she felt toward human people she'd known a long time. Part of it was that it was easier to block visions of their lives. It seemed that she had to look on purpose to pry into the past and future of these supernatural creatures, which meant they could touch her without setting her off. Part of it was that she didn't have to hide what she was or pretend to be normal. And perhaps part of it was that they had similar a survival strategy: a distancing from the ordinary human world while simultaneously trying to function within it.

True to William's word, November enjoyed a few weeks of quiet domesticity. She read a few novels. She enjoyed her catered meals and settled into a schedule, going to bed a few hours before dawn and rising in the afternoon. During the daylight hours when she was mostly alone, she explored the house until she was so used to every part of the residence that none of the rooms any longer spawned visions or specters or half-heard conversations.

Her favorite room besides the library was the ballroom, once she got accustomed to it. She hated crowds and public places ordinarily, but she loved listening to the music and watching the dancing from twenty years of lavish parties held in that chamber. She followed their footsteps and admired their shoes and their clothes, feeling like some kind of Cinderella spying on high society. She learned all their favorite dance steps, pretending to be the belle of the ball.

She did not enjoy, however, watching what usually happened once the dinner bell rang. It wasn't that the fairies and vampires were particularly cruel or savage as they fed and seduced. Self-control seemed to be expected under Lord William's roof. What bothered her was how addled the humans were, as though they were drugged, which in a sense, of course, they were. It was all a little too close to rape for her liking. She was grateful once again to be immune to being enthralled. She'd rather live with some fear than live lobotomized, without any real feelings or thoughts of her own. She'd made that decision when she'd decided to face her gift head-on and get off the drugs and out of the hospital.

November also began her self-defense lessons with Willow and Pine. They taught her along with Ben and Zinnia. Obviously, the other youngsters were way ahead of her, but they were willing to be patient. It turned out that there was a shooting range in the bowels of the government half of the building. Her tutors taught her how to shoot a handgun and a rifle. They laughed the first time she staggered from the recoil, but she quickly improved. There was an outdoor range for archery practice. November knew nothing about weapons of any kind, and she certainly had not known how much strength was required to draw a crossbow. They ordered a lighter one especially for her and promised her that in time she would get stronger and using the bow would get easier. Her aim was quite good, which gave her something to be proud of.

Hand-to-hand combat was obviously a challenge, given how weak and slow she was compared to any supernatural creature. Pine encouraged her to focus on her strengths. These strengths turned out to be playing possum and ducking. She found that when she was in "the zone," she could use her gift to see where the next blow was coming from and move out of the way, which sometimes allowed her to get a blow in under her attacker's defenses. And she was good at pretending injury or weakness to deceive an opponent.

William gave her teachers permission to give her a few weapons to carry on her person in case of emergency, so she wouldn't have to rely on her killer rosary. So she now carried a small silver switchblade and what Willow called "werewolf mace," a spray bottle full of a suspension of colloidal silver. They decided not to give her a gun, reasoning that it was be more likely to be taken from her and used against her than to be useful to her in a fight. November agreed with that assessment and was secretly relieved not to have to carry a gun. The knife scared her enough.

November began spending a few days a week working with Savita. The investigator would bring files from various bombings, and they would go through them together, November using her gift to try to tease out more information or make new connections. Photos, bomb fragments, clothing samples, videos: all were examined and re-examined. She learned all the gory details of attacks in Arizona, Texas, New York, Washington, and Louisiana. Progress was slow.

November was surprised to find that the man she'd seen apparently giving orders to Dogwood was in fact one of the first victims of an attack, escaping with moderate wounds. Savita identified him as Luka, the Lord of Arizona. "He is vicious, cunning, greedy, and powerful. He is also our brother, turned by our mother, Marisha," she added, shocking her new colleague. "He would not be above staging an attack on himself in order to deflect blame, so he cannot be eliminated as a suspect."

"Why do you and Lord William despise him so much?" November asked cautiously, not knowing quite what she was stepping into.

"There are many reasons. He took sides against our father the king during the last succession election. When our father won the throne, Luka made a token effort to get back in his good graces, but William has never trusted him since." Savita then explained that vampire kings served for life, or until they resigned, but they were elected by the Assembly of Lords. The position was not inherited, though often the relatives of kings were powerful enough to win the throne themselves. Ilyn had succeeded his wife when she decided to retire.

She continued, "Luka can also be gratuitously cruel sometimes. The rest of us in the family, we are careful with our human prey. That's what we were taught as young vampires. We take what we need and try to leave them unharmed when we are done. Luka has never had any such compunction. He sees humans as livestock or servants, whose only purpose in life should be to do our bidding, and he seems to enjoy frightening them. Arizona is a good place to be a monster. The undocumented migrant workers go missing while crossing the desert, and no one looks for them. Politically, Luka

128

fights any laws that seek to protect humans or to protect our secrecy. He is a proponent of revelation. He is not content with helping to rule our little world. He wants more, always more. He thinks vampires and fairies should rule the entire world, rather than human beings. I have long suspected he has something to do with all of this, but we don't have enough proof to convince anyone. Many of the lords fear to cross him." November had thought her own family was strange, but apparently vampire royalty had their own share of dysfunction.

Every night, it seemed, Lord William found some time in his busy schedule to spend a few moments with November. He took to sitting with her in the kitchen while she ate her last meal of the day, usually at about three in the morning. He would drink some blood out of the fridge while she ate. Sometimes they discussed her work, sometimes books or music, occasionally the events of their lives.

Gradually, she became more comfortable around the vampire leader. He made her smile. She made a point of always addressing him as Lord William or Governor. He told her she didn't have to if it made her uncomfortable. She replied, "It's what everyone calls you. If I don't, people might think I'm conceited or disrespectful." *You already pay me an awful lot of attention,* she thought to herself. *I don't want people to resent me. It would be disruptive to the balance of the household. Besides, it is accurate. You're not my dad. You're not my boyfriend. You're more captor than boss. You hold my life in your hands.* William remarked that she was awfully perceptive for a human of her age. She told him that it would be a better compliment without the "for a human" part. *Don't get close to him*, she told herself. *You have Stockholm Syndrome. You can't trust him so much.*

When she seemed very tired, if she'd been working too hard and sleeping poorly, William would offer to bite her. She found herself looking forward to those days, partly because she craved dreamless sleep, a luxury she had never before experienced, but mostly because she was falling for him. She tried not to show it too much. It made her feel foolish. She'd never had a crush before.

Lord William seemed to sense it, of course. One early morning, when he kissed her goodnight, it was on the lips rather than her forehead, and she went to bed smiling and giddy. Another evening, he brushed a strand of hair behind her ear, his cool fingertips brushing against her skin. He still had a smith's calluses preserved from his human life so many centuries earlier. It was all she could do not to throw herself at him. One night, she grew lightheaded while he was feeding and spent several blissful minutes with her head on his shoulder while he stroked her hair.

She suddenly cared about whether or not she was pretty. She finally understood why every person who walked into her tent asked about love. It was the most fun, scary, exciting and nerve-wracking thing she'd ever experienced, and every day she looked forward to seeing him. She was relieved, however, that things were moving slowly. She certainly wasn't ready to jump into anyone's bed.

Ben also made a point of spending time with her. He brought her books. He'd watch movies with her and try to put his arm around her. He was all sweetness with her now, but sometimes there was a strange look in his eye that she couldn't quite identify. November tried to discourage him without being mean, at first just to protect him, but also because she realized she was developing confusing feelings for Lord William. Ben, however, refused to be discouraged.

She couldn't bring herself to be honest about her puppy love for Lord William. She was unsure of where it was going, and she didn't want to give Ben more reason to dislike his lord. She was afraid of hurting his feelings after all he'd been through. Confrontation had never been her strong suit. Besides, she simply had no idea how to handle romance. She'd never had a boyfriend. She'd never been pursued, really, aside from some clumsy, vulgar propositions from fellow carnies. When she finally forced herself to remind Ben that given their circumstances, they could not be together, he said that he had plenty of time and could wait until Lord William inevitably disappointed her. She began to avoid being alone with him, enlisting Zinnia to assist her.

Her friendship with Zinnia continued to grow stronger. While she had been forbidden to discuss the details of her work with anyone besides Lord William, Savita, and Birch, it was nice to have someone to talk to about how difficult it was, how upsetting some of the images were. Zinnia was the only person to whom she confided about her burgeoning crush on Lord William. It was such a pleasure to have a real friend for the first time. She liked hearing Zinnia's stories about her childhood and about college life. Em also enjoyed the stories about Lord William's life and sundry escapades, some of which had become legends in the supernatural community. Her new friend's eternally sunny disposition was a nice contrast to her own more serious temperament, and her presence never failed to make November smile.

November periodically returned to the hair she had found on her mother's corpse. Having no luck doing a direct reading, she resorted to sleeping with the hair under her pillow, hoping and dreading that visions of Agnes would invade her dreams. She was rewarded one dark night with a scene that was thankfully more revealing than violent. Agnes was sitting with Philemon on a leather couch. Both were drinking steaming blood out of large wine glasses. The seer was relieved that their victim did not appear in the vision. Drinking appeared to make them chatty.

"I just can't believe what an easy time he has persuading these idiots to blow themselves up," Agnes says, laughing.

"He chooses the weak, the lonely, the young ones at loose ends. He gives them an ideology to believe in and a purpose. They're grateful for it. This is how kings have made pawns since the dawn of time," Philemon opines languidly, swirling the blood in his glass.

"Do you think he'll really be king?" Agnes asks quietly, as if frightened to express doubt of their mystery employer.

"Ilyn's spirit has been broken for 200 years. He no longer wants the throne enough to fight to keep it. Billy's still a fighter at heart, his ridiculous habit of feeding on deer notwithstanding. He's the real problem. Take him out, and the throne will fall."

"Why doesn't the boss just have his live-in spy do the job?" Agnes asks. "All this waiting around is boring," she whines.

"As if that idiot would have a snowball's chance in hell of managing to kill an old soldier like William Knox on his own. And our master still needs information from inside at least until he gets hold of that human weirdo. Dogwood's failure has set us back. And we have no idea how much information he gave them before he died. Between the human and that Indian witch, he could have done a great deal of damage. The spy only reported his capture. He had no other information for us. They had a whole night to question him before he died. Our master must be very careful right now. Besides, I thought you wanted to do it yourself," he continues. "Or at least to be there. Avenge Dogwood, destroy the father who disowned you. All that sentimental garbage."

"Well, ideally, yes," she allows. "What I don't understand is why William doesn't just turn the girl, so at least she'd have a vampire's strength to defend herself the next time we come for her."

"He's probably afraid she'll turn out a reprobate like you," he responds. Agnes throws a pillow at her lover's head in retaliation. "His main problem is that he respects the law too much. He wrote

132

the statute about only turning humans who are at least 21 years old. He and that sister of his. The penalty may only be a fine, but it offends his overdeveloped sense of propriety to violate it. Appearances must be maintained. And it's bad for him politically, what with how protective he is of the bipedal livestock. He runs a tight ship with his vassals in California: no kids, no rape, no harems, no this, no that. He'll look like a hypocrite and lose face with his underlings. His pride will be his undoing."

"Serves him right, his sanctimony coming back to bite him. I love it. A real vampire wouldn't let the law stop him," Agnes spits with distain and decades of resentment.

"Agreed," Philemon says. "It is a shame that we had to postpone the next operation due to all this nonsense with the girl. . . "

November woke with a pounding heart and shaking hands. It was the middle of the morning. She'd only been asleep a few hours. She grabbed her new computer and recorded every word of the conversation. She encrypted the file as she'd been instructed to do with all her work, and sent it immediately to Birch, Lord William, and Savita, knowing the vampires wouldn't see it until dark.

Confirmation that there was indeed a spy on the property tied her stomach in knots. The sweep of the house after the gas station attack had turned up two bugs, one in the kitchen and one just outside Birch's office. She'd used that discovery to allow herself to pretend there was no traitor in the house, that an outsider had planted them while visiting the premises on business. That piece of self-deception was no longer possible. It made her skin crawl to know that she was living under the same roof with someone who worked with the vampires who had killed her mother and the fairies who had caused her such pain, the people who might well be behind the terrorist attacks that had killed so many. If things hadn't been tense enough in the house before, she feared the coming atmosphere of distrust would be stifling. She wondered, of course, who it could be. She dreaded finding out.

She sat on her bed, curled up with her knees to her chest, resting her head on top of them. As she'd anticipated, Birch showed up in her room a few minutes later, demanding to go over every detail in triplicate. He kept running his hands through his lime green curls. He seemed to have gotten enough accustomed to November to reveal some of the feelings behind his solemn exterior.

"We shall have to proceed very carefully. It could be almost anyone. If we spook whoever it is, he may flee. Which gets rid of the problem, in a sense. But, he might do something drastic, and we won't be able to question him for information." Birch looked at her with concern. "If everyone becomes aware that we know for certain that there is a spy, your safety will be compromised."

"Yes. I suspected as much." November shivered. She had enjoyed feeling safe here inside the citadel. "As for who it is, I suppose we can cross you, your wife, and Pine off the list, right?"

Birch smiled grimly, saying, "Not really. I, of course, know that I am innocent, and that my wife is, and my son, but killing one's child in exchange for power has been known to happen. And eliminating your own spy when you fear they might be compromised has also been known to happen."

November shook her head. Obviously, she was insufficiently ruthless to understand the game being played. The fact that she was a piece on the board was more than unnerving. She kept thinking, finally venturing to say, "Philemon called the mole an idiot who had no chance of taking out a man like Lord William."

Birch nodded. "That seems to argue for one of our younger people: Zinnia, Ben, Daniel, Felix, Amy, Josue, Willow, Mary,

134

Greg. And my Pine. Though I can't imagine Greg could hide such a betrayal from his maker. He has no secrets from Savita." November winced to hear Zinnia's name. Noticing her discomfort, Birch said sympathetically, "I know Zinnia is your friend, and I would be very surprised to find out she is a traitor, but we must examine all possibilities."

November nodded. "It would be pretty easy for a fairy to kill a vampire while they are resting, wouldn't it? So if the spy is a fairy, why would Philemon say the mole would have no chance against the Governor?" she asked, hoping to eliminate Zinnia.

"All the entrances to the crypt are monitored. There are eyes on the feeds at all times. A fairy trying to enter would be caught. And even if they got past the first door, the resting chambers are locked from the inside," Birch reminded her.

They sat in silence, thinking together. "Philemon said they didn't know what Dogwood had revealed before his death. You and Daniel were present for the interrogation, right, along with Lord William and Savita? So if any of you were the spy, you would have that information to pass along."

Birch nodded. "That is reasonable." He stood up. "You and I will meet with William at dusk. Discuss this with no one." He locked his eyes on hers. "No one."

"Of course," she replied, swallowing the lump in her throat.

"Rest. And keep thinking, clever human," Birch unfolded to his impressive height and glided out the door, leaving November to toss and turn the day away.

When night fell, Birch briefed William, and the three of them went for a walk on the grounds to discuss what November had seen. They feared more bugs inside the residence. William decided to play things cool. As November pointed out, if the spy got spooked and ran, he'd likely attempt to kill or kidnap November at the same time. William decided to have Rose use the cleaning staff to steal personal objects from each the suspects. They could take things that wouldn't be missed: pillowcases and things of that nature. November would then try to see what she could sense from them, to see if the spy might be found in that way. Savita would be informed but would probably be of limited help. People knew of her telepathy and avoided touching her. Finding an excuse for her to examine peoples' thoughts without tipping off the mole was impossible.

The guards would keep an eye on everyone, recording all comings and goings from the property. Pine would be assigned to stay within earshot of November at all times. They decided that he was the least likely mole of the fairies on staff, and he owed November a life debt. He was to sit by her door while she slept. November found this simultaneously creepy and reassuring.

Birch returned to the house once the plans were made, leaving November and Lord William walking in the garden alone. It would have been almost romantic had they not been so preoccupied. They sat down on a bench, and November screwed up enough courage to lean her head against his broad, blacksmith's shoulder.

"Are you okay?" he asked. "You seem to be handling this remarkably calmly."

"I'm pretty freaked out, to be honest. I couldn't sleep at all after the vision. How am I supposed to act normally around everyone when I know there's a traitor but I don't know who it is?" November asked.

"It's to your advantage that the people in this house don't really know how a human like you normally acts. The only ones who may notice something is off are Zinnia and Ben. Even Ben may not.

136

He's not the most perceptive person," he replied, his tone betraying a mental eye roll.

"True. And my conversations with Ben are awkward as it is," she admitted without thinking about what she was saying. She winced as she realized her mistake and hoped she wasn't getting Ben into hot water.

"He's still flirting with you in spite of your discouragement?" he asked casually.

"Yes," she allowed. "You knew?"

"Of course. Everyone with eyes and ears knows. Plus, Zinnia told me that she's been helping you avoid him when I asked her about what I'd heard."

November sighed. "Of course she did. She's incapable of lying. Her ears turn blue whenever she tries." She shook her head. "I really don't see how she can be the spy, but better safe than sorry, I guess," November said with resignation. It would be difficult to get through this without Zinnia's listening ear and shoulder to cry on.

"I agree, but we must take care. If she is innocent, knowing too much will endanger her as well, and as she cannot keep a secret, she might reveal something inadvertently to the wrong person."

"Do you think it's Ben?" she asked quietly, knowing so well the antipathy between them.

"I hope it is him. It would spare me from having to kill a friend," he said with a nonchalant iciness that provoked a trickle of fear down her spine. "But honestly, I doubt it. Would you trust him with something that important? I barely trust him to pick up my dry cleaning." November hoped he was right. Some part of her prayed that it would be one she barely knew, like Amy or Josue.

William paused before continuing, "I must head back to my office, lovely girl. I don't suppose I could get a kiss goodnight?" he asked teasingly. November laughed out loud and obliged him. His hands brushed against her back and her hair for one delicious moment. "I'm glad you can still laugh. I'll see you later," he promised, wiggling his eyebrows goofily as he walked off. Somehow, that little kiss made her feel better when she had thought nothing could.

Chapter 7

November developed a fondness for the hot tub in the well-manicured back garden. It was a touch too chilly this late in the fall to swim in the pool, well-heated though it was. But the steam rising from the spa was always enticing to a girl who hated to be cold and had spent far too many hours of her life shivering for lack of money for heat. She liked to stroll out there in the late afternoon in her fuzzy slippers, wrapped up in a thick robe over the most modest swimsuit she could find. Pine would trail behind her, of course, ever vigilant. She'd soak as long as she could stand it, watching the sky or the birds, turning things over in her mind. Generally, she emerged bright pink and pruney before the sun set, so she could be dressed before the vampires rose.

This particular afternoon, however, time got away from her. The sun set, and fog began to roll in off the bay. The novel she'd brought out had been so engaging, and suddenly she looked up to see William emerging from the mist, wearing a swimsuit.

She gulped and nearly dropped the paperback into the water. Her surprise must have registered on her face, for he grinned and asked, "What? A man can't use his own hot tub of an evening?"

"No. I mean, yes. I mean, um, hi?" she stammered, grateful for the jets and bubbles that partially hid her from his eyes. She tried to look at him without looking. He was all muscle, the rest of him as pale and freckled as his face. The hair on his chest was the same bright red as the hair on his head and could not hide a couple of jagged scars. November wondered if he had acquired them before or after his first death. *Can a vampire scar?*

William slid into the water next to her, which only added to her nervousness. She looked up to find Pine, only to see that he had disappeared. William caught her at it, saying, "I figured he could use a short break."

"Right . . ." She couldn't figure out where to rest her gaze. She took a deep breath and tried to relax. *You see him every day. What is the matter with you?*

"I got your email. Nice work," he said. He seemed amused at her skittishness.

"Thanks." *What is happening right now? Did we just jump from a little kissing to making out in a hot tub? Is that what we're doing?*

He reached over and tucked a tendril of wet hair behind her ear. "Good book?"

"What? Oh, right. The book. Um, yeah, it's a page turner," she managed as he reached his hand over to her chin and gently turned her face toward his own. His hand felt so cold against her flushed skin, his lips so deliciously cool as he pressed them against hers. To her delight, she stayed in the moment rather than falling into a vision. She breathed a silent prayer of thanks that her gift worked so differently with vampires than it did with humans. She had to choose to look, and right now, she had zero interest in William's secrets.

He cradled the back of her head with one hand as he ran his thumb over her cheekbone, along her jaw, and down her throat. He whispered, "You are especially lovely tonight." His cold breath against her ear gave her goose bumps even in the steaming water.

"Thank you," she whispered back, not knowing what else to say, barely breathing as she waited to see what he would do next, hoping the steam hid them from prying eyes. His arm slid behind her back and drew her close to him.

"Of course, I might be biased by the fact that you're wearing a lot fewer clothes than usual," he continued as he ran his fangs down the side of her neck, causing her breath to catch in her throat. "Though I do wish I could see you better," he added, reaching over to turn off the jets. She tried to stifle a whimper as he kissed her collarbone. She could practically hear him smile at the effect he was having on her, which she might have found annoying had she not been so distracted.

He drew away for a moment to have a good look at her: her slender, young body flush with warmth and excitement, her blue swimsuit the same shade as her eyes, her chest swelling with each breath.

He returned his mouth to hers, and she found the courage to return his kiss in earnest, one hand pressed against his chest and the other running through his hair, feeling the soft red curls between her fingers as she came up for air. His hand crept halfway up her bare thigh, somehow stopping just shy of where she might have drawn away in fear. He ran a finger down the strap of her bikini top, moving slowly enough that she could have stopped him if she had wanted to. He traced the edges of the fabric down to the clasp on her sternum. She held her breath.

"Lord William?" came a voice out of the mist.

November jumped back as if burned, flying across the spa with a splash as she grabbed frantically at her top to make sure it was still fastened. Frustration flashed across William's face before he answered, "Over here, Birch," without bothering to hide his irritation.

Birch appeared and assessed the situation with one glance. November looked away in a vain effort at nonchalance. Birch kept a straight face as he reported vaguely, "Sorry, sir, but there is something that requires your urgent attention."

"Isn't there always? I'll be right in," he said, waving his lieutenant away. Birch nodded and disappeared back into the fog.

William turned back to November and smiled. With vampire speed, he was once again back at her side, holding her close with one hand as the other cupped her breast. She could barely breathe. "The burdens of leadership are sometimes very heavy," he murmured against her neck. "Do you feel what you are doing to me?" he asked, pressing his hardness against her, making her gasp.

And then he disappeared, leaping from the water and running toward the house faster than her human eyes could follow, leaving her alone, her heart pounding in her chest. She didn't know whether she ought to thank Birch or throw things at him. She could still feel William's cold hands on her fevered skin. She looked up at the sky, pressing one hand to her bare stomach, trying to slow her breathing, trying to ignore the throbbing between her legs. *What have I gotten myself into?* Yet she couldn't help smiling. *What have I gotten myself into, indeed?*

Finally, she dragged herself out of the water. After a cool shower during which she finished for herself what William had started, she felt almost ready to concentrate on her work for the night, hoping no one could read on her face what she'd been up to, hoping Savita couldn't see in her thoughts why she was so distracted as they studied another case file.

Life was in a precarious sort of limbo when Halloween arrived a few days later. There had been no further revelations, and November had managed to regain her calm. The vampires were planning to paint the town on the one night of the year they could let their fangs show, and the fairies were excited to go with them and

142

dance the night away with their protection. November, however, was still confined to the house. Lord William wanted there to be no opportunity for further kidnapping attempts. She was beginning to get a bit of cabin fever. She was used to living life on the road, setting up in a different town every week. The house and grounds were lovely and had come to feel like home, but she'd covered every inch of it dozens of times in the previous few weeks.

Still, confinement was preferable to mortal peril, and she was resigned to a quiet evening at home while her friends went out gallivanting. Zinnia had offered to stay in with her, but it was obvious that the fairy was craving a night of clubbing, and November told her to go ahead and have a good time. She planned to watch a movie and eat ice cream. These were not the most exciting plans for a girl who would turn eighteen at midnight, but it was certainly much better than many of her birthdays. She wondered who would get stuck babysitting her, hoping that Lord William would take the task on himself. She was equal parts excited and frightened of the prospect of being alone in the house with him.

Their little romance was progressing in stolen chunks of time, here and there, when they could find a moment alone. One particular morning had found them entwined in a corner of the garden, hands sneaking under clothes, fangs scraping across the skin of her neck, her shoulder, the inside of her wrist, until the sun had chased William away.

She was finishing up her lunch after dusk when Lord William came into the kitchen. She smiled at him, secretly hoping he might remember her birthday, but he was all business. "November," he said somberly, "there's something in the library I need you to take a look at right away." November hid a grimace and quickly got up to follow him. As serious as his face was, she feared that her task would not be a pleasant one.

He opened the door to the library, holding it for her and gesturing for her to enter. As soon as she passed through, the decked-out housemates who had made such a show of leaving fifteen minutes earlier jumped out from behind the furniture, yelling, "Surprise!" November burst out laughing, delighted and indeed surprised.

"Not much of a psychic, apparently," Josue teased as they all crowded around to wish her a happy birthday.

"You didn't have to do all this," November protested, amused at all the pink and purple balloons festooning the normally hyper-masculine library. "Thank you."

"It was mostly Zinnia, of course," Lord William admitted. The fairy in question walked over to give her recently acquired best friend a birthday hug.

"We had to do something! We couldn't just abandon you to boredom for your birthday," she said gleefully.

"I don't want you all to miss your big night out," November protested.

"Fear not; the night is young," Ben replied. "We'll go out after presents and cake, though it will be no fun without you." Lord William rolled his eyes behind the boy's back. November struggled not to laugh at that incongruously modern gesture.

Ben had bought her a Kindle Fire and gotten most everyone to buy her books for it, which November found quite sweet and thoughtful, especially given how awkward things were between them sometimes. Zinnia bucked the trend and gave her a beautiful necklace of pastel gemstones. It seemed to glow from within. "I made it," her friend told her proudly, and November was suitably impressed with her magical companion. "Fairies like to make shiny stuff that glows," Zinnia explained.

Finally, she came to Lord William's gift. She knew that it would be too much as soon as she saw the box. She opened it with trepidation to find a pair of diamond earrings that must have cost a fortune. It was far too extravagant, and she said so. "Nonsense. You'll need something to wear for the Christmas parties with the king," he countered, kissing her on the forehead. "We don't want you to be embarrassed in the company of the court. It would reflect badly on me," he said with a wink. Ben glowered behind William's back as his gift was upstaged.

After November blew out her candles and ate the solitary gourmet cupcake Rose had picked up for her, most everyone departed, leaving her alone in the house with Lord William. "Do you still want to watch that movie?" he asked once the exodus was complete.

"Sure," she said, wondering just how much of the movie would actually get watched. "Let me put these gifts away in my room, and I'll meet you in the theater."

She skipped up the stairs. This was shaping up to be the best birthday on record. She was stashing her gifts when an envelope on her bed caught her eye. She opened it, thinking it was a birthday card. Inside was a piece of paper and an antique-looking medallion, perhaps of a saint. On the paper was written one sentence that made her heart sink: "Ask him about his wife." She paused as dread poured like ice water into her open heart. She finally took the medallion in her hand and closed her fingers over it. Her stomach turned over as she was sucked into vision.

A beautiful young woman with curly black hair dances with William on the deck of a ship, by the light of another ship aflame on the sea. Her brown eyes flash. Her bronze skin glows. They kiss, and the kiss turns to more. They stand together in front of a priest, a lacy veil failing to conceal her gleaming fangs. The years fly by, the centuries, as they are bound together by a palpable love.

The woman is enjoying the company of friends, laughing and smiling. An explosion tears through the room, shredding everyone in its path. Blood and light pour out of the wounded. The dying vampires turn to piles of ash illuminated by the flashes of light from the fairy dead. The woman lays half crushed in a pool of blood, screaming in pain before she loses consciousness. She does not turn to ash.

November rose to the surface and returned to the present. She dropped the medallion on her coverlet, looking down on her hand to see the red impression it had left as she had tightened her hand around it. Dizzy, she sank to the floor and put her head between her knees, her tears dripping silently onto the carpet.

She barely heard when William called up the stairs, "Are you alright?" When she didn't respond, he ran with vampire speed up to her room. "What's wrong?" he asked, kneeling beside her. She flinched when he reached out to touch her forearm.

November reached over her head to grab the letter and the medallion, handing them both to him. "Where did you get this charm? This should be in my bedchamber," he demanded, anger in his voice.

"Someone left it for me, with that note," she said. Her voice was even, almost affectless, as it often became when she was deeply upset. Something inside her just shut down at such moments. She stared straight ahead, not looking at him.

William read the note. He closed his eyes for a moment. November could practically see the wheels turning. "My wife died in an attack, in Montana. She was there to visit some friends."

"No, she didn't. I just saw it. She passed out, but she didn't turn to ash. If she had, you would have mentioned her to me. And I would be looking at evidence of an attack in Montana when I work with Savita. But I wasn't even told that there *was* an attack in Montana. Which indicates to me that you're hiding something about it. Your wife is alive. Alive but wounded. Isn't she?" She finally looked William in the eye, and he could see that there was no way out but the truth.

"Yes," he said simply.

"How could you think I wouldn't find that out eventually? The entire reason I'm here is that I'm a psychic!" She tried to grab hold of her rage as she began to feel again. Rage was better than pain or humiliation.

"We've told everyone that my wife died, to try to protect her from a repeat attack. We think that she was the primary target. Only Savita, Birch, and my father know that she's being taken care of in secret, under a different name. It will take the better part of a year for her limbs to grow back." Em was beyond relieved to find out that Zinnia had not known. That was one betrayal that she could never have borne. "Savita warned me not to do this to you. So did Birch. Sometimes I am too arrogant and stubborn to listen when I should." November was mortified and furious at the thought of Savita and Birch being aware of this mess but glad to know that they had not approved of it. "Married vampires often take human lovers. It is normal among us," he argued weakly. "Most humans do not object."

"Most humans get mind-raped into not objecting to a damn thing you people do! And if you really thought I wouldn't mind, you wouldn't have hidden her from me. You were just hoping that by the time I found out I would be too in love with you to care. Isn't that right?" November was merciless with herself. Since her heart was breaking, it seemed better to just smash it and get all of the pain over with. William's silence answered for him. "Why? What did I do to make you want to hurt me? I've done everything you've asked of me."

"My intent was not to cause you pain," he protested.

"Really? You took advantage of a lonely child who has had so little love in her life that she's starving for it. Were you actually going to try to sleep with me tonight?" He had the good sense to look slightly ashamed. "Are you fucking kidding me? I'm an eighteen-year-old virgin who never even kissed a guy before you! Am I not screwed up enough already? Did you think I was going to react well to finding out I had sex for the first time with someone who not only doesn't love me but also is *married* and only wants to use me as a weapon? Mental stability is not really my strong suit, historically. What the hell is wrong with you?"

She couldn't sit still. She couldn't look at him. She couldn't escape, so she paced by the window like a caged animal. "You are a real piece of work, you know that? Though I don't know why that should surprise me, given the fact that you *kidnapped* me. And *bought* me. From my *mother*. What is *wrong* with me? Maybe I *do* belong in a hospital."

William defended himself earnestly, as though he actually wished to persuade her of his good intentions. She watched him with increasing incredulity as he argued, "I needed to be sure of your complete loyalty. Your love would ensure that you would stay on our side, whatever happens. I'm trying to save a civilization here. I had to find out for certain who is behind all this. I have to defeat him. For my wife. For my people. Some things are too important to leave to chance. Some things are more important than one person. You must understand, I could not entrust so much to a human without doing everything I could to ensure her allegiance."

"You've done a bang-up job of that, now, haven't you? Do you know what you could have tried instead? You could have said, 'November, use your gift to help me save innocent people from a terrorist maniac who wants to enslave the human race. Your gift will finally do some good instead of only driving you crazy and ruining everything, and you'll get to live in a house fit for human habitation and eat on the regular and pretend you have friends for the first time in your wretched life.' Maybe try *that* next time."

She was bright with righteous anger, filled with fire as she stood up for herself, full bore, with no restraint or shame or fear, perhaps for the first time in her life. As she spoke, she stepped slowly toward the vampire, who actually retreated towards the door in the face of her onslaught.

"You're a lovely girl, November. I'm . . . very fond of you," he replied inadequately. "I am sorry for your pain."

"You say that a lot. You'll forgive me if I don't believe you. You didn't love me at all. You didn't even *want me*. You just wanted my gift. How could I not have realized that? I am so stupid. So young and stupid." She had wanted so badly to be cherished for herself that she had seen love when it wasn't there. She had trusted when she should have been skeptical, which wasn't at all like her. She never trusted humans that much. In a new world, with new people, with new fears, she had tossed aside her normal caution. She did not intend to repeat that mistake.

Making one last effort to placate her, William reached out a hand towards her shoulder.

"Get out!" she commanded in a voice that could have shattered glass. "Get out," she repeated in a dangerous whisper. "And don't you *ever* touch me again." William looked like he wanted to continue with his explanations, but one look at November's face convinced him otherwise. He stepped backwards through the door, which November promptly slammed in his face.

For a long time, she just stared at the carpet. Her emotions overwhelmed her, leaving her unable to cry, unable to think. Finally, her hurt and anger settled into a stone in the pit of her stomach, and she was able to consider her situation with some lucidity.

She slid down to the floor and sat with her back against the door. She briefly considered running away. It was her first impulse, to flee from him and this strange new life of hers, this weird imprisonment. Logic prevailed, however. Even if she could get off the grounds, endangering her life to avoid seeing William, to avoid embarrassment, would be pretty stupid. Besides, she knew her fate was intertwined with these people, so what was the point in running from the unavoidable? She told herself that the humiliation and grief would fade in time. It was hard to face the fact that she would have to return to her difficult work with Savita, to go on about her business as if nothing had changed. *How do I face Savita and Birch? How do I face anyone?*

This little romance had been a source of happiness that helped her get through the difficulty of using her gift to explore these attacks. It had let her pretend that she wasn't trapped. Now that crutch was gone. She would have to do what she'd done all her life: find her own happiness in the midst of a difficult situation. Never did she seriously consider refusing to do the work. All the suffering

150

of the victims, all the evil she'd seen – if she could help stop that violence, how wrong would it be to refuse to do so in order to spite a man who'd hurt her or to escape her own discomfort? *Children will die if I stop, if I leave. Innocents will suffer. I can still prevent that.*

She was still sitting motionless on the floor when she heard a knock on her door. "It's Zinnia. Lord William told me what happened."

"Come in," November replied a bit reluctantly. She wasn't sure she wanted company until she saw her friend's face full of sympathy; she then realized that a girlfriend was exactly what she needed.

Zinnia sunk down to sit on the floor next to her. She had brought a tissue box. November gave her a weak smile. "Well prepared, I see. He told you all of it?"

"Yes. He said you needed someone to talk to, so he told me about his wife. I can't believe that Lady Esther is still alive." Zinnia shook her head. "I have to admit I'm happy about that; she was always very kind to me. I think I saw more of her than my own mother as a kid. Of course, I'm totally livid at Lord William for deceiving you. I really thought he liked you. He seemed so much happier, and so did you. I thought you were helping him get over the loss of her."

"You warned me that he could be ruthless. I should have taken that to heart. Apparently the ends justify the means as far as he's concerned. Thank goodness I didn't actually sleep with him. This would be a hundred times harder. Score one for the nuns and sexual conservatism." November started crying again. "I feel so miserable," she said, burying her face in her hands.

"I know. That's how I felt when things went south with my first boyfriend. He was my first love, and I think I jumped into bed too quickly. You know how I am. I fall in love so easily, like how we became friends in about thirty seconds." Zinnia smiled. "At least I learned from that mistake to protect my heart a little bit more. He cheated on me, so I broke it off. But I was still miserable for a while. I still missed him, missed what we had. I know it doesn't seem like it now, but you will feel better. After a while, it won't hurt anymore. And almost everyone goes through this. Most people don't end up together forever with the first person they were ever involved with," Zinnia said reassuringly, the voice of experience at the ripe old age of nineteen.

"I know. I keep telling myself that. But most people's first kiss isn't with some vampire lord who's about 900 years old and who kidnapped her and with whom she has to continue living because even scarier vampires are trying to kidnap and/or murder her."

"Wow. It does sound kind of bad when you put it like that," Zinnia replied in a deadpan tone that forced November to laugh. "At least Ben will be happy," she added.

"Oh, jeez. I hadn't even thought about that. He isn't going to give me a moment's peace." November threw up her hands in renewed frustration.

"I'll tell him to lay off. I don't know if it'll work, but I'll try," Zinnia reassured her. "*Do* you have any interest in him, with Lord William out of the picture?"

November thought about it for a moment. "I don't know, and not just because the breakup is so raw. It would be seriously awkward. I don't want to make more trouble for him. Plus, I'm not exactly confident about my judgment in men right now."

"You shouldn't blame yourself. You fell for a man with almost a millennium of experience seducing women. You didn't really have a prayer," Zinnia replied.

152

"Thanks. I think. Can we watch a movie or something? I need to not think about this for a while."

"Of course, whatever you need."

"Oh, no, I destroyed your night out on the town!" November suddenly remembered her friend's own plans.

"No, Lord William ruined my night. You are innocent. I had time to dance for awhile, so it's not a problem. All was not lost," Zinnia said with a smile, reaching out a hand to help her friend up off the floor.

As they walked down to the theater, November said, "I've had some terrible birthdays, but this one ranks pretty high on the list. And I am totally not giving back those earrings."

***

November's sleep that night and following day was disrupted by the frequent sight of Esther in her sickbed, her mangled body looking very small under the white sheets. Esther didn't look too bad awake, maybe a little depressed, but she seemed to writhe in her sleep. In another dream, November saw a human planting the note and the jewelry. She looked like one of the cleaning crew.

When November woke, she felt more sad than angry, sad for Esther and William and everyone who had been hurt in these attacks, and sad for herself as well. She supposed that if Esther had been her wife, she might have done some crazy things in the pursuit of justice herself. She was still furious deep down, but she supposed that she might be able to forgive William in time. She'd forgiven betrayals just as bad in the past, after all. She had never been one to hold grudges, but she did not forget to be wary of those who had wronged her. She just hoped she would be strong enough to maintain her dignity when she had to face everyone. The last thing she wanted was to be all weepy and mooning over William, or to have everyone looking at her with pity. She had experience acting cold and removed in order to function in spite of her pain. She would simply have to protect herself with that well-worn armor when she was forced to face her former paramour.

After a very long shower with which she tried to wash everything away, she dressed with care. She was not about to look as wretched as she felt. She hid the diamond earrings where she wouldn't have to see them and grabbed her satchel of work out of the safe before heading down to the kitchen to get breakfast before the sun went down. Pine was hanging out in an armchair strategically placed at her end of the hallway. "Anyone try to kill me while I was sleeping?" she asked with a weak smile.

"Well, there was the one guy, but I took care of it," he said with a wink, following a step behind her as she headed downstairs. It was still a little strange to have a bodyguard, even after weeks of having him as a shadow. She wondered how much he knew about the previous night. He was always circumspect, so she might never know.

"Is Birch available?" she asked as she got her breakfast together. "It's kind of important."

"I'll call his office," Pine answered, reaching into his pocket.

About ten minutes later, Birch appeared in the kitchen dressed in an impeccably tailored suit and sporting a black wig that caused November to do a double take. *How did he cover the eyebrows? Mascara?*

"I like your green hair better," she said with an amused smile.

"I do, too, young one. However, I have several meetings with humans today, and they seem not to take me seriously enough with

154

my natural hair," the fairy responded. "Pine, please give us the room." Pine obeyed without a word.

"Lord William informed me of last night's . . . unfortunate incident. I am sorry for my role in your deception," Birch said by way of apology.

"It's alright. It's not like you had any choice, and he told me you had advised against it," November said. "I don't really have any anger to spare for you anyway," she added sardonically. "Anyway, I assume Lord William has already thought of this, but I wanted to make sure that Lady Esther had been moved. Apparently knowledge of her survival is more widespread than he thought, and if whoever planted the medallion is working for the bombers, she could be in danger."

Birch raised an eyebrow. "Yes, I've already made those arrangements." He paused. "I must say, it speaks well of you that you are concerned for her safely in spite of your justifiable anger toward her husband."

"It isn't *her* fault," she replied. "I keep seeing her in her bed. Is there something that can be done for her pain?" she asked.

"She is in pain?" he asked with concern.

"I'm not sure, but I think so. I doubt she's the type to complain for herself, you know? And she looks . . . forlorn when she's awake."

"I'll look into it," he said. "So do you think the spy planted her medallion?"

"I think whoever had it done was counting on me being angry and hurt enough to change sides, maybe to run away or to refuse to help with the investigation, or perhaps just to make me more cooperative if they succeed in stealing me away."

"Plausible. Or could it have been someone with a more personal motive to disrupt your . . . romance?"

November shrugged. "You mean Ben doing it to try to break us up? Maybe. It seems like a big risk to take for a flirtation. He would have had to break into Lord William's quarters to take it. And the actual planting of the note and the jewelry was done by one of the cleaning crew, enthralled of course. She looked seriously out of it. Again, that seems like a lot of trouble to go to over a little jealousy. Honestly, I don't think Ben even likes me that much. I think to him it's just a way to pass the time and get on Lord William's nerves."

"Perhaps it is a little extreme to do this over a crush, but stranger things have been known to happen. Young vampires can be very erratic. That's why they are not permitted to live alone. And this certainly succeeded in getting under Lord William's skin. Do you know which member of the crew it was?"

"The one with blond hair and a crooked nose. I think her name is Carly?" she answered uncertainly.

"I'll have someone look for her. If she's disappeared or been killed, that would be an interesting development," he said casually. November winced at his nonchalance, hoping against hope that an innocent woman hadn't died over her. "In case you're wondering, we're going over the surveillance cameras, but I don't expect to find much if it was in fact the mole. I'll let you know if we make any progress. Please keep me updated about anything you discover in your own . . . explorations."

"Of course," she said.

"Until next time," he said, striding purposefully out of the kitchen.

November finished her breakfast just in time for Savita's arrival. November endured another apology full of sympathetic eyes. "Now I understand why you looked so concerned every time you saw us together. I should have paid more attention to that. I guess I just didn't want to see it," she told the vampire.

"Love is intoxicating," Savita replied. "Especially first love."

"Yeah, it was," November agreed. "I think I might have been more in love with love than I was with him."

"It does happen that way sometimes," the vampire replied. "Now that the secret about Lady Esther has been revealed, I've brought you the evidence from the Montana attack so that you may examine it. This one is quite upsetting, I must warn you. In addition to my sister-in-law's grievous injuries, two young fairy children were killed," Savita said quietly. "Fairy children have an empathic bond to their parents," she continued. "The parents literally felt their children die from their workplace far away from the blast." November shuddered in sympathy. "It is so difficult for fairies to have children. Their fertility has been harmed by something, perhaps human pollution, perhaps something else. Their parents had tried for two hundred years before they had the twins." Savita's eyes filled with bloody tears, which she wiped away with a handkerchief.

November shook her head. "How awful," she said. "What is wrong with these people?" she asked, not for the first time. "What can be worth all this suffering?"

"I don't know," Savita replied. "Evidently you and I are not sufficiently ruthless to understand. Dogwood did not seem to be privy to the ultimate goals, unfortunately. He was just being paid to follow orders, and he was promised carte blanche on his recreational slaughter for assisting in the bombings."

November braced herself and got to work. She took notes on every detail she observed. She grew numb, seeing the explosion over and over. It looked like a group of vampires and fairies had been having a party when one of the servers had detonated. He was a fairy with long orange hair and a far-off look in his eye. He whispered something to himself just before all hell broke loose. November watched it over and over trying to make it out. Just when she was about to give up from exhaustion, she made out his strange little prayer and whispered, "Revelation. Revolution. Rule."

Savita looked at her strangely as Em came out of her trance. "What did you just say?" she asked with unusual intensity.

"The bomber in Montana. Just before he detonated, he whispered something, like a mantra. I've been trying to make it out for an hour. It was three words: 'Revelation. Revolution. Rule.' Does that mean anything to you?"

Savita paused before answering sadly, "When my brother Luka ran for the throne against our father, that was his campaign slogan. He lost in a disturbingly close race. It appears that either he has decided to dust it off in order to motivate his cannon fodder, or someone finds his ethos very inspiring and is using it. I find the former more plausible. I doubt he would take kindly to being plagiarized."

"Philemon and Agnes were talking about their boss brainwashing young people. What would they find inspiring about that slogan?" November asked, rubbing her temples. She had a wicked headache from her hours of labor. Savita handed her a cold can of cola. "Thanks," November said, smiling. The telepath had learned her young assistant's habits pretty well over the previous weeks. November usually wanted sugar after working. Back at the carnival, Neil had always kept her well supplied.

"There are a number of reasons," Savita began to explain. "There are many supernatural creatures who view us as superior to humans and resent the measures we have to take to preserve our anonymity. They resent having to enthrall people. They resent having to always feed without killing in order to avoid having bodies to hide. They resent having to follow laws made by humans in order to avoid attracting attention.

"Additionally, there are fairies who rather despise human beings, or at least human governments. They blame humans for their declining fertility and the diminishment of their race. There are those who think we were much better off when humans lived a more primitive life. There are those who would have us take over, rule the world to serve our own interests, manage the human population like livestock. There is also the fact that many of our young ones see little opportunity for advancement in our old-fashioned form of governance. If you are not born to a powerful family, it takes a very long time to acquire wealth, power, or respect. This is a legitimate complaint. Luka is extremely charismatic. He's probably been working on this for decades. I must speak to my brother and our father. And you should take a break. Excuse me." Savita packed up the evidence and sped out the door.

November headed up to the kitchen for lunch, listening to some music on her phone. She sighed, realizing for the first time that almost every pop song known to man is about sleeping with or breaking up with someone. After lunch, she settled down in the library with a book, rocking out to Lily Allen. Em found the singer's attitude toward her exes rather empowering and hilarious. Adèle cheered her up a bit as well. Her rest was interrupted when a vision overcame her with a sudden violence.

Agnes rigs an explosive vest with an air of experience, packing the silver shrapnel while wearing thick, black gloves. Philemon sits across from her, talking on a cell phone. "Yes, the martyr is ready. He's been working in the household over a year. They haven't bothered to search him in months. They invited him to their ridiculous Thanksgiving party. Why Milton feels the need to celebrate a human holiday is beyond my comprehension." He pauses, listening. "Yes, Agnes is finishing the vest. We'll have it to him in plenty of time. Yes, sir. Of course." He hangs up, turning to his compatriot. "The party's on. No delay."

November came around curled up on the couch, clutching a pillow hard enough to leave handprints. She leapt up and ran out of the library, frantically looking for Savita or William. She ran into Ben and Zinnia first.

"Hey, where's the fire, birthday girl?" Ben asked with a grin.

"I need to talk to Lord William," November said. "I need someone to find him for me."

"Would have thought you'd be avoiding him," he replied. "I heard there's trouble in paradise."

"Shut up, Ben," Zinnia snapped. "I told you to lay off."

"Yes, it's over between me and him. That's not why I need to see him," the seer said with annoyance.

"What is it? What did you see?" Ben asked with evident curiosity.

"You know I can't tell you that. Now where is he?" she practically yelled in exasperation.

"Is there a problem?" asked Pine, appearing out of nowhere. He was quite good at that.

"I need to talk to Lord William," November explained.

160

"He's in a meeting. He gave orders not to disturb him," Pine answered.

"I know what he's meeting about. He'll want to know this, trust me," she said.

Pine studied her face. "Come with me," he said, leading her toward the official wing of the house. "Not you," he commanded when Ben and Zinnia moved to follow. He shepherded her through several locked doors and into what could have almost passed for a normal office building were it not for the armored window shutters and overabundance of security cameras. Pine ushered her into a conference room then knocked on the door of the office across the hall. When the door opened, she could practically feel Lord William's anger; it was like heat rolling out of an oven. Pine quickly explained the reason for the interruption. He then returned and led her into his master's inner sanctum. Pine, ever discreet, did not remain to hear her secret.

The office was large and beautifully appointed, of course. Lord William, Savita, and Birch were huddled around a circular conference table that sat opposite the Lord of California's desk. William had a look on his face that said, "This had better be important," as he covered up the notes they had been making. November found this more than a little irritating, as the last place she wanted to be tonight was in the same room as William Knox. She would hardly fabricate a reason to wallow in humiliation.

Wanting to get out of there as quickly as possible, she cut to the chase. "I just had a vision of a conversation regarding a planned attack on someone named Milton that will take place at a Thanksgiving celebration."

William then pulled out a chair for her. "Tell us every detail," he directed, and she obliged him.

After a very thorough debriefing, November fled to her bedroom, Pine at her side, glad to be dismissed from their brainstorming session. She had no interest at the moment in knowing anything about the plans they were making in order to win this apparent internecine war. She was exhausted from her visions and from the strain of having to sit so close to William talking business when all she wanted to do was punch him in the face or jump into his arms, or perhaps both. She collapsed on her bed with a heaving sigh, running her fingers through her hair with aggravation.

Right on cue, Zinnia appeared at her door. "First human ever to set foot in Lord William's office, eh?" she asked as she flopped down on the floor beside November's bed.

"Yeah. I feel really special," November replied sarcastically.

"How was it? Being around him?" Zinnia asked, gazing up at November with her electric blue eyes wide with concern, per usual.

"Awful. I just tried to keep my mind on the work, but I felt so awkward. I felt like everyone was afraid that I was going to make some sort of scene. So I just put on my stoic face."

"That's a stereotype we have of humans, especially young ones. We think you're all about the histrionics," Zinnia confessed.

"Histrionics got me committed. I go for hiding my feelings as much as possible," November replied.

"That sounds healthy," Zinnia commented sarcastically, finally managing to provoke a snort of laughter from her friend.

"Who all in the house knows what happened? Who knows about Lady Esther?" November asked. What she meant to ask, of course, was how mortified should she be and how much would she need to lie about what had occurred?

162

"Everyone, I think, knows that your apparent romance is over, but not everyone knows why. I think the cover story is that you weren't fast enough about jumping into his bed and he got tired of waiting." November made a face, but at least that story made him the bad guy instead of her, and discouraged others from thinking she was easy prey. "Lord William is still trying to keep Lady Esther's condition secret, but that may be impossible now. Since the person who planted her necklace seems to know, it's evidently not much of a secret."

"How long have they been married?" November asked, torturing herself a little.

"Um . . . about 500 years, on and off," Zinnia responded.

"On and off?" This new information only made November feel even more silly for her infatuation with Lord William. How could anyone compete with 500 years worth of love and trust and knowledge, a continuing marriage that had already lasted half a millennium?

"They had a few rough patches, I heard. Not uncommon, really, when you're married for centuries. It's been about 70 years since they were last separated." Zinnia paused before adding, "The last time was when he made Agnes. It was after they reconciled that Agnes ran off with Philemon."

"Oh. Wow." November suddenly had a lot more sympathy for Lord William's wayward daughter. She was amazed at William's level of emotional cluelessness.

"Yeah. I think Lord William feels pretty guilty about it. I suspect that's why he's never really tried to hunt her down, despite her frequent provocations," Zinnia said quietly.

"Is that why he hunts mostly animals? Was that over Agnes?" November asked. She'd been wondering about that. He seemed perfectly happy to drink her blood, but Philemon and Dogwood had made fun of him for drinking animals' blood, which implied that this was a well-know eccentricity of his.

"That, I'm afraid, is a bit more complicated," Lord William said, appearing suddenly in the doorway. Zinnia jumped up, chagrinned at being caught out gossiping about the boss. November just sighed. *That super speedy, sneaking-up-on-me thing is getting really old.*

"Give us the room, please, Zin," he said, and her friend looked to November to make sure she was okay before high-tailing it.

Lord William turned the desk chair around and sat facing her with his arms crossed over the back of the chair. "I wanted to make sure you were alright, and to thank you for your work today." He took a breath. "I am especially appreciative given how I have wronged you."

"I'm pretty sure I'll get over it," she replied frostily, ignoring the ache in her chest from being so close to him. She willed herself to hide her sadness. "As for the work, I don't do the work for you. I was never doing it for you. You never had to go through that ridiculous charade," she continued, with a little more heat.

"I can see that now," he said, accepting her criticism without comment. "I am not used to trusting humans with such important things. I am also not used to having to take human feelings seriously. But it is evident to all of us that you are not dissembling or holding back information. We can tell when mortals lie, and you are no liar." He was quiet for a moment before adding, "If not for me, then why? We kidnapped you and won't let you leave. We are practically strangers to you. A month ago, you didn't know us."

164

"That's not exactly true. I knew that one day we'd be comrades of some sort, since you were at my pseudo-funeral. I do the work for the dead and the people who love them, and for the people who might be saved. I do the work because for the first time my gift actually matters for something important. My whole life, I have had to look the other way when I saw bad futures for people, because there was no way for me to save them."

November was struggling to articulate something she was only herself beginning to be fully aware of. She'd been asking herself for weeks why she cared so much about this work, these people. "People almost never believed me. I had to learn not to care. But now, someone is doing something horrible to people, and my gift might actually be able to make some positive difference. I've always wondered why I have been cursed with this ability when it's never done anybody any good, least of all me. I want all I've suffered from being born like this to finally be worth something. Now all those years of pain have meaning. Nobody wants their pain to mean nothing. Even Luka knows that. That's how he gets people to blow themselves up."

"He has always been good at taking advantage," he agreed.

"Evidently it's a family trait," she replied bitterly. "But at least it appears that your cause is just rather than evil. If I find out that it isn't, you will wish you'd never found me," she vowed with a vehemence that surprised them both.

"I will bear that in mind. And I will miss our . . . whatever it was," William admitted quietly.

"We'll both just have to find other ways to amuse ourselves," she said, turning cold again to conceal her heart.

"I was never laughing at you, for what it's worth," he replied.

"So why is it?" she asked, ignoring this thread, desperate to change the subject. "Why do you mostly drink animal blood? You didn't seem to have any trouble drinking mine."

"Everyone assumes that it is because I am too soft-hearted toward humans," he said with a little smile. "They call me a self-hating vampire, a sorry excuse for a predator. The truth is, I'm terrible at enthralling. It's rather embarrassing, and it has made it difficult for me to survive this long without betraying our secret. Vampires that defective usually die young. Or are culled," he added darkly.

November gulped before asking, "But you enthralled my mother, didn't you? I saw you."

"Her mind was weakened by years of drug abuse," he explained. "It was easy to make her forget, and any damage I did would be written off as due to her habit. And I despised her, so I didn't care about harming her," he admitted matter-of-factly. "Most of the time, if I bite a human and enthrall her to make her forget, or to make her serve me and keep our secret, she goes back to her daytime life noticeably mad. In addition to the ethical issues this might pose, accumulating crazy humans near my residence would not do anything good for our secrecy. The only other option is to always kill my prey, but accumulating bodies is also . . . problematic." He shrugged.

"I should think so," she scolded. It always unnerved her, this cold vampire practicality about death, though probably not as much as it would have were she any kind of normal human being.

"You, of course, already know of our existence and cannot be enthralled. You will eventually become one of us, it seems, and in any case you are in our possession, so my deficiency presented no obstacle to consuming your blood."

166

"How convenient for you," she said, drily, not particularly enjoying being described as in anyone's possession.

"Yes, well . . ." he replied awkwardly, clearing his throat before continuing. "Because of these difficulties, generally, I only bite criminals who won't be missed and whose death will cause no surprise due to the plethora of people who wish them dead, and even them I take only rarely. A few people know of my difficulty: my father, my sister, my wife. Sometimes we will feed together so one of them can assist me. But most of the time, it's simply less trouble to hunt animals. And, very rarely, if I find a human interesting enough to turn, I will feed on her for a time until she becomes one of us."

"Is that what happened with Agnes?" she asked, her face and voice carefully blank.

"In essence," he replied with a sigh. "I thought I loved her. It turned out that I loved my wife more, and that fact destroyed my progeny. And, as I said, she did not have the temperament to make a good transition to our life."

"I'm sorry," she said.

He nodded. "I suppose you actually are. Most people in your position would not be so sympathetic."

"You are lucky that I have a forgiving turn of mind," she said, managing a brief, cold smile.

"Indeed, I am," he said gravely. He stood. "I should let you have some peace. You look exhausted." His eyes went briefly to her neck, and he opened his mouth to offer her a dreamless sleep.

"Don't say it. Don't even think about it," November said, cutting him off, denying herself a comfort that would only accentuate her pain.

"Of course," he said nodding. He halted, seemingly debating with himself before sharing his next words. "I must ask that you do not allow anyone else to bite you. It would undermine my authority and might be dangerous to you."

"Yes, I figured that out already. People still need to see me as your human right now, even though we're not . . . whatever," she answered, rolling her eyes. "And we still don't know who the spy is, and the last thing I need to do is accidentally exchange blood with whoever that is. I'm not an idiot, you know," she added with pointed irritation.

"Yes, I figured that out already," he replied with a small smile. And with that, he left November alone, with only her visions and breakup music for company.

Chapter 8

November slept fitfully, waking up again and again, tangled in her sheets, chased by bad dreams and visions all in a jumble. She felt trapped: trapped in the house whose grounds she hadn't left once in nearly a month, trapped in her apparent future as a vampire, trapped in this spider web of centuries-old plots spun by cruel strangers. For a few weeks, her infatuation with William had provided enough distraction for her to put out of her mind the fact that someone in this house was working for the enemy and intended her harm. No longer possessing that luxury, she found that she was afraid. She feared being taken, hurt, forced to help Luka do bad things. She feared failing in the use of her gift to help win this fight. She feared that when death changed her into a new creature, she would become a monster. She feared finding out the identity of the mole and the pain that discovery might cause, but she feared even more continuing to live with the viper in her nest.

It was afternoon before she finally fell asleep, so she was still dozing when dusk came. She was finally up and brushing her teeth, still in her nightgown, when Pine and Greg fairly flew into her room without so much as a knock on the door. That was the first indication that something was seriously wrong. The second sign came when Pine threw her over his shoulder as Greg moved faster than she could see, clearing her room in a whirl and hiding all obvious evidence of her existence. Previously unknown to her was a false wall in the back of her closet. It concealed a cubby into which Greg tossed all her personal belongings.

Pine rushed her out the door with Greg hot on his heels, moving so quickly that November closed her eyes tight with instinctive fear, her breath frozen in her throat. Her fairy bodyguard threw open the door to the linen closet down the hall and revealed a hidden trapdoor in the floor. He then murmured, "We're going through the chase. Don't scream," and dropped dozens of feet straight down, landing lightly on his toes. And scream she certainly would have, had she possessed any ability to draw air into her lungs. Pine barely paused before racing along a barely lit, narrow hallway, Greg following close behind. Down a few more ladders they went, emerging finally into a slightly wider but similarly ill-lit passageway.

November realized then that they were in the escape tunnel she'd intuited the existence of on her first day in the house. As they ran, November caught a glimpse of someone else in the passageway, running quickly and silently ahead of them. They finally came to a small room whose hidden door Greg secured firmly behind them, turning on the room's dim light only after the three of them were sealed in the underground tomb. The whole race had taken perhaps 15 seconds.

"Welcome to our bolt-hole," Pine said quietly as he lowered her gently to the floor. "We're about 20 feet underneath the gazebo, if you're wondering." Her knees buckled as soon as her feet touched the ground, and she wound up half in his lap. The two men helped her sit with her back against the wall, and she looked up at them in mute confusion, shaking with equal parts adrenaline, fear, and cold.

She was barefoot, wearing only a cotton nightgown that barely came to her knees and left her arms bare, and it was about 20 degrees colder down here than it was in her room. Greg took off the jacket of his suit and draped it over her, bringing a whispered, "Thanks," out of the trembling teenager who still could not process the fact that she was no longer in her bathroom. She was too freaked out to catch any visions off of the blazer, which she supposed was rather a mercy. She looked down and realized that her toothbrush was still clutched tightly in her hand. Greg gently peeled her fingers away from it, and she let it fall to the ground.

"Don't worry, you'll be safe in here. It'll only be for a little while, until the police leave," Pine said in a reassuring tone that did not quite jive with the rather dramatic sprint they had just completed.

"Police?" she managed.

Greg explained, "They found the body of one of the women who works for the cleaning crew we use, a woman by the name of Carly. They think she was killed the day before yesterday, the same day she was here to clean our house. So, they're here as a matter of routine."

November closed her eyes, sad to learn that her fears about the maid were correct, horrified to hear that another innocent had died over her gift. It also occurred to her that she should probably be careful how she reacted and what she revealed. She did not know if the two men guarding her had been brought into the loop with respect to Esther's planted necklace. She sighed inwardly. She was not cut out for this cloak and dagger nonsense.

"William asked us to hide you until they depart. He didn't want them interviewing you," Greg continued.

"He thought they might wonder why a barely-eighteen-year-old girl with a missing mom and no I.D. was living in his house?" she asked.

"Pretty much," Greg answered. Something in his voice convinced her that there was more to the story.

"What else?" The men were silent, avoiding her eyes. "Spill it," she ordered, her irritation finally subduing her fear.

They looked at each other, and Pine took a deep breath before admitting, "Someone sent in a tip to the police and the newspapers about 10 days ago saying that there was a runaway girl by the name of November living in Oakland. The individual described you, said they feared you might be a victim of human trafficking. They supplied a photo, which has been all over the news, in the papers, on the internet. Best we can tell, this was all done over e-mail, from a local coffee shop with free wifi."

Now that was a rather unexpected piece of information for the flustered young woman to take in. *Holy. Cow.* "For serious? And no one bothered to tell me?" Irritation bloomed anew. "You know, I'm getting really tired of being the last person informed about things affecting my life." The men held a guilty silence before November continued, "Who would do that? The only friend I have from the carnival doesn't even know how to use a computer."

"Presumably the same people who are looking to kidnap you," Pine answered. "This way, if you go anywhere off these grounds, you run the risk of being recognized by someone or picked up by police. That would help the enemy to find you and get their hands on you. Now half the state of California has their eyes looking for you, along with their phone cameras. Quite the force multiplier. It's pretty clever, actually. Of course, involving human authorities in an internal dispute of our realm is both illegal and very taboo. I think our spy is getting pretty desperate, which, of course, makes things more dangerous."

"That's a tad alarming," November said flatly. She was even more trapped than she had realized. Here was a good reason to be happy that she had not run away when she had found out about William's wife and his deceit. *I would have run straight into the spy's trap no matter where I had gone, thanks to the mole's little media blitz.* "But if it was the spy who did it, then why not go all the way and tell the cops that I'm in this house?"

"Actually, we think he or she may have done just that," Pine confessed further. "We have spotted people watching the gate. Humans, plainclothes police. An anonymous tip wasn't enough to get them a warrant, especially for the home of someone like Lord

172

William. He contributes a lot of money to a lot of important peoples' political campaigns. Throw in a dead housekeeper, though, and now they have enough to get inside the house." November shuddered, prompting Pine to turn to her and say, "Hey, it's going to be alright. They're not going to get anywhere near you with Greg and me around, okay?"

November nodded, feeling silly that she was afraid of the police when evil supernatural creatures were out to get her. After all, her own father had been a policeman. When she had been very small, she'd loved her father's uniform. She would sit on his lap and play with his badge. Her innate affection for police had lasted until the day they had been called to her mother's residence because the neighbors had heard November screaming from inside the trunk of the broken-down car in the yard. This fateful day had occurred a few months after her grandmother's death, and her drug-addled remaining parent had not exactly risen to the occasion of renewed motherhood.

At first, the child had been grateful for the rescue. It had been ninety degrees that day, and she had been roasting alive. But once the social worker had arrived and the police had dragged her away, screaming in fear at being separated from her only family, her feelings had begun to change. Subsequent encounters with law enforcement hadn't been much more pleasant, always charged with the anxiety that her mother would end up in jail again and that November would go back into the system. November knew intellectually that the officers had been trying to help her, but still she still assigned them some of the blame for her years-long hospitalization, and she had developed an instinctive fear of them, their sirens, their weapons, and their power to disrupt a person's whole world.

"Well, let's hope that we'll be able to get some info about Carly's murder that will help us identify the traitor in our midst," Greg said after a brief silence. "There's a fairy lieutenant in the police department, so he should be able to be of some help."

November tried to focus on Greg's words rather than on her anxiety and her frozen toes. It made November feel a little better, having something practical to think about while they were stuck in that dark room. "My examining the body is obviously out of the question, but maybe we could get hold of a personal object of hers? I might be able to see who killed her," she offered.

"We'll discuss this with Lord William after the police leave," Pine promised.

As she calmed down, a thought occurred to her. "Who was that in the chase? Running ahead of us?" she asked.

"There was no one in front of us, child," Greg replied with a raised eyebrow. "Was it a vision?"

"Maybe." *Or perhaps it was just the stress and a trick of the light. Right now, I don't even care.*

They settled in to wait. November tried to relax, closing her eyes and snuggling down underneath Greg's jacket. In spite of the vampire's chivalry and the impressive heat generated by the fairy, November felt terribly cold. She hated being cold. Their house in the winter had always been cold. Her nose was running from the chill, and soon she began to shiver.

When the light went out to protect its battery, she hit her limit. Claustrophobia, cold, fear, hunger, and lack of sleep combined to be more than she could handle. Tears began rolling down her face as she tried without success to keep her breathing even, tried to keep her companions from noticing her distress. With their acute senses, of course, this was impossible. "Hey," Pine said softly. "Let me try to warm you up, okay?" he said, putting his arm around her shoulder. November startled at the touch despite how desperate she was to no longer be cold. "I'm not going to try anything. I'm not going to hurt you. But you need to get warm. I didn't realize how chilly it was down here. We should have planned for that."

As the fairy pulled her onto his lap and began rubbing her hands between his own, November did her best to keep her blinders on. She let the fragments of Pine's life pile up around her without picking any of them up. The last thing she wanted right then was to have a vision. Once the blood had come back into her hands, she curled up against Pine with her head on his shoulder, and Greg gave her his socks to put on and readjusted his blazer to cover her again. She was still crying a little, and she was sure she looked ridiculous, but at least she wasn't quite so cold.

"Do you want to talk about it?" Greg asked gently. "It's okay if you don't."

She was silent for several minutes before everything came out in a flood. She told them of her fear of enclosed spaces, her anxiety about the mole in the house, her terror of getting kidnapped again, her anger at Lord William's deceit, her rage at being kept in the dark about everything all the time, especially this missing person nonsense. She spoke of her guilt over her mother's murder, and Carly's, and even the deaths of the fairies from the gas station. She described how trapped she felt, trapped in her life and in this house and by her gift, the feeling so reminiscent of how she used to feel locked up in that awful hospital in Idaho. By the time she finished, the tears were gone, and she did feel a little bit better if seriously embarrassed about losing her composure.

It seemed like they were trapped in there forever. In truth, about three hours passed before Lord William arrived to give them the all clear. She looked at him balefully and said nothing as she began to trudge back down the long passageway to the house proper. He tried to apologize for neglecting to keep her informed about her newly minted fame as a missing person, but she just shook her head and kept walking.

The ladders presented a bit of a problem. She absolutely refused to have the men in a position to look up her nightdress, but they for their part did not want to let her climb up behind them in case she were to fall. In the end, she had to compromise and allow herself to be carried, as it was marginally less mortifying than the alternative. This indignity did nothing to improve her black mood.

Once they emerged from the linen closet, she turned to them and thanked Pine and Greg for their help and suggested that next time they bring a goddamned blanket along. She then informed them all that she required an hour to get herself together before she wanted to exchange another word with anyone. She stalked down the hall to her room and propped a chair under the doorknob as a makeshift lock, fully aware of the futility of that measure but angry enough not to care.

It took a half an hour of blazing hot water before she felt really warm again. She dressed quickly. Her appearance was severe enough to match her mood: black turtleneck, black leggings, black boots, and a slicked-back ponytail of black hair. She looked like a severely irritated beat poet. All she needed was a pair of chunky black glasses to complete the look.

Clean and warm at last, she headed down to the kitchen, eating her dinner while reading a Harry Potter book she'd found in the library. She still found it hilarious that all seven volumes of the series were present in a vampire's elegant library, all in hardback first editions of the British version, of course.

"Snape kills Dumbledore, you know," Ben said as he slipped into the kitchen, reaching into the refrigerator for some refreshment. November flipped him off without even looking up.

"First, I've already read them all, like everyone else above the age of seven in this country. Second, I'm psychic. I always know how the story ends. The end isn't the point. It's how you get there. Third, I'm in no damn mood."

Ben slid into the adjacent stool after heating his snack briefly in the microwave. "At least you didn't have to spend an hour talking to some idiot cop about some maid you never even met."

"No, I got to huddle in a dark and freezing room for three hours wondering what the hell was going on."

"Yeah, that bites. At least the cops seem satisfied. They didn't find anything, of course. Fell all over themselves apologizing to our lord and master."

"How did he explain the fridge?" she asked. A fridge full of blood seemed like it would raise a few flags for law enforcement.

"Zinnia told them she's a hemophiliac who requires frequent blood transfusions. She's a real strong enthraller. She can make people believe anything." November's stomach clenched at that. She didn't want to mistrust the closest thing to a real friend she'd ever had, but living in this state of tension was making her paranoid.

"Where is she?" November demanded.

"In a pow-wow with his lordship." He paused. "The cops spent a really long time with her. They found a blue hair on the body," he said more softly, looking around secretively.

November felt ill. "That doesn't mean anything. The woman cleaned her room the same day she died. They come twice a week –

once during the day to do the upstairs and once at night to do the basement. They were here during the day on Halloween. She could have picked up hair from any of us daywalkers," November said with some heat. "Zinnia could never kill anyone. Not on purpose."

"Of course not, of course not," Ben agreed quickly.

"How did the woman die?"

"Strangled, apparently. With a scarf. It was probably a boyfriend or something. Humans are always killing each other for stupid reasons." He paused again, then spoke again as though having a revelation. "Unless the maid found something incriminating in someone's room that day. The spy's room, I mean. I suppose that's possible. That would make the spy a fairy."

November said, "Hmm," noncommittally. She had no intention of spilling any sensitive information in the course of this conversation, so the less she said, the better. Luckily, she was rescued by Pine, who informed her that her presence was required in Lord William's office.

The vampire governor of California was pacing like a caged animal, his hands clenching and releasing as he tried not to lose his temper and break any of the tasteful decorative items scattered around his domain. Birch was somewhat calmer, but his messy coiffure testified to the level of his tension. The stranger in the room was a policeman, obviously Lord William's fairy connection on the Oakland force. A folder was on the conference table, its contents scattered over the polished surface.

"Lt. Cyprus, this is my resident seer, November Snow," William said, finally sitting down, coiled like a spring.

"Yes, I recognize her from the Amber Alert. A pleasure to meet you," he said, tipping his hat.

"Likewise," she replied with a nod. "What is going on?" she asked.

Birch replied, "The cleaning woman was killed on Halloween, the same night you found the pendant she'd left in your room for you. She was strangled with a scarf belonging to Zinnia. Now, we know that she most likely did not have time to commit the murder that night, given that she was summoned back to the house only an hour after departing, and in that time, she was never out of my sight. However, the police estimate of the time of death runs from 4 pm to midnight, so it is possible that Zinnia could have committed the crime during the day. In addition, the police search turned up a disposable cell phone in her room that had been used to dial the victim's phone number."

November's stomach turned. "Where is Zinnia?"

"In the basement. Waiting for Savita," William answered quietly, his lips tight with anger.

"You don't seriously believe she had anything to do with this? There's no way!" November cried. It took all her self-control not to burst into tears.

"I don't want to, but we have to consider the possibility. If she is innocent, you can help us clear her," Birch replied. His ageless face was clouded with worry.

"This has gone on too long. We wanted to keep our knowledge of a mole secret so as not to tip off the guilty party or to induce him to do something desperate. It's clear now that he is desperate or foolish enough to involve humans. And it's obvious to the whole household now that there is a rotten apple in the barrel. It will soon be obvious to the entire Bay Area supernatural community, now that police have been inside my home. There is no further need for pretending. We will find the cancer and cut it out. Tonight."

November had never seen William so angry. He looked like he was moments from exploding in a fireball that would consume them all. She decided that she would never want him to be this angry with her. Everyone watched him warily, no one wanting to be the first to speak and risk drawing his ire.

"If we had something belonging to the victim, I might be able to see something. Actually going to the crime scene would work better," November ventured. "If we can get hold of the phone or the scarf, that might tell me a lot."

"I can't get my hands on the physical evidence. If you wait a few days, the crime scene would be doable. Same with sneaking into her residence to swipe a personal object. We'd need to wait a while so as not to get caught. I was able to swipe a few pictures and a copy of the crime scene report. Could you get something from the photos in the file?" Cyprus asked, gesturing toward the table.

"Probably not, but I could try," she offered, sitting down to make the attempt. The poor woman in the photos was on the floor of what looked like an abandoned warehouse. She had one of Zinnia's signature scarves wrapped tightly around her neck. Close-ups showed hands roughened by years of hard work, but she didn't see any indication of a fight. "No signs of a struggle?" she asked the policeman.

"None. She was probably enthralled, but it's not like I can put that in the report."

November closed her eyes and cast about for anything that might be of use. After a few minutes, she sighed. "Nothing," she said wearily. Lord William swore. They sat in frustrated silence for a moment.

"No, hold up," November said. "There is something that could help. I just realized that it might be significant. I had a vision, when

180

I was in the chase. I saw someone running, past the safe room, towards what I assume is an exit beyond the walls."

"Describe," his lordship commanded.

"Tall. Probably a man, but not certain." Em closed her eyes, trying to remember. It had been such a quick flash. "Blond," she said, suddenly sure. "Definitely had light hair." She shivered, her thoughts turning immediately to the resident rebel vampire. *Ben. It could have been Ben.*

"Rose or Benjamin or Pine, then, or someone else wearing a wig," William said, as he cast his mental eye over his household. Birch took pains to keep his expression impassive, but his fingers were practically making grooves in the mahogany armrests of his chair.

"Too tall to be Pine or Rose, I think," November replied to Birch's relief. "Too pale to be Pine." *Ben. It's Ben,* her instincts silently screamed.

"When did this person sneak out? Recently? Years ago? Years in the future?" Birch asked. "It might not even be related."

"I'm not sure. I'd have to go back down and look again. Even then, there's no guarantee I'd get a definite answer." She paused, thinking more about Benjamin. "I feel I should tell you . . . Ben was acting a little weird in the kitchen just now. He seemed to be trying to plant doubts in my mind about Zinnia. He was talking about how the police found her hair on the victim, how she's a really good enthraller." She almost felt bad about casting suspicion on him. Almost.

"He is certainly stupid and ignorant enough to involve humans," William replied. "I can't imagine any of the adults doing that under any circumstance." He picked up his phone and called Pine. "Guard the chase exit personally, with Greg. I don't want anyone getting out of here tonight." He hung up with no further explanation.

"What's the plan?" Birch asked.

"Well, we're not waiting for days until we can sneak November into the crime scene or steal the poor wretch's favorite earrings," William said with barely suppressed impatience.

"You could have the human and Savita examine everyone in the house," suggested Lt. Cyprus.

"That would also take days, I'm afraid," November replied.

"We could start with examining Ben, as he's now the prime suspect." Birch ran his hands once again through his hair, thinking before continuing, "That would tell us his guilt. Unfortunately, humans can't give evidence against vampires in court, so you'd need additional evidence to execute him."

"Setting aside for a moment how incredibly offensive that is, wouldn't Savita be able to give evidence?" November asked.

"Yes, but telepathy is hit or miss. There are ways to train the mind to avoid thinking about particular things while being examined. If I were going to send in a spy, I'd make sure to teach him how to do that," William explained. The room went quiet while every mind ran in circles, looking for a way to bring the mole to light in a judicially acceptable fashion.

"I have an idea," November said slowly. "You're not going to like it."

***

When Ben next saw November, twenty minutes later, she was standing outside the linen closet down the hall from her room.

182

"What's the story, morning glory?" he asked casually, leaning against the wall beside her.

November took a deep breath. "Maybe you can help me. See, when I was going down the passageway earlier, I had a brief vision of someone running down the hall. I couldn't tell who it was. So I was thinking I should go back down there and check it out, but . . ." She paused sheepishly before continuing, "I'm afraid to go down there by myself. Could you come with me?" *Is he really going to fall for this?*

"Sure," he said with a wide smile. "Any excuse to hang out in the dark with my favorite human."

Looking at his seemingly genuine smile, she wondered which way she was hoping this would turn out. Was she rooting for guilt or for innocence? As they descended, anxiety twisted her insides. She had thought to wear a winter coat this time, so at least she was warm and snug beneath a designer black wool number. *Why did I ever say this idea out loud?*

As they walked down the long passage, he asked how she was doing. "I mean, heartbreak wise," he clarified.

"Okay, I guess," she replied, trying desperately to sound normal. "It was hard to be near William at first, but there's so much else to worry about right now that I don't have time to dwell on it. Mostly I just feel stupid for falling for it. It's kind of humiliating. I've never been the love-struck schoolgirl before. I thought girls like that were silly and frivolous, like I had nothing in common with them. Apparently, I should not have been so judgmental." It felt so strange, chatting with him as though she was sure of his friendship. She felt like she was talking too quickly.

"Happens to everyone sooner or later."

The pair stopped a few dozen yards before the safe room.

"This is where I saw it," she said, kneeling to put her hands to the smooth concrete. She concentrated, seeking truth and fearing to find it. She caught the sprinter, slowed his stride. She found his face, found the scarf in his hand and the murder in his eyes. Returning to the present, she stood to face him. She took an involuntary step backward, which told the young vampire everything he needed to know. He smiled again, coldly delighted to be found out.

"Don't be frightened, November. I'm not going to hurt you. You're too valuable for anyone to hurt you. We're just going to leave this place, and I'll take you to your new home. Thanks to you, we're mere yards from a perfect escape." He reached out and put a hand on her shoulder, making her flinch. She wanted to turn away, but she couldn't stop watching his face in horror. The relaxed visage of a slacker ski bum had been replaced by the wild eyes and euphoria of a desperate man— a hungry and desperate man.

"You'll be much happier once Luka sets you free of the bondage of your human life. And you'll be part of building a wonderful new world. You'll be a hero to generations of our people. You're really very lucky." He touched her face, seeming not to notice her revulsion. Suddenly, his body pressed hers against the wall. The cold fingers of one hand were pulling at the collar of her turtleneck, tearing the fabric like tissue paper, while the other hand squeezed her arm too tightly.

"No, Ben, don't. You don't want to do this," she begged in a whisper, not sure whom she was trying to save.

"Hush, now. You liked it well enough when the lord of the manor did it," he replied with a twist of bitterness. "I can't turn you over to Luka without at least getting a taste first. It's my only chance. I doubt he's much for sharing. Magic humans are quite the delicacy, I'm told. You can scream if you want. It's soundproof down here." He smiled a terribly sharp grin as he promised, "I'll be careful."

Just as his fangs were about to pierce her skin, Ben turned his head, reacting to a sudden sound. This was November's cue to drop to the ground as William and Birch leapt from the bolt-hole and tackled Ben.

Ben never had a chance against them. His elders were so much faster, so much stronger with the centuries of life's blood and energy fueling them. The traitor howled in frustration and pain as they bound him in silver with their gloved hands. He writhed on the floor as William bent down to check on November.

"I'm fine, but I'm afraid that you owe me a new sweater." With trembling hands, she handed William back his phone, which they had used to record the entire episode.

"I'll see what I can do," he replied with a trace of a smile. "Good work, human." He helped her to her feet. "Are you sure you're alright to walk back?"

"Yeah. I was dizzy, but I'm okay now." She managed a smile that, based on William's expression, was not terribly convincing. "Really, go deal with that . . . creature," she said with revulsion. "I'll be right behind you. I'm going to need a few minutes to calm down though, before I can be useful."

"Of course."

The men began carrying the prisoner back down the passage while November walked a dozen paces behind, not wanting to get too close to her former friend. The vitriol erupting from his mouth made her skin crawl. She wanted to ignore him but feared she might miss something important. Once he started screaming about what a whore she was, she decided that blocking him out was the best course of action after all. *I really hate that word,* she thought. *Men only call a woman a whore if they're angry that they can't control her.*

The men exited the passageway when they came to a cutoff for the dungeon. Em continued to climb up to the linen closet. She just needed to get away from Ben for a few minutes. Her skin prickled. She felt cold where he had touched her. Her clothes smelled like him.

Though she'd remained calm while down in the chase, she fell apart once she reached the safety of her bedroom. She caught sight of herself in the mirror: her clothes torn, her neck bare, her cream skin and the edge of her pink bra exposed. It was then that she really began to shake all over, tears pouring silently out of her shock-widened eyes.

She told herself that all had gone to plan, that she had never been in real danger. She had thought she had been prepared to feel Ben turn on her. It had been her idea, after all, to lay a trap for her erstwhile friend. Even still, the look in his eyes had terrified her. They had been full of lust and violence and the fire of radical belief. They were a potent reminder that the enemy she'd signed on to fight was dangerous and merciless and dogged, and she feared that the next time she had to face one Luka's loyalists, she might be all alone, with no one ready to jump out and save her.

After a few minutes, she managed to pull herself together. She changed clothes and washed her face just in time for Zinnia to come barreling through the door. Her fairy friend was crying with equal parts relief and fury, not wanting to believe that Ben had tried to frame her but overjoyed that November had cleared her of suspicion. "You saved me," she kept telling November, over and over again.

186

"You'd do the same for me," the human replied. "I knew it couldn't be you. No one really believed it." November stroked her friend's back as the fairy cried on her shoulder. She glanced at the shards of images that presented themselves: Zinnia crying in her cell all alone, thankfully not in chains. She saw Zinnia's relief and shock as Ben was dragged in to take her place, her screaming rage as she flew at her former friend, Willow and Daniel pulling her away lest she kill the guilty party before he could be questioned.

"They put me in the dungeon, Em," she cried, heartbroken. "I've known them since I was born, and they put me in the dungeon."

"I know," November answered. "But what else could they do? Besides, you were safer there, and it made it easier to catch Ben." Her friend interrupted her weeping to look up quizzically, so November explained, "Ben might well have tried to kill you, to make it look as if you were guilty and had run away. With you under guard, he didn't have the opportunity. And it made Ben think Lord William had believed his ruse, which made him careless enough to be tricked into giving himself away.

"You were the last person anyone wanted to believe was a traitor," November emphasized. "That's one thing that's so insidious about this. Knowing there is a traitor in the house, everyone starts doubting each other. It weakens us even above and beyond the information he gave Luka."

Zinnia finally calmed down enough to say, "At least it's over. You caught him, and we have one less thing to worry over, especially with the king coming next month. That'll be a security nightmare."

November was about to ask her friend to tell her more about the court when they were interrupted by Savita, who quickly embraced them both and asked if they were alright. After the appropriate reassurances were made, November said, "Let me guess – he wants me downstairs."

"Indeed, we do. Are you ready to face Benjamin?"

"As ready as I'll ever be, I suppose. Might as well get it over with," the seer replied. "Is Lord William going to kill him?"

"Yes, eventually," the lord's sister replied. "He will be tried first."

"With your brother as judge?"

"Perhaps. I know, our ways must be strange to you."

"At least I won't have to testify, right?" November asked, unnerved by the thought.

Savita paused a bit awkwardly before answering, "No, humans cannot give evidence to convict a vampire or fairy." November was both relieved and offended. "There's the recording, and Birch can testify, as he was witness to your conversation."

"Are you okay, Zin?" November asked her friend.

The fairy took a deep breath and squared her shoulders. "Yes. Go ahead. Find out everything. Squeeze the bastard dry."

***

Ben looked a bit worse for wear by the time November arrived in the basement. William and Birch evidently hadn't been gentle while transporting the prisoner. It appeared that they'd grown irritated with his vocal bravado and gagged him. It looked like the whole household was in the dungeon, seeking a glimpse of the traitor, disgust in their eyes. Lord William declared that enough was enough and sent them all packing. Only he, Birch, Savita, and November remained when he closed the door.

188

The fire in Ben's eyes grew dimmer as fear began to take over. As brave as he might try to be when questioned, there was no way to fight the two magical women standing in his cell.

November almost felt sorry for him, until she thought of the gas station attack, poor dead Carly, her murdered mother, betrayed Zinnia, and her own near-miss kidnapping in the tunnel. As she sat down to begin, he looked right at her. She expected rage or hatred, but what she saw instead was more like shame, a sort of acceptance of the fact that he had lost and acknowledgement of the fact that she and her gift had prevailed this time. It was almost as if he no longer cared what happened. She soon began to see how that might be.

As she immersed herself in visions of Ben's life, November watched him get turned by his vampire father. Ben had been enthralled when he died, pain-free and unaware that his human life was bleeding away. He clawed his way out of the earth to find his maker and his sister waiting with his first vampire meal, a pretty young woman dressed to the nines.

His sister was beautiful and sad, with green eyes and perfectly coiffed blond hair. November watched Ben fall in love with her while her will to live continued to fade away. She saw Ben discover her ashes after her suicide. She listened to him wail like a wounded animal. She watched Ben go off the rails, carelessly feeding, taking no care to avoid discovery or suspicion, constantly reproved by his maker, who himself was maddened by grief for his daughter.

Finally, she saw the moment when Ben took a step too far. He killed a girl, a werewolf girl who'd caught his eye and had tried to fight back when he attempted to prey upon her. He lost control, tore her to pieces, and only afterward began to realize what he had done.

She saw Ben and his father surrounded by angry wolves, saw Ben's father offer himself to the dead girl's father in place of his child, in order to preserve the peace. Ben could do nothing to stop it, watched them tear his sire apart until the resulting rivers of blood turned to ash. She watched him scream alone into the dark once the wolves tired of mocking him.

She watched him fall further into despair, starving himself, nursing his hatreds until a man with two different colored eyes came calling. He spoke to the vampire child's pain, turned his loss and resentment into something useful. Luka led Ben down the primrose path, leading him to blame William and the rest of the vampire establishment for his loss and abandonment.

Luka told Ben that he had been right to kill that werewolf girl, that she was his enemy and deserved to die. He told Ben that his maker would still be alive if only William Knox hadn't made a peace treaty with the werewolves and charged his lesser lords with preserving it. He told him that his beautiful lover would still be alive if she'd had the guidance of a real vampire, a strong predator who could have taught her the proper pride.

Luka's seeds had found fertile ground in Ben's grief and humiliation, and by the time Lord William had come to take Ben in hand, his loyalty was to the scheming Lord of Arizona. She watched Ben making furtive calls on a disposable cell phone. Sometimes he seemed frightened while listening to the person on the other end. She supposed that Luka might be a rather impatient and exacting task master. It must have been difficult, spending so many months as a spy, all alone amongst his enemies.

She watched him enthrall the doomed maid, sending her on his errands. She watched him make friends with Zinnia and try to pump her for information, with a fair amount of success. She watched him steal Zinnia's scarf and strangle the unfortunate Carly. Finally, exhausted, and afraid to look to the boy's future, she surfaced back in the present.

190

She shook her head to try to clear it. "Was I gone long?"

"About two hours," William answered, casually sipping blood out of a beer stein. She glanced at Ben, whose eyes never left the blood and whose fangs had descended of their own accord. Young vampires had to eat often to keep up their strength, especially when injured. Ben was seriously hungry. Savita was scribbling notes in a pad, and the recorder on the table was running. They had been questioning him the whole time she'd been under. "Let's take a break," Lord William commanded, ushering everyone out of the room and locking the door securely behind him. He left the glass of blood on the table, just out of Ben's reach, of course.

He called Daniel to guard Ben as they sat in the library to pool information and map out a strategy for further questioning the spy. As the seer poured out what she'd found, everyone shook their heads. The whole thing was such a waste. "I think that's how he gets the bombers, too," November said. "He finds damaged young people and fills them full of his anger and propaganda."

"It's a shame," Savita replied. "Luka is very persuasive."

"What did Luka mean, talking about the werewolves?" November asked. Her lack of knowledge of supernatural history and politics was starting to become a bit of a liability.

Her three companions exchanged a look. "About fifteen decades ago, Lord William spearheaded a treaty with the werewolves, ending centuries filled with one war after another. There were those who felt that was a betrayal of our people, especially fairies, who had suffered most of the losses," Birch explained.

"My enemies like to call me a werewolf lover, an appeaser, a traitor to our kind," Lord William added. "The fact that I hunt animals like a werewolf doesn't help my reputation."

"Luka has long advocated exterminating the werewolves," Savita chimed in. "Ben losing his maker to the wolves was a perfect opportunity for our brother to get his fangs into a youngling. I believe several of the bombers had ancestors killed in the old wars."

"I'd hope they would be glad that people aren't still dying that way," November said.

"Forgiveness and peace aren't our strong suits, I'm afraid. But we're very good at vengeance," Lord William replied tiredly.

"What's going to happen to Ben?" November asked with a bit of hesitation.

"We will record all the evidence, and when he is no longer useful, he will be publicly executed," William answered matter-of-factly. "He will get a trial, of course."

"Execution will have to wait until the king comes," Birch pointed out.

"That's ridiculous," William snapped. "I have every right to handle this myself."

"Legally, yes. But he has the right to appeal, which means he can't be executed until his appeal is heard by the king in person," Birch pointed out. "And that's not even considering the fact that this trial will be politically very sensitive."

"A Christmas execution," November muttered. "How festive."

Chapter 9

From what November heard through the grape vine the following evening, Savita and William hadn't been able to get much more useful information from Ben after she had gone to bed. Luka had been too smart to trust a pawn so likely to get caught with any really useful secrets. The only helpful thing about Ben was that he could identify Luka as his employer, so William now had corroboration from a vampire for what November had learned in vision. Ben was, at least for now, refusing the deal Lord William had offered to spare his life in return for testimony.

Lord William then pinned his hopes for useful intelligence on Texas, but here he was again disappointed. The Lord of Texas was a proud man and refused William's offer of help after being informed of the threat against him. Savita was sent under the authority of the crown, but by the time she arrived to examine the suspect, Texas had already made a hash of things. The bomber had been easy enough to identify with the details that November had provided. They had found the explosive vest in his apartment, and he had admitted his guilt as soon as he was caught.

Unfortunately, the methods that Lord Milton favored for attempting to garner additional information were such that the kid was fifty percent dead and one hundred percent mental by the time the telepath arrived in Austin. All they got from him was that he was working for Luka's cause and that Agnes had delivered the explosives, which of course, they already knew.

The would-be bomber, who went by the name Moss, was in no condition to be able to offer evidence to help persuade the Assembly of Lords to take action against the Lord of Arizona. Lord William could be sure of support from the half-dozen or so leaders who had been bombed, along with some of their allies, but that left an awful lot of lords who had no particular liking for William or the King, and no particular reason to take sides against Luka. There were many who considered the king's hold on the throne to be weak and saw more risk in angering Luka than in angering the crown. The situation was, as Savita put it, a right mess.

The other piece of fallout from the Texas debacle became clear a few days later, when November awoke screaming from a vision of Agnes' untimely demise. Exactly how Luka had figured out that November was mining a strand of Agnes' hair did not become clear until much later. The result, however, was that when the Texas plot failed so spectacularly, Luka felt the need to relieve himself of a liability. He seemed to regret the necessity.

He killed her quickly, surprising Agnes during an innocuous conversation. She didn't even have time to be frightened before the stake was through her chest. Her face barely had the chance to register surprise at the fountain of blood before it and every other part of her turned to ash. "I'm sorry," Luka said to her remains. "I had no choice."

Pine was at November's side even before she fully came around. It wasn't the first time he'd come running after a particularly strong vision had roused a cry. As November explained what she had seen, she reached into her pillowcase, pulling free the envelope she kept pinned tightly to her pillow. She opened it to find only ash where the hair had been. Pine shook his head gravely. "Our lord will be heartbroken," he said soberly. "As if he needed any more reason to hate Arizona."

"How do I tell him?" November asked forlornly.

"He already knows," Pine said. "He would have felt her go, even in his sleep. The connection between a vampire and his children is very strong, nearly as strong as that between a fairy and

194

his offspring. He will probably have questions about the details of her death."

November nodded. "Do you think he will blame me?" she asked quietly. "If I weren't using her hair, then Luka wouldn't have killed her."

"Of course not," Pine replied. "You were doing it on his behalf. He'll blame Luka, and Philemon, and mostly, he'll blame himself."

***

Lord William looked his age when he appeared in the doorway of the music room looking for November. It was one of her favorite places to hide out when she wasn't working. She liked to sit at the piano and listen to the various past players as they practiced and performed. Often she would quietly sing and hum along. Zinnia had taken over her guitar lessons from Ben, and she tried to find time to practice each day. She found it soothing in the same way studying quieted her mind.

"I'm so sorry," she said right away, saddened at the sight of his grief-stricken face.

"Thank you," he replied, sitting down beside her on the piano bench. He started picking at the keys. "Tell me all of it," he commanded, staring at the piano.

"There isn't much to tell. They were having a conversation, and he surprised her. The stake was in her chest and she was gone before she even knew what was happening. He told her he was sorry."

"Not sorry enough. At least not yet," he growled. After a breath, his voice far less fierce, he added, "He didn't torture her for a traitor, then. That's a bit of a relief." He relaxed a little. He had been imagining terrible things.

"No, he didn't think she leaked anything. He must have found out about the hair. He knew she hadn't betrayed him deliberately, but he couldn't run the risk of my seeing more of his plans through her," she replied. Lord William nodded in agreement.

They sat in silence for a few minutes, William sunk into grief and November knowing that nothing she could say would make it any better. Finally he left her alone at the piano and hid away to grieve in private. Em could still see him, though, sitting in his resting place, weeping tears of blood without making a sound, utterly alone.

***

For a few days after William's daughter's death, the house was quiet, but soon the place was bustling with preparations for the king's holiday visit, which would quickly be upon them. Rose was the general of a small army who rendered the entire building and grounds even more lovely than usual. Tasteful and expensive Christmas décor abounded, and the residents of the house concentrated on staying out of Rose's way lest they get drafted into some project or another.

As the arrival of the court drew near, the beautification effort expanded to include members of the household, both living and dead. A trio of beautiful employees from Neiman Marcus arrived with dresses, gowns, jewelry, and shoes to try on November as she was still confined to the grounds. It was a strange experience, parading before strangers in designer clothes as they fluttered around her. It was made palatable only by the presence of Zinnia, who ordered her not to look at any price tags and defended November's decisions against the sometimes differing opinions of the fashionistas. Then there were the hairdresser and the aesthetician. Those two at least were educational, as they took the time to teach November and Zinnia how to do their own hair and makeup once they had finished trimming and styling and plucking and waxing their victims.

One evening, November was walking in the garden when she came upon Lord William, who was enjoying a rare moment of peace and quiet. She decided to take the chance to bring up a touchy subject that had been on her mind for weeks. "May I ask you something, Governor?" she asked as she approached him.

"Of course," he said, his eyes crinkling with amusement at her formality.

"Do you think maybe you should bring your wife home?" she asked tentatively. He raised an eyebrow. She soldiered on. "It seems like the secret of her survival is out, and you'd probably both be happier with her around. This has been a difficult time, and it's probably just going to get worse, so it might be good for you to have her support." She paused before awkwardly adding, "Of course, it's none of my business so I'm just going to go now . . ." She started to slide away.

His voice stopped her. "You are an odd one," he said. "Most women would not want their rival to be around."

"She's not my rival," November replied honestly. "No offence, my lord, but I don't want you anymore." And with that, she walked away, grinning, and didn't look back.

November spent some of her time during this quiet before the storm visiting Ben in the dungeon. She supposed that she should just ignore the fact that he was down there. She knew he didn't really deserve her kindness given what he had been prepared to do to her. Nevertheless, she knew what it was like to be locked up and all alone. She kept having nightmares about her own such experiences, and spending a few minutes each day talking to him from outside the door seemed to make them go away. She justified these visits by saying she was trying to see if she could persuade him to turn on Luka and to see if he would set off some useful visions. Zinnia was angry at her the first time she went, but the fairy relented when November relayed their former friend's apology for framing Zinnia. Apparently, that particular tactic had been his master's idea.

The girls both began to feel a little bit sorry for him. They saw a confused child of whom Luka had taken advantage. The rest of the house, on the other hand, seemed to be looking forward to his execution. The prisoner was kept half starving, permitted to feed only on rodents and cold animal blood. It occurred to November that her visits might well be only an additional torment, like dangling food just outside the reach of a starving animal, but when she asked him if she should stop coming, he begged her to continue. Her pleas with him to be more cooperative didn't seem to be very effective, unfortunately, and her gift showed her nothing more of use. She wasn't sure if his silence was motivated by loyalty to Luka's cause, hatred of William, fear of his master, despair, or some combination thereof.

The night November met her maker for the first time was cold and dry and smelled of wood smoke from thousands of fire places, spare-the-air day be damned. About two hours after sunset, the limousines began to arrive, and the household of the Lord Governor of California took their places to welcome the members of the court. November was the only human present and was placed at the far end of the receiving line, next to Zinnia. All were attired in business chic. Neither November nor Zinnia recognized themselves in their sober pencil skirts and silk blouses. "I feel like we're dressed up as lawyers for Halloween," the fairy joked on their way down the stairs.

November was grateful for the levity. She was growing increasingly anxious about meeting the man who would one day place her in the ground. What she'd heard about him from Zinnia was not terribly reassuring. In his younger days, he had been an extremely successful as well as merciless general in several wars. Since the queen's death, he was rarely known to crack a smile. His preferred source of blood was prostitutes, and he never saw the same one for more than a week before wiping her mind clean and sending her on her way with buckets of cash. The members of the court were said to be always jostling for position in the king's favor and for their cut of the wealth the royal businesses generated, primarily from the casinos the king owned. "The one you have to watch out for, I hear, is the Grocer," the fairy had mentioned.

At November's questioning look, Zinnia had explained. "Her name is Lilith. She runs the household, sort of like Rose times a thousand and minus any morals. She acts as hostess for the court in the absence of a queen, and she is on the king's council of advisers. She keeps the court supplied with people for everyone to feed on when they don't have time to hunt, so they call her the Grocer. She is ruthless, and she enjoys her power and her closeness to the throne. We should steer clear of her as much as possible."

With a stomach full of butterflies, November waited for the front door to open. She had been briefed on court etiquette but was terrified that she'd make a mistake. Zinnia told her to just watch everyone else and she'd be fine. At some signal her human ears failed to perceive, the waiting men knelt and the ladies sank into deep curtsies, and November followed suit.

The only one to stay still was Lady Esther, recently returned from exile, who simply bowed her head. She sat ramrod straight in her wheelchair, looking stunning even with a blanket draped over her half-missing legs. Lord William had taken November's suggestion and had brought his wife home in time for Christmas. He seemed much less tightly wound with her in the house, and his wife seemed quite taken with November. Esther knew the whole story of

November's pseudo-romance with her husband and complimented her for breaking it off so decisively. "Good on you, young one. He certainly had it coming," she had said with a twinkle in her eye. "You'd think men would get smarter after a few centuries, but no. They just get better at apologizing."

After a few moments, a deep voice commanded impatiently, "That's enough of that," and the company rose and looked up at their king.

Ilyn Zykov was tall and slender, dressed all in black, in a suit that probably cost as much as a car. His hair was also black, with a liberal smattering of grey. His features were oddly handsome in a sharp way; his face was rendered more interesting by the scar under one eye. He was fair, but November could not quite guess where his people had come from, all those centuries ago. He looked like he'd been a young man when he'd died. His eyes, however, betrayed his years.

He clasped William in a manly hug before sweeping Savita into his arms, spinning her around with her feet off the floor. Seeing his daughter almost managed to make him smile. Esther, too, brought a bit of happiness to his features, but no one else rated more than a nod. He worked his way down the line, followed by his courtiers.

As the creature who would end her life drew closer, November began to choke in an embarrassingly obvious manner. Zinnia grabbed her arm and eased her to the ground as she realized that her friend was falling into a vision. November tasted soil; she felt as though her mouth and nose were full of earth. She could see nothing; her vision turned black as pitch as she struggled for breath. She felt a hand squeezing her own, and the panic was instantly replaced by calm.

The vision passed quickly, but not quickly enough to avoid epic humiliation. As she returned to the present, she looked up to see King Ilyn, whose hand was in her own gloved one, helping her back to her feet. "So this is the little pythoness who's causing so much trouble."

November wobbled and tried to pull herself together as William replied, "Yes. Father, meet November Snow. You'll have to forgive her. Her visions often come without warning."

The king bent and kissed her gloved hand. She couldn't quite read his expression. Perhaps he was amused. November managed to say, "How do you do, your grace?" She then couldn't help adding in her own defense, "Though I don't so much cause trouble as report it, sir."

A woman snorted. She was tall and beautiful, but overly made-up, and no amount of makeup could hide her unpleasantness. She stood rather possessively next to the king, and November realized that she must be Lilith, the infamous Grocer.

"She prevents trouble, too, from what I hear from my son," added a tall, dark-skinned fairy with a waterfall of long, tight, forest green curls. She could only be Birch's mother, Hazel. "Texas certainly thinks rather highly of her. That would have been a bloodbath without her warning." November gave the king's imposing lieutenant a grateful look.

"Should we go to my office to discuss what you've seen?" William asked. November wasn't sure whether he was trying to spare her further embarrassment or if he was worried about her sharing sensitive information in so public a setting. Realistically, it was probably the latter.

"It was nothing important, my lord, really," November replied, willing this conversation to end. She didn't appreciate this new scrutiny, all these new eyes looking her up and down. She wished that William had decided to hide her in Livermore for this visit, as he'd planned to do until he realized that the secret of her existence was most definitely out of the bag and that hiding her would make both him and the king look weak.

"Oh, no, please do tell," Lilith sneered. "I'm sure we're all interested." November hesitated, prompting Lilith to add, "Afraid to reveal yourself as a fraud and a show-off, are you?" Several courtiers tittered, and November felt her face redden.

"She isn't a fraud," William replied, obviously irritated. "If she were, I wouldn't have kept her here nor presented her to my father."

"Perhaps you kept her for her . . . entertainment value," the Grocer replied amusedly, provoking further giggles in the courtiers and instant hatred in November.

Throughout the banter, the king had not ceased in quietly examining November, though his face revealed nothing about his assessment. "I've seen her reports. My children are satisfied that she sees true, and I trust their judgment." Lilith did not look terribly pleased at her master's quiet rebuke, but she quickly schooled her face. "We'd best hope she is genuine, at any rate. She may be the best hope for saving the kingdom," the king stated, never taking his eyes from November's face. His unblinking gaze was profoundly unsettling. He paused before continuing, "Enough greetings. Settle in. Some of us have work to do."

A small group walked quickly toward the offices, while the rest of the courtiers followed Rose to find their quarters. November and Zinnia escaped to the garden, followed closely by Pine. With all of these people in the house, William was taking no chances with the psychic's safety.

The two girls collapsed on a bench in an out-of-the-way corner of the grounds. It was freezing, prompting November to wrap herself in a thick wool coat provided by Pine. Zinnia, of course, could have been out there in a bikini and been comfortable. November slid off her shoes and curled her cold toes into the dirt to wash away the last dregs of her vision. "So, what did you see?" Zinnia asked as soon as November had tucked her icy feet back under her coat.

"I was in the ground, buried. I couldn't breathe. Someone in the vision, maybe the king, took my hand, and I felt better. Like, I still couldn't breathe or see, but I realized that it didn't matter anymore, since I was, you know, dead. Then the real king took my hand, and I came around. That's about it," she replied.

"Creepy. Ever see that before?"

"Nope. I suppose that's officially the second vision I've ever had of my own future, though I guess it's really just an addendum to the old burial one." She looked up through the bare branches at the dark sky before adding, "That Grocer is pretty much repulsive."

"For sure. I wanted to punch that withered old blood-sucker in the mouth," her friend loyally agreed. "Premier Hazel seems cool, though," she added. November nodded agreement, unsurprised that the powerful matriarch of a family that had produced Birch and Pine was a tall drink of awesome. "So, what did you think of the king?" Zinnia asked avidly.

"Imposing. Scary," she said after pausing to think. "I'm nervous that he thinks I'm a twit, with all the falling down and everything," she confided.

"Didn't you hear him? He thinks you're his salvation," her friend retorted. "Plus, he was totally checking you out."

"I'm pretty sure 2500 year old vampire kings don't check people out," Pine said, reminding them of his presence. He had this way of blending into the background and making them forget he was there. "But if they did, he totally was," he teased with a smile. He held up his phone. "You've been summoned," he informed November, so she dusted off her feet, replaced her shoes, and tried not to shake in them as she returned to the house, this time up to Lord William's office.

On the walk back to the building, she saw a number of humans lined up by the service entrance under the eye of Lilith, who stood by the door with an assistant with a clipboard in hand. At her inquiring look, Pine explained, "Dinner." He grimaced, seeming to find this all a bit unseemly. "There are a lot of prostitutes available in Oakland. Not as many as in Las Vegas, but plenty. And if some vampire goes too far, no one will miss them. Some of the guests will have brought their own humans with them and stashed them in a hotel. The fairies will go out hunting in the daytime, of course, since we can't feed at night and it's a lot easier for us to eat on the sly."

"Ew," she replied. She shuddered to think of how many of those poor girls might be victims of human trafficking or drug addiction or both.

"Yup." Pine shook his head.

Once she reached the office, she was greeted by William, Savita, Birch, and Hazel. After having a seat, November asked, 'Where is the king?"

"Dining," Hazel said, strain showing around her mouth. Evidently, she did not approve of the Grocer's methods any more than her grandson Pine did.

"So," William began without delay, "What did you see?"

204

"It was nothing. Really. I was in the ground. I was scared because I couldn't breathe or see. Then someone took my hand and squeezed it, and I calmed down. That's all." The vampires both had a far-away look in their eyes for a moment, along with a touch of sympathy, as they remembered their own rebirths.

"That is the worst part," Savita mused. "Not the dying. It's the waking up that is so frightening."

"So you saw nothing about Lilith?" Birch asked with a tinge of disappointment.

November was a bit surprised at the sudden turn in the conversation. "No, sorry. I probably wouldn't, unless she touched me, or I had her favorite shoes or something." Apparently Lilith wasn't very popular with this crowd. "Did you want me to try?"

"No, I don't think that's wise. We definitely don't want you to catch her attention. She is a very dangerous woman." William shook his head. "I just don't understand why he keeps her around."

"She supplies a distraction from his pain," Savita responded. "And she keeps the courtiers in line, more or less."

"You mean she encourages the king's worst impulses and she lets the courtiers skim money while I try desperately to keep the ship from running aground," Hazel chimed in bitterly. Savita's little head bob acknowledged that perhaps Hazel's characterization was more accurate.

"Anyway, November, you can go. Stay close to Pine and out of the guests' way, and once the bloodsucking starts at the ball tomorrow, hightail it."

"Yes, Lord Governor," she said primly and rose to depart.

"Thank you for saving my grandson's life, by the way," Hazel chimed in as November reached the door.

November smiled as she turned back to face the elder fairy. "I got lucky," she replied. "And he is a good friend to have."

Pine walked her back to her room. She was grateful for his presence when they passed vampires and enthralled humans in the hallways. There were lots of suggestive moans coming from behind numerous closed doors. She stiffened when she heard a scream and looked to Pine. "Nothing to be done," he said sadly. "Some enthrall them before so they won't be scared. Some like to scare them and enthrall them after so they won't remember." His voice was tight with disapproval. "They do get paid, handsomely, if that makes you feel any better." Part of her wanted to do something, but the rest of her knew that like much of what she had seen in her life, there was nothing for it. *Someday, when I'm a vampire, I'm going to fix this,* she swore to herself.

She did her best to keep her psychic blinders up, to little avail. Sex and blood flashed through her head in roughly equal measure. The worst part was the glimpse she got of King Ilyn with a rather pretty redheaded girl who seemed to have misplaced her clothes. She, at least, was not terrified. In fact, she seemed to be having quite a good time. There was an image she was going to have trouble forgetting. *I need some eye bleach,* she complained inwardly, her ears flushing bright red.

Zinnia was waiting for her when she finally reached her room. The fairy was sprawled out on November's bed having changed into her favorite footie pajamas. November pressed her lips together to stifle a laugh, prompting Zinnia to aggrievedly ask, "What?"

"First, you don't even sleep. Second, you look ridiculous," November replied with a smile.

"They're cozy. And just for that, I'm getting you some for Chirstmas." Zinnia was quite gifted at making November forget her myriad worries, at least for a moment.

They settled in for a night of girl talk and continued their gossiping until November could no longer keep her eyes open.

***

With so many people in the house the night before, and so many expected for the ball, November savored the quiet time in the late afternoon right after she woke. The vampires still slept like the dead, and the fairies were out mingling with their prey and enjoying the Bay Area's sights almost as much as they were enjoying their fellow tourists. She decided to prepare for the evening's upcoming ball by practicing dancing in her new shoes, so she headed up to the ballroom in her jeans and turtleneck with her ridiculous heels in hand.

She shook her head in disbelief when she put them on. *This is insane. This is literally insane.* After taking a few wobbly laps, she opened herself up to visions of past celebrations, allowing the music to fill her heart as she danced with ghosts, surprised and pleased that she seemed to grow slightly more graceful with practice. By the time she stopped dancing, she was reasonably sure she would be able to avoid abject humiliation if called upon to dance that evening. She laughed at herself as she returned to the present. Her giggle nearly turned a scream when she turned toward the door and saw King Ilyn standing there wrapped in a black hooded cape.

"Christ on a crutch! Shouldn't you be dead for the day?" she cried out in surprise before she'd had time to think. Her eyes flew open, and she covered her mouth when she realized what she had said and to whom she had said it. Her heart was pounding so loudly that everyone in the house could probably hear it.

Ilyn crinkled his eyes in amusement before answering, "I did not mean to frighten you. The older we get, the less rest we need during the day. The sun still burns, of course. One must take care walking by windows." He twitched the cape by way of explanation. "I heard dancing but no music, so I was . . . puzzled." He raised an eyebrow, waiting for an explanation.

"I, um, wanted to practice in my shoes?" she said lamely. "So I wouldn't embarrass myself? Though it seems I've managed that anyway . . ." she trailed off.

"Why didn't you turn on the music?" he asked, gesturing toward the tastefully hidden sound system.

"I just listen to the past. I immersed myself in a vision of a dance that already happened," she said. "I think it's kind of fun, learning all the old dances you people seem to like."

"I see," he said evenly, his face blank. The young woman had no idea what to do or say, so she just stared at her crazy shoes.

There was a long silence before November finally ventured, "I should probably start getting ready for the party. . ." She began inching awkwardly towards the door.

He suddenly said, "It has been some time since you have been bitten."

"I beg your pardon?" she managed, taking a step back away from him.

She tried to take another one but found she could not move an inch. She felt as though she was pressed against a wall, bound by some invisible force. Ilyn came closer, gently brushing her hair back away from her ear before running the tip of his nose against her jaw. Her eyes went wide, and it took all her self-control not to scream.

He sniffed her like she was a particularly expensive glass of wine before stepping away and releasing her from her invisible bonds.

His mouth twitched at her discomfort, briefly revealing a fang. "You had a falling out with my son. He has since permitted you to refuse him your blood. This will be obvious to every creature in the building tonight, as you barely smell like him at all. That, among your other attributes, will make you the object of some attention. That could be . . . problematic." And with that, he zoomed away through the doors faster than November's eyes could follow.

"Well, that was hella creepy," she whispered to the empty ballroom before beating her own hasty retreat.

She forced herself to eat something, not really tasting it. She tried to stave off her nervousness while getting dolled up for the vampire soirée. Hot rollers and makeup went more smoothly than expected, much to November's relief. She packed her little evening purse with lipstick, her rosary, and her little silver knife. She put on the earrings William had given her for her birthday. It seemed to her to be a shame to waste them. Fortunately, her hands didn't start shaking with anxiety until she started struggling with the zipper on her gown. It was a lovely dress, long and beautiful and the exact dark blue shade as her eyes. Sleeveless, it covered up most of the rest of her skin, which was revealed only by a rather demure keyhole just below her collarbone.

Unfortunately, Zinnia wasn't available to calm her down or manage her zipper. November's friend had very mysteriously explained that the fairies were meeting in the afternoon and that she wouldn't be available after dark, but that November should come out to the garden at some point in the night to see something special. Even Pine had ceased shadowing her about 10 minutes before sundown. The upshot was that she was alone when the Grocer barged in.

"I suppose that will do," Lilith began, looking her over with disdain. She had not bothered to knock, of course.

"What?" November exclaimed, taking a step back.

"You have been summoned by his grace. You'd best move quickly, as he is not accustomed to waiting." The vampire surveyed the room, seemingly disapproving of the human's somewhat lavish accommodations.

"What am I being summoned for?" November replied, stalling. *No way in hell do I go anywhere with you.*

"Presumably for the only two things humans are good for," Lilith said snidely.

November flushed with anger. "Pardon me, ma'am, but you seem to be under the mistaken apprehension that I am one of your prostitutes. You can tell him I'm unavailable."

Lilith went from disdainful to violently angry faster than the blink of an eye. With her gloved hand, she yanked November's hair back, forcing her to look into the vampire's face as she hissed, "How dare you defy me, you filthy human?" November was opening her mouth to scream for help when Lord William suddenly appeared behind Lilith's shoulder.

"Are you lost, Lilith?" he said mildly but with palpable menace. "Because I'm sure you're not assaulting my favorite human on purpose." The Grocer quickly stepped away, fear flashing briefly across her face before it was masked once again with her usual unpleasant expression.

"You need to teach her obedience," she said. "A defiant human needs a firmer hand than yours," she snapped before zooming out of the room.

210

November's knees gave out and she collapsed on the edge of her bed, putting a hand to her tender head. "Are you alright?" William asked, kneeling beside her.

"Yeah." She took a deep breath. "Does my hair still look okay?" she asked, peeking around him to see the mirror, trying to be nonchalant. William, on the other hand, looked deadly serious.

"What did she say?" he demanded.

"That I was being summoned by the King."

"What for?" he asked, confused. November just looked up at him from under raised eyebrows. "Oh," he replied, still confused. "That seems odd. You're not exactly his type. Also, he usually has better manners than to do that without my permission, though as my maker, he doesn't technically need it." William seemed a bit too blasé about this summons for November's taste. The human was only growing more angry as her fear faded along with the smell of Lilith's offensive perfume.

"Well he sure as hell needs *my* permission, and he sure as hell doesn't have it," November spat, standing up and shaking out her skirt. "When do I need to be in the ballroom?"

"Twenty minutes."

"I'll be in the garden until then," she proclaimed, pulling on her gloves, grabbing her purse, and stomping rather inelegantly out of her room.

William called out to her, "Nice earrings!" November smiled in spite of herself.

***

November stood on the patio by the pool, mesmerized. The garden was filled with what looked for all the world like delicate, glowing little birds, flittering around far too quickly to make out any details. She had never seen fairies in their alternate form, at least not in person. She'd caught a quick glimpse in vision once or twice, but the live experience was so much more amazing. She felt as though she could watch them for hours. One of them made a quick lap around her head before rejoining the others. She was certain this was Zinnia. This quick welcome from her friend made November grin all the wider. *They do rather look like Tinkerbell. I'd better not tell Zin that.*

"Beautiful, aren't they?" came a deep voice only a few steps behind her. November somehow managed not to jump right out of her skin.

Refusing to look at him, she replied, "Yes, they are," as evenly as she could manage.

He came closer, saying in a more dangerous tone, "I am not accustomed to refusals or disobedience, November." He tried to place his overcoat on her shoulders, but she shrank from him and stepped away.

She forced herself to turn and face him as she replied, "I am not accustomed to being treated like a whore, *your grace*, so I guess we're both of us disappointed this evening." She'd meant to sound defiant and strong, but it came out a strange mix of angry and deeply wounded. She felt the tears she'd smothered in her bedroom welling in her eyes, and as one escaped down her cheek, she swore and angrily brushed it away, turning her back once again to the king in the vain hope he wouldn't see it. She had always hated the fact that she cried when she was furious.

"I have caused you pain," he stated, sounding more confused than irritated now. "I do not understand."

"You don't understand why sending a *pimp* to *procure* me for your use would upset me?" November wanted to scream, but she struggled mightily to keep her voice down. "You know, the only comfort I ever found in the vision of my upcoming funeral is that the people burying me seem to care about me, that you were –" Her voice broke, and she had to swallow before continuing. "And if that weren't enough, my mother was a part-time prostitute, which fact I'm sure every one of you people is whispering about by now, and I swore I would never let anyone treat me the way people treated her. And then this woman tells me that I'm being summoned for 'the only two things a human is good for,' and it surprises you that this caused me pain." She was shaking like a leaf and only just managed to keep her gaze on his face.

"Is that what she said?" he asked, the edge back in his voice. "That was rather indiscreet of her. I'm afraid I did not make clear to Lilith the reason for my order."

"Then please, do enlighten me," she replied, but all the fire was gone from her voice. She just sounded tired. She was already wrung out, and the night had barely started. The beauty in the garden that had so cheered her now just looked alien and strange, and she realized how chilly she felt in the Christmas air. Cold as she was, she was not about to accept Ilyn's overcoat.

"I did not send her to fetch you in order to . . . make use of your person, November. I had, in fact, already fed. I don't like feeding at parties, you see. I prefer a little privacy. At any rate, I summoned you because it occurred to me after our little . . . encounter this afternoon that if you entered the ball on my arm, the guests would likely leave you alone, seeing that I had apparently staked a claim on you. Ordinarily, blood would have to be exchanged to produce such deference, but since the throne, though threatened, is still mine, the visual message should suffice. I simply wished to spare you unwanted attention from strange vampires. I also wished to spare my son the indignity of having to fend off his underlings. Every vampire of any importance in his holdings will be here this evening."

November turned her sad face back to face him, trying to see if he was telling the truth, wanting desperately to believe him. A full minute passed as he waited patiently in silence, and finally she replied quietly, "That sounds like a good idea. Thank you."

"It's rather the least I can do," he replied. He looked at her closely. "Please take my coat. You must be quite cold."

"It is a kind gesture, your grace, but I have trouble wearing other people's clothes. I tend to see things."

"Ah." He continued, "I am sorry about the misunderstanding with my servant Lilith. I'm afraid we are not used to having to be careful with human feelings. The ability to enthrall makes one rather cavalier, I'm afraid." He looked back out toward the fairies dancing in the garden. "They must think quite highly of you to permit you to witness a conclave. Humans have been killed for getting a glimpse of one, I'm told."

"Good thing I'm so popular, then, because that would be pretty inconvenient." She gave him a little smile.

"Indeed it would," he responded before offering his arm. "Shall we?"

William was waiting for them outside the ballroom. He looked relieved when November and the king came into view arm-in-arm. The hum of conversation behind the doors indicated that it was a full house. November's eyes widened as two guards threw the doors open. The room was full of vampires and humans dressed to the nines. She knew security was tight, and that every one of them had been thoroughly searched, guests, servants, and human snacks included. The whole household had been talking about the preparations for weeks.

Still, she was nervous. She hated crowds. And this crowd was composed mostly of vampires who all knew her name and had heard of her gift and would be watching her like a hawk. Then there were the humans, enthralled and creepy. She prayed that she wouldn't fall into random visions. She hoped, with some reason for optimism, that a crowd of vampires would be easier for her than a crowd of humans. The party on New Year's Eve would be even crazier, she'd been told, with out-of-state lords and their entourages added to the mix.

The moment had come, and the king entered, the most valuable human on the continent on his arm. Curtsies and kneeling ensued until the king ended the reverence by signaling the band. November began to panic as Ilyn led her to the center of the ballroom. The guests pulled back, leaving them alone in the center of the dance floor.

The king sensed her distress and said, "You'll be fine. You practiced, after all."

"You might have warned me," she hissed.

"That would have only given you more reason to be nervous," he replied in a most reasonable tone. "Relax, little one," he said. "Follow my lead." So she did, since there was nothing else to be done. She tried to ignore the eyes boring holes in her back. The song was long. It gave her the time to learn the steps and slow her heart.

Eventually, she even relaxed enough to laugh with when Ilyn dipped her or tossed her in the air. She tried to look in his eyes, but she found that rather too intense and settled for gazing over his shoulder with the occasional glance at his scarred but somehow still handsome face. By the time the dance ended, she was almost a little disappointed to have to stop. He released her and bowed slightly. She curtsied deeply, and they left the dance floor, which was quickly filled as the band played on.

Ilyn passed her off to Savita so he could work the room, and November was smiling brightly until she caught sight of Lilith's face. The Grocer's eyes were fixed on November, and they burned with hatred. Savita saw this as well, locking eyes with her father's servant until Lilith wavered and turned away. It continued to surprise November how many people were afraid of her friend Savita. She tried to shake off the feeling of doom Lilith provoked in her stomach and pasted a smile back on her face.

"I don't believe you've yet met my wife, Noemi," Savita said, steering her to a beautiful Latina vampire leaning casually against the wall in a hot pink ball gown in a style more punk than prom. Savita herself was wearing a black and gold sari.

"I'm so thrilled to finally meet you!" November cried with genuine enthusiasm. She'd caught a glimpse or two, of course, in her months of working with Savita, and her friend had told her a little about her love. She knew that Noemi was young by vampire standards, barely one hundred years old, and the couple had been together nearly all that time. Savita had not turned her. Greg was Savita's only child. Noemi's maker had turned her for love but had let her go when it became clear to them both that she had been born inclined to love a woman rather than a man. He had even given her away at the wedding.

"Likewise," Noemi replied with a smile. They continued chatting for some time. November was under strict orders to stay near vampires she knew, and she required no persuasion to comply. She felt like a goldfish in an ocean of sharks. Various vampires approached her throughout the evening, getting introductions from

216

Savita, whose presence along with the king's attention kept everyone on his best behavior. She did her best to be charming and to show loyalty to the king and his house. She left no room for anyone to think they could woo her away. She was much relieved that no one but William and Greg asked her to dance and assumed she owed that relief to her entrance with the king. She did enjoy watching the dance floor, especially when they recreated centuries-old group dances. The band, composed entirely of vampires, was, of course, wonderful. She was a bit sad that Zinnia wasn't there to see it. She wondered if Ben could hear them from the dungeon.

November tried to keep her eyes off the humans. Most were only lightly enthralled so far. It made them seem a little high. They danced and flirted, doing their job of entertaining everyone, only the few favorite companions having any idea of where the evening would inevitably take them. November was the youngest human in the room, though not by much. Some of the girls looked barely of age to drink. She found it all terribly sad. Around midnight, William came over to tell her that the fangs were about to come out. She wasn't surprised; peoples' eyes had been growing more and more predatory over the previous hour. "To the library with you, and lock the door," William ordered. "Don't come out until dawn."

"Aye-aye, captain," she said. The library doors were a lot stronger than the one to her room. Her bedroom door would present no obstacle to a vampire coming after her, either to further his ambition or because he had lost control. There would be a lot of blood flowing in the ballroom, and accidents were known to happen. After she passed through the ballroom doors, the guards shut them behind her. She walked quickly, hoping not to hear any screaming as dinner was served behind her. Her heartbeat didn't slow down until she had locked and bolted the library doors behind her. The outside of the doors were clad in silver to protect the literary treasures inside. The only way to open them was to have the single key which was presently located in William's pocket.

She'd taken over a corner of the library by the windows, with her own little desk filled with art supplies, but tonight she was too keyed up to draw. She kicked off her shoes and settled down on the comfiest couch to read. Her current project was "The Werewolf and Fairy Wars: A History in Six Volumes," an opus covering 1500 years of intermittent conflict between all three groups of supernatural creatures, from a vampire perspective. She was on Volume 3, which covered the near genocide of the fairy people and the resulting alliance between vampire and fairy. It was all rather a downer, but she wanted badly to understand better this world she'd fallen into.

Just as she began dozing under a knit blanket, and long before dawn, she heard something at the door. The tumblers in the lock were turning. The bolt lid back. Her heart skipped a beat. She pulled out both her rosary and her knife, knowing full well how hopeless she was hand-to-hand but determined not to go down without a fight. She was trying to use her gift to peek through the door when it opened.

King Ilyn raised an eyebrow when he saw November standing shoeless next to the couch, knife in hand. He raised his own hands above his head, saying, "My wallet's in my back pocket. Just please don't hurt me." November responded by dropping her weapons back in her purse and throwing a pillow at his head. He caught the pillow without using his hands and placed it gently back on the sofa.

"You're lucky the crossbow didn't fit in my bag," she said, trying to steady her breathing. "Also, making fun of little girls isn't very regal. What are you doing down here? And how did you get in the door?" she asked, belatedly adding, "Your grace," as she realized how familiar she was acting.

His lips twitched. "As I mentioned, public feeding does not interest me. You, however, do interest me. Besides, they will have much more fun without my supervision. I am not exactly known as the life of the party. And picking an old-fashioned lock is rather trivial for a telekinetic. I simply reach out and move the tumblers." He sat down at the opposite end of the couch and snatched a New Yorker from the rack across the room. "May I join you?" he asked after he was already seated with his legs crossed, magazine dropping neatly out of the air into his lap.

"Of course," she answered, a bit amused, to her surprise. She wondered if he would have left had she refused his company. She felt safer with him around, to be honest. The thought of the vampire orgy likely taking place upstairs was rather creeping her out.

November settled back down with her book, curling up once again under her blanket. She alternated pretending to read with staring at her vampire companion, trying to figure him out but lacking enough information to do so. She continued doing this until she realized that he was doing the same thing.

She found the courage to ask, "Is there something you, um, wanted to talk about?"

"I don't understand you," he replied quickly, as though dashing at a door that had finally opened. "You seem so happy most of the time. You laugh so often. I can hear you from anywhere in the house. You even seem happy around me, misunderstandings aside. In the ballroom tonight, you smiled at me whenever you caught my eye. So genuine. No one but my children smiles at me without wanting something from me, but you . . ." He threw up his hands in perplexity. "I am a 2500 year old vampire who you believe is going to end your life by drinking your blood and forcing you to drink his in return. You have been pressed into service for my cause and my house. Yet you seem neither bitter nor frightened nor angry with me, at least not about that."

"Sometimes I am all those things," November admitted. "I just let it pass through me. I let it fall away without grabbing hold of it. That's the only way I've been able to function. It's the idea of being helpless and in pain that I'm really afraid of, I think, more than the fact that I'm going to die young. I spent my whole childhood crazy from fear and from the non-stop visions I couldn't control. Eventually I found a way through it, and I chose to make happiness where I can, and to not hold grudges." November shrugged, thinking briefly of the many things she'd had to forgive.

"I just don't see the point in being miserable over a fate I can likely do nothing about. It helps that in the vision, none of you seem happy about my death. You look like you're burying a family member. It also looks like you won't have much of a choice, as far as ending my life goes. I mean, there's an awful lot blood on my dress. I must get shot or stabbed or something first." She paused, shivering slightly.

"Coming here was not exactly my idea, but quite honestly, it's the best home I've ever had. And since I've come here, my gift seems to have more of a purpose, and it seems that perhaps my death when it comes won't be for nothing, like most people's. I've watched so many people die for nothing. And all alone. At least I won't be alone when I die."

Ilyn's eyes looked sad for a moment. "I never thought to make another vampire. And I am not in the habit of killing such young humans. Not recently, anyway. Do you want to be a vampire?" he asked.

"Not really. I'm afraid of becoming a predator, of what I'll be like after, of what I might do. At the same time, the idea of being strong certainly has its appeal. But what I want has never made much difference in how things turn out, anyway. Why would it this time?" she said. "Did your children want to be vampires? Did you?" she ventured.

"I would have died otherwise, slowly and very painfully. So, yes, I chose this life when Marisha offered it to me. I already loved her. I was her favorite human, you see. She was a young vampire, perhaps a century old, and she was frightened that she would botch the process, I remember. William was too delirious to give permission or to object when I turned him. When we found him, he'd been lying on the battlefield for hours, dying of his injuries, too weak to cry for help and too strong to pass over. Now, Savita . . . she would have preferred a true death at the time, but she was too valuable. Like you, she was far too special to waste, and she had had such a difficult human life that she would have welcomed the release of death. In time, she was glad for the chance for a second, happier life, or so she tells me. But it took quite some time." He smiled sadly. He seemed very fond of his daughter.

"Luka wanted it, badly. He wanted the strength. That should have been a warning, but Marisha was too softhearted to see it, and I dismissed it. I thought the love and loyalty would come after she turned him. It often does, as the years go by. He did love her, I suppose. But never me." He shook his head, thinking of his late wife and their wayward son. "A soft-hearted vampire . . . it must sound rather unbelievable to you."

"Not really. No one is all one thing or all another." Since Ilyn seemed to be in an answering mood, she combed her mind for more questions. "Did you have children?" she asked. "When you were human, I mean?"

"I had a son. He died of fever before his third birthday. My wife died the next day. I was 19 years old."

"I'm so sorry. How sad," she said softly, reaching out a hand to touch his arm. He looked down at her hand in surprise, and she pulled it back.

"Yes, it was sad. Life was brutal and short then," he said. "So many dangers. So little medicine or protection. We were helpless in the face of disease, injury, war, disaster of all kinds. So I do sympathize with you, little one, in your fear of being helpless. I may be the most powerful vampire on the continent, but I know full well how that feels."

He turned back to his reading, so November followed suit. They remained in companionable silence until dawn, when the king retired to the crypt and the human collapsed in her bed, covered with a blanket of warm sunlight.

Chapter 10

Ilyn stops shoveling dirt and looks down at the girl in the ground, peppered with clods of earth. He tosses the shovel to William and jumps into the grave. "Bury us," he barks. William opens his mouth to question him. His father cuts him off. "I don't want her to wake up alone in the ground. It's frightening."

"We did, and we survived," William argues. "At your age, you'll be awake down there for hours before she comes around."

"Do it," comes the command as Ilyn curls up next to the corpse. So his son does.

November awoke on Christmas afternoon to find herself in a darkened room with a vampire king sitting at her desk, leafing through a binder of her drawings whilst smoking a pipe. He turned at the rustle of her sheets as she sat up. "Merry Christmas," he said matter-of-factly, then returned his attention to the binder. The only light in the room was her desk lamp. Her shutters, she now observed, were indeed light-tight.

She stared at him for an incredulous moment before throwing up her hands in resignation and returning his Christmas wishes. "Merry Christmas. May I ask what you are doing in here, your grace?"

"I wanted to examine your older work to see if anything useful jumped out at me. Savu only showed me the binder about your burial, and your recent work on the bombings," he replied after taking a pull from his pipe. "Also, I was bored," he admitted with a shrug. "The plight of the elderly vampire. We only need a few hours rest." She wanted to be irritated at his intrusion but found this admission charming in spite of herself.

"That's fine, but I would have appreciated your asking my permission. It's kind of personal. I've never shown most of those drawings to anyone."

"But you were asleep," he replied logically. "I did not wish to disturb you. Besides, I'd forgotten how soothing it is, the sound of a sleeping human breathing." So his redhead didn't sleep with him, apparently. She supposed he wasn't paying her to sleep.

"Well, that's, um, thoughtful, I guess. Next time something like this comes up, please ask."

"As you wish," he said with a nod.

She watched him for a moment, smelling the smoke. She'd always much preferred the smell of pipes to cigarettes, though she knew they were just as bad for you. "Why do you smoke a pipe? Tobacco has no effect on vampires, does it?"

"Certainly not. I began shortly after crossing the Atlantic centuries ago, in order to blend in more easily. I came to like the smell, the ritual of it. Does it bother you?" he asked solicitously.

"No, actually. My grandmother smoked a pipe, so I find the smell kind of comforting. And it's not as though either of us needs to worry about the long-term health effects," she replied with a smile and a little shrug. There were some advantages to being doomed.

"Your grandmother?" he asked, sounding amused. "I haven't seen a woman smoking a pipe in many years."

"She was a little eccentric," November answered. "To say the least. So, have you found anything interesting in my binders?"

"Just this, so far," he said, pulling out a sketch in colored pencil of a lake surrounded by snow-capped mountains.

"Oh, my lake. I see that one a lot when I'm travelling, if I'm gazing out the window. I've never known the actual location. Usually I see it from far away, like that drawing. I've had a couple of dreams from on the ground, though, in some kind of busy marketplace near the water. I could look up and see the mountains. I always thought it was funny to see all that snow but the lake never frozen over." She smiled, remembering the smell of spices and the sight of silk and camels. It was definitely one of her more pleasant recurring visions.

"The lake is called Issyk Kul. It is located in present-day Kyrgyzstan. There was a city there, on the trade route between east and west. It was important at one time. It is now buried in the water. I was born there."

"No way!" she blurted out.

"I assure you I am not mistaken," he said a little severely.

"Of course I believe you! I'm just surprised. I've been seeing that place since I was a little girl. I had no idea it was connected to any of you. I wonder what else I've seen about all of you without even knowing. Have you ever gone back there?" Her mind was a bit blown.

"No, never. I fled as a young man, when I was still living. Too many painful memories there, I fear," he said quietly. "It's quite remarkable," he commented after examining the drawing again. "Your second sight is exceptional, November. And your sketches aren't bad, either. Imagine what you might be able to do with centuries to practice, and with a vampire's strength!"

November looked down uncomfortably. She disliked the idea of being coveted as a tool or a weapon, leery of her own power.

"In the old days, a seer like you would live in a temple, surrounded by priests whose job was to care for you and to try to interpret your prophesies. People would flock to you to ask for direction, shower you with gifts. You would have been revered," he added.

"It does sound more glamorous than being a carnival fortune teller," she replied self-deprecatingly.

He looked at the shelf full of binders. "You've managed to accumulate all these visions on your own. I assume you only kept the ones that you guessed might be meaningful?" She nodded. "If only we knew what they all meant!"

"Well, feel free to look through them all." She paused awkwardly before saying, "I should bathe and get dressed."

The king failed to take the hint, simply replying, "Of course. Feel free to do so," before turning back to the desk. November rolled her eyes behind his back.

She gathered up a change of clothes and locked herself in the bathroom, trying not to grumble incredulously under her breath. She couldn't quite believe that she was standing in the shower while a vampire king sat in her bedroom leafing through her childhood drawings as though they would hold some secret wisdom of the ages. It was without a doubt the oddest Christmas day she had ever experienced.

When she emerged, Ilyn still sat unmoving at her desk. When she returned from the kitchen with her breakfast, still he remained. She read quietly so as not to disturb him. She sketched a few scenes from visions she'd had the previous day and filed them neatly away. She listened to music with her headphones, though she supposed he could still hear the music. He finally looked up toward the shuttered windows and said, "Sunset. I should head to the courtroom."

226

"You can sense that?" she asked. Ben's trial was beginning tonight. She didn't want to think about it.

"The ones who cannot don't survive long," he replied. "May I return tomorrow to continue this work?" he asked formally, carefully honoring her request.

"Of course. Try not to wake me up," she said jokingly, hoping for a smile, but, she was, alas, disappointed. The king bowed chivalrously and zoomed out the door.

Ben's trial occupied the next two nights. As a human, November was not permitted to attend, which was both incredibly irritating and a relief. She got all the details from Zinnia, of course. The king presided. Amy was relentless for the prosecution. Josue made a valiant effort, but Ben was not terribly helpful in mounting a defense. Ben refused to testify or to call any witnesses. Ilyn handed down the verdict of death by stake, disappointing those who had hoped for burning or the guillotine for a little excitement. The execution was scheduled for New Year's Day.

November did her best to avoid the visitors, especially Lilith. She kept to her room for the most part. She only ventured downstairs while the sun was shining, stocking up on a night's worth of food and replenishing her stack of books. She was taking a break from reading about the wars after coming to some quite disturbing passages featuring the king, who apparently at one time had rather a reputation for butchery and quite the penchant for decapitation. She had difficulty reconciling those images with the man she woke each afternoon to find sitting at her desk, too large for her chair, silently smoking a pipe and poring over her work.

After the king would depart, she spent a lot of time alone. Most everyone was busy keeping the court people entertained, preparing for the next party, or working on war plans, strategizing about how to get sufficient support from other lords to go after Luka.

Her trips to the dungeon to see Ben were now impossible with so many strange vampires in the crypt. She had to settle for sending him a farewell note via Pine. Zinnia was spending a lot of time helping Rose prepare for New Year's Eve and taking the visiting fairies around during the day, but she tried to stop by each evening to give her friend some company and update her on the gossip. She felt a little trapped in her room, and she eagerly anticipated things getting back to normal when the court left, but she found herself looking forward to seeing the king each day. Strangeness aside, it was probably the most pleasant holiday season she'd had since her grandmother had passed.

A steaming lake surrounded by white-capped mountains. Merchants. Plague. A policeman dies in the street. Marisha. Masks. A shining blade with a wooden inlay. Ilyn with a dozen wounds, writhing in the dirt. Zinnia throws a flower in a grave. A fairy child hides. Pine with an arrow through his chest. Savita covered in dirt, on her knees, screaming, screaming. A hundred wolf heads on a hundred pikes turn into the heads of men. A tiny body is tossed on a pyre. William and Savita and Luka curl up together in the hold of a ship, hiding from the light. Julia screams as she dies. Luka gives a bundle to a woman without a face. A shepherd stands in a clearing, guarding his sheep. Three of the sheep peel off their coats to reveal wolves beneath. They approach the shepherd, sneaking up behind him as he looks for enemies outside the flock. Their eyes glow. Their fangs drip with saliva. They make no sound as they prepare to pounce.

She woke thrashing in her tangled sheets, whimpering, Ilyn and Pine looking down on her with concern. It was the third day of Christmas. As they helped her sit up, she looked around in

228

confusion. The vision had been such a mish-mash that she was having difficulty orienting back to the present.

"Are you alright, little one?" the king asked solicitously. She looked at him blankly, not certain he was real. She reached out a hand and touched him on the tip of his nose with one finger like a curious toddler. Ilyn turned to Pine with a raised eyebrow.

"You might have to give her a minute, your grace. She gets pretty disoriented after the really bad ones. It can take a while before she starts making sense," Pine explained. November started to shiver as her sweat evaporated. Pine pulled out a clean blanket from the closet and wrapped her in it. As her bodyguard, it was hardly the first time he'd had to play the priest to her oracle. She began to rock, clutching the blanket tightly around her.

Suddenly, November spoke with quiet urgency to no one in particular, in a voice not quite her own. "The wolves in sheep's clothing. They strike at the shepherd. One at his heel. One at his heart. One at his throat. Three. Three. Three wolves in sheep's clothing."

She stopped rocking and looked up, her eyes finally in focus. She saw their faces: worried, puzzled, and in Ilyn's case, fascinated. "Well, that one was a little wild," she finally said with a weak smile. "I'm okay now, I think," she added, pulling away a bit from the two men sitting on her bed. She appreciated their care, but she still wasn't used to having help like that, and she was extremely self-conscious about being seen in such a state.

"What do you need?" Ilyn asked her. She smiled, genuinely surprised and touched. She had been certain he had been about to say, "What did you see?"

"Breakfast and a bath, then a paper and pencil," she answered.

"I'll go get you something from the kitchen," the king said, jumping up to leave.

"That's really not necessary, your grace. I'll run down there in a few minutes," she replied. She didn't want him to go to the trouble. She couldn't even imagine him going to the trouble. She was also a bit concerned that he would come back with a bowl of flour or something. After all, he hadn't eaten anything but blood since before Christ was born.

"No trouble. And don't worry, I've been paying attention. I'll get you what you always have." And with that, he was out the door.

She exchanged incredulous looks with Pine. "Did the king seriously just go to fetch my yogurt and granola?"

"Yep. Don't see that every day." He shook his head. "I'll be outside if you need me?" She nodded, and he resumed his perch in the hallway while she took a very long, very hot shower. By the time she dressed and emerged, the king was back at her desk, and her breakfast was laid out on a tray on her bed. There was also a tall beer mug half-full of blood on the desk. November wondered what had happened to the redhead.

"Thank you," she said.

"You're welcome," he replied. Rather than returning his attention to the desk as usual, he studied her as she ate. She tried to ignore him with not very much success. "Does that happen to you a lot? Such strong, disturbing visions in your sleep?" he asked.

She swallowed before replying, "All the time."

"That must be difficult. Do you remember them when you wake?"

230

"It's awful. For years I was afraid to go to sleep. I'm used to it now, though. I can usually shake it off. And yes, I remember every detail of every vision, not that they always make any sense." She didn't mention the blissful, dreamless sleep that only vampire bites could provide her. She tried to make herself forget that it was an option, but every night as she laid her head on the pillow, she thought about it with longing. "This one was a little worse than usual."

"How so?" he asked, trying not to sound too interested.

"It was such a jumble. Disparate visions bleeding into one another. Some I've already seen, cut into new ones. I couldn't make any sense of it, but I had this sense that I needed to. There was something frantic and scary about it. It's going to take some work to try to tease everything apart. And then there was that weird thing with the wolf-sheep."

"You said there were three of them and that they would strike the shepherd. Any idea what that means?" All his attention was focused on her as though she was the most important person in the world. It was a little overwhelming.

She began thinking out loud. "The shepherd is the leader and protector, right? You're a king, which is similar. If you're the shepherd, maybe there are three traitors among your people?"

"Vampires don't usually think of themselves as the sheep. We're the predators, and humans are the poorly guarded lambs," he replied. "But your interpretation does make some sense. Have you ever seen that image before?"

"I've seen sheep, scattered and bleeding. Last month, some time. It should be in the newest binder," she replied. The king found it and flipped through, holding up the page for her to see. "That's the one. Maybe the sheep are humans, and the three wolves represent the three kinds of supernatural creatures?"

"Interesting . . ." He looked toward the shuttered window. "What else did you see?"

She thought back. "You, wounded. A knife. The late queen. Luka giving someone a package. Willow, when she was little. Merchants with the plague. A funeral for a child. Zinnia throwing a flower in my grave. Savita and Lord William and Luka hiding in a ship. My dad, dying in the street. I think that's it."

He raised his eyebrows. "Well, that is quite a lot. We must discuss this more later. William and I have a great deal of work to do this evening." He drained his mug and rose to leave.

"Thank you for taking care of me before you asked about what I saw," she blurted out as he moved toward the door.

"It was rather the least I could do," he replied. And then he smiled a real smile, the first she had ever seen on him. It changed his whole face. Millennia of life's sorrows fell away for a split second. And then it was gone, and so was he.

"Oh," she said, jumping up. "You left your pipe." He was already long gone, however, so she walked out into the hallway. She held it up to Pine. "Should we go down and return it?"

"Why not? I could stretch my legs," he replied.

"Sorry I'm so boring to guard," she said as they walked together.

"Boring is a lot better than the alternative," he answered with a grin. "His grace'll probably be in Lord William's office, since he already ate."

"Why is it 'his grace' instead of 'his majesty,' by the way?"

232

"Apparently the whole 'majesty' thing is a pretty recent innovation. I think the Tudors made it popular or something. He thinks it's pretentious."

"The nouveau riche," she replied, amused.

"Vampires and fairies can be very reluctant to change traditions, in case you hadn't noticed. Plus, I think he got used to 'your grace' back when he was a bishop."

"A bishop? Really?"

"Yep. Then a cardinal. Allegedly came this close to getting elected pope." Pine held his fingers an inch apart.

While crossing the foyer to the office wing, the pair looked up from their conversation and into the highly unpleasant face of Lilith. The Grocer's eyes fell upon the pipe in November's hand. Pine quickly stepped between them as Lilith's fangs dropped. The vampire made a visible effort to regain control of herself, but there was no way to hide the murderous rage in her eyes.

November forced herself to stand her ground and not look away. "Excuse me, ma'am, do you know where I might find his grace so I could return this? He seems to have misplaced it." Her voice was respectful and sickly sweet, betraying not an iota of her fear. She smiled, all innocence. This, of course, only made the vampire angrier.

They were spared an escalating confrontation by the timely arrival of the monarch in question. With the look of an absent-minded professor, he wandered into the foyer. "Ah, November, dear, thank you. It seems I have too much on my mind to keep track of my possessions." He took the pipe and kissed her on the top of her head. Only then did he seem to notice the presence of his most senior servant. "All going smoothly, Lil?"

Her face rearranged itself. "Of course, your grace," she replied with a smile.

"Come with me, I need you to help me arrange some conference calls . . ." And with that, the vampires disappeared into the office wing.

November took a deep breath and tried to settle herself. "That woman really hates me."

"Seems to," Pine concurred, leading her back toward the residence. "You're wise to try to stay away from her."

"What did I do to provoke her?"

"With her, I doubt it takes much. You are important. You have captured the king's interest, and, evidently, his affection. You are the first to do so in centuries: vampire, fairy, or human. His isolation is part of what keeps her powerful, and she feels that the rise of someone new threatens her. If she were smart, she'd seize upon you, endear herself to you and co-opt you for her own purposes. But she is not as smart as she thinks she is." He shook his head. "That one will not go down easily, but sooner or later, the king will see her for what she is. She will take people down with her, too, mark my words."

Guests for the New Year's Eve party began arriving in town, in numbers far too large for even Lord William's domicile. Several luxury hotels in the area were owned by fairies or vampires, and they were soon packed with out-of-state lords and their entourages. Rose was in a tizzy, and even November was drafted to assist.

November then passed a lovely afternoon visiting with Birch, Zinnia, and her mother in the garden. Lady Amandier was as cheerful as her daughter, if quite a lot more level-headed. She was a staunch ally to William and Ilyn, asking Birch numerous questions about the latest developments before heading off with the rest of the fairies to feed before the celebration began.

Getting ready for the ball was certainly more fun with Zinnia around. They helped each other with curling irons and eye liner and zippers, and both came out looking like princesses. November, true to her nature, was dressed more modestly than her harder-partying friend. All she showed off was collarbone. Even her arms were mostly covered by her opera-length gloves, and only a few scant inches of back were revealed by cutouts.

Thankfully, there would be no grand entrance with the king this evening. His grace was greeting dignitaries in the foyer as they arrived and would sneak into the party after things were in full swing. Pine said that word about the king's claim on her had been spread, so she should have no problem with unwanted advances from the out-of-towners.

The ballroom was not large enough to contain this party, so it was to be an outdoor affair. The girls gasped as they peeked out a picture window when Pine escorted them downstairs. The grounds had been transformed into a wonderland. The trees were lit beautifully. Fountains glowed in Technicolor with some fairy magic no one could seem to explain. Every flower from every season was in bloom. A half dozen dance floors were scattered about, with discreet speakers bringing music to every nook and cranny. And November had been assured that the fairies had ways to keep the temperature balmy for the sake of the human "guests." Additionally, rumor had it that there would be some extremely elegant porta-potties as well as exquisitely catered refreshments for the human element. She hoped that she would be able to handle the crowd.

"My mom did pretty good, huh?" Pine commented. November grinned and nodded.

Zinnia stuck by her friend for awhile until the November told her she was free to give in to her obvious urge to hit the dance floor. The king and his children were circulating, talking up the various lords.

Lady Esther decided to hang out with November the wallflower, confined as she was to her wheelchair. November found her gossip and cutting observations about everyone both informative and hilarious, and she was thoroughly enjoying watching the dancing and listening to the music. The fairy DJ, who was evidently quite famous in EDM circles, gave the party enormous energy.

Zinnia managed to coax her onto the dance floor a few times, and November enjoyed it in spite of herself. She danced awkwardly with Zinnia and Pine, who stared aggressively at every vampire or fairy that approached her.

At one point, Savita came to fetch her, telling her mysteriously that there was someone who very much wanted to make her acquaintance. November found herself meeting Milton, Lord of Texas, who was determined to express his gratitude for her instrumental role in preventing the planned attack against him. He was not quite what November had expected for a Texas vampire. Short, portly, and incredibly nerdy would be putting it charitably. Still, it was a pleasant enough conversation, and it was always nice to be appreciated.

She caught Savita examining her closely on the walk back to the terrace. "Is something wrong?" November asked. Savita just shook her head.

Moments later, they ran into the king, who was hiding behind some shrubbery smoking his pipe. He looked terribly handsome in his obviously expensive tuxedo, a different one than he'd worn Christmas Eve. She wondered idly how many of them he had.

Savita made a discreet exit. "No dancing, sir?" November asked him, smiling.

"Perhaps if they were playing actual music," he replied a bit haughtily.

"Yeah, the club music is not exactly my scene, either," she admitted. "The fairies seem to like it. I'm sure you could ask them to play something else, being the monarch and all," she teased.

"Yes, but why ruin their fun? You look lovely, by the way," he commented. "Fairy necklace?"

"Thanks. Yes, Zinnia made it for me, for my birthday."

"Clever girl, that one."

They were then interrupted, of course, by Lilith, with one of the lords in tow. November and Pine made a quick escape before Lilith's eyes could burn holes in their heads.

Just before the countdown to midnight, November made a quick trip to the restroom. As she emerged, she saw the fangs beginning to come out as the vampires prepared to feast, so she began to move quickly toward the house without bothering to put her gloves back on. She caught a glimpse of William near a pretty blonde. Ilyn stood close to his redhead, willing to feed in public tonight, apparently. November swallowed her unexpected jealousy.

As she hurried along with Pine, one of the enthralled humans tripped in front of them. November reached out her bare hands to catch the girl and fell into a vision as soon as they touched. *A line of dressed-up humans, enthralled into zombies. Lilith with a tray of syringes, injecting each one, most not aware enough to even wince. One protests feebly. Lilith reassures her in her most controlling voice, "Hush now, it's just colloidal silver. It's good for you." The girl acquiesces with no further fuss.*

November awoke on the ground, leaping up to scream as loudly as she could, "Silver! Don't feed! They're poisoned with silver!"

Even as she opened her mouth, some of the more impatient vampires were already falling to the ground, clawing at their throats. She caught a glimpse of Amy writhing in the grass, Josue looking frantic by her side. Greg was spitting blood out onto the ground, smoke coming out of his mouth, but he did not fall. It seemed he had heard the warning just in time. Those who had not yet tasted blood shoved their human companions away. Most of the humans were too enthralled to realize that something was wrong, but a few had the presence of mind to begin screaming.

Just after November had finished uttering the last word, Lilith flew at her with impossible speed from the other side of the garden, knife in hand. November froze, eyes wide. Pine yanked her to the ground as an unseen force grabbed Lilith and tossed her in the air, an instant after the knife had left her hand.

Ilyn grabbed the dagger from where it had lodged in the grass and examined it, and a profound sadness came over his face for a moment. The wind knocked out of her, November lay stunned on the ground, her arm stinging. Zinnia appeared at her side and squeezed her hand, asking if she was alright. November managed a nod.

"Silence!" Ilyn ordered as he looked up at his former confidante dangling in the air. The crowd hushed, the only noise the cries of pain continuing to issue from the poisoned. He looked for November, his eyes softening with relief when he saw she was unharmed. When his gaze moved on, his rage grew as he surveyed the damage. Among them were scattered at least a dozen injured vampires, one already turned to a pile of ash. Those who still lived were in obvious agony. Rose had already dashed into the house and was returning with bags of clean blood. She distributed it to those caring for the afflicted. Those not busy dying or attending the suffering gathered around their king.

"Humans, sleep," Ilyn cried. The procured women all fell to the ground as one.

Lilith didn't even try to hide her guilt. "You worthless animal," she screamed at November. "You're ruining everything! For years I've waited for this chance –" Ilyn used his gift to clamp her mouth shut.

"Why?" Ilyn asked Lilith in a voice that made November shudder. His fangs glinted in the light of the trees. His face was feral. This man looked like the creature who had beheaded a thousand werewolves in one night all those centuries ago. This man bore no resemblance to the absent-minded professor who'd sat at her desk.

"He will make me a queen!" she cried pathetically as Ilyn released her jaw.

"As I would not? I assume you refer to Luka," the king said evenly. "This is his knife, is it not? My wife gave it to him in her will. Fairy forged. It's quite unique. Unmistakable." He showed it to the crowd, who murmured with anger and agreement. The mob was terrifying to behold, all fangs and rage barely held in check.
"He put you up to putting silver in their blood? To poison us all?"

For a moment, it seemed that Lilith had regained control of herself and would say no more, but her thwarted fury and the certain knowledge of her impending doom loosened her tongue. "Yes, Luka! He will be king. I once thought you were a great leader, but you are weak. He will set us free to reign over the animals as we should. The bombings were just the beginning. Tonight I have failed, but he will not be stopped!"

"And this knife? Whose life was it meant to end? Surely not the oracle child. Luka covets her too much." He smiled: a sharp, dangerous smile. "It was for me, correct? After all, it would take an awful lot of poisoned blood to kill a vampire of my advanced years. But the silver might have weakened me enough to be vulnerable to a more conventional attack. Did you intend to stake me with it, Lilith, dear?" His tone might make one think he was amused, until one looked at his eyes.

"Of course it was for you!" she screamed in rage. "I gave you centuries, for what? To watch you let your throne slip away inch by inch? To watch you be betrayed by your own son? To watch you fawn over some stupid cow of a fortune teller?"

"I'm so sorry to be such a disappointment. I assure you I intend to do much better," he replied sardonically. The crowd laughed a bitter laugh, fully on the king's side now, whatever doubts they may have had over recent months and years. "And just what else was intended to happen tonight?" the king asked in a deceptively casual tone of voice. "You don't expect me to believe you had no plans for the fairies or the vampire survivors, do you?"

She was suddenly reticent. The king made the knife fly into the air, held it a millimeter from the traitor's face. "Have you ever felt a fairy-forged blade, Lil? Highly unpleasant, I can assure you from personal experience." The scar on Ilyn's face twitched, but he received nothing from the traitor. The blade began to spin like a drill as Ilyn asked the crowd, "Should I start with the eyes?" They cheered, eager for blood. November wanted to close her eyes and cover her ears. Thankfully, Lilith's want of courage spared November the sight of torture.

"The cars," she whispered. "Bombs in the cars."

"To be triggered how?"

"Cell phone. In my purse." At that, the vampire slumped, now defeated, never again to be feared.

At Ilyn's nod, a small army of security personnel went to begin checking the line of limousines snaking along the drive while another one of them began examining Lilith's bag. "Put her in the dungeon," he told the men who remained. Before lowering her to the ground, the king wrapped her in so much silver chain she looked like a shining mummy. She screamed ceaselessly as they carried her off. The smell of burning flesh turned November's stomach.

The crowd seemed a bit disappointed. "You'll have her blood and ash soon enough," the king assured them. "Let's see if she can be of some further use against the rebel lord of Arizona first." He locked eyes with every lord in attendance before continuing. "Despite our best efforts, it seems we will have war. We'd best be as prepared for it as possible. I see some of you have filmed this sad spectacle with your telephones. Perhaps you'd be so kind as to discreetly share your footage with those not in attendance this evening who may be unconvinced of Luka's perfidy. And please do stay here until Lord William's men determine it is safe for you to leave. If you have the skills, please assist Rose and Birch in managing the care of the injured. Otherwise, please stay out of the way."

He turned away from the crowd and walked over to November. "You saved us all, little one," he said, kneeling beside her. He smiled at her for the second time, and it again transformed him. The beast was gone, the anger and the lust for blood. For an instant, he looked young and capable of happiness. The moment passed, and the king continued looking her over, trying to reassure himself.

"I'm fine. A little dizzy is all. And there's this little scratch on my arm, but there's hardly any blood," she said, displaying the slight wound. "It does kind of hurt," she admitted, wincing.

"No," Ilyn whispered, stricken. Pine swore. Tears welled in Zinnia's eyes.

"What?" she asked, suddenly frightened. "Tell me. You're scaring me," she pleaded.

Ilyn scooped her up in his arms and started running to the house. "Zinnia," he called over his shoulder, "Find Savita and send for a fairy doctor. Tell William and Hazel to deal with the rest of this fiasco."

Her head spun and her arm burned as Ilyn carried her to her bed. "Was the knife poisoned or something? What is going on?" she asked frantically. What scared her most was the wild, desperate look in the king's eyes.

He knelt beside her and pulled out the knife. It was shining and razor sharp, with a wooden inlay down the center of the blade, rendering it both a stake and a dagger. The panic left him, replaced by the calm born of surviving many crises in his long life. He knew she needed him to be calm.

"It's not so much poisoned as . . . evil. It has to do with how it's made, the magic they use, how they make the alloy with silver, how they temper the blade . . ." He hesitated, not wanting to go into the gory details of its manufacture or its effect. "A fairy forged knife creates a wound that will only heal if a powerful fairy chooses to heal it. Otherwise, it will inevitably kill its human victim. The wooden inlay is for striking vampires in the heart, of course."

"So we have someone heal it in the morning," she replied, uncomprehending.

He looked so very sad before he hid his feelings behind his customary stoicism. "You might not last that long. And even if you do," he continued after a pause, "you might wish you hadn't. The

242

pain . . . it will get much, much worse. I myself lasted perhaps twenty minutes before I began begging to die. Fortunately, Marisha soon found me and transformed me into a vampire. The fairy had attacked me in order to hurt her, you see, and the fairy lost both his life and his weapon in return . . . Of course my wounds were more numerous as well as much deeper . . . but I was also much larger and stronger than you are." By this point, the room was filling up. William, Savita, Zinnia, Esther, and Pine had joined them.

"You should turn her. Now," William said without preamble. "Screw the law I wrote. Pay a fine. There's no way she'll make it to morning." The evening's events had put him in a ruthless mood, apparently.

"She's too young," Savita protested weakly.

"She's older than you were," came William's retort.

"And I was too young! And we all paid for that, as I recall. How many innocents died as a result? Hence, the law."

"But we can't just let her die!" cried Zinnia, trying with limited success to hold herself together.

"We aren't going to let her die," Esther said firmly.

The pain was becoming difficult to ignore, as was the distress of her friends. November tried to think rationally. The thought of becoming a vampire that night made something within her cry, *No!* "This isn't how I die," November said with quiet firmness, cutting though the argument. "It isn't supposed to happen this way. And I'm just not ready. So you're all just going to have to do your best to keep me alive until dawn. That's what? Five or six hours?"

"Most of us aren't ready when the moment comes to die," Ilyn said. "And what does it matter how it's supposed to happen?

What's wrong with sparing you suffering from this wound if you're just going to end up one of us anyway?"

"It's important somehow, my staying human a little longer. I don't know why, I just know that it is," she stated with a sudden conviction. The more she thought about it, the more convinced she was. Her other sense was fairly vibrating with the certainty. "I am sure. I wish I weren't, but I am. And I'm the psychic, so we're just going to have to go with that."

She looked each of them in the face in turn, feigning a bravery she did not feel, but knowing there was no escape. "If I am literally about to die, then go ahead and make me a vampire, but you must do your best to keep me alive until the sun comes up." Pain shot through her arm and into her chest. She pressed her lips together. "Regardless of what I might say later."

She looked up at Ilyn, wondering if he was about to overrule her, wondering if he was preparing to drain her blood and her human life away. She wasn't much afraid of that, she realized. She would be sad about it, but she trusted him. She was just afraid that to die now would be a mistake, perhaps a fatal one.

"Alright," he said, looking in her eyes and finding her resolute. "I think we have to trust your judgment."

"No!" cried William. "It's too risky. We can't afford to lose her! You must do it, or I will." Ilyn fairly growled in reply.

"It's my life, not yours. I'm more than your chess piece, *my lord*," November spat with uncharacteristic vehemence. The pain was starting to get to her. "Now I don't know how long I'll be coherent, and I'd like to get out of this dress. The men will please leave. I'd like the king and Pine to please return in 15 minutes, and the doctor, if he's here by then." She did not think William's presence would be very helpful. He looked like he was about to start smashing furniture. The men reluctantly obeyed and continued arguing audibly in the hallway.

Zinnia and Savita helped her out of her dress and into a nightgown. Esther supervised from her chair, telling them from experience how to move November without causing her additional pain. "The satin one with the buttons, please," November requested. "I don't think I can lift my arm." The wound had turned angry, her whole upper arm red and throbbing now, too heavy to move.

She struggled not to cry out as her friends dressed her, helped her to the bathroom, and got her back in bed. She leaned back against the pillows trying to catch her breath so she could tell Zinnia and Savita, "I'm not sure how long you two should stay. It's not that I don't want you to, it's just your gifts might make it hard for you when things get really bad."

Zinnia began to cry again. "But you're my best friend. I should be here."

"I know, but you're an empath, and she's a telepath, and I don't know if I can handle this if I'm worrying how it's affecting you, too." Zinnia gripped her hand. "I won't hold it against either of you, really."

"She's right," Savita said quietly. "My father and Pine will certainly stay, and Lady Esther. She won't be alone."

"You can stay for awhile, but when King Ilyn tells you to go, you should go," November managed. Speech was becoming more difficult. She laid her head down and tried to ride the pain. She noticed when the men returned and conferred with the doctor, who did not seem terribly optimistic.

She murmured that she'd like someone to take down her hairdo from the party. The pins were sticking in her scalp; this had become intolerable all of a sudden. To her surprise, it was Ilyn who began gently disentangling her hair, combing it smooth with his fingers. It was very soothing.

She opened her eyes when the doctor asked for permission to put in an IV for hydration. She nodded agreement and offered her arm. "No sedatives, please," she whispered. "Bad visions from those. I'm already getting intrusion," she added, looking fixedly at an empty corner of the room.

"Intrusion?" asked the king.

"That's what I call it, when images from visions start mingling with the present and I can't really tell the difference between what's real and what isn't. There's somebody standing in the corner. A little kid." He had the king's mouth. Her voice was oddly affectless, and she tore her eyes away from the specter.

Dr. Cedar's eyes widened. "Alright, then, no sedatives. I doubt they'd do much anyway, and human painkillers would have no effect, I'm afraid," he replied.

Ilyn pulled a chair up to the bed. She looked at him and managed a faltering smile. "You'll stay? The whole time?" He nodded and took her hand. "Please don't leave me alone," she begged, suddenly desperately afraid.

"Of course not. I'll stay," he promised. "I'd stay forever." She looked at him, confused, uncertain whether she'd heard him correctly, until she was overtaken by a wave of pain that arched her back and wrung a cry from her throat.

"Here we go," Pine said, stone-faced and knuckles clenched to white.

Chapter 11

"It's all my fault," came Pine's voice, despairing. "If I had just been a little faster. . ."

"Nonsense. I kept that viper in my nest for 200 years. Hazel tried to warn me, as did my children, and I wouldn't listen. The blame is mine," Ilyn replied, determined to take all the responsibility for November's injury.

"It was my job to keep her safe. She trusted me. Lord William trusted me."

Ilyn studied the young fairy sitting vigil with him. "Do you love her?" he asked in a deliberately casual tone, noticing how hard Pine seemed to be taking this turn of events.

Pine raised his eyebrows. "Yes, but not the way you mean, sir. I'm gay."

"Ah. Do you have someone?" The king seemed uncharacteristically talkative and curious about matters of the heart that evening.

"I did. He died a few years ago. Old age. We had nearly 50 happy years together. I have the gift of illusion, so his family and friends thought I aged with him."

"What about him? Did he knew what you are?" Ilyn sounded a bit scandalized.

"Yes. I broke the law," Pine admitted. "He was my mate. I wasn't going to lie to him his whole life, our whole life together."

"You aren't the first to break that law, I suppose." He shrugged before adding, "You won't be the last. I'm sorry for your loss, truly. You still wear the ring?"

Pine nodded, looking down at the scuffed gold band on his left hand. "I can't seem to manage to stop wearing it."

"Neither can I. And it's been centuries." The king shook his head. "Sometimes I think it's easier for us vampires. We can make the humans we love immortal, so we can have more time. But then they can still die, and it isn't any easier for having had more years with them."

"Life always contains loss. I believe in finding happiness where I can, for however long it lasts," the younger man replied philosophically.

"November said almost the same thing to me the other day."

"Maybe that's one reason the two of us get along so well." The men lapsed into silence. Pine screwed up his nerve and asked his king, "Do *you* love her?"

He looked sharply at the much younger man. "I don't believe that I'm capable of feeling . . . for a human . . . I know her suffering grieves me. I know I enjoy her company, which is more than I can say for anyone else since my wife died. I know her gift is remarkable. But how do I compare this child to a wife I loved for thousands of years?" Ilyn looked down at November, who looked so very small and fragile as she whimpered and trembled, insensible, in his lap.

"You don't. You can't. It isn't fair to either of them." Pine managed a half-smile as he added, "If you do pursue her, please do try not to hurt her, your grace. I'd hate to have to take a swing at you. It was all I could do not to break Lord William's nose for leading her on."

"You and me, both," Lady Esther interjected, looking up briefly from her high-speed knitting. It was a miracle the yarn didn't catch fire.

"I shall take care. Your grandmother would be irritated if I had to kill you for raising your hand to me. That would be most inconvenient." The king closed his eyes for a moment. "I should probably just leave her alone, for her sake. She'd be so much better off if we'd never found her."

"Someone else would have found her, wanted to use her. Better us than Luka or the wolves," Esther said. The king knew she was correct, but it was a difficult truth to believe as they watched the innocent seer suffer for other people's sins. They lapsed into silence.

The girl in question heard very little of this conversation. November had been trapped in agony for hours now. When she wasn't screaming, she was murmuring incoherently in foreign tongues or keening like an animal caught in a trap. She gripped Ilyn's hand like a vice even as her strength waned. The king now held her in his arms as though she were a sick child, her feverish head leaning on his chest when she curled into a ball, or else cradled in his palm when she arched her back in pain. She seemed somewhat more comfortable with him than lying in her bed, though it was hard to tell for certain. She was by then unable to speak coherently, so they had been spared her pleas for mercy, at least, after the first hour had passed. The hardest part for Pine had been the ten minutes she'd spent calling out desperately for her mother.

Needing something to do, Ilyn sang her songs he'd thought he'd forgotten: some from his human life, some he'd learned later. Pine and Esther found it quite touching. Ilyn was not exactly known for gently crooning lullabies. It helped pass the time, and drown out the moaning, and his voice seemed to give November some comfort.

That's what he told himself, anyway, to justify this unseemly gentleness.

Later, she would struggle to describe the visions she'd seen in the throes of her delirium. The one mercy that night was that she'd be able to remember so little of it. She was accustomed to recalling her visions in precise, excruciating detail. She was unable to forget anything from her real life, either. But that night would stay with her only in fragments of memory, flashes of vision, a brief period of convalescence, and the memory of the kindness of those who had cared for her. She would remember the pain not at all.

Her temperature was starting to climb again. Dr. Cedar pumped her full of useless fever medication and saline solution to prevent dehydration. Ilyn held cold, wet cloths to her head and neck, to little avail. She was a furnace. Ilyn gazed down at her dark hair now soaked with sweat, then looked mutely at the doctor. Cedar shrugged helplessly. "I've given her everything I have, and we're keeping her from getting dehydrated. We've only got the last ditch, old-school remedies now if the fever gets any higher: shaving her hair, cold baths. She's already at 104. Much higher, and we have the risk of brain damage."

This was sadly all too familiar to the king, who'd watched many die of fever over his long lifetime, including his human wife and child. He told himself that it didn't matter, that when she started to fail, he could simply make her a vampire. He told himself that it would be better that way, that she would be stronger, that she could start her new life, that the two of them would be family then, and on a bit more equal footing. Nevertheless, he knew that he wasn't any more ready to kill her than she was ready to die and rise again. He wasn't sure why, but he knew it to be true.

"You'd best send down for some blood for me and Esther," Ilyn requested at some point, his fangs half showing. "I am finding it difficult to be hungry this close to her," he admitted matter-of-factly, his teeth just inches from her neck, his cheek resting on her hair.

After eating, he again stroked her face with the cold cloth, battling indecision. "We'd better cut her hair now, before she starts seizing," he said. "It'll be easier now than trying to do it if she's thrashing. We might hurt her. And send Willow down for enough ice for the bath." Willow was keeping watch in the hallway.

"Such a shame," Esther said sadly as they plugged in the clippers. "She has such lovely hair."

"It'll grow back," Ilyn said. "If she lives." He stroked her hair one last time before he began. "But yes, it is sad." And November's long, black tresses fell to the floor. She took no notice at all. Ilyn tried not to think of his human wife. Nadi's red hair had never had the chance to grow back. He could still see her long braids in a pile on the dirt floor.

Ilyn proved prescient. November's febrile seizures began when her fever spiked ten minutes later. Into the ice water they went together, Ilyn holding November carefully, keeping as much of her immersed as possible while ensuring her head stayed above the water. It would have looked funny if it hadn't been so deadly serious: the ancient and dignified king in the bath in his tuxedo pants and shirt, the jacket and tie long since discarded, the girl in a nightgown splashing water up his nose. Pine occupied himself with refreshing the ice as it melted. "She hates being cold," Pine commented morosely. She wasn't crying out anymore. The most she could mange now was the occasional whimper, which was somehow more frightening. Esther watched quietly, able to do little but hope for the girl who had tried to help her from afar.

This is how they passed the rest of the night, monitoring her pulse and temperature all the time, hoping against hope for dawn to come. "I've never wished so hard for sunup," Esther muttered.

"It's almost here," Pine said. "Willow's right outside. I'll send her down to get my grandmother."

"And you must go to ground, Esther," the king admonished. "I don't want you to jeopardize your recovery trying to stay awake past dawn."

"I know, I know," she replied to her father-in-law. "I just want to know that she's alright."

"You'll know. You'll know when you hear the screaming," Pine said grimly. "It's going to be a rough road back from the brink."

With that, Esther took one last look at the girl and wheeled herself to the elevator. Pine carefully lifted November out of the bathtub and carried her back to her bed, where Ilyn wrapped her in a dry blanket, partly for modesty's sake, as her soaking wet nightgown had become transparent. Fairies and vampires didn't much care about nudity, but he suspected November wouldn't want to exhibit herself to a crowd.

Ilyn took no notice of his own wet clothes. He knelt by November's side and paid attention only to the approaching dawn and to her faltering breath and pulse, willing them to continue long enough to reach daylight. Hazel rushed in, joining Pine, Ilyn, and Cedar. Willow and Zinnia waited anxiously in the hallway. The other vampires waited uneasily in the crypt.

Finally, light's first blush arrived, and Hazel placed her millennia-old mahogany hands on the human girl, who even near death was again clinging to Ilyn's hand.

November said later that the heat of the fever had been nothing compared to the fire that had burned through her as life poured back into her dying body. The pain was as sharp as anything she had suffered that night, but the quality was different somehow: the pain of birth rather than of death. Pine had been correct: she screamed with a newfound power as Hazel pulled her out of the grave.

As she healed, she regained enough consciousness to realize what was happening and stopped trying to fight the process. It was so much easier somehow, once she knew that the pain would soon end. Finally, suddenly, the anguish disappeared, leaving only a dull ache throbbing softly through her bones. She opened her eyes, dizzy and confused, not knowing if she was surrounded by reality or delirium.

She looked over and saw Ilyn. She reached out and touched the tip of his nose to try to see if he was real, just as she had done days before. He laughed with relief. It was a wonderful, seldom-heard sound. It brought a weak, transient smile to November's weary face, and it set Pine grinning from ear to ear. Hazel hugged her grandson and collapsed into a chair, exhausted by her efforts. Zinnia rushed in at the sound, weeping with happiness, and ran to her friend's side. November looked around in a daze, not speaking, not sure where she was or what was happening, but seemingly relieved.

"Alright, everyone, let's give her some space. She's out of danger, but she needs to get some rest," the doctor admonished.

November then glanced over at Dr. Cedar in his white coat; he was filling a syringe from a vial. She was seized with an irrational panic. Suddenly, she was a terrified little girl again, in a hospital she hadn't seen in years. "No, please, I'll be good, I promise! I'll take my pills. I'll eat. You don't have to! I won't scratch my eyes anymore, I swear. Don't drug me! Don't put me in that room!" She struggled to escape her blanket, tangled up, trying desperately to flee. She tore at the IV line still attached to her arm.

Ilyn swiftly freed her from the blankets and took her by the shoulders. "Look at me, please, November. It's Ilyn. You're safe here. You're not in a hospital. You're not in danger. You're at home. You're safe at home. He's not giving you human drugs. It's just vampire venom, so you can sleep without seeing anything."

He kept saying these things, over and over, until she finally seemed to hear him. She threw her arms around him and buried her face in his neck, sobbing noiselessly. Ilyn looked startled for a brief moment, unused to such displays of emotion. He quickly recovered and wrapped his arms around her, stroking what little was left of her hair until she stopped shaking and raised her head. While she was crying in Ilyn's lap, Willow had taken the opportunity to change the sheets, and Zinnia had pulled out a fresh nightgown.

November looked around the room, her eyes resting briefly on her friends as well as on empty spaces filled with people only she could see.

"Are you alright, brave girl?" Pine asked, crossing the room to kiss her on the forehead. She reached out for him weakly, patting his arm reassuringly, but said nothing. She cocked her head and squinted at him as if puzzled.

"Em?" Zinnia asked, kneeling at her feet. "Say something, please." November gently touched her friend's hair and managed a twitch of a smile, but said nothing. "Why isn't she talking anymore?" Zinnia asked the doctor with alarm.

Cedar cleared his throat. "She's been through a great deal. As I said, the patient needs rest. There will be plenty of time to talk to her later. She spoke when she was . . . altered, so there's no physical damage to her ability to speak. I'm sure she'll feel better after she wakes up."

"How long will she sleep?" the king asked with concern.

"I'm not sure. I've never done this before, injecting someone with vampire spit." Cedar wrinkled his nose in distaste. "Frankly, I'd be more comfortable using a normal sedative, but since that's not an option, Lord William suggested this."

November shrank with fear as the doctor approached, but she didn't protest or flee.

"Do you want me to stay until you fall asleep?" the king asked her quietly. She started at him for a long moment, then nodded. The men turned their backs as Hazel and Zinnia helped November to change. She was so weak that it was like dressing a baby. Ilyn placed her in the bed and gently tucked her in. Dr. Cedar administered his potion, and November soon closed her eyes, still holding the king's hand.

She woke up in a sunny garden, surrounded by flowers of every type and season. Every surface in her room was crowded with vases. Afternoon light glinted off the crystal. As she struggled to sit up, Zinnia jumped up from the floor to help her. "She's awake!" her friend cried, and Pine rushed in from the hallway.

"Morning, sleepyhead," he said with a hopeful smile. "Feel any better?"

There was a long pause. She opened her mouth, but made no sound. Then she nodded hesitantly. The two fairies exchanged a worried glance. "Are you hungry?" Zinnia asked. "You slept 36 hours; you must be hungry."

November nodded again. "I'll go send down for something," Pine said. "Zin, why don't you help her get cleaned up and dressed?"

November was cooperative as Zinnia helped her to and from the bathroom, but she never quite seemed all there. When her friend placed the toothbrush in her hand, she managed to use it, carefully, as if trying something for the first time. She had no opinion about what clothes to wear, but she helpfully held up her arms for her sweater and stepped into her jeans.

The only time she showed any real reaction was when she caught a glimpse of herself in the mirror. She reached out toward her image, and her face briefly twisted in horror at the state she was in: her pallor, the livid scar on her arm, her missing hair. She'd always thought that she had pretty hair. It had been her sole vanity. For a moment, she seemed about to cry.

"It's okay, Em. It'll grow back. They had to cut it. Your fever was so high," Zinnia tried to explain. "I can make it grow back faster, if you want. It actually looks kind of badass, if you ask me."

November pulled her hand away from the mirror and looked at her friend with confused eyes before she withdrew back into herself again.

Inside herself is where she stayed for days, never speaking, but communicating and understanding when it suited her. At first Zinnia and Pine tried to fill the silence, catching her up on events.

"We've never left you alone. Everyone's been by to see you, too, to check on you and pay their respects. There are even more flowers downstairs that wouldn't fit," Zinnia began, as November slowly began to eat her breakfast.

She reacted to that information with a hint of surprise. Humans usually didn't rate much respect with fairies and vampires. The courtiers certainly had never shown her any consideration before.

"You saved a lot of vampire and fairy lives the other night," Pine explained further. "They want to show their appreciation. More importantly, they want to ensure that you're on their side when things hit the fan. Also, there's a certain degree of sucking up to the King going on, since everyone knows you have his favor."

November didn't know quite what to make of any of that. "Speaking of the King, he's been checking on you every hour on the hour," Zinnia reported. "He stayed the whole day yesterday. Slept on the floor holding your hand, with half a dozen fairies guarding you both. Every time he tried to leave, your vitals went haywire. Dr. Cedar says that with all the fairy magic you absorbed, you seem to have bonded to him like fairies do when they're born. You seemed more stable by nightfall last night, so he's been able to come and go. He'd probably be here right now, but he told us to open the shutters. Thought some sunlight would do you good."

"His security detail freaked. As did Lord William, when he found out last night. Vampires who survive for thousands of years don't tend to take such chances," Pine elaborated. The mention of Ilyn seemed to catch November's attention for a moment, but then she returned to her food.

From Zinnia and Pine, November learned that Ben's execution had been postponed in the midst of all the excitement. After she'd finished interrogating Lilith, Savita had been sent to Luka's mansion in Arizona in command of a large contingent of federal knights. They'd found the place deserted and were currently searching for clues to where they might have gone.

"Hey, why are people so afraid of Savita, anyhow?" Zinnia interrupted.

"Well, there's the mind reading, for starters. Scheming people like their privacy," Pine began.

"And?" Zinnia asked when Pine hesitated to continue.

"They say she has the ability to enthrall supernaturals, even to the point of forcing them to commit murder or suicide." Pine accentuated this tidbit of information with spooky hand gestures. "Blood kin are immune, they say. I've never seen her do it, myself, but my grandmother tells stories."

"For real? Wow. She could be seriously powerful if she wanted to be. Like, rule-the-world-as-a despot powerful." Zinnia's eyes were wide.

"Yep. Lucky thing she's not a monster like Luka. She avoids using both her gifts as much as she can. She wishes she didn't have either one of them, I think. Anyhow, as for Lilith, she's going to be dead pretty soon, I imagine," Pine continued, getting back on topic. "They must be about through asking her questions if they sent Savita to Arizona. Quickie trial and execution, I expect. Unless they wait to try her at the Assembly of Lords, so everyone sees proof of what Luka's been up to. Though I suspect that those who refuse to believe it have already chosen Luka's side, or are well compensated for staying neutral."

"Is that a lot of people?" Zinnia asked.

"Enough for trouble, I'm afraid."

"So what will the king do next? Will he go back to Nevada?"

"You'll have to ask him when he comes."

Darkness was falling, and Zinnia turned on some lamps as she replied. "I'm surprised he isn't here right now."

The conversation trailed off as the fairies looked with concern at their silent friend. She had finished eating and was just sitting there, staring at the wall.

"I wonder if she saw bad things, when she was . . ." Zinnia said quietly to Pine, unsure if November was even listening.

"It certainly seemed like she did," Pine replied. "From what little I could make out of what she was saying. For a while there, I would swear she was speaking Old Fairy."

"Do you think it would make her feel better to draw?"

"It's worth a try," Pine replied, grabbing a notebook and pencil and placing them in November's lap. The girl registered their presence, looked up at Pine, and grinned her thanks before taking up the pencil and returning to her own world. "At least she seems to know who we are. That mean's she's still in there, right?" her bodyguard asked her best friend.

"She's in there," the empath replied with assurance. "It's just going to take time for her to get back to normal. She's kind of blank right now. I don't think she's ready to feel much yet. Every so often, something gets through, but I think she put up some walls that night, to protect herself. She's just not ready to take them down yet." Zinnia seemed to be trying to convince herself as much as Pine. "I really wonder where the king is," she added, watching November begin to sketch.

November wondered, too. As she turned her thoughts to him, she could see him clearly. Ilyn had gone out to feed. He was sitting in the back of a limo, drinking from a woman in a business suit. He didn't seem that into it, which somehow pleased her. It wasn't like most of her visions, which felt like trespassers. This one was comfortable and reassuring, like when you hear your grandmother cooking in the next room and you know that it means you're both okay.

It was strange. She'd never been able to just think of a person and see where they were and what they were doing. She needed something of theirs: hair, jewelry, a piece of clothing, and even then, it was hit or miss. Now, however, she seemed somehow linked with the King. She tried to remember what her friends had been saying earlier about her vital signs worsening when Ilyn tried to leave. It was so hard to pay attention to details; her focus seemed so fragmented.

For a moment, she hoped he would come see her when he returned. But that hope came with the pain of possible disappointment, so she cut it off and went back to drawing, letting her mind wander and drift. Her last coherent thought before letting go was that she probably shouldn't tell anyone that she could see him.

She spent the night like this, filling sheets of paper with disjointed images, tearing them off, dropping them to the floor, and beginning again. She stopped only when someone took the pencil out of her hand and placed food in front of her. Several people came by to check her progress: William, Hazel, Cedar. She heard worried whispers but didn't bother listening to them. William tried to talk to her for a moment. He was determined to explain his behavior the other night, when he'd threatened to turn her himself. She managed to give him a reassuring smile. She didn't really remember why she was supposed to be mad at him.

The person who did not come was Ilyn: not that night, not the next, not the one after that. She knew he was still in the house. In one of her more lucid moments, she'd heard Willow and Pine discussing the fact that Hazel and most of the court had returned to Las Vegas to plan for the upcoming Assembly, but Ilyn had stayed to make war plans with William.

She tried not to wonder why he didn't come. Perhaps he didn't care about her as much as he had seemed to. Perhaps now that she was out of danger, he had more important uses for his time. Perhaps he had seen so much of her human weakness that she now repelled him. Whatever the reason, part of her wanted to despair. Part of her was angry. After all, she'd suffered because she was protecting him and his people. The rest of her was still numb and was willing to wait to see how things played out.

Ilyn certainly featured prominently in the fragments of vision she could recall from her ordeal, as well as her few actual memories from that night. She remembered being curled up against his chest as he sang to her. She remembered him holding her in ice cold water. She remembered clutching his hand for dear life. She had never held anyone's hand like that. With humans, the contact led to visions she didn't want. With vampires, she didn't see much unless she chose to look. With Ilyn in particular, when the visions did come, they weren't disorienting and painful and nauseating like everyone else's. They were somehow comfortable and familiar, even when they were upsetting. She couldn't understand it.

She kept making the same drawings over and over: Ilyn dying, Ilyn as a young human throwing his dead son on pyre, Ilyn with his wives, Savita's rebirth, William's human death. A number of her visions featured the knife that had caused her such damage: Marisha killing a fairy and taking his knife, Luka killing a number of people with that same knife.

One vision of Luka stuck out in her mind, because it seemed so strangely gentle. He was using the same knife, that cruel weapon, to cut ropes that were binding an injured young girl. She'd obviously been badly abused, but apparently not by him, as she looked at him as though he were an angel. November wondered who she was.

The most disturbing visions were those of the knife's manufacture, which involved quenching the hot metal by plunging it into terrified fairy captives, who proceeded to die screaming. The wooden inlay was carved from a stake used to execute vampires. Those particular images haunted November for some time.

Sleep did not come easily during her recovery. Visions, nightmares, night terrors, panic attacks – these all conspired to wake her every few hours. Pine or Zinnia would come running and sit with her until she fell back asleep, as though she were a frightened child.

Even so, she made quick progress. She began talking in her sleep. One morning, Zinnia put some music on, and November began singing along without seeming to realize she was doing it. Excited to see improvement, Pine and Zinnia kept up a constant soundtrack of November's favorite musicians: Florence Welsh, Regina Spektor, the Devil Makes Three, Adele, Josh White, Lily Allen, Ingrid Michaelson, Son House, Bob Dylan, Pink, the Be Good Tanyas, Catey Shaw.

As she grew physically stronger, they took her on longer and longer walks outside. They watched a movie in the theatre. She picked up her guitar again. She spent less time drawing in trances. She began communicating more, writing out some of her messages, and yet, no conscious words passed her lips.

One early afternoon, she woke up to find a few drops of blood on her pillow. She reached out to touch them, thinking she must have had a nosebleed in her sleep. Instead, she plunged into a vision of the night before.

The king kneels by her bed, studying her as she sleeps. Zinnia and Pine quietly sneak through the door. Ilyn's eyes turn cold. "I believe I told the two of you to wait in the hallway," he says without turning his head.

"Why are you doing this to her? Staying away while she is awake? Why are you doing it to yourself?" Zinnia asks, practically distraught.

"My decisions are none of your concern, child," he replies.

"She asks for you in her sleep. Every day," Pine says with quiet seriousness. "It's the only time she talks."

"Every time she hears a footstep in the hallway, she looks for you. For a moment she brims with love and hope, and when you don't appear, it curdles to pain. And then she pretends she doesn't care. She'd be recovering so much faster from her trauma if only you would help her." The empath is wringing her hands. "How can you do this to her? You feel something for her! I can sense it."

"A vampire does not love a human. It's like loving a butterfly. They're pretty and fragile and understand nothing and then they die. Now get out," he growls with fangs bared, finally turning to face his tormentors, "before I do something you'll regret." Having said their piece, they flee their king's wrath.

As soon as he is alone, he drops his forehead down to rest on November's bed. An hour later, when he finally rises to leave, he leaves behind two tears of blood on her pillowcase.

November looked around her room as she came back to the present. Something thawed inside of her. She wanted to laugh and cry at the same time. So, she got in the shower to muffle the sound, and that's exactly what she did. When she finally emerged, she felt clean and raw and renewed. She felt like herself again, just sharper and harder somehow, with the softness all burned away by the pain of Lilith's attack.

She stood for a long while, examining herself in the mirror, reflecting on the previous days. She had been hiding from her pain. She could see that now. She had been afraid of feeling, so she had walled her heart up and felt nothing. It was a coping mechanism she had used many times before, but this time, she'd nearly lost herself in it altogether. She had survived New Years Eve only to refuse to live, and regardless of how the rest of her day played out, she was determined not to continue that mistake any longer.

She got dressed in an embroidered white tunic and leggings, a Christmas gift from Savita called a *kameez* and *churidar*. With long white sleeves and a smattering of gold embroidery, combined with her shorn scalp and illness-heightened cheekbones, she looked like some kind of avenging angel or warrior monk. She briefly considered wearing some makeup to cover up her pale skin and dark circles but quickly rejected the notion. She wanted to be herself, the way she really was.

Zinnia's classes were back in session, so only Pine was waiting for her in the hallway. "Let's take a walk," she said to him nonchalantly. She didn't wait for his reaction to hearing her voice before she headed purposefully down the hallway.

"Yes, ma'am," he replied after a shocked pause and leapt up to follow her. "Where are we headed?"

"The copy room in the office wing."

"Okey-dokey," he said as they took the stairs two at a time.

"It's where he hides until the other vampires wake up, when he wants to be alone." Pine raised a questioning eyebrow, but she did not elaborate on how she had come up with that tidbit of information. They entered the government wing, passing a few busy fairies who widened their eyes but did not question the human they now called the Oracle.

When they entered the cavernous supply room, Pine turned to her and asked, "Now what?"

"Now we wait." November lifted herself up to sit on a scarred wooden desk hidden in a remote corner of the room. This was where the King spent his solitary hours these days, reading or working on his laptop or staring off in thought. She'd tried not to spy on him over the previous days, both out of respect and out of her fear of feeling things, but she hadn't been able to resist the occasional peek. There was something strangely endearing about a king hiding out amongst the highlighters and paper clips.

They did not have to wait too long. The king must have smelled her and heard her breathing from out in the hallway, as he already looked guarded when he caught sight of her sitting on the desk. He looked accusingly at Pine, who quickly spoke to defend himself. "I said nothing to her. This was all her idea." The king cocked his head toward the door, sending November's bodyguard into the hallway.

He looked at the seer, sitting on top of his desk, her arms wrapped around her shins, her chin resting on her knees. To his shock and relief, she spoke. "I've missed you." Happiness and relief skipped across his face for an instant before his customary hauteur returned.

He fought with himself before responding frostily, "I'm quite busy. If I wished to see you, I would have summoned you."

She smirked at him a little. "Not too busy to spend an hour leaving vampire tears on my pillow last night." He closed his eyes for a moment, horrified that his weakness had been witnessed. She continued more gently, "I'm sure you have your reasons for wanting to keep your feelings secret. I can hardly blame you if you're trying not to feel anything. That's what I've been doing ever since I woke up. I've spent whole years of my life like that. Not as many as you have, I suppose. I've screwed up the courage to choose to live again. I'm pretty sure that if I can do it, so can you."

"Are you calling me a coward?" he asked with some heat. "You understand nothing." He looked like he wanted to break something, or a lot of somethings. He brought his face very close to hers, his fangs gleaming and sharp. She supposed she should be frightened, but she wasn't.

"Like a butterfly?" He had the good grace to step back and look slightly abashed. "Look, I can't pretend to understand what it's like to be you. Objectively, us having any kind of romantic relationship would be pretty inappropriate. I'm not asking you to declare your eternal love for me. I don't want to jump into bed with you. You've known me about two weeks, and you're about a million years old. That would just be stupid.

"But the fact is, I'm happier when you're around, and I think the same goes for you. You earned my loyalty the way you took care of me the other night. Bloodthirsty vampire you may be, but you've been nothing but kind to me. You stayed when I needed you even though you barely know me. I've never had anyone take care of me the way you and Pine and Esther did. I've always suffered all alone, but you stayed. Without your help, your care, I would never have survived Lilith's attack. You were my anchor. I would have chosen oblivion without your voice to lead me back. Even if my body had survived, the rest of me might not have.

"And then there's what I know of the future, a future when you will spend a day buried in a grave so that I won't be afraid when I wake up to a new life in the dark." She took a deep breath. "I just feel safer when I'm near you."

"You're not," he replied darkly. "You are a fool if you love me, and the more fool to trust me."

"Look, I feel secure with you and uneasy when you're gone. I feel like I'm at home, like you're some kind of sanctuary. The fairies seem to think magic from the knife and from the healing has something to do with that, that it bonded us somehow, like fairy children bond with their kin."

"So it isn't real," he concluded starkly, "what we – what you're feeling."

"That's not what I said. Of course it's real. I mean, fairies really love their families, right? They said that the magic can't make something grow if the seeds aren't already there. They think it just speeded up something that was already beginning," she replied, and reached out tentatively to touch the scar on his cheek, so similar to the one on her own arm. He pulled away. "Now, if you didn't want me at all, that would be one thing. If you thought I was ugly or stupid or weak, I would be sad, but I would get over it. But knowing that you feel something that you're trying to suppress out of some need to protect me or you or both of us – that I have trouble accepting. After what I just survived, I don't want to waste any time or any chance to be happy."

"Vampires of my age do not have feelings about human children," he said in a hard voice. "You forget your place. This conversation is over."

"My *place*? My place? What, are my words not worth listening to?" she asked. "Or do you just hate yourself so much that you think you don't deserve to be happy?" Her face flushed with anger.

In the blink of an eye, he grabbed November by the shoulders and shoved her against the wall. "I caution you, do not provoke me further," he whispered through bared fangs.

She still wasn't afraid, merely furious. "You do realize that you're not the only person you're consigning to loneliness? I don't have the option to go find someone else to be happy with. No one is going to get near me for fear of offending you. Except, perhaps, your enemies. I'm not even allowed to leave the house." To this, he said nothing.

"You know, I'm starting to think I was better off in the carnival. First your ridiculous son pretends to love me when he doesn't, and now you pretend not to care about me when you do. I save your life and countless others. I suffer and nearly die for you people. I offer you a chance to be happy again. And what do I get in return? Threats and scorn. You're an emotional cripple and a pathetic excuse for a man." Still, he said nothing. He merely clenched his jaw.

"Fine," she spat, "have it your way. Enjoy your endless misery, *your grace*. I'll go find some other way to be happy." Ilyn stepped back when she tried to shove him away. "Know this: if you think I'm not worthy of you while I'm alive, you're sure as hell not worthy of *me* after I'm dead."

She strode toward the door and turned back to add, "And if you ever lay a hand on me in anger again, so help me God I will make you wish you hadn't." And then she was gone.

November found Pine waiting around the corner. One look at her face was enough to prompt him to say, "That could have gone better."

"Your king needs a shrink."

"No comment," the fairy replied. "Are you alright?"

"I need to get out of this house before I lose what's left of my mind."

"We'll all be leaving to go Las Vegas tomorrow or the day after, I think," Pine answered.

"Not soon enough. I won't sleep another night in that room. I'll go stay in the Livermore house until we have to leave. We're flying out of Livermore anyway, right?" She stopped and turned to look straight at him. "Can you make that happen for me? Please. I thought this place was a sanctuary, and now it feels like a prison. I have reached the limit of my tolerance, and if I don't get a break, I will flip a lid in the middle of this Assembly."

"I think I can manage it. I'll go talk to my betters," Pine promised.

"Thank you," she said sincerely. She squeezed his hand. "I don't know what I'd do without you and Zinnia."

"It isn't that he doesn't care about you. He's just not ready to let go and start over. And I think he genuinely believes that you're better off without him. You know that, right?" Pine said gently.

"Well, maybe he should have thought about that before he made me love him," she retorted. "Don't worry, I'll go back to feeling sorry for him once the rage wears off. Speaking of which, any chance this fairy magic thing will also wear off? It's putting a serious cramp in my ability to remain infuriated."

"It doesn't fade for fairies. It just grows stronger over time. But I've never heard of it happening to a human before, so who knows?"

"How encouraging."

By the time Pine returned with permission to head out to the ranch, November already had a bag packed. An hour later, the two of them were shooting arrows into hay bales and watching the sky get dark behind the hills. November felt a bit more free already. Even the car ride itself had been a little thrill, though she'd had to curl up on the floor of the back seat until they got on the interstate. She hadn't even minded the traffic between Pleasanton and Livermore.

To her happy surprise, Savita appeared as soon as it got dark. She'd given up the search for Luka until the Assembly ended. The trail had gone cold.

Savita must have been warned by Pine or her brother, because she was careful to avoid the king as a topic of conversation until November brought it up herself. They were sitting on the stone patio behind the house: November, Pine, Savita, and Noemi. Greg turned up as well, joining them after he chased down a coyote for supper. They lit the gas heaters for November's benefit and sat around while she snacked on fruit from the garden. "Savita," she demanded bluntly, "what can you tell me about these crazy men you're related to?"

"Hey, now," Greg protested.

"Present company obviously excepted," November allowed. "You are definitely my current favorite," she added, smiling.

Savita laughed. "William and Ilyn can be a bit hard to take," she answered. "My father wasn't always this difficult. Marisha's death undid him. She kept him young, somehow. Most vampires of their age, they become sort of ossified. They stop being interested in changing, in the world that's changing around them. But Mother always kept up with the latest human doings, and somehow, she never quite got as heartless as most of us do. You frighten him because you make him feel things he thought he'd long since left behind, like love and happiness and guilt and concern. He thought he was done with all of that. Of course, his human life wasn't easy, either."

"I saw him placing his wife and his son on a pyre, when I was unwell," November said sadly. "And I saw when Marisha turned him, but I didn't see anything in between."

"He was a mercenary. In his grief, he wanted to destroy things, and the constant wars obliged him. I think he meant to get killed, but he was just too good at warfare. When he met Marisha, she was moving over a battlefield, feeding and putting the doomed out of their misery. He was terrified to realize what she was, but still, he found her beautiful, and so gentle," Savita replied, obviously telling a story she'd heard many times. "She truly was strangely gentle for a vampire. Perhaps because she was an empath, like Zinnia, which is a most unusual gift for our kind. It is difficult to reconcile empathy with our . . . predatory nature."

"And Lord William?" she asked.

Pine and Savita laughed. "He's actually better than he was. Esther's tamed him a bit. Even when he was human, he was egotistical, quick-tempered, and cavalier with women. I think he'd bedded every woman within a day's ride of his village before he got killed on the battlefield."

"Why did your parents turn him?" Noemi asked curiously, breaking into the conversation.

"After the battle, the two of them went looking for the wounded who might be saved. These were their men, after all, fighting under their banner. William was too far gone to live, but not too far to change. He was a very good blacksmith, and a brave soldier. He'd served them well and loyally for years, so they chose to give him a new life. I think they also thought it would be good for me to have a friend nearer my own age." She sighed before continuing. "It was hard for me, leaving India and coming to Europe with them, though that was my own fault. Sometimes I had to pretend to be a servant Ilyn had picked up on crusade. It was humiliating."

"How was it your fault?" November asked. Her three companions exchanged glances. "Sorry, I shouldn't be prying. It's none of my business," she apologized.

"It's alright. You'll hear about it sooner or later," Savita said softly. "I was very angry when I was first turned. I did not want to be a vampire, but Ilyn forbade me from killing myself. You see, in the first few decades, it is almost impossible for us to disobey our makers. This helps us survive our early years. And I was so young when I died. I was quite volatile. Anyway, one night I lost control and slaughtered a lot of people. Innocent people. Enough of them that we could no longer stay in India, as it was impossible to cover up adequately. So we headed to Europe and eventually wound up in Scotland for awhile. That's where they made William and Luka." They were all quiet for a moment. It was hard for November to picture Savita doing something so horrible.

"What about Luka?" November finally asked tentatively.

"Ah, the black sheep. He knew what we were even before he died. He was a scribe, worked closely with Ilyn on the accounts and such. He never left the castle, and saw no one but us and the other servants, so we stopped bothering to enthrall him after awhile. He was crippled, you see: born with twisted legs. He'd have wound up dead or a beggar if a priest hadn't felt sorry for him and taught him to read in Latin and to do figures. We found him in Italy on the way from Asia to Scotland. Ilyn bought him from the priest.

272

"He served my parents from the time he was eleven until he was about forty-five and Mother finally changed him. He had first asked them years before, but it took Marisha some time to convince Ilyn.

Finally, when he took a bad fever, Mother brought him over. He wanted physical strength to go with his intelligence. He wanted strong legs, to be stronger than all the humans who had ever looked down on him. He wanted power and money and women."

"Don't we all?" Pine interrupted to cut the tension. "Okay, maybe not the women in my case."

Savita smiled. "I liked Luka. We understood each other. We both knew what it was like to be humiliated. William, of course, that was another story. Even when he was human, William was everything Luka despised and envied all at once: this burly blacksmith, the strongest man in the village, a different woman every week, half a dozen bastards, arrogant and highly competent, so everyone put up with it. And the worst part was how kind William was to Luka. William designed a sort of wheelchair for him, built it himself one Christmas without even being asked. Luka hated having to be grateful to him. And when they turned Luka, so soon after making William, rivalry was inevitable."

"Do you love him?" Pine asked curiously.

"I did, until he started blowing people up," she answered sadly. "Maybe I still do." With a deep breath, she changed the subject and turned to Greg. "What about you, *raja*? Would you like to share your story?"

"I was born in Georgia a slave. I ran away. Savita found me dying in a ditch. I'd gotten wounded in the course of my escape. Infection had set in, of course. She offered me the choice of a quick death or a new life in freedom. Obviously, I chose the latter," Greg

273

said matter-of-factly. "We helped slaves escape to Canada until the Civil War came and went."

"That's when we started migrating west. Eventually, all of us wound up all the way out here," Savita concluded.

"How did you two meet?" November asked Noemi and Savita.

"I grew up on a ranch in Southern California," Noemi answered. "I married and had a child, as was expected of me. My maker was riding through our land one night. He saw me sitting on the porch, sewing. He decided that instant that he had to have me and stole me away, changed me that night. Felipe is a very impulsive, passionate man, even now. At least he let my kin find me and bury me that day, so they wouldn't think I had run off and abandoned them. That gave me some comfort, but it was hard for me, at first, because I missed my family so much. I had no desire for my husband, but I still loved him. He was a good man, gentle and hard-working and patient with a wife who shrank from his touch. And of course, I loved my little girl. That was the worst part.

"But Felipe was kind to me, taught me how to survive in this life, and I was happy enough. I didn't realize what had been missing in my life until I met Savita." She turned to her wife and smiled. "Felipe realized I was smitten even before I did myself. He loved me enough to let me go."

"Is that all of you in the family?" November asked Savita, fascinated by the tale of their history, which was filling in a lot of gaps between glimpses she'd accumulated over the previous months.

"Esther is William's progeny as well as his wife. He found her while he spent some time as a pirate. Ilyn also has two older children, Raina and Emil, siblings we haven't seen in centuries. They elected to stay in Europe when we left for adventure in America. They came to visit after Mother died, but we haven't

274

heard from them since. They probably have some children, but I've never met them. They've mostly been living in Russia, I believe. For a time, Raina ruled Persia."

"Does Luka have any children?"

"No. His disdain for human beings only grew once he was one of us." Her face darkened. "There was one girl, poor child, whom he tried to turn. She was like you, a prophetess. He found her in Spain, just before they were about to burn her for a witch. She failed to rise. It was a terrible disappointment to him. He's always said that he was searching for someone worthy of the honor, someone special," Savita replied, glancing at November and quickly looking away.

"Someone like November," Pine stated flatly, his honesty crashing into the middle of what had been a very pleasant evening.

"That is likely his intention, to make her his child," Savita admitted. "We must do our best to shield you from that fate," she added in November's direction.

November felt suddenly cold. "Wait, you said something a few minutes ago . . . that you can't disobey your maker for the first few years. So if Luka were to . . . kill me and make me come back, I would have to do whatever he wanted? He could force me to help him to terrible things? And I wouldn't even be able to kill myself so he couldn't use me?" Her hands twisted in her lap.

Everyone nodded and grew quiet. Savita spoke first. "It is a very bad thing indeed, to have a bad maker. We were all lucky enough to have parents who did not abuse their power over us."

"We got lucky in the gas station, that they sent such a young fairy that you were able to kill him, and we got lucky again that Ben was so inept," Pine said in the most serious tone November had ever heard from him. "We got lucky that you were able to see Lilith's plan before more people got killed and before she could spirit you away. But if that luck runs out, we need to be able to find you before Luka harms you or turns you."

November slowly raised her head, instinctively knowing that this conversation was going somewhere she wasn't going to like. Pine pulled a vial of blood out of his jacket pocket.

"No way," November said quickly, shrinking back into her chair. "Not gonna happen."

"It will help us find you," Pine argued. "Just one sip of the king's blood. That's what they required of me, before the king and Lord William would give permission for you to come out here. They made me promise that I'd get you to drink this."

"I already had Lord William's blood," she retorted.

"It was one drop, and it was months ago," he replied evenly. "It won't work anymore. We're about to travel, which increases the opportunity for Luka to try something. We can't risk it."

"Why does it have to be his?" she asked, beginning to panic.

"He's the oldest. His blood has the most power. With my blood, if he got you a couple of hundred miles away, I might lose you," Savita explained gently.

"Can't you just put some kind of chip in me or something?" November asked, grasping at straws.

"They only work from close by, and he'd just cut it out of you anyway," Pine answered a bit brutally.

"If you make me do this, I won't sleep for a week. I'll wake up screaming. I'll see him all the time. It's bad enough, all this fairy magic and his ridiculous behavior. Now this, on top of it? I'd rather be back with my mother," she said with some heat.

"Unfortunately, that isn't an option," Pine replied, cool and implacable.

"November, please drink it. I wouldn't be asking you to do something this difficult if I didn't think it was in your best interest," Savita said, leaning forward, trying to persuade her.

"Are you sure it's not because I'm your family's favorite weapon at the moment?" November responded, anger now winning out over fear.

"Perhaps that would have been true before I knew you, before I worked with you on those bombings. Before you saved the life of my only child, as well as countless others." Savita knelt on the ground next to November's chair.

Quiet Greg finally chimed in. "I hate that we are pushing you to do something against your will. November, I owe you my life, and I don't want to see you lose yours. Please just drink it. We'll all help take care of you after, we promise."

"Sometimes, choosing to live is the most difficult thing you can do," Pine said gently. "You know that better than any of us. It would be a shame for you to have fought so hard to recover only to die at Luka's hands because we couldn't find you fast enough. Please, November."

November looked into their faces, and what she saw there was sincere concern, even a hint of fear. She closed her eyes for a moment. "You tell him. You tell him that I don't know if I can forgive him this."

When she opened them, she stood up, grabbed the vial, and drank it down without saying a word.

Savita caught her before she hit the concrete.

Chapter 12

Ilyn kneels by a pile of ash, weeping, rending his clothes. Ilyn standing next to a pyre, weeping, rending his clothes. Ilyn teaches a little boy how to fish. Ilyn holds Savita as she cries silent tears of blood. Ilyn runs down a long hallway, surrounded by smoke and screaming. Ilyn helps November down into her grave. Ilyn cries on November's pillow. Ilyn sings to her in the bathtub. Ilyn on battlefield after battlefield. Ilyn in bed with Marisha. Ilyn marrying Nadi. Ilyn screams, stabbed again and again. Ilyn feeds on an endless parade of humans. Ilyn gives William his blood. Ilyn and blood. Ilyn and death. Ilyn and birth. Forever.

It was nearly an hour before the Oracle came around. With Greg's help, she sat up. They had moved her to the living room during her extended vision. Savita put a straw in her mouth, and she sucked down a full glass of orange juice.

"Are you alright?" Pine asked.

It occurred to November that he uttered that phrase an awful lot. She said nothing in reply. Instead, she stood up, looked down at herself to make sure she was steady enough to walk, and headed toward her room. Her companions looked at one another, uncertain. Pine stood up to follow her. Just as she reached the door, he stopped her. "Please, say something. Anything. November?" he begged, desperately worried that he'd derailed all her progress.

She looked at his anxious face and had mercy on her friend. "You can also tell him that he made me cry." Then she stepped into her room, closed and bolted the door, threw herself down on the bed, and was true to her word. She sobbed into a pillow until finally, exhausted, she fell asleep.

She woke often from her troubled sleep, as she'd expected. The third time, she sat up, heart pounding, wondering if she'd screamed, and over her labored breath she heard quiet voices in the hallway.

"Of course I have a key," Savita said softly, "but I think you should just let her sleep."

"I want to make sure she's okay," came Zinnia's strained voice. "She was seriously upset. I could feel it all the way in Berkeley."

"I felt it as well," Ilyn's voice added. He sounded terribly agitated. November's heart skipped a beat at the sound of his voice, hope rising for the instant before she remembered the day's events. "There has to be something you fairies can do about this," Ilyn continued. "This isn't supposed to be possible. I can't stand it, this connection with her. I feel like I'm losing my mind. It's only gotten worse since she drank my blood. I've never heard of giving blood having an effect like that, not in all my years." He sounded as close to panic as a vampire of his age could get.

At his words, November's fury bloomed again, and she strode to the door and swung it open. "I don't much care for it myself, *your grace*," she said in a voice dripping with venom. "And I'm ever so sorry to have inconvenienced you with my unfortunate survival the other night as well as my following your order to Pine this evening. By the way, thanks so very much for making one of my only friends do that to me. That was super classy of you. Now if you wouldn't mind getting the hell out of this house, I need to get back to bed. I think I can fit in a thousand more nightmares about you before breakfast, though I might have to cry myself to sleep again first." And with that, she slammed the door and locked it again.

November heard footsteps, then silence. She was seething, relieved to be alone again, when she heard a tentative tap on the door. "Please, Em," Zinnia whispered. "Please let me in. The others have gone. I just want to make sure you're alright."

November sighed; then she went to let her best friend in, bolting the door behind her. "Do I *look* alright to you?" she asked in a harsh voice as she got back in bed.

"You look awful," Zinnia replied, climbing in beside her to give her a hug. "Pine filled me in. You don't have to talk about it if you don't want to."

"Thanks, Zin. I'm sorry for sounding so mad. And thanks for coming," November replied, trying not to start crying again. "Can you stay?"

"As long as you need."

With Zinnia in the room, November managed to fall back to sleep and get a few hours of rest before more dreams made it impossible. It was a beautiful day, which helped lift her spirits. She decided to enjoy the warmth and the sunshine by having breakfast outside. Zinnia stuck close to her side but didn't ask any prying questions, for which November was quite grateful. Pine did the same, looking vaguely guilty. Finally, November asked Zinnia, "Don't you have school? I don't want you to get in trouble over me."

"Mom pulled me out," she answered sadly. "There was a bombing last night of a house being rented by several vampires and fairies who were students at a college back East. All four of them died. One of their parents is lord of Ohio. Whoever did it spray-painted 'Traitors' on the street in front of the house. Some people think that getting a college education means we're trying to live too much in the human world, having too much respect for their intellectual achievements or some garbage. My mother is afraid I could be targeted, too, because of her politics and my friendship with you. So I'm on leave until this all plays out."

"I'm sorry, Zin. That sucks."

"Not your fault. Besides, I couldn't really concentrate anyway, with all this mess going on. Too much drama," the fairy replied.

"Seriously, though. Hey, do either of you have any idea when we have to fly to Nevada?" November asked.

"Last I heard, tomorrow night," Pine answered.

"And what exactly am I going to have to do there?" the seer inquired, wanting to be prepared. She was in no mood for more surprises.

"I'm not sure. I'll find out all that I can. One thing is for sure – no parties for you."

"Thank God for small favors," November said, managing a little laugh. Pine smiled at the sound of it, and Zinnia looked much relieved.

"The lords are pretty spooked, I hear. A few are making secret sleeping arrangements. Most are bringing frozen blood along. I heard a rumor that the lord of Kentucky is bringing a hundred caged squirrels for snacks, but I think that's just a joke at his expense," he added with a slight smile. "It's possible that they might want you to examine Lilith before they do her in." November made a long-suffering face. "I know, I know. It would suck. But maybe you might see something useful."

"She's just so gross," November complained. "Honestly, examining that knife would probably be more useful, since it belongs to Luka."

"Yeah, about that . . ." Pine began. "It seems to have disappeared."

November twitched at that piece of news, her hand rising of its own accord to rub the scar on her arm. It still ached, a little less each day. "How is that possible?" she demanded.

"There was a lot of commotion that night. It's an extremely valuable weapon. Very old. They don't make them that way anymore, thank God. The king was livid, of course," Pine said, shrugging. "Anyone could have grabbed it."

Finished with her breakfast, November turned to her work. "I need to draw," she told her friends, and they knew she was done talking for a long while.

When she was finished, she took a walk to the gate at the end of the long driveway. After a little while, once the sun had set quite spectacularly, Greg joined her.

"You want to run." It was a statement rather than a question. November looked up at Greg and didn't bother to deny it, nor did he bother to tell her that running would be at best an empty gesture. He knew that she knew.

"I am having trouble seeing much difference between Luka and Ilyn. Other than that Ilyn hasn't blown anybody up. Lately."

"Not that I often agree with my grandfather, but at least Ilyn doesn't want to rule the world, commit genocide against the werewolves, and enslave the entire human race," Greg offered.

"No, just the ones he wants to make use of." She shook her head. "The things I've seen him do, the things he's said to me. . . and I can't stop thinking about all those girls at the parties. I'm supposed to be on his side because he's the lesser of two evils? But then he's kind to me sometimes, and I don't know how to reconcile it. And now I have this magic tying me to him, a tie I won't escape even after I die, according to my vision. I can't . . . I just can't. I don't want to be like him."

"You don't have to be Ilyn *or* Luka. Though there is one thing I think my Uncle Luka has right." November looked up at Greg with more than a bit of shock before Greg continued, "Revelation. The only way to be a truly ethical vampire, or fairy, is if our prey gives informed consent. Which they can't do if they don't know we exist." November nodded, allowing that he had a good point. "At any rate, there is more than one way to be a vampire. You could feed solely on animals, like Lord William. Or, you could do what I do when I feel the need to drink human blood directly from the source."

"Which is?"

He bent down to whisper in her ear. His breath was cold against her skin as he confessed, "I break the law. I bite people who know." He grinned at her surprise.

"But how does that work? How does word not get out over all those years?" November breathed, fascinated.

"It started with some people whose lives I saved, when I was young. Savita and I helped them escape slavery, like she helped me. They asked what they could do for me in return. I could somehow tell I could trust them. So, I told them, and they gave me blood freely, and they kept my secret. Over the years, I saved a lot of people from a lot of different things. They have children, grandchildren they teach about me, who want to know me, in case they ever need my help. Symbiosis."

"Who knows? What if you get caught?" November whispered conspiratorially, peeking around for eavesdroppers.

"I'm sure Savita knows, but she pretends not to. And nothing good," he replied. "William is utterly committed to the law. It would mean exile at best. But I hate enthralling people. It's too much like slavery. I have a real problem with slavery. As you might imagine." Greg's kind features turned fierce for just a split second, just long enough to make November's heart skip a beat. "There are stories, legends of a community somewhere, where vampires, fairies, werewolves, and humans live together honestly. Nobody thinks it is real, but I just love those stories, you know? Like a vampire garden of Eden, where we lived in peace before we all learned to hate and hunt each other."

They stood together in silence for several minutes before November worked up the courage to say, "In my vision, it looks like Ilyn turns me. . . but what if you did it instead?" The words came out in a tumbled rush, as she tried to shove them out before she lost her nerve.

"Oh, November . . .I wish that I could, but it just isn't a good idea," he replied gently, like a potential date trying to let a girl down easy. November looked at her shoes, mortified. The vampire knelt down next to her, gently turning her to face him. "Hey, it's not like that. It's not even that I'm afraid the king would be livid, which he would. Whatever, we could run away to another country. But turning someone into a vampire is not as easy as the stories make out. It doesn't always work, and my track record . . . I've tried twice and lost them both. I swore off of it. And Ilyn's made at least four and never lost a one at rebirth, and those are only the ones I know about."

November looked down at him questioningly. "Humans and fairies have miscarriages and stillbirths, sometimes, right? So do we. Sometimes our progeny don't rise, even if we do everything right. Sometimes they rise, but they are sickly and waste away, or their minds aren't right. And just like with the fairies, it's happening to us more and more. Rumor has it the werewolves are having the same problem, not that they'd tell us."

"The fairies?" she asked. She vaguely remembered someone saying something to her about fairy infertility.

"Zinnia's parents lost five before they had her. Pine and his ex-wife stopped trying after four because they couldn't endure another loss."

"How awful. I can't imagine." She swallowed the tears that sprang to her eyes.

"I think Ilyn is just the safer choice. If I tried and you didn't make it . . ." he trailed off. "But I promise, I'll help you, if you really do wind up one of us."

"Thanks," she said with a crooked half-smile. "Just don't let me hurt anybody."

Her lanky companion unfolded himself. "Come on, we should get inside. You must be cold." She took his arm, and they walked back to the house, both wondering what life might have been like if things were just a little different.

***

November had never been on an airplane before. She suspected that she had now been spoiled for life as far as air travel was concerned. They were sitting on a private jet, on their way to Las Vegas to finish preparing for the Assembly. The king was sitting at the front of the plane, talking on the phone. November was doing her best to ignore him. Ben and Lilith both had been transferred during the day to prevent any attempts at escape, and the plane had returned in the evening for the king and his entourage. Zinnia was sitting across from November, resting. Fairies didn't sleep, but they

286

had this way of zoning out when they had a quiet moment with nothing to do. Most of William's other people were also making the move to Nevada, flying separately as a security precaution. Greg would be staying behind to hold down the fort in Oakland. Ilyn and November were accompanied by security staff, with Pine and Willow assigned watch over the human.

The oracle and the king had already had one argument that evening. There had been the issue of her reward. It turned out that there was a tradition that a person who saved the life of the king could name his or her reward. Generally, of course, these would consist of money, land, lordships, priceless jewels, and other items of that nature. November had no interest in such things. Upon reflection, a strange notion popped into her head. She requested that Ben's life be spared. She wasn't sure why. The idea just came to her, but once it did, she was sure it was the right decision. She, however, could neither understand nor explain why. After all, she was the one Ben had tried to kidnap. Ilyn had not been pleased and had done his best to talk her out of it. In the end, he trusted that her gift was involved and would not lead them astray, and he agreed to her request, saying in a strained voice, "Perhaps we will find a way to make use of him."

On the plane, the remains of a gourmet lunch sat on the table next to her, along with a fresh glass of cola just delivered by a lovely fairy flight attendant. November looked out the window down at the lights on the ground as they approached the airport. Her ears popped as they descended. Take-off had been a little frightening for her, which everyone had found amusing. The current view of the Strip was pretty amazing, which was a good distraction from her nerves. "That one's his," Zinnia said, reaching over to point. "That one, too." November was suitably impressed.

"Could you help me with my wig?" she asked once they were safely back on solid ground. She'd removed it once they were in the air; it itched something awful. With her face still on telephone poles throughout Northern California, they'd chosen the closest thing they could find to the opposite of her own hair: a sleek, strawberry blonde bob with heavy bangs. Her shorn head certainly made dealing with the wig easier. Add a pair of designer glasses, tasteful jewelry, and expensive clothes, and she was unrecognizable as a scruffy, dark-haired runaway.

They were whisked from the plane to a waiting limousine flanked by SUVs for the short drive to Ilyn's primary residence at the Tayna Spa and Casino. They came through a private entrance, of course, bypassing the crowds on the gaming floor and in the lobby. Even the back hallways were spectacular. It was apparent that no expense had been spared in the construction and decoration of the complex, the flagship of Ilyn's financial empire.

Zinnia and November were delivered to the rather large suite they were sharing. It was, in Zinnia's always elegant parlance, "Ridonk." It was certainly the work of someone with very good taste and a great deal of money at his or her disposal. Everything was perfect: the cream color of the upholstery, the cool stone floor of the bathrooms, the placement of the furniture, the smooth way the curtains opened and closed.

Even so, something about the place was nagging at November. She wandered around for a long minute, trying to put her finger on it, until she finally opened the door to take a look down the hallway, and it hit her. She looked at the room number on the door, and the details came back in a rush.

"November, are you alright?" Pine asked, right on cue. November decided that he should have t-shirts printed with that sentence on the front.

"I need to talk to the king," she said with quiet resignation.

"I very much doubt that is possible right now," Willow answered in a rather disbelieving tone.

"Then someone do me a favor and tell him that there's going to be a fire in the hotel," she replied with brisk annoyance and closed the door firmly, irritated that Willow would think she'd want to see him if it wasn't an emergency.

The fancy, extra long bathtub with its own pillow beckoned to her. She wanted to heed its siren call, but instead had to wait to see if she'd be summoned once her news reached the king. After about fifteen minutes, just as her irritation reached critical levels, there came a knock at the door. She took a peek before unlocking it and was surprised to see that the king had instead come to her. She opened the door and stood aside for him to enter. Lord William was just behind. They strode into the living room, Ilyn's eyes seeming to study every feature in search of an imperfection while studiously avoiding looking at the human.

Before November could even sit down, Lord William began with the questions. "What's all this about a fire? When will it be? How does it start? When did you have the vision?" November ignored him and opened up her most recent binder of work, pulling out the relevant pages.

"I first saw it the night before last. I saw the king, alone in a hallway filled with smoke, seemingly searching for someone. I heard crashes, alarms, and screaming. As you can see, the number on the door matches my room number, and the filigree around the peephole is the same. This leads me to believe that the fire will happen here." She spoke quickly, in a businesslike tone that betrayed none of her extremely mixed feelings about being so close to the vampire monarch.

"We have excellent fire suppression technology," William mused. "And the security screening is thorough. I don't understand how someone could get enough fuel in here to start a significant fire."

"Well, someone will," November said. "Is there any way to move this thing somewhere else?"

Ilyn shook his head. "That is not feasible," he replied. "We're talking about hundreds of people who would need lodging. And who knows how safe the alternate site would be?"

"If they know about a specific threat, a lot of them will take it as excuse to just go home. We need them to see the trial, to vote to support action against the rebel," William added.

"Surely you're going to warn people?" November asked, shocked by their seemingly cavalier attitude.

"We have developed a very good plan for quick, daytime evacuation, coordinated with each delegation," Ilyn assured her. "They knew the risk when they came here. Believe me, after what happened in Oakland, we are taking every precaution. We'll have guards everywhere. A whiff of smoke or fuel, and they'll set off every alarm in the place."

"That is somewhat reassuring," November replied. "There's one other issue this brings up that I should probably point out to you. For me to have seen this vision, I must not be in the building when the event occurs. I can't see my own future, remember? And since I have no plans to make a run for it . . ."

"You're afraid someone's going to make off with you?" Ilyn finished. She nodded. "Let's increase her guard," he told William. "Keep the two on the door and add a man each in the elevators, lobby, and the stairwells. And six guards on her when she leaves the room." William nodded. "Is that everything?" the king asked November.

She looked him in the eye for a long moment before answering coldly, "Yes, that's all." The vampires blew out the door. "Don't bother thanking me or anything," she said to the closed door before finally drawing herself a very hot bath.

The Assembly opened with a minimum of pomp, given the circumstances. The first major order of business was Lilith's trial, where she was judged by a jury composed of twelve randomly selected lords, since it was the crown itself who was the wronged party in a case of treason. Not surprisingly, they quickly voted unanimously to convict. What was surprising was their choice to invite November to attend the execution.

"They did what, now?" she exclaimed to William when he paid her a visit to give her the news.

"They want to meet the great Oracle. You're famous, and we've been holding you close," he explained with a shrug. "So, to hell with precedent."

"I don't want to be there," she replied.

"Look, if it were up to me, you wouldn't be. But there are several very powerful lords on the panel, and the king really does not need to be disagreeing with them right now," William said with earnest exasperation. "We need you to do this."

"Fine," she said, throwing in the towel. "Just tell me I don't have to wear a prom dress."

The king himself came to escort her. November would have preferred some warning on that score. Her chest got tight whenever she saw him, and she wasn't sure if she wanted to slap him or kiss him. No, scratch that – she definitely wanted to slap him. And yet, she got the strangest feeling of comfort just being near him. She was beginning to find fairy magic tremendously irritating.

"You look lovely," Ilyn murmured when she opened the door. She was wearing a grey cashmere suit with a slim skirt that stopped a few inches past the knee. A pale pink blouse provided a splash of color, and her stubble of hair was covered by a chic black turban. She was wearing William's earrings again, as they were the only ones she owned.

"Thanks," she replied shyly. "So, just how awful is this going to be?"

"You mean the execution?" Ilyn asked.

"Yes, the execution," she said, almost laughing. "Not the incredibly awkward conversation in which we are currently engaged."

"Well, that depends on the method of execution she chooses," Ilyn explained as they began walking down the hallway, surrounded by a phalanx of bodyguards.

"She gets to pick?"

"That is our tradition if the jury deadlocks. They couldn't decide between burning at the stake and dismemberment followed by decapitation."

"Classy."

She was silent for a spell as they rode the elevator up to the roof. They emerged to bows from the assembled dignitaries. Once Ilyn acknowledged them, everyone returned to their milling about and networking while simultaneously staring at November. It was a different kind of stare than she was accustomed to from supernatural people. It was more of a respectful, appraising gaze, as though they were trying to get an idea of how powerful she might be, rather than how her blood might taste or how she might be seduced. The lord of Texas, already one of her fans, strode over to pay his respects and introduce some of his allies. Bodyguards were constantly within reach, not just Pine and Willow, but half a dozen from Ilyn's own guard. She was glad for them: the roof was closely packed, but the guards forced some breathing room around her, refusing to let the crowd press in. In one corner of the roof stood a stage topped with a wooden stake, for now empty of the condemned woman. The sight chilled November's heart. It felt viscerally familiar; she knew not why.

A number of people came up to thank her. Some had been at William's house the night of Lilith's attempted attack and credited November with saving their lives. Others had had friends or family there that evening and were similarly grateful. Others were simply glad she had helped get rid of Lilith's poisonous presence in Ilyn's court. November was all smiles, as gracious and charming as she knew how to be, and grateful that the entirely non-human crowd wasn't taking too much of a toll on her mental shields. It was kind of gratifying to have her gift so appreciated by strangers. She felt less like a freak and more like a treasure. It was almost enough to make her forget the unpleasantness that was to come. Pine smiled at her during a lull in her receiving line and murmured to her, "We take life debts seriously, you know. You made yourself some powerful allies on New Year's Eve." *Yes*, she thought, *but some powerful enemies, too, I'll wager.*

Finally, the crowd hushed as Lilith emerged, flanked by guards. She held her head high, but her eyes were wide and her gait unsteady. An aisle opened up in the crowd, and she was forced to walk a hissing, spitting, shouting gauntlet. November kept well away from her. Ben was brought out, too, apparently to witness the fate of his fellow traitor, but drew considerably less attention, being comparatively much less despised.

As they bound the condemned to the stake with silver chains, a slight smell of burning flesh wafted over the crowd. A hush came over the assembled witnesses as the king stepped up to the stage, his day minister at his side. "In what manner shall you die, Lilith Roosebeke?"

Her reply was inaudible to November, but plain to the crowd around her, as they muttered such phrases as, "Stake, eh? Deserves a lot worse."

"And by whose hand shall you die, Lilith Roosebeke?" the king demanded. Most of their condemned chose a friend or ally, that a friendly face might be the last they saw. Lilith had few friends, even among those secretly loyal to Luka. She had, after all, failed her rebellious master. Again, her voice was too soft for November's human ears, but the crowd let out a hue and cry, and everyone turned to look in her direction. *Oh, no.*

Pine turned her way, his face alive with surprise. "She chose you, Em."

"I don't want to do it," she protested. "This is ridiculous. The king should do it. I decline. I refuse."

"You must," Willow stated flatly. "It is our way."

The crowd once again opened up an aisle, this time for the oracle. *Why is she making me do this?* November asked herself.

As she walked toward the stage, Pine and Willow flanking, the crowd applauded her, then began cheering. Ilyn looked at her apologetically. "I had no idea she would do this, little one," he said, placing the stake in her hand, showing her how to hold it. It was the first time he had touched her since their falling out, and November was freaked out enough to be grateful for the help.

"How do I do this?" she whispered, her voice shaking as much as her hands were.

"Stab her in the center of the chest, as hard as you can," he replied. Lilith looked at them both with contempt mixed with envy and desperation.

November stood before her and felt strangely sympathetic. She knew what it was to be helpless and alone. "Why did you choose me?" she whispered to Lilith.

"Because you've been here before," she replied cryptically.

"What?" November asked, confused, sure she had misheard. But Lilith would say no more. She simply closed her eyes and waited for the final blow.

"Now, little one," Ilyn urged gently.

So, November took a deep breath, pulled back her hand, and drove a sharp wooden stake into her enemy's chest. As the blood of centuries began to pour forth, Ilyn picked her up at the waist and swung her out of the way so that not a drop of that awful woman landed on her. Almost immediately, the blood turned to ash, and Lilith was no more. November dropped her stake, squeezed her eyes shut, and covered her mouth and nose, not wanting any part of Lilith inside of her. Ilyn gave her his silk handkerchief and walked her quickly to clean air. The crowd released its anticipation and its rage in a cheer loud enough to make her ears ring. Cries of "Long live the king!" alternated with that of "Oracle, oracle!" Fangs began appearing in vampire mouths, provoked by the excitement of the execution.

"Well done, little one," Ilyn praised her before turning toward Pine. "This would be a good time to get her out of here, before they start looking for food," the king instructed her entourage, who swiftly ushered her back into the building. Zinnia followed close behind, taking her hand to squeeze it in support. With great relief, they collapsed in their room.

"Wow, Em, you're a slayer now. A fairy and a vampire under your belt. I can't believe she made you do that." Zinnia shook her head in disbelief.

"You and me both," November concurred. She didn't bring up Lilith's cryptic final words. She wanted to hold them close for awhile, worry them a bit, roll them around in her head. It wasn't until that moment that November started to shake. *I just killed someone. On purpose. She's dead now. Like, permanently.* Zinnia, sensing her distress, moved to sit next to her friend.

"Hey, there was no getting around it. She was dead before she even said your name. Besides, after what she did to you, she seriously had it coming," Zinnia said reassuringly.

"I know," November sighed. "But I just looked a woman in the eye and killed her. And people cheered." She leaned her head against Zinnia's shoulder, not crying, simply overwhelmed and exhausted. "I'm never going to have a normal life again, am I?"

"Did you have one before?" Zinnia asked gently.

"No," she admitted. "But nobody died because of me, directly or otherwise. And there were no geriatric vampires waxing hot and cold, or magic knives, or forced exchanges of blood, either."

"Fair enough," her friend allowed. "You know, if I thought there was any way to get you safely away from this, I would do it. Sometimes I couldn't care less about the war and the kingdom. The

296

whole situation is terribly unfair, and you don't deserve any of it. I'm pretty sure Pine feels the same way. He is super upset about everything you've gone through."

"I know," she said, smiling gratefully at her friend. "But, per usual, I am at the mercy of forces beyond my control. And I am seriously sick of it." She flopped back onto her bed before continuing, "So, what happens in the Assembly now?"

"The lords meet in private session tomorrow night to determine a course of action against Luka. Mom will need me to be an errand runner, so you'll be on your own up here, unless they summon you to ask questions about your visions. I wouldn't think they would, but after tonight, anything's possible."

"I'll pray for a boring night, then!" November replied. "Hey, what's going to happen to Ben?"

Zinnia looked around furtively as though afraid of being overheard before revealing, "They're sending him with a message for Luka, one last offer for him to give this up and accept exile rather than risk war."

"But if he knows where Luka is . . . I don't understand," Em replied.

"Oh, he doesn't know. He would have spilled by now, believe me. After you almost died, that kid became an open book. No, the king's people just assume that Luka's people will find Ben and snatch him up. They'll just put him on the street. They'll try to track him, but of course, Luka's people aren't going to be careless enough to lead our guys to the secret base or whatever."

"But Luka will kill him," November protested.

"Maybe. Probably," Zinnia responded, unconcerned. To her, Ben deserved to die after what he'd done to them all. "So it's true, then? You asked the king to spare him as your reward?" November nodded. "Why?"

"I'm not sure. I mean, I kind of felt sorry for him, what with Luka taking advantage of how screwed up he was, but I don't think that's why. The idea just, sort of, came to me," November replied.

"Well, at least this way he has a chance, I guess," her friend said a bit skeptically.

"I guess."

Shortly thereafter, Zinnia's phone buzzed, and she returned to her mother's side where she had been spending almost every hour since they had arrived in Las Vegas. This left November to the task of calming down enough to eat before taking a much-needed bath and tumbling into her comfortable bed in her favorite white nightgown, hoping against hope for a dreamless sleep.

A dead woman in threadbare clothes swings from a noose as birds peck at her dead eyes. A young girl screams at the hands of merciless priests. A woman rides a horse dangerously fast, her hair streaming behind her, her belly round with pregnancy. A fairy, silver-haired and silver-eyed, addresses her troops from horseback. A woman, running, becomes a wolf mid-stride. Lilith and Ilyn, arm in arm. Lilith and Ilyn, feed together.

She slept exceptionally poorly, even for her. This was not too surprising, given the execution in which she'd just played a starring role. It seemed she couldn't sleep more than an hour without jerking awake, shaking, sweating, occasionally screaming. Pine came to check on her more than once. In the end, he just sat in the room with her, which made her feel a little better, or at least, less alone. When she finally gave up on sleep, she opened her eyes to see him still sitting in the little armchair next to the television, his eyes trained on her, watchful and concerned.

298

"Morning," he said as she sat up in the bed and turned to check the clock. "Had enough tossing and turning?"

"Yeah," she said. "Maybe some food and some sunshine will make me feel human again."

"Do you want to check out the atrium? There's a café down there, and it usually isn't too busy this early in the afternoon," Pine offered.

November smiled. "That sounds cheerful. Let's do it."

She dressed carefully, not wanting to look like a slob if she ran into any of the dozens of important fairies she had met the previous night. She might have been beyond caring about politics, but she still had her pride. She no longer felt like an imposter in designer clothes, but she was still acutely aware of the luxury of them. She put on a little makeup, mostly to cover up the constant dark circles that plagued her pale face. Then she stood staring at her hair, wondering how to hide it this time. It was growing back out pretty quickly, but it was still only barely an inch long. "Eh," she said out loud. "What the heck?" She found some gel, spiked it up all crazy, and called it done.

Pine smiled when he saw it. "November Snow, trend-setter. It'll be on the cover of Vogue in two months."

"Right," she replied, rolling her eyes. "As if fairies have room to talk about weird hair. Shall we?"

The atrium was quite impressive: all glass and water and green plants quite out of place for the desert. She especially liked the waterfall. Most of the restaurants and night clubs at the resort had their entrances off of this central space. It was still afternoon, so it wasn't yet swarming with the people who would fill the place after dark. There were some families with children, and a number of fairies who nodded politely to her and kept their distance when they saw her formidable entourage of fairy guards.

All the vampires were, of course, still resting. November wondered what Ilyn might be doing. He was usually awake by 2 or 3 pm. She immediately caught a glimpse of him alone at a desk, drinking cold blood from a mug, his lit pipe lying forgotten in an ornate ashtray. *Stop looking for him*, she told herself impatiently. *He doesn't want you. He doesn't deserve you.*

After a light meal, she returned to her room to change before heading to the pool complex. She was in desperate need of relaxation after the previous evening's violence and endless bad dreams, so she thought she might as well take advantage of the fact that she was trapped in a fancy hotel. The resort boasted four different pools and a number of steaming whirlpools. November chose the very well-heated salt water pool. It was located in a shady sort of grotto underneath a stone overhang, and with most everyone catching the last few rays of sun beside the outdoor pools, it was mostly deserted. Only one other woman began swimming laps as November floated aimlessly in an attempt to wash away her tension.

Suddenly, a hand closed around November's ankle like a vice, jerking her violently underwater. She kicked out frantically, struggling to escape as her assailant pulled her ten feet to the bottom of the pool and held her there. Unable to keep her eyes open in the salty water, she heard rather than saw her guards dive into the pool. Her lungs began to burn as her security team worked quickly to disentangle her from her attacker. Strong hands tugged her in several directions. Finally, just as she began to panic and her vision began to darken, she felt herself being pulled toward the surface.

The next thing she knew, she was on the pool deck, coughing and gasping for breath as Pine pounded on her back. The whole episode couldn't have lasted more than twenty seconds. She said a

300

silent prayer of thanks for fairy speed. She looked around to see Willow and two other guards dragging away a dazed-looking fairy. "Who? Why?" she managed to ask between coughs. She began to tremble, and Pine wrapped her up in a towel.

"That fairy from the gas station – you know, the one you killed in the bathroom? Apparently that's his mother," Pine explained. He shook his head. "I'm sorry we didn't see her as a threat in time to head her off. I should have been suspicious – no fairy chooses shade when the sun is still out. Do you think you can walk? I'd like to get you back to the room before anything else goes wrong."

"Yes, let's go," she agreed in a weak voice, standing unsteadily and pulling on her bathrobe. "Better get me back in my cage before Dogwood's sister gets here with a machine gun or Lilith's hairdresser shows up with a chainsaw," she added in a voice made stronger by bitterness. "Maybe Ben's old college roommate can stab me with a ski pole." Pine pressed worried lips together as he led her back to the elevator.

Back in her room, just after sunset, she lay curled up in her bed, buried under a pile of blankets, still in her bathing suit and wrapped up in a robe. She just couldn't seem to get warm. On the other side of her locked door, a whispered conference was taking place. She heard it all with her gift rather than her ears, though she was too upset to give them her full attention. She cried soundlessly, her fist in her mouth, as they argued over her in the living room.

"How could you let this happen?" Ilyn asked, furious and pacing, his ire directed at Willow and Pine.

"The assailant was cleared to enter the hotel by your people, as well as the security in her own delegation from Maine. No one suspected her of anything. We neutralized her within seconds of her making contact with November," Willow protested. "There's also no indication she was sent by Luka. He wants the girl alive, after all."

"Is she injured?" Savita asked with characteristic calm.

"It looks like just a few bruises," Pine answered. "But she refuses to see a doctor or let us heal her. I would say guess the pain is more mental than physical."

"What is she thinking?" William asked his older sister.

"I cannot tell from here. I've told you many times: she's not as easy to read as other humans. I have to make physical contact to get much of anything, and I very much doubt my telepathically assaulting her would improve the situation at the moment," Savita replied with some irritation.

The meeting was interrupted by the arrival of young Zinnia, who was decidedly less calm than Savita. She slammed the door before demanding of her king, "What the hell did you do this time?"

For a moment, Ilyn's hackles went up, and he seemed about to take the blue-haired fairy to the woodshed. Zinnia was uncowed in the midst of her fury. Finally, he relaxed as though acknowledging his guilt, and all he said was, "It wasn't me, this time. At least, not proximately."

"That gas station kid's nutbar mother tried to drown her in the pool," Pine explained sucinctly to Zinnia.

"In theory, that should make her pissed off and frightened," Zinnia answered.

"But she's not?" Pine asked quietly.

"No," Zinnia said, looking accusingly directly into his eyes. "This is more like--."

302

"Despair," Ilyn finished for her.

"I think today was just one more thing on top of everything else. She's barely sleeping. That nonsense at the execution last night shook her up, I imagine. It's not as though she's accustomed to dispatching people," Pine added. "She's overwhelmed."

Zinnia picked up the thread. "She feels trapped and alone, and she has little hope that her situation will improve. If we don't take better care of her, she's either going to make a run for it or one of us will find her swinging from a chandelier."

"If it were possible to set her free, I would," the King replied sadly.

"Well, maybe you should tell *her* that," Zinnia retorted.

"I don't think seeing me will make her feel any better," he replied.

"She'd be hard-pressed to feel much worse, Father," Savita countered gently.

"You two need to manage her," he said to Pine and Willow. "Handling a human servant should not be my problem."

"If you weren't worried about her-- if you really didn't care – you wouldn't be standing here," Zinnia said. "You can tell yourself all you want that this is beneath your dignity as a vampire or whatever," she continued, rolling her eyes, "but you and I both know the truth." She crossed her arms stubbornly, adding, "Either go talk to her, or go away and give her some peace. She doesn't need to be hearing all of us talking about her behind her back."

Ilyn made up his mind. "Get back to work, the lot of you," he ordered as he strode toward the bedroom door.

November squeezed her eyes shut when she heard the tumblers in the lock moving. *Please just make me invisible. Make them all go away.* Ilyn walked toward her, stopping next to her bed. She was expecting him to coldly lecture her form on high, but to her surprise, he knelt next to her bed.

"November?" he asked quietly.

She lifted her head away from her knees and opened her eyes. Anger bubbled up past her hopelessness. "What do you want? Do you need me to cut Ben's head off with a hatchet or something?" Her voice was sharp and brittle.

"I am sorry about last night," he said. "If I'd had any idea that she would choose you . . . I suppose she thought it was a chance at vengeance, forcing you to do it."

I don't know about that, she thought, but she said aloud only, "Why are you here?"

"I wanted to make sure you were alright," he replied.

"I will live to be used another day," she said flatly, "so you can go ahead and get back to more important things."

"Little one, you have every reason to be angry, but –"

"I am not your little one! You are so patronizing!" she yelled, suddenly sitting up in her bed to face him, eyes blazing. Her robe slipped off her shoulders, revealing her bathing suit and the physical evidence of her very bad afternoon. Ilyn winced when he saw the livid bruises from her underwater struggle.

"And damn straight, I'm angry," she continued without pause. "You know, the reason I helped Savita, that I helped all of you, was that I felt badly for all the people Luka has hurt and killed, and I thought it was worthwhile to help stop him. It was nice to think that maybe my gift finally meant something.

"And the longer this goes on, the less I can see why I should care who gets to be king of the leeches. And I thought I had a home now, and friends. But then you have to go and use my friends to try and control me. Sending Pine with your blood – how could you do that? You should have at least done it yourself.

"And to top it all off, now I find out that when I do get turned into a vampire, I'll be even more of a slave than I already am, under the control of a man who thinks that because I'm human I'm not worthy of being loved. I have *nothing* to look forward to. Before you showed up, I had made my peace with my fate, and now that peace is gone. You have left me with nothing. What the hell did I ever do to you to deserve this?"

She pressed her lips together, trying in vain to stop the tears her tirade had set free. *And I so hate that I cry when I'm angry!*

"Nothing," he responded softly. "You've done nothing, and you don't deserve any of this. But in my experience, hardly anyone is free, and deserving has precious little to do with what people get." He looked at her beseechingly, but she refused to meet his eyes, drawing her knees back up to her chest. "When I sent Pine, I thought it would be easier for you that way, given the tenor of our last conversation."

"It wasn't. Are you sure you weren't making it easier for you instead?" she replied, unusually merciless.

"Possibly," he admitted after a moment. "Perhaps it was a mistake. I seem to be making a lot of those recently."

He ran his hands through his hair, seemingly having picked up the habit from Birch. "And as for who is 'king of the leeches,' I wouldn't much care myself if I thought Luka would be satisfied ruling his own. But he is greedy, and he has greater designs. He would make slaves of the entire human race. He would exterminate the werewolves, who, my history with them notwithstanding, don't deserve to die for old grudges. I've done enough evil in my life that I don't want to see more done. I can't just step aside and facilitate Luka's violence. I ask that you continue to help us, even though we don't deserve it, even though we've made your life a prison. Of course, if you refuse, I'm not going to do anything bad to you."

She said nothing, his words worming their way through her anger and fear. "As for the life you anticipate having after your death, I take it that someone told you of the bond, the tie that binds maker and child in the first few years?" the king asked.

"It came out that night when they were all trying to convince me to drink your blood," she affirmed, swallowing the fresh rage that welled up whenever she thought of that evening. "I would have appreciated knowing about that sooner."

"I've never abused the bond with any of my children, lit— November. I have used it only to protect them, and their prey. Learning how to feed safely, adapting to the vampire life – these are difficult things. Once my offspring were able to fend for themselves adequately, I set them free. I would do the same for you, November, if and when the time comes. I swear it. Besides, I have many children, which weakens the maker's control. You have enough legitimate things to fear. Please don't let this be one of them, brave girl."

November finally looked up at him with hard, studying eyes. After an eternity, she nodded and said, "You can see why I might have difficulty trusting you at the moment."

"Indeed."

"Alright," she replied. "Thank you for coming to talk to me instead of delegating it." And with that, she curled back up under her covers, still not ready to face the world.

"It's rather the least I could do," he said, standing up to leave. He reached out a hand to touch her, but stopped short when she stiffened in anticipation of the unwelcome contact. He lingered at the door, looking at her, looking for something, but she had already closed her eyes and tucked her forehead against her knees, hiding her face under the covers. He silently took his leave.

The remainder of the day was quiet. Zinnia clucked and fussed over her for a little while before having to return to her duties as a page. Confined to her suite, November finally managed to rouse herself enough to bathe, change clothes, and order some room service.

The talk with Ilyn had helped her a bit. She had to give him some credit for that. She tried to distract herself with movies and books, but found more peace in drawing some of her recent visions. They seemed unusual to her, a seemingly random assortment of women from disparate time periods, featuring none of the people playing parts in the current political and familial drama. And yet, they seemed important and familiar and somehow related, but she couldn't say how. She started a new binder for them.

By three in the morning, she was exhausted and sore, and she tired of waiting for Zinnia to get back. Off to bed she went.

A rough night's sleep came to a rougher ending as November awoke in the late afternoon, shaken frantically by Willow. "Em, we have to go, right now. You're in danger, and the king is moving you to a more secure location."

November sat up, brought instantly awake by Willow's intense, worried voice. "Where's Pine?" she asked, disentangling herself from the sheets.

"Securing the path to the car," Willow replied.

"Where are my shoes?" November asked, unable to recall in the rush where she had left them.

"No time, come on," Willow insisted, grabbing her by the arm and pushing her toward the door. The fairy warrior held a dagger at the ready.

The hallway was empty. November's hair began to stand on end. Something was badly wrong. They turned a corner and saw some unfamiliar fairy faces. Willow pressed her into a doorway. The group passed them by without even a glance, as though November and Willow were invisible. As soon as the group was gone, Willow continued propelling November down the corridor, leaving her no time to wonder at Willow's little trick.

They approached the elevators, one of which had been propped open, waiting for them. When they were nearly there, Pine appeared from a hidden corner: crawling, desperate, severely injured, an arrow running straight through him.

November screamed in shock and horror and tried to move toward him. Willow yanked the girl violently back to her side and threw a knife, which buried itself in Pine's chest. He looked up at November, his eyes full of guilt and sorrow and, without a sound, he disappeared in a blinding flash of light.

"No!" November screamed again, struggling to break free from Willow's iron grip. She barely felt the prick of the needle the fairy inserted into her neck. She was unconscious before she could draw enough breath for another scream.

Chapter 13

A woman burns at the stake, the flames licking her feet while the smoke chokes the life out of her. A terrified fairy child hides as her kin are butchered by wolves. Ilyn shovels dirt onto Savita's corpse. Marisha drains Luka's blood, his mismatched eyes open wide, a smile on his face. Sunset over the desert. Flies on Julia's face. Willow on the phone. Zinnia throws a flower into November's grave. A fairy child lies in shock surrounded by destruction. Ilyn and Luka make their way toward her. Luka picks her up and cradles her to his chest, strokes her hair, murmurs words of comfort. A little girl with a pockmarked face gazes at Luka as he drains her blood. She asks if he is an angel. He laughs. A fairy carries an unconscious girl over her shoulder, turning to fire a crossbow one-handed at those chasing her through a parking deck. She is herself hit, more than once, but she does not so much as stagger. She reaches her getaway car, tossing the girl into an open trunk as she turns to finish off her enemies before speeding out into the daylight.

November woke into a terrifying, bone-shaking darkness. It took a long while before she was lucid enough to realize that she was in the trunk of a car. She tried to move her limbs but found that she was tightly bound at both ankles and wrists, her arms pinned painfully behind her back. Her mouth was taped shut. An icy ball of fear filled her stomach. Her mind was running a frantic loop, whispering again and again, *Willow is a traitor. She killed Pine, and she is going to give me to a monster.*

She wondered how long she'd been out, where in the world they could be, how much of a head start Willow had. She wondered how much the pending fire at the hotel would slow down a rescue attempt, if in fact Ilyn's people were unable to prevent it. She wondered if anyone would come for her at all.

She cried for a while, but that made it difficult to breathe through her nose, so she stopped, wishing fervently for the tape over her mouth to disappear. She tried to use her gift to look outside the car, but Willow was driving impossibly fast through a rural landscape entirely foreign to her. Rolling around in the trunk, the speed was terrifying. She experienced a moment of sympathy for the unfortunate Dogwood.

Her heart raced when the car slowed to a stop. She simultaneously hoped and dreaded that the trunk door would open. When it did, she blinked her eyes, blinded by the bright sunlight. Willow looked down at her, her face in shadow. "No screaming-- do you understand?" November nodded.

Willow pulled her from the trunk, more gently than November had expected. The fairy removed the gag and wiped her captive's face with a damp cloth. Thankfully, her kidnapper had had the courtesy to slather her lips with petroleum jelly before taping her mouth. The fairy held up a bottle of water, which November gratefully sipped. Willow removed it too soon and bent to cut the plastic tie around her ankles with a pair of hedge clippers.

She led November a few paces from the car, holding tightly to her elbow. "You try to run, I will catch you, and I will make you wish you hadn't. Now do your business." November squatted and relieved herself in the dirt, face burning with anger and shame. She took a look around the deserted turnoff, unable to keep herself from hoping for someone to come to her aid. There was no one.

She could guess why the fairy had done this, so she felt no need to ask. She berated herself for not seeing the danger months earlier, when she'd learned what had happened to Willow's family at the hands of werewolves. Willow swiftly bound and gagged her again and put her back in the trunk, dosing her with more drugs while ignoring November's whimpering attempts to plead with her from behind the tape.

Just as the hood was closing, November caught a glimpse of two glowing orbs floating several yards behind her kidnapper. With a flash, they transformed into two heavily armed fairy soldiers. Hope filled her, and she fought the drugs in an effort to stay awake. She could hear arrows glancing off the hood, then gunshots as Willow pulled her own weapon. Her hope was short-lived. Their pursuers quickly fell at the hands of Willow's experience and determination. The drugs dragged November back under, and Willow made another narrow escape.

Under the influence of the sedative, her nightmares were even more disjointed and relentless than usual. They were a crazy quilt of clashing time periods and encounters that had never happened and never could.

Julia pours tea for Marisha in what looked like a Roman courtyard. Ilyn buys cotton candy at the carnival and gives it to her, standing in bright sunlight. Willow's childhood self screams inside the house of mirrors.

The next time they stopped, Willow left her in the trunk while she hijacked someone's car. Only after she had the new car running did she transfer her victim, so quickly that November barely got a look at the unfortunate soul whose life Willow had entirely drained. He was reduced to a blackened husk. November screamed behind her gag as the trunk door slammed shut and the pharmaceuticals sent her back into a spiral of confusing visions.

As the winter sun beat down on the hood, the air in the trunk grew uncomfortably warm and close. Sweat matted November's short hair to her skull, and her thirst grew intolerable. Once the sun set, however, she quickly became chilled and longed for the warmth of the day to return. She so hated being cold.

She heard the ring of a cell phone a few times, and conversation too muffled for her to understand. She supposed that Willow was checking in with her master and receiving instructions. The car slowed once more, and her heart hammered as she feared they had come to their destination. Instead, she heard a door quickly open and shut. Willow immediately took off again with a squeal. To her surprise, she made out a familiar voice in the cabin of the car: their new passenger was Ben.

November tried to marshal her gifts and focus her mind on them, struggling to push away the fog of drugs and hunger and make out what the two traitors were saying to each other.

"I thought you would run," Willow commented. "I thought for sure someone would have to hunt you down."

"What would be the point?" he replied matter-of-factly. "I must say, I'm surprised, too. You. You were another agent. Reliable Willow. I cannot believe it," Ben said, incredulous. He gave a bark of bitter laughter. "You couldn't help me out after I got caught?"

"Stuff it. I would put you in the trunk if it weren't currently occupied," Willow replied flatly. "Your incompetence had no bearing on my mission. I have been under cover for over a century, and I wasn't about to jeopardize that for an idiot newborn vampire who couldn't manage to do anything without giving himself away."

"Fair enough," he allowed, not seeming to care enough about his fate to actually be angry about it. "Why don't you just kill me and deliver this letter yourself? Save him the trouble," he asked almost hopefully. Evidently he wasn't looking forward to an encounter with Luka.

"Because those aren't my orders," she replied impatiently. "Are you seriously going to talk the whole way? Do I have to pull your tongue out?"

"Sorry. I've just been talking to walls for months, that's all," he responded quietly. "Do you mind if I ask one question?" He construed her lack of a reply as acquiescence. "Why? I mean, haven't you worked for them for, like, hundreds of years?"

Willow heaved a sigh. "They betrayed me first, when they made peace with the animals that killed my kin. They are not worthy of anyone's loyalty." November had a strange feeling that she was leaving something out.

"Fair enough," he said again. "I assume November is in the trunk? You smell like her." Willow just nodded. "Is she okay?" he asked, trying and failing to keep the concern out of his voice.

"She'll live," Willow replied, adding, "Look, if you know what's good for you, you will forget any feelings you have for her. She's Luka's now. If he lets you live, and that's highly unlikely, you had better keep your little crush to yourself." Ben said nothing. He just looked out the window. Willow turned on some music.

They switched cars one more time, to an SUV that had apparently been left for Willow in a planned location, as there was no murder involved in this swap. Since the vehicle had no trunk, the prisoner was instead tossed unceremoniously onto the floor in the back. The windows were heavily tinted, and the sun had long since set. There was no way anyone would see her.

"Oh, jeez, Willow? Is all that really necessary?" Ben asked, breaking his silence of several hours when he saw the sorry state November was in. "Those ties are cutting into her, and it looks like you beat the crap out of her. How much of a fight did she put up?"

"Most of those bruises are from yesterday when some deranged fairy tried to drown her, and I'm not taking any chances after how many times this has been botched in the last six months," the fairy answered in a hard voice.

Ben looked at November with sad eyes. She met them with her own eyes full of fear. He looked awful, even more gaunt and worn than she remembered. She wondered if he was grateful that she'd asked for his life to be spared or if he wished that he'd gotten his execution over with. Of course, November hadn't know that Ilyn would so warp her request by sending the prisoner to an almost certain death.

She could tell he was considering doing something unwise as he shifted his focus from her to the driver, and she could see the moment when he admitted to himself that he didn't have a prayer of taking the much older fairy in a fight, certainly not without getting November killed in the ensuing high-speed crash. She tried to smile her understanding through the duck tape before turning her gaze out the window to the moon high in the sky. At least it was something prettier to look at than the inside of a trunk. She wondered if she would ever see the sun again.

November had no idea how many hours this journey was taking, though she thought it had been early afternoon when they left the hotel and it was now well past sunset. She couldn't be certain she hadn't missed a whole day somewhere. As disoriented as she was from the drugs, the visions, the thirst, and the imprisonment, she knew very little for certain. She knew that the road had gotten rougher; the additional bruises forming all over her body told her that much. She assumed they must be in the middle of nowhere, for she heard no other cars going by. Her numb limbs and the screaming pain in her shoulders told her that she'd been bound for a long time. She knew she was frightened and hungry and alone.

She thought of Pine, there one moment and then gone in a flash of light. She tried not to cry. She thought of Ilyn, who showed his attachment to her yet denied it to them both. The thought that she might never see him again, or worse yet, that she would see him as an enemy, made her want to break things in grief and anger. She prayed that he was safe, that all her friends were safe. Her well-justified anger had melted away in the heat of danger, and all she felt was longing and forgiveness and sympathy. She imagined that he was with her, singing one of the songs he'd used to comfort her at the new year. She could almost smell the pipe-smoke in his clothes.

They stopped for gas. It was a two-pump, cash-only, pay-inside kind of place. A couple of other cars were parked there. Kids were hanging out, sitting on their trunks, drinking soda and smoking. Willow turned to her and said, "If you try anything, I will kill everyone here." She then turned to Ben. "If you try anything, I will hurt her and make you watch."

After she slammed her door and entered the tiny store, Ben turned once again to November. "I'm so sorry," he whispered, over and over. "I'm so sorry. I'll find a way to stop him. I'll find a way to help you. I will. I'm so sorry." He looked so desperate and sad. The cocky frat boy had turned old and haunted. Even if she hadn't been gagged, November had no idea what she would say. It was hard for her to believe that there was anything Ben could possibly do to save her, given his track record. And yet, it was a comfort to hear a sympathetic word in such a desperate moment. Later, she would feel a pang of guilt for having doubted him. Ben was the kind of person it was easy to underestimate.

Willow returned and started pumping the gas, ending Ben's monologue. They got on the road again. Bad asphalt turned to gravel and then to rutted dirt. November was bouncing around something awful, finally prompting Ben to insist that Willow move her to a seat and belt her in. "Willow, she's going to get a concussion if this goes on much longer, and if she vomits with that gag on, she could choke."

After a moment of thought, the fairy pulled over, unbound her captive's wrists, tore off the gag, strapped her into a seat, and rebound one arm to an armrest, all without saying a word.

"Thanks," November murmured as the vehicle resumed its race down what had to be the worst road in the continental U.S. She leaned her forehead against the cool window glass and tried not to throw up. Ben looked around for something to use as a make-shift sick bag, coming up with only his hat, which he placed in her lap with a shrug. She gave him a shadow of a smile before she commenced dry heaving. She was momentarily grateful for the fact that she hadn't eaten anything all day. Thankfully, after a while the road smoothed out a bit and her nausea passed. Exhausted and numb, November gazed out the window into pitch blackness. They hadn't passed another car in hours.

Suddenly, they were driving on smooth asphalt instead of dirt. It seemed so quiet, and November wondered why the road had suddenly resumed before realizing that it probably meant that they were getting close to their destination. With a screech of its breaks, the S.U.V came to a stop. Willow emerged, clipped November's wrist free, and pulled her out of the car, dragging her still-bound feet in the dirt. "Look," the fairy said. "We're almost home."

November followed her kidnapper's pointing finger. Her heart sank as she took in the fortress at the end of the road. A flat-topped mountain rose above the rest of the canyon-cracked desert. The cliff was almost vertical, its rocky face illumined by moving searchlights meant to reveal anyone foolish enough to try the climb. No windows glowed to break up the monotony of the wall; even the scrub brush had been burned away to minimize handholds and hiding places.

She could see a large, fortified gate at the base of the installation, which appeared to have been carved from the rock. It appeared that there was not a single place to force an entry other than the main entrance or perhaps the roof. She identify what looked like a water tank and radar or satellite dishes on top of the structure along with towers dotting the circumference of the roof, prepared to locate and rain fire down on any force approaching from above or below. She supposed the Gatling guns must have been modified to take silver and wooden bullets, then wondered how she could manage such calm speculation while this view snuffed out all the hope remaining in her heart. She could make out small objects flying around the installation like so many bees around a hive. She gasped when she realized that they were people: fairies and vampires on aerial patrol with what appeared to be rocket launchers at the ready.

It was obvious that the road they travelled was the only land route into the base, surrounded as it was by a barren, formidable landscape creased with cliffs and canyons. She wondered briefly whether it was beautiful by day and decided that it probably was. A few hundred yards down the road, about halfway between them and the fortress, stood a heavily-armed and guarded checkpoint securing a drawbridge over what looked to be a wide chasm. Willow held her up by her arm, letting her take in the view before she began speaking. "I want you to see this so that you know that there is no escape in your future. Even if anyone survives to come for you, which I highly doubt, they will never be able to get into the fort, and there would be no way to get you out. It will be impossible for you to escape on your own. I'm not doing this because I want to see you suffer, November. I like you, honestly. I simply want you to accept your fate, because it will be much easier for you if you do. If you do as you're told and accept that Luka is your master now, he will treat you well. He will cherish you as a treasure. If you fight him, he will not coddle you like Ilyn and William did. He will do whatever is necessary to break your will."

November kept her eyes on the landscape as helpless tears began to flow. Willow's voice softened slightly. "Soon you will be one of us, and in time, you will understand that our cause is just. You will be proud to be part of our victory, the new world we're going to build. You will be a hero to generations of our people, a beloved queen. Time will pass, and all of this will be a fading memory. You will learn to be happy again."

Finally, November spoke. "I would rather you just killed me."

"I know," the spy replied. "But you are far too valuable for that." The fairy shook her head. "They don't deserve your loyalty, seer. They have failed you, again and again, just as they failed me. If they hadn't, you wouldn't be here, would you?" Willow carried November back to the car.

"One more time," she said, pulling November's arms behind her back again and placing tape once more over her mouth. "Forgive me," she said, pulling out a black hood and placing it over November's head. After an initial shudder of fear in the darkness of the hood, November was almost grateful to have the privacy to weep without being seen.

They stopped at the checkpoint by the bridge. November could hear voices as Willow convinced the guards of her identity and the value of her two pieces of cargo. She could hear the gears grinding as the bridge was lowered. They drove on for a few minutes. Finally, Willow stopped and turned off the vehicle. Strong hands lifted November out of the car. Someone placed her over his shoulders like a sack of potatoes and carried her a long way, first through the frigid night air and then into some kind of structure. Too terrified and exhausted to concentrate, she was unable to use her gift to peek through the bag on her head. Between the gag and the hood, she began struggling to breathe, which only added to her panic.

Finally, after being carried down long corridors and up and down spiral staircases, she heard a door swing open, and she was deposited on a cold stone floor. Hands gently removed the black hood and swiftly ripped off the gag, drawing a loud gasp of pain. November looked up and gazed with fear into the mismatched eyes of Luka Lazzari, erstwhile Lord of Arizona.

Chapter 14

"Ah," he breathed, gently grasping her chin to look in her eyes. "It is you, after all this time. I knew it. I am so glad Ilyn didn't turn you. It would have been such a shame to have to attempt a redraining and transfusion. It can go so badly wrong."

She looked at him mutely, fear and pain and confusion swirling around her face. He laughed and pulled out a familiar knife of gleaming silver, inlaid with blood-darkened wood. An instinctive panic filled her at the sight of it, a blind, animal urge to flee, though flight was impossible. "Shhh," he said, cutting the plastic ties constraining her limbs.

It was an oddly familiar gesture. For a moment, when she looked at her hands, they looked like someone else's. The fingernails were missing. The moment passed, and her hands were once again her own. "No fairy wounds for you today. You're safe at home, now. Well done recovering my knife, by the way, Willow," he said, "and for delivering her in good condition. She was in a lot worse shape the last time I found her, I must say. Though I do think the binding might have been overkill. Her wrists are badly bruised. And the gag – look at her poor skin. She's just a human girl, after all, in body anyway."

He took his attention off November for a moment to rise and kiss Willow on the forehead. "I am so proud of you, my darling."

The fairy smiled and embraced him before answering, "Perhaps I was overcautious, but given how difficult it has been to obtain her, I thought I'd best err on that side. And I would not underestimate her, my lord. I've seen her do some rather improbable things."

"Like killing a fairy with a rosary?" He laughed again. "That was splendid, I agree. Extremely inconvenient," he added toward

November in a mock scolding tone, wagging a finger in reproach, "But still, splendid."

He clucked his tongue at the welts on her wrists and began massaging her dead limbs. She flinched and tried to pull away from his touch, which was, again, impossible. She tried unsuccessfully to stifle a whimper of pain as the blood began to return to her arms and legs. "It's alright, kitten, we'll get you warm and fed and you'll feel much better."

There was a thick, woolen blanket warming by the fire. He snatched it up, wrapped his prisoner in it, lifted her as though she was a small child, and placed her in a large, high-backed chair set at a long plank table. He took the matching chair at the head of the table, just to her right. "Broth first," he commanded.

November hesitated for a moment. Soon, her brain caught up, and she realized that if Luka Lazzari wanted to drug or poison her, tricking her into drinking soup would hardly be necessary. It took both her shaking hands to bring the steaming mug to her lips. After a few swallows, she began to feel a bit more in command of her faculties. She was still terrified and confused and ached all over, but at least she was on the way to no longer being frozen, starved, and dehydrated. She opened her mouth and managed to rasp out, "Thank you."

"Oh, see how polite she is, Willow? And most humans these days are so rude. Delightful." When November finished the broth, Luka rang a bell. A human girl entered. She wore a simple, warm-looking, long-sleeved dress with thick stockings but no shoes. She was obviously enthralled, and November could see numerous marks from vampire bites old and new. She set the plate before November, and looked to Luka for instruction. He dismissed her with a wave, at which she curtsied and hurried out of the room as fast as possible.

November looked down at the plate to find half a roast chicken, heavily buttered mashed potatoes, and bright sautéed green beans. The smell alone was enough to bring tears to her eyes after her ordeal in the trunk. There was a napkin, but no silverware.

She forced herself to look up at her captor. "May I please have a knife and fork?" she asked softly, forcing herself to look into his mismatched eyes.

"Oh, I'm afraid not, kitten," he replied with a condescending smile. "We find it best not to allow our humans cutlery. It cuts down on unfortunate incidents."

November looked down again at the plate, fully aware that this policy was likely less a safety measure and more likely a way to humiliate her by making her feel like a savage in front him. Still, she was hungry, and she would need all her strength in the days to come. She placed the napkin in her lap and deftly tore the chicken into dainty pieces. The chicken and beans were easy enough to eat with her hands. She decided to use the bread to scoop the potatoes. She tried to eat slowly and neatly, striving to give no sign of her desperate hunger nor the hot feeling of fear that grew in her chest the more Luka studied her. She said nothing until she had eaten everything on her plate and drained the milk in the tumbler that had accompanied it. After all, if she displeased him, there was no way of knowing when the next meal would come.

And she fully intended to displease him.

Luka's gaze upon her was relentless, and she wondered what he was looking for. She forced herself to look around the room, to try to see what the room could tell her about the man. The chamber appeared to be a large study. The table at which she had dined was half-covered with books and maps and papers in various languages. A large desk occupied one corner of the room, complete with laptop and tablet, and one wall was lined with bookcases. The remainder of the roughly carved stone walls were covered in many places by tapestries and paintings. There was a sitting area by the fire furnished with two heavy armchairs of brown leather with seats so deep she knew her feet wouldn't touch the ground. The ceiling had a dome of glass in the center with a retractable cover, and the moon shone brightly down into the chamber. She finally noticed that classical music was playing from a turntable in the corner. The room seemed strangely cozy for the lair of a villain like Luka.

The man himself was fairly unremarkable. He was of average height, medium build, with brown hair shot liberally with gray above a high forehead creased from years of concentration as a human scribe. He was dressed like a religious brother, in a long black cassock with a high collar. His long fingers were stained at the tips with what November sincerely hoped was ink. His most striking features were his eyes, of course, shrewd and intent, one green and one brown. A hawkish nose and a cruel mouth completed his intimidating face. He wasn't exactly handsome, but he had a cold sort of charisma, and his features certainly commanded one's attention.

"The food was to your liking, my dear?" he inquired, finally breaking the silence.

She nodded. "It was excellent, thank you." It was a struggle to force out the words through trembling lips.

"Yes, we captured a very good chef some years ago whom we put to work overseeing the kitchen. You'll find we take great care with our animals. They are well fed, well clothed, and well housed. The vast majority of them are content and live long and pleasant lives, far better than their previous ones," he opined, as though a farmer discussing his sheep. His casual superiority made November's full stomach churn. "I feel I must apologize for the ineptitude of some of those in my employ. Lilith was under the strictest orders to bring you to me in pristine condition. Alas, when you caught my father's eye, she could not control her jealousy. She failed me twice that night. She is lucky her death was not at my hand, or she would have known much more suffering."

Not having any idea what to say, November searched for words. She swallowed and said, "I assumed as much."

"In spite of the trouble you have caused to me and my plans, kitten, I have no desire to see you suffer. It is not your fault my brother got to you first. That failure belongs to me," he said magnanimously.

He seemed to expect a reply, so she said, hesitatingly, "I'm relieved to hear it."

He smiled wolfishly at her before responding, "Yes, I should think so. Now, November, in between filling your head with lies about my character, did any of my relatives bother to tell you what you are?"

"What I . . . they just said that humans like me are rare, that I have a special gift." November was puzzled at the turn this conversation was taking. She had been expecting to be interrogated about Ilyn and William and her visions.

He gave a bark of laughter. "True enough, if incomplete. Do you mean to say that you still believe that all you are is a teenage carnie from a trailer park? A human child of a whore, barely grown, who has somehow become enmeshed in a supernatural power struggle, guiding the plans of kings and lords when she ought to be studying for the college boards?"

Pride reared up in her, and she lifted a defiant chin. "I'm not ashamed of who I am or where I come from," she retorted without thinking how her defiance might be perceived.

"Good for you, kitten," he said indulgently, to her relief. "I came from the gutter, too, and I applaud your sense of self-worth. But have you really never wondered why you were so unlike other humans, other children? Why you feel so removed from them? Why you are so comfortable with supernatural creatures and so ill-at-ease among the mortal? Why your relationship to the passage of time is so unusual? Why you have so little fear of death? Why you can send your soul out of your body on reconnaissance and bring it back again?" He seemed incredulous.

"My gift – the nature of my upbringing— they isolated me from other people," she protested haltingly.

"Human beings do not see the future, November. They do not read minds. They cannot affect the weather. They can't fly or bend spoons. They cannot resist thrall. They have no supernatural gifts whatsoever. Fairies are born with gifts. Vampires acquire them when they are reborn, the lucky ones. Werewolves, rarely, acquire them when they are bitten or come of age. Humans lack them altogether."

"Savita could read minds when she was human. And her sister could tell fortunes," November protested.

"Exactly, my dear. Savita has never been human," he replied with a smile. "Nor was her sister." He shook his head. "I wonder why Savita didn't tell you. William, I understand him not knowing it. He is tragically ignorant. Ilyn, I thought, was better read, or would have tasted it in your blood, since he had so much of Savita's and might recognize its similarity." He shook his head again.

She must have betrayed something in her face, for his next comment was, "Don't tell me my father hasn't tasted you?" She just looked at him. "Truly?" he asked, incredulous, looking back at Willow for confirmation.

"I think he feared upsetting her. William has fed on her, a few sips, months ago, but not Ilyn," she replied with a hint of amusement.

"What a sorry excuse for a vampire he is," Luka said in disbelief. "I don't know why he bothers anymore." He pursed his lips in amusement and gazed silently at his captive, drawing out the suspense.

Unable to contain her frustration any longer, she finally demanded, "Fine, then, what the hell am I?"

"A demon," he said, as though this were the most obvious answer in the world.

She looked at him, disbelieving. "You're saying I'm possessed? I have heard that one before, you know, along with people yelling 'freak' and 'witch' when I tried to go to school."

"Your body is possessed, silly girl. *You* are the demon possessing it. If you don't like that word, you could go with wraith, spirit, whatever you wish. The bottom line is that you are a non-physical supernatural being with the honor or misfortune of being tethered to one body after another for all eternity. When one body no longer operates, you move on to another, taking possession of it at the moment of its conception. For all we know, you've been fairies and vampires and werewolves as well as human beings. You're not eighteen years old. You could be eighteen hundred, or eighteen thousand. You could be as old as creation." He seemed terribly earnest, almost professorial.

"This is crazy," she whispered, disbelieving.

"Is it? It is any crazier than the fact that you can see the past and predict the future? Crazier than dying and climbing back out of the ground? Crazier than people who can fly or bleed light or turn into wolves?"

"I am a person. I'm not some kind of . . . supernatural parasite." *He's just trying to manipulate you*, she told herself. *Savita would have told you if it were true.*

"Why in the world would you rather be a human than a goddess?" He seemed genuinely puzzled.

"If this is true, then why don't I remember all these other lives?" she asked slowly, trying to remain calm and formulate coherent questions.

"Oh, but I think you do, in a way," he countered. "Who knows how many of your visions of the past might be of your own lives? As for not consciously remembered every detail, perhaps it is a coping mechanism, or aids in the survival of the host body. That much of a past could be a burden to one's mental health, I expect. Savita remembers more the older her current body gets, or so she's told me." He studied her for a moment. "You still don't believe me. Have you ever looked at your eyes by fairylight, November?"

At her shake of the head, he raced invisibly fast around the room with a whoosh of displaced air, shoving aside her dinner tray and placing a mirror before her on the table. He picked up a delicately folded piece of paper patterned in violet and yellow. He pulled at it gently and it unfolded into a little cylinder the size of November's hand. With no bulb and no flame, the magic lantern glowed magically from within from the moment it was unfolded. He stood behind her chair and draped a blanket over them, blocking out all other sources of light. The vampire leaned over her shoulder, uncomfortably close. "Look in the mirror and tell me those eyes are human."

She looked at the glass, her image gently lit by the fairy lantern. Her irises remained the deep blue to which she was accustomed, but the whites of her eyes were now replaced by the same midnight blue. This blue, which looked like a becalmed lake by normal light, now looked like a night sky running in fast forward. Pinpricks of light flashed and flickered and whirled around like stars speeding in the heavens. Her pupils, black by day, glowed with the blue-white of a hot flame. She wanted to believe it was a trick, but she knew in her heart that it was not.

November dropped the mirror and jumped back in her chair. Those eyes were not human.

"Maybe everyone's eyes look strange by fairylight," she protested feebly.

"Don't mine look the same?" the vampire asked her, amused by her reaction. She darted a glance at his face and nodded. He pulled away the blanket, and her eyes returned to normal as the ordinary light returned. "The eyes are the only thing that says the same, from body to body. You should see Savita's. They're nearly as spectacular as yours. Hers glow gold with red sparks."

Luka spun her chair around to face him. He looked down at her, saying, "Now I'm sure this is a great deal for you to have to take in all at once. We can talk further tomorrow evening. I'm sure you will have many questions. Dawn is approaching, and we have a little business to attend to first." November shrank away from him as he bent to sniff her hair. "You reek of my father. I must say, I don't care for it."

Willow chimed in. "They had Pine strong-arm her into drinking some of his blood just a few days ago, so they could trace her. It looked like at least an ounce in the vial."

"He didn't even do it himself? Have her drink straight from his wrist? Does he take no joy in anything?" Luka asked, once again incredulous. "I do hope he'll be brave enough to come for her himself, if he lives that long. Not that the blood will be any help to them in finding her, thanks to you." He turned back to his new pet soothsayer. "You have a new master now, kitten. I'll wait until tomorrow to bite you, so you can regain your strength. But tonight, I need you to drink a few sips of my blood."

Panic returned. She struggled to think of a way out, her mind racing. "You don't want me to do that," she protested desperately. "I'll see things you don't want me to know. I'll learn your secrets."

"That would only concern me if there were any chance of your escaping my control, which I assure you, there is not. I want you to see visions of my future; that is part of your usefulness, after all." He rolled up his sleeve and prepared to bite his wrist.

"No!" the girl cried instinctively, "I won't!" She could not face the reality of this monster's blood coursing through her, visions of his sins filling her mind.

He clucked at her. "I promise you, you will. Why make it harder on yourself? Cooperate, kitten. If you don't, I shall have to punish you. I don't allow defiance." He gazed down at her face, which was already wet with terrified tears yet still full of the fight rising within her. "You always have been too brave for your own good, kitten. So much fight in you. You made those Jesuits torture you for hours and gave them nothing. You will make a fine vampire. Willow, some assistance, if you please."

Before she could blink, November was on her back, pressed against the table with enough force to smash the mirror into pieces. Willow held her down by her shoulders while Luka tore into his wrist and pinched his victim's nose closed. As the seer thrashed, shards of glass tore through her nightgown and cut deeply into her back. She held her breath as long as she could, but soon enough, her mouth opened seeking air, and Luka's blood poured in. Forced to swallow lest she choke, she finally gave up fighting, and her tormentors loosened their hold on her. "There, now," Luka said soothingly, stroking her brow. "That's a good girl. Almost done now." His skin healed, and the flow of blood ceased.

She curled into a sobbing ball on top of the table, blood soaking through her nightgown. The last thing she heard before succumbing to the visions was Luka's instruction to Willow: "Heal her at dawn, strip her, and put her in one of the cubes. Perhaps a day down there will put her in a more cooperative frame of mind. And grow her hair back while you're at it. I like to have something to grab hold of."

A little girl, broken, lies in the dark, waiting for death. Luka cuts her bonds, takes her blood, gives her his. Her eyes are deep blue, flecked with starlight. She is happy to die, not understanding that she can't. Juana. He calls her Juana. Luka, crippled, pulls himself along in a contraption made by his enemy. Ilyn, running, surrounded by smoke, calling her name. Luka, killing Agnes. Luka, digging a hole in the ground and climbing in, covering himself with dirt. Luka and Savita, feeding together on dazed humans in a hovel. A werewolf, strapped to a gurney, howling as he changes form, howling in pain at what they do to him. Two werewolves tear each other to pieces while a crowd watches with Luka, laughing. Rubble where a building once stood, the dust still billowing. An old woman, burning at the stake, a cross in her hands. A young woman, throttled at a crossroads. A girl on horseback, fleeing. An oracle in a temple, surrounded by pilgrims. A young girl running in the woods is suddenly a wolf instead. Luka pulls a hatchet out of Willow's skull. A fairy flying, with eyes like the night sky. Explosion after explosion. Scream upon scream. Rivers of blood.

She woke up in darkness black as pitch. She reached up to touch her tender scalp, finding her long locks restored. She felt for the cuts on her back, but her skin was once again unbroken, though it crackled with dried blood. As her awareness returned, she realized that she was naked, freezing cold, and utterly alone. Claustrophobia clouded her mind with fear, and she began to shake. She told herself to focus. She tried to give herself tasks, to calm her anxious thoughts. This was a method she'd often used when placed in isolation at the hospital. Explore the space, she told herself.

She used her ordinary senses first. She felt around next to her. The floor was thickly padded. She crawled until she hit a similarly padded wall a few feet away. She moved along the periphery, finding the door and a drain that reeked of human waste. She could feel air circulating from a vent in the ceiling. She realized that if she was still, she could hear faint voices through the air ducts. This calmed her a bit. She wasn't entirely alone after all.

Exhausted as she was, she was afraid to sleep, afraid of the visions that would pounce on her. She sat in the center of the room and drew her knees into her chest for warmth, then cast out with her sixth sense, trying to get some idea of the layout of her enemy's fortress.

She found dormitories full of addled humans. Some were sleeping, some reading or watching movies. Others were performing chores. They seemed healthy enough, but zombie-like. She continued exploring. The whole place seemed to be carved out of a mountain, a warren of tunnels and man-made caves, five or six floors worth, packed with vampires and fairies and human livestock.

She found a few surprising things, including a helicopter, a laboratory, and what appeared to be an auditorium. She found several padded cells like her own, one of which was occupied by a man obsessively banging his head against the wall. She wondered what his transgression had been.

Finally, she stumbled onto a heartbreaking scene: a small group of people, isolated from the others, leather cuffs around their necks and attached to the wall by shining chains. She gasped in distress when she saw that one of them was a child. At first, she couldn't figure out what made them different from the others. Then they began to howl, the sound echoing through the ventilation system. *Luka is keeping werewolf prisoners.* As their aching song faded, November's heart filled with dread. Whatever the governor of Arizona was keeping them for, it couldn't be good.

When her mind returned to her tiny prison, she tried to think of something, anything, to distract herself from the fear and the cold. She began to sing, softly at first, then with growing volume, trying to fill the space and warm her body. She finished a song and grew quiet. In the silence, she heard a voice. "Keep singing, sister," echoed quietly inside the vent. So she did; for how long, she had no idea. Eventually, her body succumbed to its hunger for sleep, though she woke often, crying out in distress.

The door opened, the light blinding her for a moment before someone shoved a black bag over her head and hauled her to her feet, propelling her into the passageway. She stumbled, her limbs stiff from cold and from sleeping on the floor. "Morning, Oracle. Hope you like the accommodations," came Philemon's cruel voice on her left. "You look delicious. This walk will be the highlight of everyone's day." November's stomach clenched and her face flushed hot with humiliation at the thought of being paraded naked through the halls.

"Stow it," Willow snapped from her right, strangely protective of her charge's feelings.

They seemed to walk forever, past endless twists and turns and up a spiral staircase until they finally removed the bag from November's head. She blinked in the bright light, finding herself in a large bathroom with dozens of toilet stalls, sinks, and open showers. It was clean and bright, covered with white tile.

Willow pointed to the stalls, and November stumbled over to relieve herself, once again mortified that they were listening to her. In her brief moment of privacy, she tried to steel herself for battle. She told herself that this was part of Luka's punishment, that he wanted to humiliate her, and that the best course of action would be to refuse to let it get to her.

Willow handed her a basket of toiletries when she emerged. "Thank you, Willow," she said casually, as though the situation were the most normal thing in the world. She then proceeded to ignore them entirely. She walked over to the sink and carefully brushed and flossed her teeth. She then strode purposefully over to the showers and was pleasantly surprised at the piping hot water that washed over her. She sighed with relief as the water drove the cold out of her limbs and washed off the accumulated blood, sweat, and tears of her days of torment. Just as with the previous evening's meal, she didn't know when her next shower would come, and she was determined to enjoy it as much as she could manage. Thankfully, the rushing of the water mostly drowned out Philemon's comments about what he would do to her if he were Luka. She stood under the water until Willow ordered her out, handed her a towel and a comb, and pointed her toward a bank of blow dryers along one wall.

Once she was dry, Willow handed her some clothes: a long-sleeved v-necked tunic, a skirt that came down to her calf, and a pair of knee-high wool socks. No shoes, and no underwear. *He wants you to feel vulnerable*, she told herself. *I am vulnerable*, her mind replied.

The sack went back over her head, and she was again dragged through the halls and stairways of Luka's headquarters. She expected to be brought back to the study, but instead she was taken to a small, well-furnished suite. The far wall was taken up by a four-poster bed with dark blue linens, an armoire, and a nightstand. The portion of the room nearest the door featured a fireplace with an overstuffed couch in front of it, a well-stocked bookcase, and a sitting area with two comfortable-looking chairs and a round table which was taken up by a generous breakfast tray and a stack of art supplies. There was also an arch leading into a large bathroom to the right of the bed. The message was clear: good girls get to stay here; bad girls get locked up in a dark hole and bathe with Philemon.

"If you need anything, knock on the door, and a guard will check on you," Willow instructed. "And for God's sake, do as you're told when Lord Luka comes."

"I was rather hoping she'd piss him off," Philemon replied, hatred in his eyes. November supposed he blamed her for his woman's death.

November finally turned and looked straight at her mother's murderer. "I'm sorry about Agnes, truly," she said, surprising herself. "Despite what you did to my mother. But it's not my fault your master killed her."

Something blazed in his face, but quickly disappeared. He said nothing and rushed out the door with a faint whoosh. Willow soon followed, bolting the heavy door loudly behind her, and the captive was again alone. She assumed she was being watched somehow, by camera or who-knew-what fairy device.

She sat at the table, and as she had done the previous night, deliberately ate every morsel on the plate. She noticed that the fairy lantern from the night before was folded carefully in the center of the table in from of her, a little gift from Luka to remind her of what she really was. She had no idea what time it was or how long she'd been in the cube, but she was certainly hungry. She wondered how long Luka would leave her alone to stew and frighten herself. She decided that she would be better off occupying her mind and turned to the art supplies, opening the sketchpad and pulling out a charcoal pencil. It was time to purge herself of some of Luka's poison.

She tried her best not to draw anything she thought would hurt her friends, but it was always so hard to tell what visions meant. The drawings of the women she was coming to think of as herself were fascinating and frightening all at once. Many of them she had seen before without knowing they had any significance. It seemed she'd had a number of bad deaths, but she was comforted by the strength she saw in these women. It made her feel a little less weak and helpless. She wished she had access to her binders to see what other clues about her true nature might be found there. The vision that really made her heart pound was of a collapsing building. The details of the rubble were obscured by the cloud of dust that enveloped the sight. *Please, God, don't let it be Ilyn's casino*, she pled silently. *Please don't let my friends be in there.*

She drew until her hand cramped, then curled up on the sofa in front of the fire. It felt good to be warm. She had been avoiding thinking about what she had learned and the hopelessness of her situation. It was too overwhelming, but she could not run from it forever. *I am not a real human being. Savita knew what I am, and she didn't tell me. He's going to bite me. He's probably going to rape me. Even if they come for me, they'll never be able to get me out of this place. All my friends are going to die. He's going to kill*

*me and make me his vampire slave child bride. Do not cry. Do not
let him see you crying when he comes.*

There was, predictably, nothing in the room that she could use to
kill herself, even if she was brave enough to do it, which she soon
acknowledged she wasn't. There were no belts or straps, nothing
breakable or sharp. She was utterly trapped. She looked for Ilyn,
struggling to quiet her mind enough to reach out for him, but her
anxiety and the distance made that impossible. She felt utterly
alone.

She thought about Luka's revelation of her identity. She
wondered how many loved ones and how many treasures she had
lost in her long series of lives. Had she borne children? She was
glad she couldn't remember. She wondered what the point was of
the endless cycle. She wondered how many times she had learned
her true nature only to forget it again. She wondered if she had
come to terms with it, come to accept it or appreciate it or
understand her purpose. Why would God make her this way, to live
and die again and again and never know peace? Had she done some
great wrong? How could she repent of it if she had no idea of the
nature of her sin? Was there something she was supposed to do?
How would she know what it was?

When her captor finally joined her, he found her asleep on the
sofa, exhaustion having overcome her once again. She raised her
head when she heard the door close behind him and quickly sat up,
wary and still.

Luka laid an iPad on the table and looked at the piles of paper
she'd produced. "Very industrious," he commented with approval.
She watched him and said nothing. "And how did you find the
room, and your breakfast?"

"Very nice, thank you," she replied in what she hoped was a suitably meek tone. *Use what you have. String him along. As long as your heart beats, there is a chance.*

"And how are you feeling? You look much better." His gaze made her yearn for another shower.

"Old," she replied, truthfully. Luka laughed.

He sat down on the sofa, turning to face her as though they were old friends. "And have you thought of any questions or comments about the information I shared with you last night?"

"I think I believe you," she said after a pause, "about my not being human. There's a whole stack of women there. I think they're all me."

"Excellent. A good first step," he replied approvingly.

"How long have you been looking for demons?" she asked.

"Most of my life. At least seven hundred years."

"And all you've found is me?" she asked, puzzled. "Surely there are more than me and Savita out there."

"I have found a few others, but most were, shall we say, extremely unstable. Not at all suitable for turning into a vampire. And it is rather like looking for a needle in a haystack. I've examined thousands of frauds, more than I can count." November tried not to think about what might have happened to all those mediums and spoon-benders and faith healers who'd been faking it.

"How did you know I was Juana before you even caught me?" she asked.

He shrugged. "Ah, you know her name! Well done! It was merely a hunch, and a hope. Ben's descriptions of your abilities matched the reports of the priests who examined you five hundred years ago. I have been waiting for you for a long time," he said, almost tenderly. November shivered. "Speaking of Ben, you have a visitor. Send him in," he called to the guard.

She found herself face to face with her former friend. He still looked awful: gaunt and sad and hopeless and a little bit afraid. "Ben tells me that he owes you his life, kitten," Luka said in an artificially light tone. "Tell me, November, why would you choose his life for a reward?"

November had the distinct feeling that the wrong answer would lead to a very dead vampire. She went with most of the truth. "I felt sorry for him, because of his sister and his maker. I thought you took advantage of him, of his youth and his grief. I thought that if anyone had bothered to take care of him properly, he wouldn't have gotten into such trouble. I guess I know what it's like when adults fail children." She left out the part about her instinctive feeling that somehow his life would be helpful to her own.

Luka examined each of them in turn. Finally, he said exactly what his father had said: "I suppose we'll find a use for him." Looking at the lowliest of his servants with contempt, he added, "It seems you owe the Oracle twice over, boy. You may go. And stay away from my seer." Luka flashed his fangs briefly in warning. Ben gave November a ghost of a smile and disappeared out the door, which locked loudly behind him.

"Now, show me your work," he ordered.

November fetched her stacks of paper. She didn't think there was anything in them that would hurt Ilyn or the rest of her friends. She was terrified that she would somehow inadvertently help Luka, but she couldn't very well pretend she hadn't seen anything, and God knew she needed to draw to get the visions out of her system.

338

She assumed that the eyes in the sky would report if she made a drawing and destroyed it. She knew she was a pretty bad liar, even to human beings. She only hoped that she would be able to cover up anything she saw that would be a danger to her friends. She handed her work to the vampire, sat down, and waited for his reaction.

"Now you do realize that if I catch you deceiving me, the consequences will be dire," he said with quiet menace without looking up from her sketches.

"I expected as much," she replied, staring at her hands. Luka took the sketch of him in his broken human body and tossed it into the fire.

"Is this past or future?" he asked about the one of him frantically digging a hole for himself in the ground.

"I'm not sure. If I see it again, I'll try to get more details on the clothing, which helps me figure that out."

The vampire glanced briefly at the drawings of the women, then held up the drawing of Ilyn in the hotel hallway. "Tell me about this one."

She swallowed. "There is smoke, screaming, crashing noises. He's in the hotel."

"Upstairs or in the vaults?"

"Upstairs," she answered truthfully. Luka's resulting smile made her shudder.

"Well, that is good news indeed," he said, savoring the words. "And this one?" he asked, holding up the sketch of the ruined building.

November's heart sank, seeing where this line of inquiry must be leading. "A building, collapsing. I couldn't see enough detail to identify it. Too much dust," she replied.

"I have something to show you, kitten." Luka picked up his iPad. "Let's take a look at the news, shall we?" Apparently the desert fortress somehow had excellent wireless internet access.

And with that, November knew that her fears had come to pass. She watched a tourist's cell phone footage of a private jet crashing into the Tayna Casino on a bright afternoon. The resulting explosion was violent enough to indicate that the plane had been packed with high explosives, according to the newscaster's analysis. The anchor continued, "Hundreds are missing, including casino magnate Ilyn Zykov, who according to witnesses risked his own life helping victims to safety. Casualties would have been higher save for the fact that the complex had been partially evacuated due to a faulty fire alarm twenty minutes before the terrorist attack. No group has taken responsibility for the attack, so reminiscent of the Al Qaeda attack on September 11th. Rescue efforts continue as federal investigators begin trying to determine how the attack was planned and carried out . . ."

November shook like a leaf, the faces of her friends flashing though her mind as she wondered if any of them had survived. The thought that Zinnia could be no more, and Savita, and all the others, was more than she could bear, and fear for Ilyn filled her heart. *Surely I would know if Ilyn were dead*, she told herself in desperation. *Surely I would feel it.*

She didn't realize she was crying until Luka caught a tear on his finger and brought it to his lips. "No one is coming for you, November," he said gently. "They are all dead or nearly so, and even if any survive, why would they risk their lives for a seer who couldn't save them from such a disaster? Their time is over. It is my time to rule now, and you will be at my side. In time, you will accept this. In time, you will see that this is all for the best." November remained silent, no longer weeping, but her body still shaking. "They tell me you love my father. Is this true?"

"Maybe," she whispered, too heartbroken to lie.

"I am told that he spurned you." She nodded in affirmation. "I admire your loyalty, kitten, but he was not worthy of your love. Weep for him now, and then forget him. Forget them all." He stood to leave. "In a few hours, after you have time to grieve, I have something special planned. My people will want to celebrate this great victory for our kind. I will send for you." November didn't even hear the door close behind him.

She sat for a long time, feeling hollow. She looked for Ilyn, but all she could see was darkness. She prayed for her friends. She prayed for herself. It had been a long time since she had prayed, but she supposed it couldn't hurt. Her fingers itched for her rosary, but she thought she would probably never see it again. *Perhaps it would be better to lose all hope. It would be easier to just snuff it out*, she told herself.

And yet, she was sure that she would have felt Ilyn's death, even at this distance. She knew that her vision of her own burial was a true seeing. Thousands of time it had come to her, unchanging.

Whatever Luka intended, whatever he might do to her, however broken she might become, she knew that it would be Ilyn who brought her to her next incarnation. This was her fate. She had always known it. So, rather than snuffing it out, she blew on the ember of her hope until it was a little flame, and then she hid it away where no one could see, where it could keep her warm in the dark. And she prepared herself for battle.

She knew she must present a certain face to Luka, to make him think she had begun to accept her fate as his prized possession. She must seem fearful, which was easy enough to mange given her near constant state of terror. She must act as though she needed him, to appeal to his vanity and his obvious loneliness and need to be important. She must act sad, but not too sad. She knew she must keep her eyes open and look for any opportunity, any chance to make possible an escape. And when her friends came, she knew she must be ready.

She knew they would come, whoever was left. They would not abandon her, she was certain of it. Luka thought they would blame her, and that they would not repay her loyalty in kind. But November knew better, because she knew that at least some of them loved her, not just her gift. Most of all, she knew she must stay alive as long as possible. *As long as my heart is beating, I have a chance.*

A human servant brought her some food, and she dutifully ate it. She pulled out a math textbook and began working problems to quiet her mind and pass the time. She dreaded finding out what these people did to celebrate. She was certain it would be a thousand times worse than the parties at Lord William's house, and those were already pretty bad. Finally, the door opened, and someone entered. Her heart fell as she saw that her escort was Philemon.

Determined not to show any fear, she stood and walked to him. To her surprise, there were no cruel comments. He handed her the black bag, which she pulled over her own head without protest. He took her elbow and led her out the door. She could hear other people in the corridors. They were all heading in the same direction, moving much more quickly than she could walk. After a few minutes, everyone had moved ahead of them, and November and Philemon were alone in a stairwell. Philemon pulled off the hood, and she found herself pressed against the wall, looking at a very intense and fangs-bared vampire. Already anxious, she went cold with fear, expecting him to take his vengeance for Agnes.

Instead, in a desperate voice and with grief in his eyes, he demanded, "Tell me what happened to my Agnes."

She took a deep breath. "Luka killed her because somehow he figured out that I was having visions based off of a hair she had left on my mother's body. Maybe Willow found out and told him? Anyway, I guess he couldn't have her participating in his plans anymore for fear of giving them away, so he staked her out of the blue, in the middle of a conversation. It was very quick. She didn't really even have enough time to realize what was happening," she said, hoping his wife's lack of suffering would be a comfort to him. Instead, he was outraged.

"He slaughtered her like a human? He didn't even give her a chance to fight?" She shook her head. He let go of his prisoner, who clung to the wall as her knees buckled and she slid to the floor. "He told me William killed her for you, to gain your loyalty."

"No," she said. "William wept for her. He felt everything she suffered and everything she did was his fault." She almost wanted to comfort him, this monster who had murdered her mother. He seemed so undone.

Suddenly, he came to some sort of decision and turned back to her, grabbing her arm with a grip that would bruise and hauling her back to her feet. He threw her back against the wall and growled, "If you ever tell anyone about this conversation, I will tear the flesh from your bones. Are we clear?"

"Crystal," she whispered.

"Good." And with that, he shoved the bag back over her head and dragged her up the stairs to the place where hope went to die.

Chapter 15

What November had thought was an auditorium was actually a killing ground. She could feel death before she was even shoved through the heavy double doors. Still shaking from her heart-to-heart with Philemon in the stairwell, her legs failed her again as images of brutal violence flooded her mind. Philemon guided her to the ground far more gently than she would have expected. "I just need a moment to get used to the room," she whimpered through the hood, trying not to get washed away by a tidal wave of blood. After about ten minutes of being buffeted by horror, she resurfaced to find herself looking into Willow's worried face.

"I told him he shouldn't bring her here," the fairy whispered to Philemon, who was leaning against the wall. "All we need is for her to lose her damn mind. But, no, he wants to show her off, and 'acclimate her to our ways.'"

"Your concern is touching," November murmured. Willow looked relieved and helped the seer to her feet. November looked around, a bit disoriented and dreading the scene on the other side of the doors.

"I need to put these on you," Willow said almost kindly, holding out two pairs of golden shackles. November shrank from her, retreating until her back was against the wall. "It's okay. See, they're loose, and the chains are long. They won't hurt. It's just for show: this is his triumph, and you're his war trophy. You know, like in Roman times." November just looked at her. "I don't want to hurt you," Willow beseeched her, "and I don't want him to put you back in the hole again. Just hold out your wrists. There's no way around it." So November held out her arms, and Willow avoided her gaze as she chained her wrists and ankles.

"Come on, girl, he's waiting," Philemon said, holding the door open. November shook off Willow's help and entered under her own power, which she considered a victory. The chain on her ankles was long enough to permit her to walk almost normally, though running would have been impossible.

Her eyes now took in what her mind had already seen. She stood on a wide landing at the top of a set of bleachers. To her left was a tasteful sitting area where Luka was enjoying the party with his most senior people. The bleachers were packed with the rest of his employees, the ones who were not milling about on the floor below obtaining refreshments. Said refreshments were dipped from three galvanized tubs full of blood which sat underneath three tightly-bound human beings who had been suspended upside-down before having their throats slit. Two of them were dead when she walked in, and the third stopped breathing as she watched. It was all November could do not to start screaming. She prayed that the bloodletting was over and that these three would not be replaced by additional unfortunate souls once the drinks ran out.

Luka caught sight of her and beckoned her. She walked slowly, trying not to fall. As much as she was trying to hide her feelings, he must have seen the bleak look in her eyes, as he took pains to assure her, "They felt nothing, kitten. No pain. No fear. We practice humane slaughter of our livestock whenever possible."

She nodded mutely, not trusting herself to speak and fearing she would vomit if she opened her mouth. He was drinking steaming blood from a crystal goblet, jubilant about his victory. News footage played on a huge plasma screen opposite the bleachers. He gestured for her to sit on a nearby divan, and she gratefully availed herself of it. She tried to prepare herself for whatever was coming next. She was beginning to feel numb, and she welcomed it.

Once the vampires had all been fed, the corpses and tubs were removed from the floor, and Luka stood to address his loyal troops. November knew she should pay attention. She tried to focus on the words, but she simply could not process them. All she could do was look at the bloodstains on the concrete, all that remained of three human beings who once had pasts and families and friends and dreams, only to be turned into the vampire equivalent of beer kegs. She prayed that she had never been so callous in whatever lives she'd led, and she prayed that she never would be.

Finally, some of Luka's words made it through, and they only deepened her despair. "Soon, we will control this land together with all of our vampire and fairy brothers and sisters. Now that the leaders of our enemies have been decimated, we will restore unity among our people. We will cleanse this country of the werewolf vermin. For those humans who bend the knee to our rule, we will be the wise shepherds they so desperately need. Those who resist, we will cull from the herd. We will restore the natural world that the humans have despoiled with their foolishness and greed by imposing upon them a simpler lifestyle more suited to their true station. We have taken the first steps in building a better world, but there is still much work to be done. You will be heroes, remembered for generations. Are you prepared for revolution? For revelation? For rule?"

The cheers of Luka's people snapped her out of her frozen state, and she looked up to see Luka motioning for her to stand and join him. As she struggled to stand, paralyzed with fear and disgust, Philemon took her elbow and pushed her forward.

"You have heard stories about the Oracle found by our enemies. You have heard rumors of how they used her to disrupt our plans, to delay our quest for a better future. You have heard that she is a true seer, the first we've found in many centuries. All of this is true. It is my joy to tell you that tonight, after our greatest victory to date, thanks to your sister Willow, this weapon is now in *our* hands." Luka pulled her forward to stand next to him, displaying her proudly like the prize of war she was.

He then forced her to her knees, eliciting another cheer. November concentrated on looking straight ahead and remembering to breathe. Her face flushed red, and tears threatened to spill past her eyelashes. Luka's troops were screaming and stomping on the bleachers, riled up by the speech and the blood and the victory. Luka raised a hand for silence. "And two nights hence, when the moon is full, I shall drain her and give to her my blood, and she will rise again our newest sister."

More cheering followed, resolving into a chant. "Claim her! Claim her!" they shouted over and over. November's stomach clenched even tighter. *Please don't scream. Please don't faint*, she begged herself.

Luka turned and looked down at her with a shrug and a smile as if to say, "I have to give the people what they want," before pulling her roughly to her feet. Keeping a tight hold on her arm, he grabbed a fistful of her hair and yanked her head back with enough force to rattle her teeth. He breathed in deeply of her scent, savoring the moment before he plunged his fangs into her neck. Despite her best efforts, she cried out with pain and fear as he tore into her flesh.

William had taken tiny sips from small punctures made by the tips of his fangs, leaving wounds not much larger than a needle's. This was a real bite, a predator's bite, with no gentleness about it. As she grew dizzy, Luka disentangled his hand from her hair and supported her back as he drank several large swallows of her blood. When he was finally finished, she slumped against him, her head resting helplessly on his shoulder as he licked her wound until the flow of blood stopped. The fact that she needed her assailant's support and care in order to stay upright made her hate him all the more. Before he turned to half-carry her back to the divan, he cried out to the crowd, "Let the games begin!"

She found herself sitting with her head still leaning against Luka, a goblet filled with fruit juice pressed into her hand. She managed to raise it to her lips without spilling it and drained it without stopping for a breath. The rush of sugar cleared her head a bit. Luka had his arm possessively over her shoulder. She wanted so badly to pull away, but she was beginning to see that she might be able to turn his proprietary feelings about her to her advantage. It seemed like he wanted someone who would not only be in his control but who also would actually need him, who would depend on him in a personal way. So she leaned into him as though it didn't turn her stomach, and she tried to put out of her mind how much she wished for the vampire who smelled like pipe smoke instead the one who reeked of brimstone.

"You did splendidly, kitten," he told her in the way one might over-praise a small child or a particularly stupid dog. "You just rest now."

She lifted her head with great effort and screwed up the courage to look down to the floor of the hall, but she couldn't make out what was happening. It was all a blur. "What's happening now?" she asked timidly.

"Fencing tournament," Luka answered brightly. "I expect they're moving too quickly for you to follow. There will be hand-to-hand sparring as well, and then something special for the finale." November shuddered to think what that might be. She hoped desperately that it would not involve her.

She watched the activity below with disinterest and an unnatural calm brought on by the vampire venom in her veins. If it weren't for all the cheering, she might have fallen asleep. She found her gaze drawn to the news coverage. She gathered from the closed captioning at the bottom of the screen that many of the hotel guests had been evacuated before the plane even hit. Someone had pulled a fire alarm twenty minutes before the attack.

November wondered who had realized that something was amiss. Perhaps Ilyn had taken her warning more seriously than she realized. Of course, the news couldn't tell her if they'd managed to get the vampires out in the middle of the day. Every so often, they would flash Ilyn's photo on the screen, lauding him as a hero for remaining in the building to guide victims to safely.

A loud noise startled her into awareness. A tough-looking metal gate was descending from the ceiling, separating the bleachers from the floor. She looked to Luka for an explanation. "Steel coated with silver," he explained. "It's time for the finale. Wouldn't want the wolves to get loose, now would we? The alpha of our little wolf pack made the mistake of killing one of my men last week. Obviously, he has been suffering for it ever since. Now it is time to put him down, as entertainingly as possible." His smile chilled her.

A noisy rattle began below, and November watched as a rolling cage packed with half a dozen prisoners was pushed out of the tunnel. They were dressed in rags, frighteningly thin, obviously despondent, and defiantly proud. Their condition made plain that werewolves were not worth tending in the same way as human livestock. There was a little boy, no more than five years old, who had the eyes of an old man. November couldn't tear her eyes from his as the tears she'd been suppressing all night began to roll down her cheeks. The boy noticed her chains and raised his hand just a little, an almost invisible wave of encouragement. She wiped her tears hastily away, hoping Luka wouldn't notice the exchange. All of the adults were looking intently at the screaming crowd, scanning it as though memorizing faces for future retribution.

Luka did not fail to notice her weeping. "They don't deserve your compassion. Who do you think betrayed you to the Inquisition when you were Juana, hmm? Werewolves have always excelled at betraying their fellow supernatural creatures to human authorities. They had no compassion for you then, and you were an innocent girl of twelve or thirteen as I recall."

"He's just a little boy," she protested softly.

"Nits make lice," he replied, patting her knee paternalistically. "Soon, you will understand." She said a silent prayer that she would not.

One young man stood out from the others. He held himself tall, calmly taking in the scene. He gazed at the blood stains on the floor, at the hate-filled crowd now grown quiet with anticipation. He looked for a long moment at November and her chains and gave her a smile as though they were conspirators.

The young man called up to Luka, "Why not make this more interesting, bloodsucker? Come down and join us." November looked up with a start as she recognized his voice from her day in the box. *Keep singing, sister.*

"Not tonight, cur," Luka replied. "Your father is the star tonight."

"I thought the star was your pretty little body snatcher there," he replied with a grin. November winced at his name for her. "Sees the future, does she? Has she seen the part where I kill you?"

"Your father is the one who dies tonight, Hector," Luka said with a fang-filled smile.

"Your demon sings like an angel, did you know?" the werewolf replied, stalling, trying to delay the inevitable. Luka raised an eyebrow at her, demanding explanation.

"I sang in the cell when I came around, that first day I was here," she quickly explained, trying to avoid trouble. "He must have heard me through the vent."

"Ah. Well, then we must hear you later. Perhaps you can sing a memorial hymn in honor of the dead mutt," the vampire replied. Her heart sank. That was all she needed: more attention and humiliation. *Why did he have to bring me up at all?* she thought, but when she saw the desperate look in Hector's eyes, she forgave him. He was just trying to forestall his father's slaughter. Luka, however, was done letting the wolf delay the inevitable. "Begin," he ordered.

From the tunnel below the bleachers came an unholy howling that set November's teeth on edge. Some primal part of her knew that sound. It made her want to howl back. A snarling mass of fur burst out onto the floor, herded by fairies with long cattle prods. He was enormous, easily twice the size of a normal wolf, heavily scarred and missing an eye. Another growling sound soon followed, and three coyotes came tumbling out. The wolf made fairly quick work of them, though they did manage to wound the larger beast, eliciting cheers from the crowd whenever the wolf howled in pain.

The spectators' features were twisted with hatred, especially Willow's. November looked around for Ben, who also had much reason to hate the wolves, but she couldn't find him. Every vampire's fangs were showing, their mouths watering at the scent of wolf blood.

The werewolves made to watch this display began to shift forms, as the smell of blood and the nearness of the full moon forced their transformation. Desperate to aid their leader, they threw themselves against the silvered bars of the cage, adding the smell of singed fur and skin to that of blood and excrement.

The only one who did not change was the little boy, of course, who had not yet reached puberty, the time when werewolf children generally began revealing their heritage. He remained in his trembling human form, eyes squeezed shut, hands balled into little fists over his ears. November's stomach clenched. She wanted to turn away but knew that it would not save her from seeing. Besides, something made her want to bear witness. She felt like the condemned man deserved that at least.

The wolf tore into his kill with a desperate hunger, but before the Hector's father had a chance to swallow more than a bite, the gate to the tunnel opened again, and a mountain lion stepped into the fray to continue the torment. The parade of vicious animals continued for an hour, each battle more difficult for the werewolf as he accumulated wounds. A bear followed the mountain lion, and a pack of wolverines followed him.

Even a werewolf's remarkable healing ability could not keep up with the onslaught. Finally, unable to continue the fight, the condemned creature collapsed half-dead in the middle of the carnage, shifting back into his human form as he fell, revealing a slight, middle-aged man, naked and grizzled and covered with wounds. The other wolves howled and reverted as well.

November remembered a conversation she'd had with Pine months before, when he had tried to explain the antipathy between the supernatural races. "They style themselves as protectors of the innocent," he had explained. "They feel justified in killing us because we prey on humans. The fact that most of us only kill as a last resort is lost on them. They're also fond of getting humans to do their dirty work. Every witch hunt in history, they've had their fingers in it. Why do you think suspected witches were tested by

352

immersion in water? You can't drown a fairy or a vampire, so we were guilty as charged. We sure as hell burn, though. And if humans die in the process? Collateral damage, unfortunate but necessary. They especially enjoy murdering fairies because if a werewolf takes a fairy life, it extends his own, sometimes by decades. They resent our longevity and feel justified in murdering to take it from us. Every fairy living has had loved ones or ancestors slain in the night by a werewolf. Every vampire knows someone dragged from his resting place by them, condemned without trial to die screaming in the sunlight." She wondered if the cycle would ever stop.

In the end, Luka's men hanged the poor man, hauling him up with a noose of silver chain, without even the mercy of a quick fall and a broken neck. His family was forced to watch him twist and twitch for the better part of twenty minutes, listening to the catcalls and glee of their enemies.

November placed one hand on her neck, swallowing convulsively, the scene before her alternating with flashes of a vision of her own hanging centuries before, in another life. She saw a slight old woman, swinging in the wind at a crossroads, strangling slowly from a too-short fall, a crowd screaming its condemnation of a witch. Finally, both the phantom and the flesh-and-blood victims gave up their struggles and swung limp.

She was overwhelmed by the sadism she'd witnessed that night, at the very limit of her strength, when Luka turned to her and said, "I think this would be a good time for a song."

She was about to beg for his mercy, to plead exhaustion. She simply couldn't face anything more. But when she looked at the wolves in the cage, their grief and rage and hopelessness, she decided that if she could give them any kind of comfort, she would try. "You wanted a funeral type song, sir?" she asked with as much fake meekness as she could manage.

"Yes, I think that would be best," he replied, pleased to think she was going along with his taunting of the werewolves.

"I can only remember the words to one at the moment," she replied. She struggled to stand up on shaking legs. She started with a weak voice which grew more powerful as she managed to ignore everyone but the grieving wolves. She drew a deep breath before beginning.

Some bright morning when this life is over

I'll fly away

To that home on God's celestial shore

I'll fly away, fly away, oh glory

I'll fly away, in the morning

When I die, hallelujah by and by

I'll fly away

When the shadows of this life have gone

I'll fly away

Like a bird from these prison walls I'll fly

I'll fly away

Oh how glad and happy when we meet

I'll fly away

No more cold iron shackles on my feet
I'll fly away

Just a few more weary days and then
I'll fly away
To a land where joys will never end
I'll fly away

I'll fly away, fly away, oh glory
I'll fly away, in the morning
When I die, hallelujah by and by
I'll fly away

She sang with all her heart, her voice filled with sadness and hope and defiance, knowing that she herself would never receive the gift of peace after death. She wanted to remind the wolves that even if this life had no mercy for them, the next one would. She wanted to make them feel that though their leader was dead, he was also free.

She finished, trembling, and looked up at Luka for his reaction. He smiled his creepy smile and said, "But, kitten, there is no freedom in heaven for you."

"I know," she replied softly. "That's why I thought it would amuse you." She hoped against hope that he wouldn't see her true motives, her desire to stand with the wolves in their grief. She had no strength left to survive his displeasure.

To her relief, he threw his head back and laughed. He tweaked her nose as he said cheerfully, "You are going to be so much fun, kitten." And with that, November promptly collapsed in a heap. The last thing she saw was Hector in his cage, raising his hand to give her a little salute.

She woke twelve hours later to find Willow in her room and the shackles gone. The fairy looked relieved as November sat up in bed. The fairy handed her prisoner a plastic cup of water, asking, "How do you feel?"

"Better for having slept," the girl replied after finishing the water. "Is he upset with me for fainting?"

"If he were, you'd be in the box. No, he was worried that he might have pushed you too far, that you'd wake up crazy or something," Willow admitted.

"How touching," the girl replied in a voice dripping with sarcasm. Willow said nothing in reply but called out to the guards outside, "Tell him she's awake and lucid." Willow then told her, "He's given me permission to take you outside to the garden for a walk. He wants you to have the chance to say goodbye to the sun. He fears there won't be time tomorrow. It's almost sunset, so we should hurry. You can eat and bathe when we return."

November shivered at the reason, but her heart leapt at the chance to see something besides stone walls. Willow gave her a pair of bedroom slippers to go over her wool socks, covered her with a cloak, then slipped the black bag once again over her head and led her to the roof. The edges of the garden featured thick, chest-high walls topped with eight feet of metal bars and razor wire. Even these stark reminders of imprisonment could not destroy the view of the sunset over the desert. November found herself smiling in spite of herself. If this was to be her last sunset, at least it was a pretty one. The garden itself was handsome enough, a green oasis and unexpected respite.

There was a small group of humans taking the air under the gaze of watchful guards. They seemed to be doing yoga. At one end of the roof, another handful of humans appeared to be constructing a small stage at the direction of a short, red-haired fairy. Three of the workers lifted up a wooded structure and anchored it to the platform. It consisted of a central wooden beam with two arms angled downward. November began to wander over to see what they were doing when Willow blocked her way. "You don't want to go over there," the fairy cautioned.

November was turning to ask why not when she realized the reason: they were building this for her, for the next night. "He's going to attach me to that . . . that cross thing?" she asked in revulsion and disbelief.

"It's just so everyone can see you. They couldn't bear witness if he drained you lying down," Willow said in a weak attempt at comfort. "It won't hurt. You won't be hanging from it. You'll just be standing in front of it, attached so you won't fall." She shook her head. "I thought they were putting it up tomorrow. I wouldn't have brought you out here to see that."

"Is that supposed to make me feel better?" November demanded angrily. "I'm going to get murdered for public amusement. Tomorrow night." The reality of her predicament was beginning to hit her as she watched the hammers swinging. Fear and panic and rage and grief fought for supremacy as she began to tremble.

While she watched the sun finish dipping below the horizon, her tears began to fall. *This isn't how it's supposed to happen. Ilyn is supposed to save me from death, to drain me reluctantly. I'm supposed to die with people who love me. I'm not supposed to be gleefully executed by a monster like Luka. They'll come for me.* *They have to. I don't die like this. I have seen it. Please don't let me die like this,* she prayed as her trembling increased.

"It isn't a murder to us. It's a birth, a joyful occasion," Willow protested at the sight of her weeping. She reached out to put an arm around November's shoulders, which were now shaking with silent sobs.

November jerked away from the fairy, anger flaring at her touch. "Oh, are we friends now? You killed Pine. You brought me here to die."

"I did not want to kill Pine. He was my friend. Sometimes sacrifices have to be made for the greater good. And I brought you here to live. You would be dead if you had been in the hotel." Willow came close again and placed one hand on each of November's shoulders. November stood still this time but could not look her kidnapper in the face. "Soon you will understand. Now let's go back inside. You must be getting cold." *I am cold,* the girl realized, and she slowly followed Willow toward the door, with one last look at the nearly full moon rising.

Just before Willow slipped the hated bag back over her head, November glimpsed something odd: three of the exercising humans fell to the ground. Before she could ask what was going on, Willow ushered her quickly back inside the fortress.

Back in her room, breakfast sat on her table. She sat down to tuck in to what might be one of her last meals, preparing to savor the oatmeal with maple sugar, fruit, and a mug of hot chocolate. Just as she was about to take a bite, a blur swept into the room and knocked the spoon out of her hand. It was Luka himself. She looked at him with puzzled surprise.

He grabbed her shoulder, spun her around, and demanded, "How much did you eat?"

"None of it, yet. Why?" she asked, her hands prickling with fear at his frantic demeanor.

He looked to Willow for confirmation, and she nodded. "We just got back in. What's going on, my lord?"

Luka studied November another moment and finally relaxed his iron grip. "Someone's poisoned the humans' food, or the water. We're not sure yet. But they've all collapsed. Half are already dead, and the rest soon will be." His eyes burned with his fury.

November stood up and took a step back from the table, as if to avoid contamination. *Those poor people*, she said to herself. She thought a moment and said a silent prayer for them. "It can't be the water. I drank some over an hour ago, and I'm fine."

"I gave you bottled water," Willow countered. "Ben brought it by before dawn, as you slept. He said there was a problem with the cistern, a crack in a pipe or something."

"Did he?" Luka asked, eyes narrow and voice dripping suspicion. He clicked a button on his phone. "Find me Ben. Yes, the idiot youngling. Now." He did not wait for a reply. In a flash, November found herself pressed against the wall, the vampire's hand and fangs at her throat. "Tell me you didn't know about this in advance," he said with quiet, dangerously precise diction.

She could barely take in enough air to reply. "Of course not!" she answered hoarsely. "I would never sit by and allow such a thing," she managed to protest, her honest horror at what had been done evident in her face.

Luka studied her closely before releasing her. "I thought not," he replied, fangs once again hidden. He straightened her tunic and patted her on the shoulder. November found a seat, hoping no one could hear her knees knocking. Luka began to pace. He turned to November. "If you examined the cistern, could you tell if he poisoned it?"

"Probably," she replied honestly, "Especially since it most likely just happened today or last night. I assume it's fed by a well?" He nodded. "I should check that, too, just to be sure."

"Let's go," he said, beckoning Willow.

"Sir?" she asked, slightly confused. "You will accompany us?" She was accustomed to a master who liked to delegate.

"I'm not letting her out of my sight if I can help it," he replied, taking November by the arm. "And you will be with her every moment I am not. Tomorrow night she will become mine forever. I'm taking no chances until then, even if this is all the doing of that moronic boy." With inquiring eyebrows, Willow held up the black hood, at which Luka rolled his eyes. "I think we can dispense with that, given her abilities. She probably could draw a map of the place by now anyway." Luka wrapped his prize up in a cloak and bundled her out the door.

The three of them started quickly down the hall, trailed by three more guards. Philemon caught up with them and delivered the news that they'd done a complete head count, and the only people missing were Ben, a tower guard, and two of the drawbridge guards.

"I should have known," Luka said, sounding irritated with himself. "I should have killed him as soon as I had the chance. I thought that he could be useful. Evidently not."

As they hurried back up to the roof, November got to see with her eyes what she'd only heretofore glimpsed with her gift. They passed by the human dormitories, whose walls along the corridor were made mostly of glass so as to facilitate the surveillance of the guards. Now it afforded her a view of the dead and dying. Many were convulsing, backs grotesquely arched. "Oh, God," she murmured, horror-struck, wanting somehow to help them. She reached out helplessly and touched the glass. There were so many of them, many hundred humans kept to feed Luka's troops. All were dead or nearly so.

Luka looked at her as he sensed her distress. "We've already enthralled them into oblivion, and there is nothing more to be done. They're feeling no pain, kitten. They feel safe and warm and unafraid. We're not complete monsters, you know." So she tore her eyes away and hurried along beside him, swallowing her tears. "It's not a nice way to die, strychnine, and it doesn't take much. We keep it around for the rats," he explained further.

"Why couldn't the fairies heal them during the day?" she asked before she could stop herself.

"Most of the humans slept all day and woke at dusk. It was only then they were poisoned. We did not realize what was happening to them until it was too late," he replied. "Even if we had, there were too many of them. It would have weakened the fairies too profoundly."

Another question struck her, which this time she managed not to voice. *What about the werewolves?* She tried to look for them, down through many floors to the dungeons she'd glimpsed, but to no avail. It was instead Willow who asked, as they emerged onto the roof, "My lord, what about the wolves?"

He answered, "No food or water for them today, so they are still among the living. For now." November couldn't tell if Willow was disappointed or pleased that they had lived to suffer another day.

They walked over to the water tank. November closed her eyes and placed her hands upon it. Once she was able to quiet herself, she was swiftly rewarded with a vision of Ben climbing up to an access hatch and pouring several bottles of something into the water. He looked determined rather than frightened. With one look back, he murmured, "I'm sorry. It was the only chance."

November pulled her hand away, and looked back to her keepers. She nodded confirmation of Ben's guilt, telling herself that it was not too much of a betrayal given that he had already revealed it by fleeing. She couldn't understand it. What was the point of murdering all those people? And he couldn't have been sure that November would avoid ingesting the poison.

"It was him. Three bottles of poison. Judging by the sky, maybe a couple of hours before dawn?" she reported. "He killed the guard over there first," she added, pointing to one of the towers. Luka swore under his breath.

After a cursory check of the well and the kitchens, where November found nothing of note, they headed to Luka's office. The stains of her blood were still just barely visible on the wooden table, and November had a glimpse of one of the humans scrubbing it vigorously the day before. There was a tray on the table, and a bottle of water, but she couldn't bring herself to eat for thinking of the dead and dying. She took a seat by the fire to warm her chilled bones, trying to disappear. She still didn't understand what was going on, or why. That is because she was continuing to think of the dead as people. Everyone else, of course, was thinking of them as supplies.

"We'll have to break into the reserve blood, then, to feed the vampires? They can't eat tainted blood," Willow asked her master.

"He unplugged the freezers and slashed all the bags before dawn. Nothing edible left. The fairies will go after the garden in the

362

morning, I suppose. Younglings first, in orderly fashion. Put Barley in charge of that. He doesn't suffer fools. I'll have to let people go hunting in the desert in small groups as well as send to the ranchers for resupply," he said, worry written on his face. "We won't have fresh livestock until tomorrow night at the earliest. No one will starve, but the young ones will be difficult to manage to say the least."

"Do you think he had a plan? I mean, to take advantage of the weakness caused by our lack of food?"

"I doubt Ben could conceive of a plan for picking up my dry cleaning," he replied acidly, sounding remarkably like his brother for a moment.

"But Ilyn or Hazel—" Willow protested.

"Are dead, most likely. We will be careful, of course, but I am not overly alarmed. This a child's ham-fisted attempt at vengeance. He will pay for it, of course. How far do you think he could have gotten?"

"He's a flyer," Willow said, "so, pretty far if he fed first, and no way to tell which direction."

"Put out the word to our friends," he ordered. "Million dollar bounty. I want him, preferably alive. I want Philemon in charge of resupply. No stealing along the way by the young ones. They'll be hungry."

"Of course," she answered. Luka dismissed her with a wave. Willow gave a short bow and left, leaving November with a sinking heart, alone with her enemy.

Chapter 16

"You must eat, kitten. You lost blood last night, and you must keep up your strength," Luka admonished, smiling down at her. They had just fed some of everything to the wolves, to make certain Ben hadn't poisoned the food as well. Luckily, he hadn't. So the wolves were still alive, and at least they'd gotten to eat.

She did as she was bid, rising and moving to the table. Breakfast tasted like ash in her mouth, for all she could see were the dying. Even still, she ate it all. She drank some of the bottled water, saving some for later, not knowing how much they had around.

She considered recent events, rolling them over in her mind. What if she had drunk it? Or bathed in it? Ben couldn't have been sure she wouldn't. She hoped that if he was willing to take such a risk, to kill all those innocent people and endanger her, that he was up to something important enough to justify that action, at least in his own mind. She didn't think anything could justify it in her own. *Please let him know what he is doing*, she prayed. *For once.*

She realized that Luka was staring at her. He moved from his desk to the chairs by the fire and beckoned her with a crooked finger. As she moved to sit in the chair across from him, he patted the footstool close beside him, commanding her to sit there instead. She did so, swallowing nervously, and he spoke. "Willow tells me that your trip to the roof this afternoon upset you."

"When did she tell you that?" she asked, looking at her hands, avoiding his eyes.

He held up his phone. "Texting – so useful, don't you think? I remember the days of messengers and carrier pigeons and waiting months for replies. And e-mail, so convenient – you know, I'm already receiving overtures by e-mail from the surviving lords," he said in a confiding, gleeful tone.

She quailed inwardly at that unsettling tidbit. *Fair weather friends*, she thought. He pocketed his smart phone. "You've been crying. I can smell it." He moved to sit next to her at the table. "I hope you don't think I sent you up there meaning to upset you. I had forgotten that they were building the scaffold. I suppose the fairies will have to finish it." He reached out and placed his hand upon her own. It took all her strength not to snatch it away again.

What in the world am I supposed to say to that? No problem, sir, looking forward to my murder? "I've had a lot to process in the last few days, that's all," she answered quietly, staring down at his cold hand on top of her own. She knew she ought to take the opportunity try to look into his life, but she couldn't bear to do so, nor did she think she had enough presence of mind to hide what she was doing. "I, um, never thought my death would be so public. Though it seems I've been executed more than once before."

"I should think so. People are so easily frightened by magic. You do rather have the air of a witch, a bit of a glow," he said with a flamboyant hand gesture. "Even the humans sense it. But, kitten, please don't think of this as an execution. This is a joyous event! I am giving you a great gift. I simply want all my people to celebrate it with us."

"That's what Willow said," she responded, not knowing what else to say. *Joyous, right.*

"You should listen to her. She's the closest thing I have to a daughter, until you rise. She will be part of your family."

No way in hell does that happen, she swore to herself. "You took care of her, after her family died, didn't you? I saw you pick her up off the ground." *Keep him talking as long as possible. Talking means he's not doing anything worse.*

"Indeed, I helped raise her, along with my kin. The family was all together then, living on the east coast, before Ilyn became king. After the rift with my parents, when I settled in Arizona, I asked her to stay with William. I knew that eventually, I would have need of her there. And that eventually, my brother would disappoint her. He's always been too soft on the wolves." Luka's mouth twisted with distaste.

"May I ask, why didn't you leave her with Ilyn?" she asked. She was afraid he would be offended by her questions, but instead, he seemed pleased at her interest, as if he'd just been waiting for someone to regale with tales of his own brilliance.

"Because I considered him the lesser threat. Without my mother, he had no agency, no drive, no fire." November wondered, not for the first time, if Luka had had a hand in his mother's death. "You might have given it back, I'd wager, given the chance. But that's no longer a problem," he added with a shark's smile. "You are a remarkably resilient girl, you know. Most people in your position would be incoherent with terror. But then, I suppose you've had to be adaptable: so many lives, so many deaths." He finally removed his hand from hers and lifted it to briefly touch her hair. "Of course, I can smell your fear, but still, you hide it well."

"Um, thank you?" she managed uncertainly.

"I'm not going to rape you, if that's what you're worried about," he said in a conversational tone, as if they were discussing a menu. Some of the tension left her body, and her breath came a little easier. *Why, yes, that is exactly what I am afraid of, fancy your mentioning that.* He continued touching her lightly, here and there, curiously, as if examining an expensive suit he was thinking of buying. "Not that I don't enjoy a spot of sexual violence now and again," he said with no shame, as if admitting a minor vice like watching reality television. "But you," he continued, touching her hair in the creepiest possible fashion. "You, I want willing. I want to win all of you, heart included. And I will have that, in time."

November continued looking silently over his shoulder, avoiding his eyes, trying to keep her face blank. "Besides, I shouldn't bite you again so soon after last night," he said, softly brushing his fingers against the fresh marks on her neck. She shivered. "Your blood is so delightful, it might be difficult for me to stop. And without teeth, well, how very boring the coupling would be." He brushed the back of his hand over the scar on her upper arm, and she winced as pain shot though the healed wound. "Ah, poor girl, is that where she cut you?" November nodded. "She's lucky you already killed her. Now, then," he said, changing the subject. "Any interesting visions since last we spoke?"

"Not really," she replied. "After I'm bitten, I sleep without dreaming." *Thank God for small favors.*

"Any more visions of your previous selves?"

"I think I've been a fairy and a werewolf both," she said. "But I've never seen myself as a vampire. So I guess I haven't experienced that before . . ."

"Oh, good. What fun we'll have corrupting you, kitten," he replied. November swallowed her disgust.

Their strange tête-a-tête was interrupted by a strong knock on the door. Willow entered in a hurry. "Trouble with the younglings, master. There have been several fights, and a number of them tried to feed on the downed livestock and have fallen ill. The captains are having trouble maintaining order."

"How disappointing," he replied with evident irritation. "I suppose I must make some examples. And we need to burn the bodies before anyone else does something idiotic. For heaven's sake, who eats spoiled meat? Sometimes I am surprised younglings can tie their own shoes." He turned back to his captive. "Alas, kitten, duty calls. I'll have Willow escort you back to your quarters." November tried not to show her relief as Willow whisked her out the door.

They moved quickly down the halls, Willow looking very alert, almost nervous. "What's wrong?" November asked, picking up on her tension.

"You're the only prey available. One of them might do something stupid," she replied.

"I don't understand. They all fed just last night. I've seen people go days between feedings. A week, even."

"Not newborns in the first year. And being in groups only makes it worse. It sets off their survival instincts. They subconsciously see the others as rival hunters, increasing the urgency they feel to find blood. And younglings are well-represented in his lordship's ranks." This November already knew from watching the suicide bombers. "Young fairies, on the other hand, become more lethargic, to conserve energy." A bell began ringing. "All call," Willow explained. "Our lord is summoning everyone to read them the riot act and get them under control, give the makers the chance to issue orders to behave to their progeny. That will help, but the captains have so many children that it dilutes their power over them."

They heard crashes and sounds of shouting up ahead. Willow swore, grabbing November by the arm and doubling back down the corridor. Groups of irritated and hungry predators kept forcing her to change course to avoid them. "We should have stayed in Master's office," she said under her breath.

Their route grew so circuitous that to November's surprise, they were soon close to where the werewolves were kept. Their luck ran out when out of a door burst a vampire with a rat held in his teeth. The moment he saw November, he dropped the vermin, and his eyes went wild. He lunged toward her. Willow easily threw him aside, ordering him to stand down, but he could not hear her. He lunged again. This time, Willow broke his arm. Before he could try again, Willow quickly keyed open the dungeon door and threw November inside to safety.

She landed hard in the middle of the floor, scraping her hands bloody on the rough concrete. She looked around her. Against the walls, a half-dozen chained werewolves stared at her. Her head spun for a moment, as she was subjected to flashes of the various unfortunate souls who had lived and died in this particular hole. She finally opened her eyes again.

The little boy finally broke the tension, silently raising his hand in greeting. "Hi," she whispered in reply, holding up her own hand.

"We hear it's a bit of a mess out there, demon," Hector said. "At least we got to eat. Though there is a marked lack of beverages. I really must complain about the service." He gave a sardonic smile.

"Well, I'm glad you got to eat, at least, but the cost was quite high, I'm afraid," she replied. "And my name is November," she added wearily.

"They all died, then, November?" he asked quietly. She nodded sadly. "Over you?"

"Evidently," she answered with trembling lips. "At least partially." Tears pooled in her eyes.

"And I take it some of the vampire babies are going a bit nuts out there?"

"Evidently," she said again. "I suppose that must have been the idea. Why are there so many of them, anyway? The, ah, vampire babies?"

"They make good cannon fodder. He has his senior people create his army for him, to supplement the older recruits. Newborns have a hard time disobeying orders from their makers, you know," he replied.

"So I've heard," she responded somberly. "And lucky me, I'll be Luka's first. No siblings to dilute the bond." She rested her suddenly weary head in her palm.

"And his lordship intends to kill you tomorrow?" Hector asked, his voice bitter.

"Yes, I believe that's still the plan," she managed to reply without shuddering.

"So if someone's coming for you, they're coming soon?" She nodded. "Do you think they'll come?"

"God, I hope so," she replied. For an instant, all the fear and grief she'd been holding back poured over the dam and threatened to wash her away. She swallowed a few times and got control of herself. "If they do, I'll do everything I can to get that door open," she promised.

Hector laughed. "I doubt your friends will be inclined to set us free. Luka stole you from Ilyn, did he not? Ilyn the Scourge, killer of a thousand wolves?"

"They'll do it if I insist." She looked him straight in the eye, and apparently her confidence was persuasive, as Hector conceded the point. Em continued, "If they're too late . . . if they come after he's already changed me, if you get the chance, could you try to make sure I get staked before he makes me do something awful?" She angrily wiped away a tear. "Please."

Hector looked her over, appraising her, and finally deciding that she meant it. "I'll do my best, miss," Hector promised.

November then caught sight of the little boy's arm. It was covered in burns from the silver shackle binding him to the wall. At least he only had the one chain; the others were much more thoroughly tethered. She crawled over toward him, tore the lining out of her skirt, and began wrapping his wrist to protect it from the silver. At first, he shrank from her in fear, but he relaxed once he realized what she was doing.

"They'll just take it from him as soon as they notice, and then the both of you will be in trouble," one of the women scolded her.

"Let her be," Hector countered. "It'll give the skin a chance to heal, save him from another infection. You hide that when the fairy opens the door, Carlos." The boy nodded and curled up protectively around his arm. November just sat, looking at him. He was so small. "Move away, November. She's finished the bloodsucker off," Hector warned, and November scurried back to the center of the room.

Willow opened the door, barely a hair out of place. "Out. Now," she ordered, and November complied, careful not to look back and give away her concern for the werewolves. The vampire so interested in eating her was now a pile of ash on the floor. "I was trying to keep him alive," Willow offered, "but he was quite determined." As soon as the door was locked behind them, Willow picked November up, threw the girl over her shoulder, and ran at full speed, not slowing once until they were behind the heavy, locked door of November's quarters.

November spent a long while curled up on her sofa, staring into the fire. Willow kept watch, taking her eyes from her charge only to check her phone for updates. They could hear occasional noise in the halls or through the vents but otherwise were undisturbed. November appreciated the quiet. It allowed her another chance to try to find Ilyn. She stared into the flames and let her mind drift to clear her thoughts, and then she closed her eyes and thought about the king. She listened in her mind to the songs he had sung to her as she had suffered from the cursed blade. She smelled his pipe smoke, saw the shine of his hair, felt the pressure of his hand on her back when they had danced together.

And finally, it came, just a glimpse: *Ilyn and William and Zinnia, standing next to a truck on a deserted road, talking to Ben.* It was just a flash, and then it was gone, but it was all November could do not to jump up and sing. *They're alive.* She glanced at Willow, who was texting and had noticed nothing. *They're coming. But when?*

She nearly jumped out of her skin when a loud knock sounded. Willow braced herself for trouble, but it was Luka who unlocked the door, followed by two fairies bearing boxes of food and bottled water. They placed their burdens on the table and were dismissed. "Any word from Philemon?" Willow asked as November tried to be invisible by the fire.

"He'll have a refrigerated truck full of human blood here by tomorrow dusk along with a couple of trucks full of live chickens." Willow made a face. "I know," he said. "Revolting. However, according to our engineer, it will take several days to get the cistern and plumbing sufficiently clean to provide drinking water for a new herd of humans. There's no point in getting the livestock here only to let them all expire. We'll have to make do for a few days on short rations."

"Are you sure you still want to have her turning be public? The young ones might still be pretty on edge if they're still hungry," Willow warned.

"The captains have things under control now, and they will be fed before the festivities begin," he replied in a definitive tone. "But perhaps she should be in place before our people assemble rather than having her walk through the crowd as planned."

"That sounds safer," Willow agreed. November silently gave thanks that she would at least be spared that particular humiliation. She had found Lilith's running of the gauntlet rather horrifying. "Is Mark very upset about Henry?" the fairy asked with a twinge of guilt.

"He knows it's his own fault for not getting hold of his progeny and issuing proper orders. You did what was necessary," Luka replied, seeming unconcerned about the loss of one of his vampires.

"I know. I just don't like killing babies."

"To your credit," he replied before turning his attention to November. "And how are we doing, kitten?"

"Fine, thank you," she answered, ignoring the revolting pet name with great effort. "I was a little spooked by that business in the corridor, but I've calmed down."

"Splendid," he answered absently. "Back to work for me, then. So much to do, and all these complications. Willow, keep her here all day tomorrow. We take no chances. This should be enough food and water, yes?"

November looked over the provisions and nodded. "More than enough."

"Have her bathed and ready by dusk," he ordered Willow. "Carrot and Ivy will bring water directly from the well to heat in the fire, as strychnine can be absorbed through the skin."

Willow smiled. "The old fashioned way. How ever did we manage?"

"Servants," he replied with a smile of his own. He walked over to November and took her by the shoulders. She tried not to shrink from his touch. "Until tomorrow, my dear, when you become one of us," he said, kissing her on the forehead. "Don't be frightened. It barely hurts at all." And with that, he left.

"What time is it?" November asked her fairy keeper, not sure if she'd answer.

"Nearly dawn."

"Maybe I should have a snack and then try to get some sleep." Willow nodded.

She savored the bread, fruit, and hard cheese she found in the boxes, along with the clean water for which she had a newfound appreciation. Then November curled up in the bed, which was warm and comfortable. The previous early morning, she'd already passed out and had been tucked into it by someone else. She'd been sedated enough by Luka's bite that she'd slept peacefully. This time, however, was different. She was anxious and frightened, unable to settle, wondering if her friends would come in time, wondering if they would be successful or if they would only add to the list of people dead because of her.

When she finally dozed off, she discovered unhappily that this room had possessed a previous occupant: a young man, a demon,

374

like her, she suspected, but less stable, and older, maybe 30 or 35 years old. The clothes read nineteenth century. He had been beautiful and tormented, and Luka must have decided that he would make a bad vampire, for one night, he had killed his prisoner. It was a gentle murder, as murders go. The victim saw it coming, but he didn't fight. He seemed relieved. Then she saw a child, a little boy of about ten years old. It took her a moment to realize that this was the same person, that Luka had kept him in this room for twenty years or more before giving up on him. Willow had to shake her awake when she started screaming. After that, she didn't try to sleep anymore. It seemed a bit of a shame to waste her remaining hours of human life on sleep anyway, if, in fact, she really was to die that night. Willow watched her carefully, not even letting her close the door when she used the bathroom.

She curled up again on the sofa, staring into the fire. Visions came and went. She dozed occasionally, always waking with a start. She ate when she got hungry. She sketched a little. She thought about what she would say to each of her friends if she ever got the chance. She tried to think of how she would try to behave up on the roof. She didn't want them enjoying her fear, but she didn't want to spend her last human moments with her mind adrift and numb, the way it had been so much of the time during her childhood sufferings. She finally decided that she would try to focus her mind on good memories, on times of love and happiness from her life, few as they might be.

Eventually, fairies began showing up with huge pots of water, which they set in the fire and used to fill the bathtub. Once it was full and steaming and capped with sweet-smelling bubbles, November immersed herself in the scalding water and stayed submerged for what had to have been hours. They kept replacing the water as it cooled. Willow seemed in no real hurry. It was only early afternoon. Somehow, the water made November feel peaceful and calm. She always had liked feeling warm. *There's nothing I can do about whatever is going to happen. All I can do is be ready to react in the moment. There's no point in torturing myself with fear between now and then. I'm going to just be. Just be.*

When she finally emerged, Willow dried and curled her hair as November sat wrapped in a thick bathrobe. It was all oddly maternal. *I feel like I'm getting ready for the prom . . . the evil death prom.* "It really isn't going to be that bad, November. Everyone tells me that the only pain is the initial bite. Then there might be a little nausea or dizziness, and then you'll feel a little cold. But once you start drinking his blood, you'll be warm and you'll just sort of drift off."

"That's not the part I'm afraid of," November replied quietly as Willow's deft hands styled her dark hair.

"You're afraid of what comes after?" Willow asked sympathetically.

"Yes."

"You won't be alone. We'll teach you how to feed, how to enthrall, how to survive," Willow reassured her.

You aren't the ones I want helping me! All she said out loud was, "I don't want to be a part of his war."

"You won't be on the front lines, November, and I doubt there's going to be much of a war. With Ilyn and William gone, our people will coalesce around Luka, and he intends to welcome all comers to his government regardless of their previous loyalties. Even Savita has contacted him."

That bit of intelligence made November's heart skip a beat. *How could Savita possibly be on Luka's side? She must be deceiving him.* She elected to reserve judgment until she had more information. Of

376

course, November alone knew that Ilyn still walked among the living, fully capable of putting up quite a fight.

Willow continued, "And as for the rest of Luka's plans, they will unfold slowly with a minimum of bloodshed. Humans are a valuable resource, after all." November elected to say nothing, swallowing her horror, knowing that Willow was incapable of understanding her concerns for human beings and werewolves.

Willow moved on from hair to makeup. She was subtle, managing to make November look fresh and healthy rather than exhausted and frightened. She seemed uncharacteristically cheerful, happily humming as she prepared her prisoner for sacrifice. She certainly seemed to buy the whole "murder as celebration of life" line. It occurred to November for the first time that Willow might be completely out of her mind.

When the fairy pulled out the snow white dress she was to wear to her execution, November could not hide a small smile. She wrapped well-worn memories around herself, thinking of the girl in a dark blue dress, the girl awaiting burial, surrounded by friends. The vision that had terrified her, that had haunted her childhood— this vision now became her comfort and her armor. *This is not the dress I die in. This is not the dress I rise in.* "You like it?" Willow asked hopefully.

"Yes, it's lovely," November answered cooperatively. *It's actually a little bit Bride of Frankenstein, but whatever.* Willow helped her put it on, carefully protecting her hairdo. Looking in the mirror, November thought she looked like a child bride or a virgin sacrifice. She supposed they intended her to be both. To her surprise, she found the dress had a pocket. She slipped the fairy lantern into it, on a whim. She found it a comforting thought, that she could carry some light in her pocket when she went to face the dark.

Then it was time to wait. November wound up doing what she guessed most people did when waiting for death: she got down on her knees and prayed, careful not to mess up the dress. She prayed that Luka's plans would be foiled. She prayed for the safety of her friends. She prayed that no one else would die because of her. She prayed for courage. She prayed that there was a reason for all of this: for her gift, for her incessant reincarnation, for her being drawn into this long-brewing conflict. She prayed that there was a purpose for her in all of it and that she would learn what that purpose was. She prayed that she wouldn't do anything terrible. She prayed for the werewolves, for freedom and an end to their suffering.

"I didn't know you were so religious," Luka commented, startling her out of her contemplation. She hadn't even heard the door open.

She looked up at him and replied, "Neither did I."

"Rather surprising given your track record with priests." He helped her to her feet and examined her from head to toe. "Perfect," he said, pleased as punch. "Well done, Willow." The man himself was dressed in his usual black, impeccably pressed. "I'll send Philemon to help you escort her up in just a little while. He's almost done supervising the feeding." The vampire bent to kiss November on the cheek. She couldn't suppress her shudder. He laughed at her discomfort. "See you very soon, kitten." And with that, he departed.

November was grateful that she did not have too long for her anxiety to build before there was another knock on the door. Philemon keyed in the code and entered, a fairy stranger at his side.

"Philemon. Persimmon. It's time, I take it?" Willow greeted them, rising to meet her comrades.

"It is," Philemon replied, just as he buried a hatchet in Willow's skull. Willow fell to the ground, insensible, light bleeding around the blade. November stepped backwards in shock. "Don't scream," he ordered. November obeyed, hands over her mouth, trying to slow her racing heartbeat.

The fairy called Persimmon stepped forward with a concerned expression, asking, "Em, are you okay?" She looked at him in total confusion before the unfamiliar features resolved into those of one she'd thought she'd lost forever.

"Pine?" she whispered in disbelief. "How?" Before he could answer, she threw her arms around his neck. "I thought you were dead. I saw you die. Thank God! Oh, Pine," she said fiercely, holding him tightly as she could, as if she feared he would vanish again. "How is this possible?"

"Power of illusion," he replied as he squeezed her back. "Comes in handy when your partner repeatedly tries to kill you. I'm so sorry I couldn't stop her, Em. I tried. I really did."

She stepped back and held his hands tightly. "Not your fault. And you're here now."

"This is all very touching," Philemon interrupted snidely. "We haven't much time before we're expected topside."

Pine stepped over to Willow, pulling out a knife to finish the job Philemon had started.

"No!" November shouted without thinking.

"She'd have seen us both dead, November. She's a dangerous enemy," Pine counseled.

"I know, but—" she began, shaking her head. "I don't think it's all her fault. I think he took advantage of her pain, warped her from her childhood. She's insane."

"Of course he did. That's his gift: he sees inside people's hearts, knows their deepest fears, desires, and pains. That's why he is so good at manipulating people and gaining their loyalty. That doesn't make Willow any less dangerous," Pine replied. He moved closer to his former friend.

Willow's eyes fluttered. She struggled to move her hand, as though she was planning to pull the hatchet from her skull. The three of them watched her eyes register Pine's presence and his weapon and saw the fear and shock dawn in them. Then, without a sound, she disappeared.

Philemon spoke for everyone after a shocked pause. "What. The. Hell. See what happens when you hesitate?"

Pine swore. "*She's* the hider. Well, I'll be damned. No one figured it out in all these centuries. Must be how she survived that attack on her village when she was a kid."

"That certainly does explain a lot," November said. "But she's still there on the floor. Couldn't you just stab at where she was?" November asked, making vague hacking gestures with her hands.

"Nope. Won't work. It keeps her invisible and shielded," Pine shrugged. "Fairy magic. What are you gonna do?"

"Well, at least she's not going anywhere with a silver ax in her head," Philemon said, uncharacteristically looking on the bright side. "She'll die of it sooner or later. And now we don't have to worry about hiding her half-dead body. So, can we get on with destroying Luka now? I'm a little impatient to avenge my wife," he said with his accustomed acerbity. In reply, Pine shimmered slightly and turned into a perfect copy of Willow, minus the hatchet.

"Excellent. So, here's the plan, weirdo," Philemon continued toward November, who was still staring in amazement at her not-dead friend in the guise of her not-dead enemy. "We go through the motions of this shindig until the moment of truth. We need to get all Luka's people on the roof, you see, if we have any prayer of living through this and getting away clean. When he starts biting you, that's when the fighting starts. The vampires have all been fed slightly tainted blood, which they will start to feel the effects of right about when your friends start trying to kill them all. The fairies will be hampered by the fact that it's nighttime and they can't suck the life out of anybody. Pine will get you out of the way. Try not to get yourself killed. Or do; I don't really care."

"So you snuck everyone in using the trucks with the provisions?" she asked, trying to piece it together. She had to admit, she had not expected Philemon's betrayal of Luka to happen so quickly or to be so complete. She hadn't even been sure the vampire had believed her explanation of Agnes's death.

"Obviously," he replied with a roll of his eyes. "I can tell why you're such a sought-after soothsayer."

"Was the poisoning your idea?"

"No, Ben does get credit for that much. I, however, came up with how to best capitalize on it when I caught him coming up from the basement with rat poison. Now, we really must go."

So up they went to the roof, empty but for the men at the Gatling guns. Her escorts walked November up to the platform where they bound her to her strange cross. She felt clumsy with anxiety and cold. Her feet were bare. They took their positions to either side of her.

Soon they were joined by the arriving assembly. All of Luka's people were in attendance. Even the flying guards broke from their aerial patrols to witness the festivities. The wolves were brought out, heavily chained in silver, to enjoy their tormentor's moment of triumph. November wondered if Luka planned to finally let his minions tear the wolves to pieces. She also wondered where her friends could possibly be hiding. She felt hyperaware, noticing every breath, every beat of her heart, every splinter in the wood, every scratch from the rope.

Luka himself was last to arrive, of course, processing through his adoring followers like some kind of rock-star bridegroom. They cheered for him. She could not wrap her mind around how much they loved him. She wondered if he returned their love at all. At the sight of him, November felt even colder. *But you're not alone,* she told herself. *They came for you. Keep your wits about you. Breathe.*

Too soon and not soon enough, Luka stood in front of her. He smiled his awful smile. "It's time," he said, brushing the back of his hand against her cheek.

"You are a monster," she said, unable to restrain herself. "And I hate you."

He laughed at her. "I know, kitten. You'll come around. Now, scream for me." And before she could blink, he had sunk his fangs into her neck.

Chapter 17

She did not scream for him. The screams came later, and most of them were not hers.

November gazed over Luka's shoulder as he drank, barely registering the pain of the bite or the twisting of his fist in her hair. She noticed neither his icy hand on her back nor the cheering of the crowd as he swallowed her blood. She was distracted by shadowy figures rising slowly through the air just outside the roof's boundaries, four ghosts floating silently upward, waiting for their moment, bows in hand.

She did not see them with her eyes, for she was the well-lit star on stage and they were in the pitch dark of the balcony, but see them she did. William, Savita, Greg, and Hazel, lifted skyward by their king, stood in midair next to the corner gun towers, poised to strike, prepared to kill or die to save November and their house. For a moment, November could have sworn she smelled pipe smoke. Suddenly, she wasn't cold anymore.

Philemon's attack came quickly. He could no longer check his rage. He allowed his master only a few sips of blood before falling upon him, stake in one hand and silver blade in the other. His angelic features twisted with hatred, and his eyes called a shark to mind. Luka's instincts alerted him in the nick of time. He pulled away from November, her blood dripping from his mouth, and he managed just barely to evade Philemon's weapons as he drew his own vicious dagger. They became a savage blur: Philemon frantic with rage and grief, Luka fighting for his life. November could barely make out which killer was which as they flew across the roof in a manic dance. She rather hoped they both might perish.

Before the crowd could even react to the change in the evening's program, the four phantom invaders had taken the gun towers for their own, killing the gunners with only the twang of the bows to mark their deaths. As the invaders turned their newly-captured weapons toward those assembled on the roof, Pine quickly freed November from her ropes and pulled her down to relative safety between the scaffold and the roof's wall. He had also dropped his magical disguise, much to November's relief. Pine disguised as Willow was one of the evening's creepier features, which was saying something. She wondered if Luka had seen the transformation and now knew that the real Willow was missing.

Members of the crowd began to cry out as they registered what was happening; they started pulling weapons and looking for cover. Some of the less-courageous tried for the door, which they found to be locked and stronger than it looked. A few moved in to try to help their leader in his fight against Philemon, but they were whirling about so violently that those who got close only succeeded in getting themselves injured. Those who fired arrows or bullets at the towers found their projectiles batted out of the air by llyn's unseen hand. A sizable number of Luka's people appeared to be dizzy and disoriented; a dozen fell to their knees, disabled by vertigo courtesy of Philemon's tainted blood delivery.

November tried to catch her breath while she crouched next to Pine; she wished her head would stop spinning. Her friend held a gauze pad against her punctured neck. "Are you alright?" he asked gravely, for the millionth time. *He totally needs that t-shirt. He can put "I'm so sorry" on the back. Christmas present!* She nodded weakly and closed her eyes for a moment, wanting desperately to sleep. "Stay with me," he said, shaking her gently. "I know it's hard, but you need to try to be alert if you want to get through this in one piece." She forced her eyes back open. "That's the way," Pine encouraged her. "Deep breaths."

384

As November listened to the sounds of battle and struggled to still her shaking, Ilyn vaulted over the wall and landed lightly, with the grace of an acrobat. He had used his telekinesis like a certain superhero's webs, pulling himself up the side of the fortress, swinging from the invisible lines of his own thoughts. He looked at November as though she were a miracle before gathering her up in his arms. He said nothing. She squeezed him tightly in reply, too giddy with blood loss and relief to formulate a sentence herself.

Their reunion was, of course, interrupted by the battle in progress. November jumped as howls rose from the chained wolves. "The werewolves! Ilyn, you have to free them. Please!" He looked at her for a moment, eyebrow cocked incredulously. "Look at them, your grace! They're innocent, and trapped, and they're going to get killed if you don't do something."

Ilyn rose to get a look at the chained prisoners and shrugged, hesitating no further before raising his hand and unlocking the shackles. He used his gift to pull away the silver and sent the chains flying through the crowd, taking down several of the fairies and vampires in their path. The former prisoners looked over to Ilyn, surprised by his assistance. He gave them an ironic little bow. Hector smiled at November and saluted Ilyn before changing form and joining in the fight, along with the other adult wolves.

"Carlos! Over here!" November called. The small boy stood frozen in the midst of chaos, his fellow wolves too charged by the battle and the full moon and their sudden freedom to stop and get him out of harm's way before seeking vengeance on their captors. "The little boy! Look!" she cried as a stray arrow careened towards the child.

Ilyn batted down the projectile and snatched up Carlos, pulling him through the air towards their hiding place. The poor child was terrified, eyes wide and full of tears as he flew above the turmoil. As

Ilyn gently put him down, he shrank from the vampire. November took his hand. "They're my friends. They won't hurt you. They're good ones, I promise." He responded by jumping into November's lap, burying his face in her neck, his arms and legs locked tightly around her. Just skin and bones, he weighed almost nothing. November hugged him tightly. His wrist was still wrapped with the scrap of fabric from her skirt.

"I must go fight. Pine, keep her safe," Ilyn ordered, and he disappeared in a blur before November could say anything more. Ilyn raised his hands and began to pull weapons from the hands of Luka's soldiers, mangling them before tossing them over the wall to the desert floor far below. His people continued using their captured guns to cut swaths through the crowd, careful to avoid November's refuge and their king, as well as Philemon and Luka. Ilyn had given his word that they would allow Philemon to kill his master himself, if he could. That had been the price of Philemon's assistance.

By the time November's friends in the gun tower ran out of bullets, well over half of Luka's people were dead or severely wounded. Greg and Hazel continued firing arrows from on high, while William and Savita descended to fight at closer quarters. Savita began to sing in a foreign tongue, sending those close to her into a trance from which they would never emerge. She made her way grimly across the roof, swinging a silver scythe as though cutting grain, surrounding herself with a cloud of ash and light as her victims fell helpless before her, an invisible terror wrapped in a fog of death. William fought gleefully from the opposite corner of the roof, ax in one hand and mace in another. He was a juggernaut, and no one could touch him.

Luka's people fought desperately, but most were young and inexperienced and hampered by Ben and Philemon's ploy. The only ones who could escape were the flyers. A dozen or more of them flew about above the battle, helpless after Ilyn took their weapons, looking for any chance to save their friends, and mostly failing. It was a slaughter.

A number of the more mobile survivors moved for the shelter of the platform, finding November and her companions there. Pine stood to fight them off, aided by one of the wolves. November was somehow certain it was Hector. November turned, using her body to shield Carlos as fairy and wolf fought on the same side for once. They worked in tandem to hold off the weakened but desperate attackers.

One of the vampires slipped past their defenses and went for November and the child. With but a moment to spare, November snatched up a dropped ax and swung wildly for the attacker's neck. The vampire disappeared in a cloud of ash. Once November and Carlos had finished coughing, they saw that their refuge was once again free of enemies. Pine grinned at her, calling out, "Nice one," over the noise of the battle. Hector howled at her almost cheerfully before heading back into the fray.

Philemon and Luka's duel slowed to visible speeds as both vampires began to grow weary. Luka had a slight edge in age and strength, but Philemon was fueled by his thirst for vengeance. They were fairly evenly matched, and each had bloodied the other several times in the preceding minutes. Wounds appeared and healed again and again.

As they circled each other warily, Luka got his first good look at what was happening to his people. Despair briefly flashed in his eyes, turning quickly to cold steel and determination. His loss fueled him, and he now had the advantage. He attacked with renewed vigor, driving Philemon back until his former servant tripped over a fallen weapon. Luka's knife, the same one that had wounded

November so grievously many weeks earlier, soon found Philemon's heart.

The younger man fell to ash, his justice denied. In the next moment, one of the strongest flyers swooped down low to snatch his master out of danger. Luka clung to his back as they soared into the air above the fray.

Greg directed his fire at them, fire they managed to evade until the remaining flyers coalesced around Luka, providing a shield and receiving instructions from their master. Greg began picking them off one at a time. Luka and his companion began evasive maneuvers while the rest of the aerial force dove to the ground, huddling in the darkness outside the fortress, sheltering against the walls where the fighters on top of the roof were unable to reach.

Ilyn turned his attention to his wayward son, pulling him down out of the air. Hazel killed the flyer with one well-placed arrow, and Ilyn flung Luka against the ground, pinning him there. Pine, November, and Carlos cautiously left their hiding place to witness the confrontation. They stood by Hector, now again in human form, his leg bleeding and eyes wild. Carlos took his hand. They were the only wolves remaining.

The bodies of their fellow prisoners lay scattered on the roof, the only visible evidence of the night's violence as the ash that remained of their tormentors blew away. One was still breathing, a woman, mortally wounded.

November went to her, knelt, and took her hand, trying to use her white dress to staunch the bleeding. The woman smiled at the fruitless gesture as she breathed her last. November sat back on her heels and looked down at the blood on her hands. It seemed pointless: all of this death, ever her shadow, ever attached to her heels.

Luka was friendless on the roof of what had once been his secret sanctuary. His people were nearly all dead: blowing ash, spent arrows, dead wolves, and brass shells were the only signs that they had ever existed.

Yet Luka laughed at the victors. "You have won the day, Father, but I will win the war. You've burned this crop, but I have other fields to harvest, and I can always sow another." He looked at November almost mischievously. It made her stomach turn. "I shall have her, too, mark my words. I have hunted her for 500 years. I will hunt her for another 500 if I have to. I warn you: do not change her. I have taken precautions."

"I should have staked you before you rose," Ilyn said with disgust, barely hearing his son's words. "Only my love for Marisha protected you. She would despise what you have become."

Ilyn lifted a bow and notched the arrow. As he drew the bow, the hiding flyers reappeared, shooting through the air at breathtaking speed, one weaponless flyer taking aim at each of November's rescuers. Luka's last remaining soldiers crashed into each of November's friends, knocking them to the ground in a blur of tangled limbs.

In Ilyn's moment of distraction, he lost his mental grip on his son, and one of Luka's men pulled his master once again to the safety of the sky. Pine struggled to shield November. Luka's last man grabbed them both, dropping Pine as he hauled November high into the air. Ilyn quickly dispatched his attacker, as did William, Savita, Hazel, and Greg. From the air, November saw the resulting flashes of light and swirling ash.

November screamed in fear as they rose higher and higher, until her friends on the roof looked like insects. Between the thinness of the air and her mortal terror, the girl struggled for breath. She screamed again as she and her assailant suddenly fell several dozen feet. She looked at the vampire and saw that he was bleeding in half a dozen places, failing to heal, his eyes starting to glaze over. He was not long for this world. It was all he could do to stay up in the air with the silver poison sapping his life.

Luka and his flying partner circled them as Luka assessed the situation. The undignified piggyback ride would have been funny in any other context. It was evident to Luka that the vampire carrying November would not get very far. "Alas, it seems we must part for a time. Don't worry, kitten. I'm sure dear old dad will catch you. *A la prochaine* . . ." he said with an awful smile. And with that, he and his man took off into the night. An instant later, November's vampire captor died his second death, sending her plummeting toward the ground.

Ilyn did indeed catch her, of course, before she could even scream again. He gently halted her fall and lowered her slowly back down to the roof until she alighted in his arms. She shook like a leaf, her lips pressed together so tightly that they nearly disappeared. She could scarcely register what was happening around her. All her energy went into breathing and not falling utterly apart.

Hector required some persuading to come along with vampires and fairies, but he had little choice. He would not have gotten very far on his injured leg, and they were truly in the middle of nowhere. Fortunately, he was the only one of the group who had been seriously wounded. He hated to leave the bodies of his companions, but there was nowhere to bury them and no time to waste. In the end, he settled for cremation, and Pine helped him quickly arrange the remains and set them alight.

They all scrambled into Luka's abandoned helicopter. As the helicopter took off, with William and Pine at the controls, November struggled to control her fear, Ilyn's reassuring presence

390

notwithstanding. Carlos, also frightened, took her hand and held it tight, which helped her to be brave for his sake. Quarters were close in the helicopter cabin, and between that and the deafening noise, November was desperate for the flight to be over even as it had just barely begun.

They rose into the air and began to fly away, leaving Luka's no-longer-secret stronghold behind them. The smoke from the hastily arranged funeral rose in spirals into the starry sky as the helicopter disappeared into the darkness. The take-off had frightened November anew, but she was grateful to escape the smell of burning flesh. The floodlights from the fortress were visible for a long way, a strange beacon in the middle of the empty desert.

Just as November began to relax, one of Luka's injured flyers made one last effort to stop them. He appeared unsteadily beside the helicopter, bleeding light in several places. He reached out, grabbed a handhold by the door, and aimed a pistol at Ilyn. His hand was surprisingly steady even as the rest of him trembled with the effort. November and Carlos screamed in unison as William and Pine turned the helicopter sharply, trying to shake off the attacker. Hazel threw a knife which found its home in the fairy's throat. He screamed, dropped his weapon and clutched at his neck, then plummeted to earth.

Gradually, November calmed down, and her teeth began chattering more with cold than with fear. Ilyn wrapped her up in a blanket, and she closed her eyes to rest for a bit, Carlos's hand still in hers. They flew for over an hour before alighting near a beat-up VW bus with a unique paint job. As they climbed down from the chopper and walked over to the vehicle, November shook her head, bemused in spite of the night's toll. "What?" Ilyn demanded, feigning offense.

"Just doesn't seem like your style," she replied, managing a little smile.

"Beggars can't be choosers," he said, helping walk over the uneven ground to the vehicle. "We're trying to blend in." There she found Zinnia and Ben waiting nervously. Zinnia immediately folded November into a tight hug, murmuring her relief that her friend was safe. Ben hung back, unsure how to behave surrounded by so many people he had betrayed before turning coat again to help them in the end. When Zinnia pulled back, November gasped. Her friend looked just terrible.

"What's wrong?" November exclaimed.

Zinnia's face contorted as she struggled to swallow her tears. "My mother . . . she . . ."

"Died in the hotel," November whispered, suddenly seeing it in a flash. "Oh, no. I'm so sorry! I'm so sorry," she cried, enfolding her friend once again in her arms.

"She just kept going back in to save more humans, and I tried to tell her it was too dangerous, and –."

Zinnia began to sob. November held her until she regained her composure. The fairy's tears left an electric blue stain on the shoulder of her white dress. Zinnia finally calmed down enough to look around and notice the strangers. Her nostrils flared warily at the scent of wolf.

"Hector and Carlos," November explained. "Unfortunately, they've enjoyed far too much of Luka's hospitality."

"Any enemy of Luka is a friend of mine, I guess," she said after an uncertain pause, nodding at the pair in welcome. She caught sight of Hector's leg and winced. "I can fix that in the morning if you want." Hector seemed shocked at her offer, as did Hazel, who now

392

that they were out of the helicopter was keeping her distance from the werewolves. Zinnia knelt down in front of Carlos. "Hi," she said, holding up one hand to wave. "I'm Zinnia." The boy turned his head shyly away, hiding his face against November's leg.

"Come," William said with gentle firmness. He placed a hand on Zinnia's shoulder. He was the closest thing to family she had left, November supposed. "We must get moving." He got behind the wheel, and everyone scrambled aboard. To Hector's evident surprise, Pine helped the injured werewolf into a seat.

Ben finally spoke up. "Did you get Luka?" Ilyn gave his head a quick shake. Ben dropped his gaze to the floor.

"Where are we going?" November asked wearily.

"Good question. We need to find somewhere to rest nearby, somewhere the vampires can go to ground. And we sure as hell don't have any friends in Arizona," Hazel replied, ever practical.

"I do," November replied. Everyone looked at her in surprise. "I have a friend here," she explained. "From the carnival. His name is Neil; he sold funnel cakes. In the winter, he lives on his parent's old farm, in the country, outside of someplace called Wilcox. He made me memorize his address and phone number in case I ever needed to run away from my mother during the off season."

"I remember him," William said. "Seemed protective of you. Real suspicious of us when we started asking questions."

"I remember him, too," Zinnia said. "He loved her, for sure."

"Well, aren't you popular?" Hector commented wryly, looking up from examining his injured leg.

"It wasn't like that," November protested. "I remind him of his kid that his wife took with her when she ran off."

"Regardless of the exact nature of his affection, it seems as good an option as any," Ilyn said decisively.

November gave Neil's address to William, who programmed it into his phone and gave his verdict. "We'll make it in plenty of time, the way I drive," he grinned fiercely.

"Do we warn him?" November asked. Everyone shook their heads.

"Safer not to," William replied.

So, off they went. The seats in the modified Volkswagen lined the walls on the sides of the cabin. Carlos sat between Zinnia and November, with Ilyn, of course, on November's other side. After a little while, Carlos looked up at Zinnia and said in a sweet little voice, "Did your mommy die?" November had never heard him speak before.

"Yes, she did," Zinnia answered sadly.

"Mine did, too, when the bad vampires came," he replied sympathetically before he clambered up unto her lap. "You'll see her again in heaven," he said confidently before curling up against the fairy's chest and closing his eyes. Zinnia looked like she might cry again; then she wrapped her arms around the little boy, leaning her cheek against his filthy hair. She sang fairy songs to him softly until he fell asleep.

"That's the first I've heard him talk in months," Hector said quietly once the boy began to snore.

"He's not your son, I take it?" Zinnia asked, stroking the little boy's filthy hair as he slept.

394

"No. There were two small packs in Arizona before Luka decided to finally wipe us out. As you know, we tend to keep to ourselves except for festival times. He was born into the other one. I didn't meet him until Luka's men threw him into the cell maybe six months ago, along with the only other survivor of the raid on his people. She didn't last long." Hector's voice was filled with sadness and smoldering anger.

"I'm surprised he didn't drive you out years ago. He was always opposed to the peace," Ilyn commented sympathetically.

"We've been trying to flee for generations. Packs in neighboring states were disinclined to cede us any territory or allow us to join them," Hector replied bitterly. "No pack leader wants an influx of strangers eroding his power base, and they especially don't want extra alphas hanging around."

"I'm sorry," Ilyn somberly replied. "As I am sorry for those you have lost."

There was a pause. "You are . . . not what I would have expected," Hector said. "We tell our kids stories about 'Ilyn the Scourge' coming for bad little boys and girls when we want to scare them into behaving themselves."

"I'm growing mellow in my old age," Ilyn answered. That comment provoked barks of laughter from Hazel and his kin, all except Savita. She stared solemnly at nothing, seemingly deaf to the conversation swirling around her. "Daughter, are you alright?" he asked quietly, reaching over to touch her hand. She looked up at him and simply shook her head. "I'm sorry you had to fight, dear one." She nodded but said nothing. Greg looked at his mother, worried.

"How soon do you think we need to worry about Luka coming for us?" Greg asked to break the heavy silence that followed.

"He'll need time to regroup, surely," Hazel answered. "Though, I suppose he might send a few men on the off chance they'd do some damage."

"He'd have to come himself in order to find her through the blood bond," Ilyn said, "Though I suppose he might just take some guesses as to where we might go. And he'd surely want to take care not to kill November. Now that they've exchanged blood, his obsession with her will only be stronger."

November was seized with anxiety. She was not ready to contemplate future threats. She was not ready to think about the danger her existence caused to strangers and friends alike. She certainly did not want to be reminded of how Luka had forced her to drink his blood or of how much of her own he had swallowed. The fact that she knew she must reek of him made her want to gag.

Her companions continued their conversation, untroubled by the constant bumps and high speed. "We might be wise to avoid Las Vegas and Oakland for a few days, since that's the first place he would look," Hazel opined. "Then there's the complication of your being recognized in Vegas when everyone thinks you're dead, your grace."

"Georgia?" suggested Zinnia. "My betrothed is there. Not that I actually know him."

"He might offer you sanctuary, if he still lives. Not sure about the rest of us, though," William replied.

"Texas has also offered shelter," William called from up front. "He hasn't forgotten November's help."

"Too close," Ilyn judged. "Luka has friends in Mexico."

"Maybe she should drink some more of your blood, Grandfather, or any of ours, really, and dilute the effects of Luka's, make it harder for him to find her," Greg suggested. "I wonder how much of his she had."

"Enough talk," Savita said with a quiet authority. "You're upsetting her." These were the first words she'd uttered since the battle in which she had slain so many.

Ilyn turned his attention to November and realized that his daughter was correct. November was shaking again with fear and worry, suffering silently. "I'm sorry, little one," he said, cradling her head against his shoulder. "You're only just out of danger and we're already fighting the next battle."

"Why don't you sleep a little? You're so tired," Zinnia suggested. "It's okay. You're safe now. You don't have to hold it together anymore." She squeezed her friend's hand.

So, with their kind permission, she did just that. She wept silently into Ilyn's shirt until it was soaked through, then she fell into the deepest of sleeps. She didn't even wake up when they got to Neil's farm.

The farm had first belonged to his grandparents, who'd had ten children. They'd added rooms haphazardly as their family grew, giving the place a charmingly organic appearance. Consequently, the house was far too large for a single man, and the upkeep was a constant project for him. He kept the place nice and tidy, though, out of pride and a sense of obligation to his parents who'd left the property to him rather than his brother. The porch still had three rocking chairs in good repair, though Neil's wife and daughter had been gone for years. The land was leased out to ranchers, mostly, as Neil had no knack for farming or livestock.

Neil was a chronic insomniac and thus still awake when a mysterious vehicle made its way up his gravel drive at around four in the morning. He met his unexpected visitors at the door with suspicion in his eyes and a shotgun in his hands. His heart dropped and his expression turned to grief and worry when he saw November unconscious in Ilyn's arms.

"It's alright, Neil, she's just sleeping. But she's been through rather a lot. She thought she might find a safe place to recover here. Was she wrong?" Ilyn said by way of greeting.

"'Course not," Neil replied after a wary moment, stepping aside to allow them entry. "Come in." His eyes narrowed as he examined the strange bunch. The hair stood up on the back of his neck as something within him warned that these were not ordinary people. "Jesus, man," he exclaimed when he saw Hector's leg. "You need a doctor."

"It'll wait," Hector assured him, limping along with Pine's help, his arm around the fairy's neck. They seemed to have forged a bit of a bond. "Plus, doctors tend to call the cops for bullet wounds, in my experience," he added with strangely cheerful honesty.

Neil raised his eyebrows at that but was distracted by the next casualty of Luka's evildoing. "What the hell happened to him?" Neil asked with alarm when Zinnia crossed his threshold with Carlos still wrapped around her neck and waist. In the bright light of Neil's home, the child looked even more wretched.

"I don't know, but whatever it was," Zinnia replied sadly, "it was bad."

Neil stared at her for a moment. "Do I know you?" he asked her confusedly, not quite remembering her, of course, since she had enthralled him months before.

"We met at the carnival one time," she admitted, supplying no details.

Neil looked around at the bizarre group gathered in the large living room of his ramshackle house. "Humph. Is someone going to explain what's going on?" he asked. "Haven't I seen you on TV?" he added to Ilyn. Everyone looked at the king, waiting for him to take the lead. He lay November gently down on a sofa, turned back around, and seemed to make a decision. He went with the truth, though incomplete.

"My name is Ilyn Zykov. I own casinos, among other things. One of them was destroyed a few days ago in a terrorist attack, which is why you've seen me on television. My son Luka is the one who orchestrated the attack. He wants to, shall we say, take over the family business, and I am unwilling to give it to him. November has been in my employ since she left the carnival."

"Doing what, exactly?" Neil interrupted suspiciously.

"Serving as my soothsayer. Nothing untoward, I assure you," Ilyn answered. "You are aware of her gifts, I presume?"

"We never talked about it. She didn't like to, you know? But I could tell she wasn't fakin' the whole psychic thing," Neil admitted. "Creeped people out, but not me. I just thought she was special."

"Well, then you must understand how valuable her ability might be. Luka is also aware of her value and absconded with her. Hector and Carlos here were also victims of his penchant for kidnapping. We liberated them along with November earlier this evening. As you can see, November was rather heavily drugged during her captivity. I do not yet know what other mistreatment she may have suffered." Here his voice grew thick with anger. He calmed himself before continuing. "Now we need a place to hide and rest until we can catch a flight to somewhere she'll be safe."

"This worthless son of yours – is he dead?"

"Unfortunately not," Ilyn replied.

"He'll come for her again?" Neil asked gruffly.

"Most likely, and soon. Sheltering us might well endanger you," Ilyn answered forthrightly.

"Stay as long as you want," was Neil's steely-eyed reply. "I've got four extra bedrooms and a finished basement, if that suits you."

"That will be perfect. Thank you for your hospitality. Now, let me introduce everyone," the king replied. Once all the head-nodding and hand-shaking was concluded, everyone scattered and found places to rest. Ilyn put November in Neil's daughter's old room, still decorated with purple curtains and pictures of horses. Pine stayed with her has she slept, as did Ilyn until almost sunrise.

Neil cleaned and bandaged Hector's leg, after which Hector took a guest bedroom. He slept uneasily on the soft mattress after months of captivity, falling into an exhausted sleep only after moving to the floor. Zinnia stayed with Carlos as he slept in another bedroom. The boy spent a good twelve hours curled up on her chest like a baby. The vampires settled into the basement for the day, of course, barricading the door from the inside for protection. All rested, not knowing how soon danger would reappear.

Chapter 18

It was such a relief for November to wake slowly, warm and calm and safe. She opened her eyes to see a patch of late-afternoon sunlight falling across her legs, little motes of dust dancing in the light. She saw that someone had changed her into some purple and pink plaid flannel pajamas. She wondered idly what had happened to her dress. She hoped they had burned it. Whatever they'd done with it, someone had removed the fairy lantern from the pocket and left it on the nightstand. Her rosary sat next to it. She smiled. She turned her head to see Pine sitting across the room, and her smile turned to a laugh. Pine looked relieved to hear the sound.

"What, you don't think I look awesome?" Pine asked, standing and turning to better model his ridiculous ensemble. "Neil had to scrounge in the attic for clean clothes for everyone to wear while we wash our own. Apparently, he was quite hip circa 1970." Pine was sporting an epic pair of lime green bellbottoms along with an orange paisley blouse. "You should see Savita's outfit. She looks like she belongs on a commune, courtesy of Neil's sister. The king looks like a cowboy undertaker. As for Lord William, I have two words for you: lumberjack chic."

November sat up in bed and took stock of herself. She was pleased to find that she felt pretty decent, other than being ravenously hungry. "He stayed by your bed until dawn, you know, and Hazel practically had to drag him away to rest in the basement," Pine reported. November knew he referred to the king. She reached out to look for him and found him dead to the world, ramrod straight on his back underneath a foosball table. He looked strangely fragile.

She was moved by the image, but still, she replied, "If he's only able to love me when I'm asleep or about to get killed, that isn't going to work for me."

"He's afraid of you. And for you," came Zinnia's voice from the door. She sounded uncharacteristically subdued, but she had a smile for her friend. November leapt up to hug her. "I am so glad you're alright," the fairy said fiercely.

"Right back at you," November replied. "I was so afraid I'd lost you all." She pulled away for a moment to look at her friend. "I'm so sorry about your mother."

"I know," she replied and squeezed her hand. "But right now, let's worry about you. Do you have wounds that need healing? Do you want to talk about what happened?"

"Not really, but I guess I should."

"The king could sense your suffering. I could, too, a little," Zinnia said. "It was awful, but at least we knew you were still alive."

"For the first couple of days, I couldn't find any of you with my gift. All I could see was the hotel coming down. I felt so hopeless. When I finally caught a glimpse of some of you in the desert, it was all I could do to hide my joy from them."

"Were they terribly cruel to you?" Zinnia asked worriedly.

"Some of the time. They would go back and forth, kind one minute and terrible the next. I guess that's how you do it, right? When you want to break your prisoner?" She shook her head. "I expected it from Luka, but Willow . . . that was almost worse. She's a true believer. She'll do anything for him, no hesitation. And I think she's probably mentally disturbed."

"I should have seen it coming. Or Lord William should have," Pine said, reproaching himself.

402

"Not your fault," November countered. "Anyway, it could have been a lot worse. I could have been raped, or maimed, or turned into Luka's vampire. It was mostly fear and humiliation and getting knocked around. And having to drink his blood." She shuddered at the memory.

"That's plenty," Zinnia said sadly.

"Yeah," November replied. She sighed. "On that cheerful note, let's take a break for breakfast. I smell bacon," she said with somewhat forced cheer.

Pine showed her to the kitchen, where they found Carlos and Hector eating Neil out of house and home. Zinnia sat down next to Carlos, who brightened immediately. Hazel was "taking a walk." November supposed that there would be an awful lot of dead animals in the vicinity by the time they departed. Neil was at the stove, happy to be cooking for hungry people and secretly pleased to have a full house in the loneliness of the off-season, even if the circumstances were odd. November ran and gave him a huge hug, which he returned, spatula still in hand.

"It is so good to see you!" November exclaimed to her old friend. "Thank you for taking us in."

"I gave you my address in case of trouble, and it sounds like you've had plenty of it," was his reply. "Now sit down and eat, and you can tell me everything later."

November sat down next to the two werewolves. Carlos smiled shyly and showed her the pancake Neil had made him in the shape of Mickey Mouse. Hector nodded to her but was too busy chewing to speak. The werewolves had gotten washed up. They were both in clean clothes, Carlos wearing a faded concert t-shirt of Neil's that came down past his knees. Hector was about Neil's size, so he'd hit the borrowed-clothes jackpot and landed some duds from the current decade. It looked like someone had given them both haircuts.

Hector had a bandage on his leg that was suspiciously free of blood, and November was certain Zinnia had made good on her offer to heal the wolf. November knew that their invisible trauma would be far more difficult to fix, but the food and care did seem to have perked them up. She soon dug into her own breakfast, the most delicious she could remember ever eating, made so enjoyable by the fact that she had feared never to eat anything but blood ever again.

Once she had eaten her fill and the others had moved on to the living room, Neil's questions began. She tried to be as honest as she could without using the words "fairy" or "vampire" or "werewolf" or "demon." She told him about her mother's murder. "Two lowlifes killed her over a watch," she said, which was more-or-less true. She was glad that her shirt covered the awful scar on her arm so she didn't have to explain that.

"I was hoping you'd call and let me know how you were doing," he scolded once he had gotten the highlights. "Those 'missing' posters had me pretty worried. My brother told me CPS had come for you, but then the news said you were a runaway . . ."

"I'm sorry. I should have called," she apologized. "I didn't find out about the posters right away, and there's been so much going on, and I didn't realize that you would worry."

"Are you sure you're okay? I mean, kidnapping – that's pretty heavy. Did they hurt you?" Neil asked fiercely.

"Just scared me, mostly," she fibbed. "I'll have some bad dreams, I expect."

"These people you're with – they seem a little odd. But awful attached to you," he added, trying to be fair.

"That's a pretty accurate description," she replied with a rueful smile. "I've gotten pretty attached to them, too. I don't have to hide what I am from them."

"Well, you watch out for that Ilyn guy – he's got eyes for you, and he's way too old to be looking at a girl your age," he counseled.

"Seriously, though, he's not going to try anything," she replied, laughing. Of course, she didn't tell Neil that Ilyn was too old to be looking at a girl of any age, nor that, as it turned out, she herself was not as young as she appeared to be.

As soon as the sun set, the vampires surfaced. Neil noticed that none of them ate any food, just as he'd marked Pine and Zinnia's abstinence from breakfast, but he said nothing. Ilyn made a beeline for November but didn't seem to know what to do once he'd found her. "You are well?" he asked her awkwardly.

"Yes, thank you," she replied with a bit of a smile. He reached out and brushed a hand lightly against her cheek. Then he fled without saying anything else. November sighed and rolled her eyes.

Greg, William, Hazel, Savita, and Ilyn congregated on the back porch, presumably to form some kind of plan, she hoped.

Ben, excluded from the meeting, sat awkwardly in an armchair in the living room, watching Zinnia playing with Carlos on the floor. Pine stayed close to November, as usual. Hector was brooding by the fire, his leg miraculously improved. Neil stayed silent about noticing that, too. Ben stared at November. She, in return, didn't know what to say. How could she thank him for killing all those innocent people? But if he hadn't done it, she would probably be worse than dead. She finally settled for asking him if he was okay.

"I'm relieved you're alive," he answered, "but I'd be better if Luka were dead."

"I think we can all get on board with that sentiment," she replied with a strained smile. "What are you going to do?"

"I don't know. I assume Luka has a bounty on me, so I can either live on the run or wait somewhere nice for the inevitable."

"I'm sure they'd give you sanctuary," she offered, tilting her head in the general direction of the conclave then in progress on the porch.

"It'd be more like house arrest. I mean, how could they ever trust me? I wouldn't trust me, either," he said morosely. "I don't know that I can bear to be around all of you anyway. It's just too painful."

"I'm sorry," she said sincerely. He gave her a crooked half-smile before walking out towards the basement stairs to find the solitude he now preferred.

November, feeling antsy and uninformed, went back through the kitchen to eavesdrop on the porch conference. They noticed her, of course, but kept right on going, which she appreciated, as it made her feel like less of a pawn and more of a player.

"You should have killed him and let her fall," William said with his typical ruthlessness.

The group made general sounds of protest. "That would have been dishonorable," Hazel scolded. "November is under our protection."

November inserted her own comment as she came through the door, saying, "He's right. Luka dead is of more benefit to the universe than me alive, as far as I can tell." At Ilyn's stricken look, she hastened to add, "Not that I'm not grateful to be alive. But I'm really frightened about what he might do, especially now that he's backed into a corner."

"What's done is done," Ilyn declared, striding over to November and placing his cloak on her cold shoulders. He looked at her like a drowning man looks at a lifeboat before turning back to the group. "He was at the very limit of my range anyway. I couldn't be sure of my grip on him or of my aim. I'm satisfied that I made the right choice. The question is what to do now."

"We hunt him down," William declared. "Without Willow's magic, it will be harder for him to hide."

"I wouldn't be so sure that Willow is out of the picture," November cautioned.

"Pine said Philemon left a silver hatchet in her head!" William countered.

"I had a vision a few nights ago of Luka pulling a hatchet out of the aforementioned head," came November's reply. "She's a survivor. She's also completely loyal to Luka and two thirds crazy to boot. I wouldn't count her out."

"I just can't get over it," Ilyn said sadly. "Willow. I used to read her stories every night before dawn. Marisha would take her riding on her favorite horse."

"I think it started that night you and Luka found her. He purposely worked to win her love, so he could use her later. Luka was the first one to pick her up after her family died. I think there's some kind of fairy magic bond there," November ventured.

"That's impossible," Greg said.

"Tell that to your king," Hazel said. "I didn't think it could happen between a human and a vampire either, but here we are." She cocked a head in November's direction.

"Was Willow why you couldn't find me without Ben and Philemon?" November asked.

Ilyn nodded guiltily. "The blood was useless. Willow must have enchanted the place when it was built. We had no idea she was a hider. We thought that gift had died out. It was always rare, and I haven't heard of a hider in centuries. We would never have found the fort without Philemon leading us there. I put you through drinking my blood for nothing." November grimaced at the memory.

"Besides needing to worry about Willow, Daphne wasn't there. If Luka had her miss his moment of triumph, she must be off somewhere doing something both important and awful," Hazel pointed out.

"Who's Daphne?" asked November wearily.

"Luka's Second. A night-powered fairy, a very rare gift. Means she can feed and heal others at night as well as by day. She's a very dangerous woman," Greg answered.

"Well, where are we going to go?" William asked, getting the conversation back on track. "I say back to Oakland. We're fortified and well-staffed. He won't dare come at least until he's had time to regroup."

"Your house is also in the middle of a city, surrounded by innocent people," Savita pointed out, chiming in for the first time. "And he took down the hotel with one enthralled human and a stolen airplane full of C-4."

"Only because he made sure November wasn't in it first," William countered. "He won't risk a bombing anywhere she might be."

"The Livermore ranch?" November asked.

408

"Hard to defend. Hard to escape," came William's reply. "Wouldn't want to stay more than a night."

"Should we split up?" Pine asked from the doorway. "No, bad idea," he said in answer to his own question. "He'll just go for November."

"He'll be able to find me anywhere?" November asked with quiet dread.

"Until the bond wears off. At least 6 months, depending. How much did he make you drink?" Greg asked.

"A lot," she answered, looking down at the floor, remembering the desperate, choking feeling of being forced to swallow Luka's blood. Her skin crawled. Greg gave her hand a comforting squeeze.

"Or you go ahead and turn her. Not as though anyone cares about the law at this point. No government, no law. She dies: the bond is broken," William said pointedly to his father. "Makes it much easier to hide her."

"No," Ilyn said shortly. William began to protest but was silenced by his father's glare. "How soon can Birch send the plane for us?" the king continued.

"The feds have grounded every private plane in the country because of the attack. There's talk they might lift the ban by the day after tomorrow, but who knows?" Hazel replied.

"Should we drive?" Greg asked.

"Too risky, being caught on some road in the middle of nowhere," was William's assessment. "No cover. At least we have walls here. The oldest part of the house is stone construction."

"So we stay here until he can send the plane," Ilyn said reluctantly. "And we hope our black sheep is in worse shape than we are."

The water was scalding hot when November finally made it into the shower, for which she was grateful. The planning meeting now concluded, the vampires were out hunting in pairs for their breakfast, which gave November the chance to get cleaned up. She'd come back to her borrowed bedroom to find a box of clothes that Neil's wife and daughter had left behind, along with towels and toiletries. She had smiled at Neil's thoughtfulness before shucking her pajamas.

Now she stood beneath the shower head, scrubbing herself raw, turning bright pink. The comfort of hot water thawed her frozen calm. She finally broke down into tears when she realized that she was washing her hair for the fourth time because she couldn't get the smell of Luka out of it.

She got out of the shower feeling better for her little breakdown. The fear and grief was beginning to transform into a well-banked, slow-burning, and righteous anger that would serve her better. Clean, dry, and dressed, she felt a bit more in control. Images of Neil's teenage daughter flashed before her; she was currying her horse.

November rooted around in the desk until she found a pair of scissors. When a knock came at the door, she was standing in front of the bedroom mirror, the scissors in one hand and a lock of hair in the other.

"Come in," she called, expecting Ilyn or perhaps Zinnia. She smiled with surprise to see Greg standing in the doorway.

"King Ilyn's still out feeding. I thought somebody should check on you," he explained.

410

"Thanks," she replied, gesturing for him to come in. Greg perched somewhat incongruously on the edge of the little-girl bed.

"So, what's with the scissors?" he asked in the sing-song tone of someone who is worried about provoking a crazy person but trying to sound nonchalant.

She looked down. "Oh, right. You didn't think I was going to try to hurt myself or something, did you?"

"It has been known to happen with traumatized people, you know," Greg replied.

"I was just . . . see, he made Willow grow my hair back, and now I don't like it because it's how he wanted it, and it smells like him, and I was just thinking I might cut it back off, but now I'm not sure, and --." Her cheeks bloomed an embarrassed red at her outpouring of angst, and she shrugged her shoulders and sighed. "So, there's that."

"It's your hair. You should do whatever you want. You're beautiful either way, believe me. But maybe today isn't the day to be making major changes, or to do something to yourself just to spite Luka. As brave as you are, you're still traumatized, and you need time to recover."

She put the scissors down and sat down next to the vampire on the bed. "Fair enough." She turned her head to look at him. "Thanks for coming to help save me. You could have died."

"It was rather the least I could do. You did save my life on New Year's Eve, remember? At rather great cost to yourself, as I recall."

"Still, thank you," November insisted with a smile.

"You are welcome." They sat silently until Greg caught her staring down at her hands, pulling her sleeves over her wrists. "What's wrong, November?"

She hesitated. "I just keep seeing . . . Luka had these shackles, you see, and he made me, so everyone could see – it was just so humiliating." November found she couldn't continue. Silently, she leaned her head against Greg's shoulder and closed her eyes to hide the tears, not seeing Greg's face darken.

"Well, that I can certainly empathize with," he replied softly after a long pause. "You don't ever forget how that feels. But, at least knowing what it is to be in chains will help you understand the importance of freedom for all people. That's how it is for me, anyway."

November looked up at him gratefully. "I suppose that's a good way to look at it."

"It beats shame. He's the one who should be ashamed, anyhow, not you," he replied with a stern insistence.

"I know," she said, smiling briefly. "Thanks for the reminder."

A throat cleared. The companions looked up to find Ilyn at the door. The king raised a suspicious eyebrow at how cozily they were situated. "I'd like a moment, Gregory, if you please?" he said silkily. His grandson moved to comply, but not too quickly. November stood to give Greg a hug before he left, and Ilyn's eyes followed him all the way out the door.

November looked up at Ilyn incredulously at this display. "What was *that* about?" she asked, simultaneously amused and offended.

He didn't answer. He simply sat down next to her on the bed.

412

"I don't belong to you. He's my friend," she said firmly, not willing to let this slide. "I'm not your property. I'm not even your girlfriend. Your grace," she added belatedly.

He snorted. "Please, I hardly qualify for honorifics now," he replied, ignoring the substance of her statement. "I'm a king with no crown, no court, no kingdom. Ilyn will do for now, though I suppose I'll have to change it again, now that everyone thinks I died in the hotel."

"What's your real name?" she asked, curious.

"It's unpronounceable. I never use it. I wanted to forget my human life. I've used a lot of Russian names, sometimes Polish or German. I was pale enough to pass for European after I was turned."

"That's sad, don't you think? You shouldn't have to hide who you are. It's not good for you," she replied. "Maybe someday you'll tell me what your name was." She began to reach out to take his hand but stopped short, still wary.

They sat in awkward silence. November didn't understand how she could feel so glad to be near him and yet feel so uncertain. They sat six inches apart. Part of her wanted to fly into his arms, but she wasn't about to show her feelings, not after what had happened the last time she had taken that chance. Vampires weren't the only ones with pride. She cleared her throat. "Did you want to talk about something?" she finally asked.

"I wished to apologize. You have suffered greatly for my mistakes, and I am terribly sorry. I will understand if you wish me to stay away from you as much as possible."

"Is that what you want?"

"No," he said with a quiet desperation. "But how could you not hate the sight of me?"

"I was angry before, about the things you said to me, about your making me drink your blood. But while I was with Luka, and I thought I was going to die, I let it all go. I don't think you were deliberately cruel to me. You seem to regret it, and I've forgiven worse. I'm just glad you're not dead."

"When I . . . rejected you, you must understand, I had no wish to harm you. It's been centuries since I felt much of anything at all. But meeting you – something in you called to me, awakened me. That is . . . disturbing. Numbness is so much easier than caring. When I was a young vampire, happy in my new love with Marisha, I couldn't understand the jaded old vampires, so bored with life, walking around dead inside. Then the years went by . . ." He shook his head before continuing, "Then there's the vampire's pride, and habits of centuries. We pretend we're of more value than humans because how else do we bear what we are, what we do, what we see? Watching people die year after year? Killing what we used to be in order to stay alive forever?"

"So you've decided that you . . . care about me? As a person, not a weapon? Even though I'm only human?"

"Yes," he replied. "If I saw no value in your humanity, I would follow William's advice and make you a vampire now. There must be a reason that I . . . hesitate." He looked at her questioningly, as if she in her youth could explain something this ancient creature couldn't understand.

"And if I didn't have my gift, would you still . . . feel things?" she asked.

"Probably not," he began. At her stricken look, he hastened to add, "No, that's not what I meant. It's simply -- you wouldn't be the person you are without it. It has shaped you. And we would almost

414

certainly never have met without it. But if you woke up tomorrow and couldn't do it anymore, I would still care for you. I think."

Good enough for now, I guess, she thought. She was ready now to talk about her experiences in the previous days. She told him everything; she minimized nothing to spare his feelings. There were no tears; she had spilled them all in the shower, and they'd been washed down the drain. She described her terrifying kidnapping, the painful hours in the dark, Willow's ruthlessness interspersed with her strange moments of kindness.

She told him of her fear and humiliation and of the suffering of the wolves and the humans at Luka's mercy, of gagging on Luka's blood and shivering naked in the cold. She told him of her unexpected compassion for Philemon, a strange moment of connection with her mother's murderer that had made her own rescue possible in the end. She told him about her new ability to find him with her gift. She described the panic she felt when her inability to tune into him made her think him dead. She told him about the moment her hope had returned. She told him everything she knew about Luka's views and plans for the future.

Finally, it was Ilyn's turn. He spoke of their frantic drive across the desert, their tense efforts to locate her, fruitless until Ben and Philemon appeared. He told her how on the day Willow stole her away, Pine had dragged himself to a fire alarm, pulling it in time to allow people to evacuate in the twenty minutes between Willow's escape and the crash of the plane into the hotel. Ilyn told her of his frantic search for her, his despair when he realized that she was gone, and his rage when Pine told him who had betrayed them. He described his own narrow escape and Amandier's refusal to leave. He counted for her the dead and missing: 87 vampires, 29 fairies, 107 humans. Without November's warning and Pine's alarm, it could have been markedly worse.

Of the dead vampires, 6 were lord governors who had refused his pleas to make an escape plan after November had shared her vision of the fire. The survivors had fled to their homes, fearful of losing their holdings to local rivals in the confusion, wanting to protect their fiefs in case of further action by Luka, wanting to be prepared to switch sides if it became advantageous. There would certainly be fighting for control of the newly lordless states.

All hope of a unified response to Luka had gone up in smoke. Other than a few close allies who remained loyal, there was little confidence in Ilyn among the lords. Rumors were swirling that Ilyn was dead or gravely wounded, or that he was himself behind the attack in order to defame his son, or to grab land. The kingdom was in shambles.

There was a sad silence, finally interrupted when November replied with a weak smile, "But other than that, then, things are going okay?" Ilyn raised an eyebrow, then laughed, surprising even himself.

"At least you live," he replied. He looked down at his hands. "If he had killed you, made you his, I do not know what I would have done," he added, looking up to gaze at her intently.

"Killed us both, hopefully," she replied in a flat voice. She was as serious as the grave.

"I'm not certain I could have," he admitted.

"There's something else I should tell you . . ." November began, drawing in a large breath. "Did you catch what Luka said about searching for me for 500 years?"

"I assumed he meant he was searching for someone *like* you. He always had an interest in . . . unusual people. Like Savita, for example. He was always fascinated with her, wanting to understand how her gift worked when she was human. He went through a lot of wise women and soothsayers and spoonbenders over the years. It never ended well." Ilyn shrugged as if to say, "Kids today and their crazy hobbies and the rock music."

"Yeah, well, apparently, he was being literal. Luka is of the opinion that I am an ancient demon who has possessed a succession of humans, fairies, and werewolves for centuries, maybe millennia. He thinks I was, among other people, a girl named Juana whom he found and tried to turn during the Inquisition. She was staked before she could rise, much to his consternation. He thinks Savita is a demon, too."

A double eyebrow-raise communicated Ilyn's lack of faith in his enemy's theory. "I'm afraid I find this rather difficult to believe," he replied.

"Yeah, so did I," she said. "Until he showed me my eyes by fairylight, and which point I freaked the heck out." She grabbed his hand. "Turn off the light," she commanded. Ilyn raised his eyebrows again. "Humor me," she said, and he complied, flipping the switch without moving a muscle.

She pulled the lantern out of her pocket and lit her face with it. "There," she said. She looked at him, chin tilted up, eyes open wide.

A slow smile snuck onto his face. Rather than recoiling from her, as November had feared, he bent to look more closely, gently sweeping her hair back from her face. "Well, I'll be damned," he whispered. "I thought I'd seen everything." He laughed with a child's delight. Finally, he pulled away and she broke the moment.

"I take it other people's eyes don't do that?"

"No, they do not," replied the dumfounded vampire.

"So, yeah, not completely human, then," she summarized.

"Do you remember these supposed other lives?" he asked, full of childlike curiosity, just as he had been back in Oakland looking through her binders. He looked like he was bubbling up with questions.

"I've been having a lot of visions about them recently, and I've seen some of the same women throughout my childhood. I thought they were ancestors, or maybe just random visions. I didn't realize that they were somehow *me*. Luka claimed Savita also remembered some things, that he told her of his theory centuries ago."

"Why didn't Savita tell me about this? I can't believe I didn't notice that about her eyes after all these years," he said, shaking his head. "Even with our sharp senses, we look but we do not see."

"Apparently, the light has to be just so, only fairy light," November replied.

"Savita?" Ilyn called softly. "Come to me." He reached out to summon his daughter.

A half-breath later, Savita opened the door. She stood, a shadow framed in the doorway, lit from behind by the hallway light. Observing Ilyn and November on the bed, the fairy lantern between them, she sighed. "Well, now you know," she said quietly before shutting the door and joining them on the bed.

"Oh, darling, why did you not tell me?" Ilyn asked, reaching toward her. His daughter's eyes were no longer their familiar deep brown but rather a swirl of ruby and gold, lit from within.

"I simply didn't want to believe that Luka could be correct about what I am. It means I am even more of a monster than I even knew. It means that even when this life is over, there will just be another one to ruin. There's no escape at all, no peace. Not for me. Not for

418

my sister. Besides, what difference does it make?" Savita replied hopelessly.

"We're not monsters," November countered. "It's not as though we asked to be born this way. There must be a reason we exist." She shook her head. "I wish you would have told me. So I didn't have to find out from Luka of all people."

"I wanted to spare you. Knowing didn't make things any easier for me," Savita replied, looking down at the coverlet.

"You're not evil, either one of you," Ilyn stated flatly. "I've seen evil plenty of times, believe me, and neither of you qualify. Besides, the ancient Greeks didn't think *daemons* were evil. In Islam, *jinns* can be good or bad. There are good *asuras*, too, according to your own countrymen, Savita."

"You were the one who staked Juana, weren't you? When Luka tried to turn her?" November asked, giving voice to what she had suspected for days.

Savita nodded. "I hated to betray my brother, but I feared how Luka would use her . . . you. I wanted to save you from him, even though I loved him. I feared what he would make you into. And I thought . . . what if you were my sister? I never saw Juana's eyes by fairy light, so I thought, maybe . . ."

"But I'm not?" November guessed.

Savita gazed downward, looking like she was about to cry again. "No. I wasn't sure, at first, of course. Not until I saw your eyes in the fairy light, at the garden party. I'm not sure if I was disappointed or relieved." She shook her head. "I should have told you. I just couldn't. I told myself that it would do no good, your knowing. And then Luka took you again, and I thought we would be too late to save you, too late for me to confess what I withheld—"

"But you weren't. I'm fine. And the truth is out. We just have to figure out what it all means." November reached out a hand to her. "And you won't have to stake me the next time I get turned into a vampire, because it won't be by Luka."

"You still think that can't be prevented?" Ilyn asked.

November shook her head. "I'm going to get mortally wounded, somehow. The choice will be to let me die or change me. I've decided I want you to change me if it comes to that. I wasn't sure before Luka took me, but I am now. Look, I don't want to be born again not knowing what I am or how to handle my gift. My childhood was a nightmare until I got some control over the visions. I don't want to have to fumble through it all again, all alone, in constant danger from Luka without even knowing it. Luka needs to be stopped, and I need to see that through. Dead and reborn as a crazy infant, I can't do that."

"I hope you're wrong," the king replied with sad eyes.

"There's a first time for everything," November replied, not feeling very optimistic.

The three of them emerged to find Hazel and William deep in whispered conversation in the hallway.

"Well, then, what do *you* think we should do with the pup?" William asked, sounding exasperated.

"It isn't our responsibility. Hector should make arrangements for him once we get to California," Hazel replied. "Put him in touch with the local packs. It's not as if I don't have enough to worry about right now."

"What about Zinnia?" November interrupted.

"What *about* her?" Hazel asked, confused. "This is a werewolf matter. I mean, she can't possibly keep him! When he hits puberty and the transformations begin, he'll want to rip her throat out." Her phone rang yet again, and she excused herself. "Birch, dear one, what's the word?" she demanded, zipping down the hallway.

November turned to the three vampires. "I don't know if separating them is such a good idea," she said.

"There's no avoiding it," Ilyn replied. "Every fairy she meets will reject her if she tries to raise this child. Every werewolf will reject him."

"What if they're, you know, bonded already or whatever you call it?" November demanded.

"That's impossible," Savita said, not sounding quite as sure as she intended.

"I've been hearing that a lot lately," November said. "Her mom just died, right? Maybe it leaves her open to it? I mean, just look at them."

They returned to the living room, standing in the doorframe as they watched Zinnia and Carlos. They were curled up together on the sofa, Zinnia reading to him patiently as he ate a huge bowl of ice cream. The connection between them was strong enough to nearly be visible. Judging by everyone else's concerned faces, they could see it, too.

***

Luka pulls a hatchet out of Willow's head. Light pours out, blinding. A red-haired fairy drops to her knees to heal her sister-in-arms. Willow's wound closes and her eyelids flutter open. A young Spanish girl is dragged from her bed. The President stands at a

podium. Ilyn fills William's grave with dirt, Marisha at his side.
Agnes falls to dust. Savita screams, covered in blood.

Exhausted, November had returned to bed, but she found little relief there. Without fresh vampire venom in her veins, sleep was a pitched battle and November lost. She didn't get more than a half hour's rest at a time before something awful trespassed in her head. At one point, her screaming woke up every sleeping person in the house, and Zinnia had a heck of a time getting Carlos to go back to bed. He insisted on coming in November's room to make sure she was okay first.

Ilyn was there to comfort November every time she woke until dawn came. "I would offer to bite you," he told her quietly at one point, while she tried to stop shaking from a vision of Luka. "But you lost a lot of blood yesterday. I don't think it would be wise." She nodded her understanding and closed her eyes, praying for sleep. Ilyn left her side reluctantly as dawn kissed the sky.

November finally gave up mid-morning, showered to wash off the cold sweat from her disturbed sleep, and dressed. She pulled once again from the top of the box of discarded clothes, not really caring how she looked, grabbing blindly.

At the bottom of that box was a blue party frock. It was over a decade old, but classic and chic enough to still be worn in decent company. It was a lovely cocktail dress, as out-of-place in that ramshackle house as an orchid in a pigsty. That's probably why Neil's wife had bought it: the dress was exactly as out of place there as she had been. She'd only worn it once or twice. They hadn't exactly gone to a lot of parties.

November never found the dress, buried as it was under all the other clothes. Even if she had, she might not have recognized it, all clean and pressed and folded neatly. It looked a lot different on a corpse, stained with blood.

Similarly, November didn't recognize Neil's garden when he gave her a tour that morning. It looked so different in the light than it had in her many visions of her nighttime burial. It was a desert garden, planned to survive Neil's long carnival absences in the summertime. It was about what she would have expected, mostly cacti and succulents. There were some lovely old trees planted by his parents and grandparents and carefully tended until their roots had grown deep enough to find water on their own. It was handsome and austere and practical, rather like Neil himself. By day, it had none of the gothic beauty it possessed in her visions of it. Perhaps November's exhaustion also contributed to her inability to see what was right in front of her. So fresh from peril, perhaps her mind tried to protect her from seeing the new danger she faced. Whatever the reason, no premonitions cast shadows on that bright and sunny day: her last day.

Chapter 19

"So, what are you going to do?" November asked Hector after she returned from her promenade in the yard. She was sitting with Pine on the back porch, eating a muffin, drinking coffee, and watching Zinnia play tag with Carlos. Neil had found some work to do in the garden.

"Don't know," Hector answered tersely.

"You should come with us," Pine advised. "No pack is going to want to take you. They will wonder why you survived when every other wolf in Arizona perished."

"I'm aware of that," Hector replied in a voice more like a growl.

"Also, we like you," November piped up.

"Also, we like you. Plus," Pine continued undeterred, "with us, you'll be on the inside of any fight against Luka. You'll get your chance to help get justice, protect your people."

"That argument I find more persuasive," the werewolf allowed with a quick flash of his teeth.

"Then there's him," Pine said, gesturing to Carlos. "He needs a wolf around. Maybe no one else besides us has noticed that Zinnia's bonded to him, but our betters are going to pick up on it sooner or later."

"Ilyn, William, and Savita have noticed. Hazel seems intent on pretending not to," November interjected.

"Well, there you go," Pine said. "And a fairy raising a werewolf? Not going to be popular. They're going to run into a lot of trouble on all sides. And the kid's going to need a wolf role model. No other wolf will accept him now, even if they did separate."

"It is not possible for a fairy to bond with a werewolf," Hector insisted. He sounded like he was trying to persuade himself as much as anyone else.

"Yeah, well, someone forgot to tell them," Pine countered. "There seems to be a lot of misbehaving fairy magic lately."

"None of this is my problem." By now Hector was grinding his teeth. "It cannot be," Hector stated flatly, then fled into the house.

"Well, that could have gone better," Pine commented drily.

"He's been through a lot," his friend replied.

"Speaking of which, so have you. How are you doing?"

"Okay, I think," she answered honestly. "I assume you heard about the whole demon thing."

"It made the rounds. Don't possess me."

She threw a pillow at him. "Not funny."

"A little funny?" he asked, giving her a hopeful puppy look until she relented and smiled. "Seriously, though, you must be kind of freaked out."

"Not really. I was, at first. But I've sort of accepted it now. The whole thing does kind of explain a lot: the psychic business, my sense of otherness. I mean, I always felt sort of old. I never acted like a kid, even as a toddler, according to my grandmother. It weirded people out. The church nursery refused to keep me."

"It's always the quiet ones," he said with a smile.

"Besides, whether Luka is right or not, it doesn't really matter what I am. What matters is what I choose to do," November shrugged.

Zinnia and Carlos joined them on the porch. Pine tossed the boy a snack and a bottle of water. Carlos smiled shyly but kept his distance. He was still understandably leery of the vampires and fairies, Zinnia excepted. Neil turned up as well. They sat companionably as the sun began to go down.

Neil suddenly piped up. "If any of you need a snack, there's some coyotes north of the main road could use clearing out," he commented nonchalantly as he sipped a beer.

Everyone slowly turned to look at him, silent and astonished. "What, did you think I was blind as well as stupid?" Neil asked. "In close quarters, it doesn't take long to see you're not ordinary people. City people have an easier time pretending you're not real, but out here in the country, we've all heard about bloodless carcasses, or sheep turned to black husks. My grandparents had stories to curl your hair. "

"We could make you forget," came Hazel's voice from the doorway. She'd been holed up in the house all day, thinking and consulting with Birch on her third throw-away cell phone of the week. Everyone tensed. "But I don't suppose it's necessary." They all relaxed. "You have been a good friend to us. It would hardly be fair to repay you thus. No one would believe you, anyway." She came and sat down on the steps. "Good news: we're cleared to fly. We leave for the airfield at midnight."

"That is good news, but I admit, I'll be sad to see you go," Neil said. "It's nice to have a full house again."

"Much thanks for your hospitality," Pine replied, everyone then murmuring their agreement.

426

"It might be best if you left before we do," Hazel suggested delicately. "Perhaps go to your brother's house for a week or two. If our enemies have tracked us, the most likely time for them to try to attack will be tonight, when we are on-the-move and more vulnerable. I would hate for you to be collateral damage."

"I'm not running from my own home!" Neil protested.

"It's just for a few days," November said. "Please, enough innocent people have died over me. I couldn't stand it if you got hurt, too," she pled, sounding close to tears.

The prospect of November crying was more than Neil could take, of course, so he agreed to the plan. He packed a bag and pulled out just after sunset, after saying his heartfelt goodbyes and giving Hazel the key to the gun cabinet.

"Thank you for everything," November called out, waving as he stood near the door.

"You're welcome," he said in a worried voice. "Be careful."

"I will," she promised, knowing that she could be as careful as she wanted without making herself much safer. Judging by the look on his face, Neil knew that, too.

The vampires rose, but no one went hunting. They'd fed well the night before, and they worried about being seen or smelled in the surrounding country. The living ate their fill from Neil's larder, and everyone hunkered down to nervously pass the time until the scheduled departure. Carlos turned out to be very fond of board games, soundly beating Hector, Pine, and Zinnia at Candy Land. William and Hazel argued strategy for the coming struggle. Ben brooded, per usual.

November drew, pouring out the images from recent days, visions that had filled her to bursting. She sat on the couch, her back

427

against the arm of the sofa and her legs bent to hold a sketchpad she'd dug out of Neil's daughter's desk. Ilyn sat beneath her bent knees, watching her and her paper with an intensity that would probably have been uncomfortable had November possessed enough spare attention to notice it.

The psychic's right hand flew across the page, sketch after sketch appearing beneath it. Some were of the hotel, its destruction, and those who perished. Luka's werewolf prisoners appeared, as did some of the humans dying of poison. A number of her antecedents appeared as well. She'd taken to calling them "The Octobers" in her mind, since they came before November. Ilyn's eyes widened in surprised recognition when a silver-haired fairy with a jeweled crown appeared, but he said nothing. Eventually, November ran out of steam and out of paper and simply sat quietly, her eyes closed, enjoying a precious moment of calm and safety.

Eventually, the moment arrived. It was time to go.

***

Wooden bullets with a silver core are the ammunition of choice for most supernatural bounty hunters, since properly aimed they worked on all supernatural creatures and humans besides. Forster followed this convention, but he was unusual in that he preferred to do his killing at a distance. Most vampires enjoyed a close kill, but Forster's weapon of choice was a long-range sniper rifle fitted with a scope that doubled as a video camera to record evidence of his success as proof for his employers. Under certain circumstances, getting a sample of the ash as proof was unwise.

This seemed to be one of those times, as the target was surrounded by an unexpected bounty of friends. Or, perhaps, as seemed more likely, he was their prisoner. There was the smell of werewolf, too, which struck him as odd. No matter. Downwind and well-hidden, Forster's presence was undetectable even by the sharp senses of those he hunted. Had the tow-headed boy vampire been alone, Forster might have merely injured him and tried for the live capture and the higher price, but surrounded as he was, a simple kill was a safer bet.

The crowd gave him pause, and he considered bailing. Going for the kill was risky. They might pursue. A wiser man would have changed his plan. Forster, however, was a bit of a risk junkie; moreover, he didn't know when he would get another chance, and he really needed the money. He also had no idea that Luka's lost prize psychic was present. Nor did he know that telekinetic Ilyn was in their midst. Forster wasn't much for keeping up with politics.

Forster had been waiting, silent and motionless since sundown, calm with a vampire's preternatural patience. Finally, the front door opened and individuals began to emerge. As expected, to Forster's consternation, they were clumped together for protection. He decided that firing a few rounds might be a useful way to flush out a youngling. In his experience, they tended to react rather foolishly to danger. So, he took a shot, aiming at the little werewolf pup. Just before he pulled the trigger, the human girl cried out, turning to look for danger and throwing herself in front of the boy, thus alerting the rest of them to the threat she had sensed.

While the more experienced of the group hit the dirt, the blond boy turned to look in the direction of the shot. He was rewarded with a bullet to the chest. He looked down and back up again, in either confusion or relief. He collapsed to dust before he could even cry out. Forster then began shooting at the others, hoping to thin out the group and lessen the risk of pursuit. Unfortunately for him, Ilyn was now on alert and caught the bullets in midair. Forster fled, job well-enough done, or so he hoped. As he ran, he texted his successful report to his employer.

Down at ground level, Carlos was fine, huddled under both Zinnia and November. November lay unmoving with her face in the dirt. Zinnia turned her over with a cry of alarm.

Once the supernatural creatures were certain there would be no more shots coming, everyone began standing up around her. She lay motionless on the ground, looking up at the sky. She touched her stomach, and her hand came away wet. She looked for Carlos and Hector and was overwhelmingly relieved to see that they were whole. "It's mine, right?" she asked weakly, holding up her bloody hand, just to be sure. All was stunned silence for a moment, as various combinations of horror, anger, and pity swirled across the faces above her. Then things began to happen very quickly.

"In the house, now," ordered Ilyn, "In case he is foolish enough to come near. Keep away from the windows. William, Greg, Savita: Go. Find him. Bring him." He sounded as dangerous as November had ever heard him, even more terrifying than he had sounded on New Year's Eve.

His son and daughter disappeared in a flash. Greg, his face full of regret, took a moment to squeeze November's hand before speeding off behind them. Zinnia and Pine hesitated, wanting to stay with their friend rather than go in the house. Carlos had his arms wrapped around Zinnia's leg, hiding his face in her trousers. Hector had a wild look in his eye.

Ilyn looked at them, standing frozen. "The boy doesn't need to see this," Ilyn said to them with uncharacteristic gentleness.

"Take him inside. It's okay," November whispered. They complied.

Ilyn and Hazel knelt beside November. "Does it hurt?" he asked, pulling a stray lock of hair out of her mouth and tucking it behind her ear.

430

"I can't feel anything," she whispered. "I'm numb below my ribs. Thank God for small favors."

"Hazel? If we get her to a hospital, can she make it to dawn?" he asked with desperate hope.

She shook her head as she continued examining November. "I think it hit her spleen before it severed her spinal cord. She'll bleed out before we get there. She's got, maybe, half an hour at the outside." She turned to November, "I'm sorry, child, there is nothing I can do for you."

Ilyn's face was motionless, but tears of blood welled in his eyes. "Since moving can't make things much worse, let's get her inside where it's warm," Ilyn said decisively, needing something to do to delay facing the inevitable.

He and Hazel gently lifted her and carried her into the living room, laying her down in front of the fireplace and covering her with his cloak before kneeling once again at her side. The others had taken Carlos to the kitchen. November could hear Zinnia trying to comfort him and explain what was happening. Hazel started a fire going.

Unfortunately, November could also hear Pine and Hector arguing. "If he changes that poor girl without her permission, so help me God, I will kill him, I don't care how old he is," the werewolf declared.

"I'm telling you, he wouldn't! And if he did he'd have problems with me, too. Now calm down, man, you're going to freak out Carlos even worse," Pine replied, trying to talk him down.

Hazel went to inform everyone about the unfortunate prognosis, giving Ilyn and November a much-needed moment alone.

He looked down at her, helpless for one of the few times in his long life. "Oh, little one," he said softly, "I am so sorry."

"I don't blame you," she said, honestly. "I've known this night was coming since I could walk. But I did think I had a little more time," she admitted, tears filling her eyes. "And I am scared of what will come after."

He looked like he was struggling with himself, before finally managing to say, "If . . . if you would prefer to die, if you don't want me to change you, I would . . . I would abide by your wishes." He looked as though the words in his mouth were made of glass.

She shook her head weakly. "I already told you that I have work to finish. I don't want to be born not knowing and have to figure everything out all over again. Meanwhile, Luka would be hunting me down while he destroys the world. I just have to trust that this is happening for a reason, that God has a purpose for me as a vampire." She paused. Breathing and talking were becoming more difficult. "As long as you're there, and everyone else, I can do it. If you can all help me. But I don't want to be like . . ."

"Like me?" he finished.

She closed her eyes, unable to face him as he spoke that truth for her. "Please don't let me do anything I'll regret," she begged.

"I will do my best," Ilyn replied, knowing that what she asked would be impossible.

"I'm worried about what Luka said, about how he took precautions," November confessed. "What could he have done?"

"He was almost certainly bluffing," Ilyn responded in a voice more sure than he felt. "And we really have no other choice."

By now, the bloody tears streaked Ilyn's face, and he did not bother to wipe them away. Pine, Zinnia, and Hazel snuck back in. "Do you want us here?" Pine asked softly.

"Yes, please," November said weakly. "I love you all," she murmured. Zinnia looked stricken, but she held herself together for her friend's sake. She could collapse later. Everyone sank to the floor, surrounding her with love.

"Ilyn," November said. "I think time is running out. I'm so tired."

The king lifted her gently into his lap, cradling her head against his shoulder. Ilyn bent and quickly buried his fangs in November's neck before he could think too much about it; he began to drain the life from the only person who had made him feel anything in two centuries. Under other circumstances, he would have been delighted by her blood, but he could barely taste her as he focused all his attention on his race with her fluttering heartbeat and ragged breathing.

For her part, November was floating, lightheaded but feeling no pain, feeling as comfortable and safe as it was possible to feel while bleeding to death. She was a little surprised when Ilyn pulled away and bit his wrist, holding it to her mouth. It seemed like dying should take longer. He had to coax her to begin drinking, but as soon as she tasted his blood, a terrible thirst took over, and she drank eagerly, desperately. She whimpered with an infant's impatience each time Ilyn had to pull away to reopen the wound. When her thirst was finally satisfied, her head fell weakly back to his shoulder.

It was then that the visions began, all a jumble, a mishmash of Ilyn's life, her own previous lives, and the perilous future. "On, no," she whispered. "No, please. No. I can't do this." She began to struggle frantically to rise from her deathbed, desperate to escape the visions and her long-sealed fate. Her friends were horrified. They tried to quiet her, but she was beyond hearing their voices.

"The maker's vows," Hazel reminded Ilyn, who was staring in despair at his now-terrified victim.

Ilyn looked at Hazel, paralyzed for a moment before remembering the words he was expected to say. He squeezed November's hand. She could not feel it. "With my blood, I give you life immortal. With all my strength, I will protect you. With all my knowledge, I will teach you. With all my heart, I will--" He hesitated before continuing, "I will love you. This is my solemn vow."

November looked up, gazing straight through him. "Where is my mama? I want to go home. Mama?" she murmured pleadingly. Ilyn closed his eyes, wishing he could cover his ears. How many times had he heard the dying begging for their mothers?

"You'll feel better when you wake up," Ilyn promised, "And then we'll go home." He then kissed November's lips tenderly, tasting her blood and his own mingled together. She smiled and opened her eyes for the last time, able to see everyone's faces once more as the light grew dim. A moment later, her now-rasping breath fell silent, and she faced the end of her human life peacefully, with her eyes open wide.

Ilyn sat stoic and still as a statue, his eyes now dry, while somewhere in New Mexico, Luka screamed in rage as he felt the life ebb from his lost prize. Ilyn carefully lowered November's body to the floor.

Pine held Zinnia as she collapsed into sobs. "It's okay, Zin. We'll see her tomorrow."

"But she won't be the same!"

434

"No one stays the same forever," Pine said gently. "Even human, she would have changed as she grew older. She will still love us and need us, and now she will be stronger. She'll be a hell of a lot sturdier than you, actually, and that's a good thing, given what a shoddy job I've done of protecting her." He closed his eyes, trying to hide his own pain.

"She didn't deserve this," Zinnia said, despondent. She gave Ilyn a look filled with blame, but said nothing else.

"In my experience, people rarely get what they deserve," Hazel softly replied.

Ilyn pulled out his handkerchief and wearily wiped the blood from his face. "Hazel, we obviously must stay until tomorrow at the earliest. But the wolves should leave ahead of us. November might lose control if she smells them right after she wakes." He sought refuge in the details, as he had always done. Old habits can be useful in times of crisis.

"I know. I already informed my son that they will arrive tonight and he is to send back the plane to get us tomorrow. He's arranging for extra animals at the ranch for November, and he's working to procure some human blood. I'll have someone find her food for when she wakes tomorrow night."

"She won't forgive me if I let her kill an innocent," Ilyn replied warningly.

"I know. We will do our best to avoid it. We should prepare her for burial," Hazel urged gently. "Do you want me to clean her up?"

"I'll do it myself," he replied quickly. "I just need a few moments." He retreated, intending to sit in the basement to compose himself, but he stopped short when he ran into Carlos and Hector in the hallway.

Carlos held out a blue dress. It was obvious the boy had been crying and was frightened of Ilyn, but he screwed up his courage to address the vampire king. "I found this in a box in her room. Do you think she'd want to wear something pretty for her funeral?"

Ilyn was taken aback, and his eyes once more filled with bloody tears. "Yes, I do. Thank you, child," he managed.

"Hector says you are making her a vampire," the boy continued bravely.

"That's true," Ilyn answered. "It was her choice," he said pointedly, glancing at Hector. "She wanted to keep fighting Luka."

"Then why are you sad?" Carlos asked. "I thought vampires liked killing people, anyway."

"That rather depends on the people in question, in my case," the king replied. "As for my sadness, I . . . suppose it is . . . irrational."

"Will she still be my friend, even though I'm a werewolf?" Carlos asked worriedly.

He hesitated before answering. "Yes," Ilyn finally said, not sure if he was lying. "I am quite sure she will. Now, you and Hector are going to go ahead of us to California, and we'll meet you there after November rises tomorrow. It will be safer that way. Baby vampires are very hungry when they wake up."

"What about Zinnia?" Carlos demanded, suddenly panicked, looking around for her.

Zinnia, overhearing, joined them from the living room. She knelt next to Carlos and wiped away her own blue tears in order to tend to him. "I'll be there soon, I promise. But I need to be here for November. She is the closest friend I ever had."

"She died protecting me," Carlos said guiltily.

436

"She protected me as well," Zinnia replied. "That bullet might have killed me, too, young as I am."

"I'm sure she was glad her death did so much good," Ilyn managed to say, swallowing his grief and rage in order to comfort Zinnia and the boy, because that's what November would have wanted him to do. He turned to Hector. "Pine will take you to the plane. I know you are uneasy about staying with us, but I ask that you remain with the boy at least until Zinnia arrives."

"I will," Hector replied. As Ilyn turned to walk away, the werewolf added. "I'm sorry, bloodsucker."

Ilyn walked away, wordless.

Ilyn's private mourning was soon interrupted by the arrival of his progeny with sniper in tow. Forster looked quite a bit the worse for wear, and the sight of Ilyn full of grief and guilt and righteous anger did not make him feel any better. If it was possible for a vampire to blanch, he certainly would have. Someone was most assuredly going to pay, and Foster knew it would most likely be him.

"Name?" Ilyn asked languorously after a pregnant pause, looking as though he was bored already with his prisoner. Savita put a hand on the gunman's shoulder and closed her eyes to concentrate on his thoughts. Forster flinched at her touch.

He considered keeping his mouth shut but thought better of it. "Forster," he admitted.

"Explain yourself." Ilyn pulled a sharpened stake out of his inside jacket pocket and began using it to idly clean under his fingernails.

The prisoner's words came tumbling out. "Lord Luka put out a bounty on this Ben kid. A big one. Didn't think he'd be in company like this." Forster swallowed convulsively.

"Obviously not," Ilyn replied, voice dripping disdain.

"Are you . . . are you King Ilyn?" the prisoner managed to ask.

Ilyn raised an eyebrow. "I was." He leaned in. "Should have shot me first, boy."

"Look, I . . . I'm sure we can work this out. I mean, I only killed the traitor and the bloodbank, so, like, no real harm done, right?" the terrified vampire stammered.

Ilyn's eyes were daggers. He leaned in close to his prisoner. "Certainly few tears will be shed over Ben. I'd raise him and kill him again myself if I could. The . . . human . . . on the other hand, was rather more valuable. Perhaps you heard rumors about an oracle discovered on a carnival midway? The one Luka kidnapped for himself and intended to turn?" Forster's eyes widened as he realized the magnitude of his error. "I'm quite certain Luka would be very unhappy that you killed his prize. Perhaps nearly as unhappy as I am. I must confess, I was rather. . . fond of her."

"He didn't say anything about the girl when he posted the bounty, I swear! I wasn't even aiming for her. She threw herself in front of that mutt," Forster protested desperately.

"And how were you to collect your payment?" Ilyn asked, abruptly changing the subject. "Were you to meet somewhere?"

"Over the internet," Forster answered, startled into truthfulness.

"Get every detail of how Luka communicates with these mercenaries and how he pays them," Ilyn ordered his people. "I have other business to attend to."

William cracked his knuckles. "My pleasure," he said, smiling. His personality flaws notwithstanding, he really had rather liked November.

438

***

Ilyn had seen and perpetrated a great deal of violence over the millennia. Nevertheless, it pained him to see the wound in November's stomach. Her scars were also rather upsetting. There was the fresh mark on her arm from the fairy blade with which he was already intimately familiar, along with others more mundane, inflicted mostly by her mother or by herself.

He had removed her clothes and tossed them into the fire, first retrieving her rosary and lantern from her pockets. Zinnia had brought the prayer beads for her from Las Vegas, carefully secreted in an envelope. He let the silver burn his hand before placing it in his own pocket for safekeeping. November would never be able to touch it with bare hands again. He then used his gift to pull the bullet from her body. He wondered if she would want to keep the silver portion and placed it in a plastic bag for her. The splinters of wood joined her clothes in the flames.

He then carried her back to the bathroom adjoining the bedroom she'd been using. He laid her down in the bathtub, careful not to crack her head against the porcelain. He had done this before, preparing his wife and son for burial when he had been human. The task was only slightly easier with indoor plumbing. He bathed her carefully, wiping away the blood and tears and bodily soil. He taped a thick pad of gauze over the entry wound, which continued to leak blood. He brushed her hair and her teeth, then dressed her in the blue dress and carried her out to the garden, to the spot he thought was prettiest. He gently propped her up against a tree. The tangled roots supported her as he paced out a grave, marking the boundaries with the shovel someone had found in the barn.

A trickle of blood had leaked once again from November's mouth, and her wound had begun to stain the dress in spite of the bandage. *So much for cleaning her up*, he thought. But what did it matter? She would probably make a mess of herself anyway during her first feeding after she awoke. Everyone did.

Ilyn's own suit looked like it had been worn by a butcher, soaked as it was in her blood. He was beyond caring. He didn't bother wiping her face again. What was the point? He left Zinnia to sit with the body so November wouldn't be alone. Hazel was cleaning up the blood inside the house. The living room was filthy as a charnel house. He couldn't bring himself to close her eyes.

The erstwhile king returned to the basement. When his children reported that they had gotten everything they could out of the assassin, Ilyn said, "You're lucky we are the ones who found you. Luka would not have been this generous." And without another word or hint of hesitation, Ilyn staked the hired killer and turned to leave without so much as a backward glance. "See if Neil has a shopvac for the ash, will you? I'd hate to leave him a mess," he said absently as he climbed the stairs. Forster's remains slowly settled to the floor.

It was awfully quiet in the garden as William dug the grave. His movements were sure and rhythmic, with the ease born of repeated practice. Greg came out to pay his respects before going hunting for November's first meal. He was glad to have an excuse to miss the burial. Even though he knew she'd be rising soon, it would have been painful to see her disappear beneath the dirt. Even after a few centuries as a vampire, Greg had not grown comfortable with the death of innocents. He silently promised November that he would help her adjust to her new life. His own first years had been difficult.

Neither did Hazel stay to see the psychic put to ground. She could not bear the look on Ilyn's face, so she accompanied Greg on the hunt.

Zinnia cried quietly. As vampires and fairies left no bodies, she had never been to a burial. Fairies had a memorial ceremony, but in all the craziness, there hadn't yet been time to mourn her mother. So she wept for Amandier as well as for November.

Once she came outside, Savita simply sat, silent and exhausted and sad.

Ilyn sat by November with his eyes closed, keeping his thoughts to himself, looking like a statue, too wrung out to even bother keeping up the pretence of breathing. It had been a long time since he had buried someone he cared about. William, it had been. That poor young man had been bloody, too, cut to pieces in a pointless battle over a worthless patch of dirt. Savita, though, she had been whole. Some plague or other had been draining her life when he drained her blood and replaced it with his own.

He thought of his human wife and child, dead for so many centuries. As long as it had been, he could still remember the taste of his tears and the smoke as he put them on the pyre. He had tried to throw himself into the flames; relatives had struggled to pull him away as he screamed for his family. The widower had been 19 years old then, when his hair had started coming in gray.

William finished digging. "It's nearly dawn, Father." He was trying his best to be gentle as he hurried Ilyn along, but gentleness did not come easily to him.

The ancient vampire roused himself. He moved slowly, gently lifting November's body and placing it carefully into the grave. He straightened her dress. He finally closed her eyes. She looked so small. Zinnia threw a flower into the grave, her face stained with streaks of blue. Ilyn demanded the shovel from his son and began filling in the hole; he changed his mind and joined November in the ground over William's protests. Now there was no need for relatives to pull him away from the fire; this time there was no reason he could not accompany her into death.

He looked at November one more time as William began to bury them. He closed his eyes and curled protectively around the girl, hoping that she wouldn't be afraid when she woke up in the dark earth.

The sun rose. The dead slept. The living waited, standing guard as the sun rose high and warmed the earth and the seed within it. The living waited, as the sun descended and the air grew cold. And when the sun finally set, the seed sprouted and the dead stirred. Two pale hands burst out of the ground, clutching one another, their fingers intertwined. Life rose from lifelessness: a miracle. A curse.

About the Author

In addition to her work as an indie author of paranormal fantasy, A.M. Manay is a former inner-city chemistry teacher, a singer, a yoga enthusiast, a Clerk of Session in the Presbyterian Church (USA), and a mother through domestic open adoption. She has a passion for increasing diversity in popular culture and for strong heroines who stand up for themselves, make their own decisions, and don't depend on romance as their reason for being.

Be the first to know about the release of the upcoming sequel as well as bonus material about your favorite characters by

Signing up for the fan email list: ammanay.net/Contact.php

Following the author on Facebook: facebook.com/ammanaywrites

Following the author on Twitter: @ammanay

Following her Amazon author page: amazon.com/author/ammanay

If you enjoyed the book, please consider posting a review on Amazon or Goodreads. If you found an error you'd like the author to know about, or have a question or comment, feel free to email her at author@ammanay.net.

Book Group Discussion Questions

1. How is the author's portrayal of vampires similar to or different from other vampire stories or movies you've enjoyed in the past?
2. If you could have a power like many of the characters, which one would you want? Which seems the most useful?
3. What event in the book shocked you the most?
4. Who is your favorite character? What about him or her appeals to you?
5. Which character angered you the most? Why?
6. If *She Dies at the End* were made into a movie, who should play your favorite character?
7. With which character did you most closely identify? Why?
8. Which character do you wish you knew more about?
9. Which character are you most attracted to romantically? Who is your "book boyfriend" or "book girlfriend"?
10. Was there an image in the book that stuck with you?
11. If you knew you had lived past lives, would you want to remember them? Why or why not?
12. What do you think happened to Marisha, Ilyn's late wife? How do you think she died?
13. Do you think November and Ilyn could ever have a healthy romantic relationship? Why or why not?
14. Did you learn anything from the story and its characters that could be applied to your own life?

10/22/15

Made in the USA
San Bernardino, CA
13 October 2015